PRAISE FOR *HOLLY BANKS FULL OF ANGST*

"There are many novels about women struggling to fit into upper-class communities, but debut author Valerie manages to create a story that feels fresh, with sparkling dialogue . . . A unique and over-the-top look at modern motherhood, full of funny and cringeworthy moments."

—*Kirkus Reviews*

"Valerie's witty, rollicking novel is an ode to modern motherhood . . . A charmingly cautionary tale of the pursuit for domestic perfection."

—*Booklist*

"Debut author Valerie's excellent take on modern motherhood illustrates a mother's attempts to keep up with the Joneses. Full of humor, including a bout with one too many detox cookies, an online psychic, and a cat doula, Valerie plays out the drama of being a wife and a mother. Perfect for fans of Laurie Gelman's Class Mom series and the TV show *Desperate Housewives*."

—*Library Journal*

"Julie Valerie does a great job relaying the anxiety that comes with starting your daughter in kindergarten in a new school and a new town. And she does it with the perfect mix of humor and humility."

—Laurie Gelman, author of *Class Mom* and *You've Been Volunteered*

"Seemingly perfect lives are usually anything but, as the eponymous protagonist of *Holly Banks Full of Angst* quickly learns. A sharp, witty, and altogether unexpected story about how striving can lead you straight to the end of your rope, Julie Valerie's debut is not to be missed."

—Camille Pagán, bestselling author of *I'm Fine and Neither Are You*

"*Holly Banks Full of Angst* is a must-read for any mother who sometimes feels inadequate—and what mother doesn't? With themes of new beginnings, the quest for perfection, motherhood, and marriage, Valerie delivers lessons in hospitality, humanity, and hope, gently reminding us that we're all works in progress. If you're looking for a fun escape filled with humor and heart, look no further than *Holly Banks Full of Angst*."

—Lori Nelson Spielman, *New York Times* bestselling author of
The Life List

"You will love the time you spend with Holly Banks in the Stars Hollow–esque Village of Primm. Holly is the perfect heroine: flawed, impulsive, and self-deprecating but also deeply relatable, lovable, and hilarious. This book is pure fun (but be prepared to cry a little). *Holly Banks Full of Angst* is the perfect read for anyone who has ever wanted to stick it to the Pinterest Mom."

—Suzy Krause, author of *Valencia and Valentine*

"With wit, whimsy, and an artful sleight of hand turn of more than a few phrases, Julie Valerie's frothy cautionary tale of suburbia on steroids is like a finely crafted cocktail: effervescent but complex, sweet but with just a hint of bitter, and packing a potent punch. I'll have what she's having."

—Josie Brown, author of *Secret Lives of Husbands and Wives*
and the Totlandia series

"With astonishing wit, razor-sharp dialogue, and pitch-perfect pacing, Julie Valerie has created a masterpiece about motherhood. *Holly Banks Full of Angst* is absolutely hilarious yet also deeply poignant, with some of the best lines I've ever read. Both satire and upmarket women's fiction, this novel will be beloved by readers everywhere."

—Samantha M. Bailey, author of *Woman on the Edge*

"Our plucky heroine, full of quippy asides and enough anxiety to keep us all up ruminating at three a.m., imagines herself the star of her own movie (because of course she dreams of ditching her SAHM life and fulfilling her long-lost film student aspirations). Personally, I would title her movie *Mean Girls for Moms*, and you'd find me at the premiere, front row center!"

—Lindsey J. Palmer, author of *Otherwise Engaged*, *If We Lived Here*, and *Pretty in Ink*

"Ever wonder what would happen if Liane Moriarty could channel the late Robin Williams? Me neither—until I read this astonishing debut, a modern allegorical marvel. Valerie absolutely skewers Parenting While Privileged and pulls it off without preaching or condescending, thanks to the irresistible, inimitable heroine, Holly, the (questionably) sane person in the insane (but wholly recognizable) world of Primm. I tore through this inventive, compulsive read, pausing only to catch my breath and wipe my eyes at passages so outrageously hilarious I could not believe what I was reading. So come for the humor, but stay for the honesty. Valerie imbues the narrative with sincerity and with truths so bald that, at times, the world fell away around me. I'm on my feet and clapping: brava!"

—Sonja Yoerg, *Washington Post* bestselling author of *True Places*

"A fresh voice in fiction, Julie Valerie hits it out of the park with her debut novel, *Holly Banks Full of Angst*. Wise and witty, it's filled with humor that takes some wildly comical turns at times. Lead character Holly Banks, a newcomer to the idyllic Village of Primm, is every mom who feels inadequate because her home isn't Pinterestworthy and she's a less-than-perfect parent—totally relatable, in other words. Her good heart, which shines through even when she's screwing up, ultimately triumphs over her good intentions gone awry. Love, love, love this novel and can't wait to read the next one by Julie Valerie."

—Eileen Goudge, *New York Times* bestselling author

THE *Peculiar* FATE OF HOLLY BANKS

ALSO BY JULIE VALERIE

Holly Banks Full of Angst

THE *Peculiar* FATE OF HOLLY BANKS

Julie Valerie

a novel

LAKE UNION
PUBLISHING

This is a work of fiction. Names, characters, organizations, places, events, and incidents are either products of the author's imagination or are used fictitiously. Any resemblance to actual persons, living or dead, or actual events is purely coincidental.

Text copyright © 2020 by Julie Valerie
All rights reserved.

No part of this book may be reproduced, or stored in a retrieval system, or transmitted in any form or by any means, electronic, mechanical, photocopying, recording, or otherwise, without express written permission of the publisher.

Published by Lake Union Publishing, Seattle

www.apub.com

Amazon, the Amazon logo, and Lake Union Publishing are trademarks of Amazon.com, Inc., or its affiliates.

ISBN-13: 9781542007993
ISBN-10: 1542007992

Cover design by Liz Casal

Printed in the United States of America

For Andrew Michael Michael

He who labors diligently need never despair, for all things are accomplished by diligence and labor.
—Menander, Greek dramatist, best-known representative of Athenian New Comedy

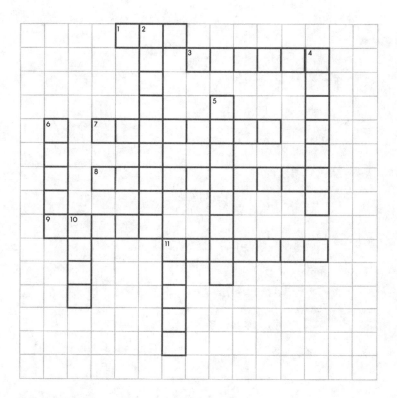

ACROSS

1. it has a key and a legend

3. typesetter's dot

7. reader's place keeper

8. branched hanging light

9. you can skip one on a lake

11. twisted treat

DOWN

2. navigational tool - sextant forerunner

4. botanical sculpture

5. plant prized for its scent

6. half-full or half-empty

10. chickadee's perch

11. nom de _____; pen name

1

September

"Struggle!" Holly shouted as she tried catching hold of the dog, but it was early on a Saturday morning, and she didn't want to sacrifice the cup of coffee in her hands, nor did she want to drop the *Primm Gazette* tucked beneath her armpit lest the store coupons fall out, so out plowed their chocolate Labrador, Struggle, with no collar to grab on to, leaving Holly staring after her, irked about the hot splash of freshly brewed vanilla hazelnut coffee now staining her shirt. *Freaking dog.*

Holly loved Struggle, but Struggle was barking like there was no tomorrow, off to greet the gallant, sixty-something-year-old Houston Bonneville-Cranbarrie as he tried but failed, yet again, to retrieve his own *Primm Gazette* from the end of his driveway—without the assistance of the Banks family dog. Who, yet again, wasn't collared but was instead wearing Ella's ballet tutu around her neck: a wiry, bristled wreath of pink tulle, making Struggle look like a dog clown, except scarier, because she was barking like a four-legged Pennywise.

Ugh! Holly kicked herself for not being more careful.

What's with all the dumb luck lately?

She was hoping to relax with a cup of coffee. Maybe scan the *Primm Gazette* for news of the coming Scrabble tournaments. Maybe solve a crossword puzzle. And maybe, just maybe, before prepping the house for Ella's playdate with Talia, find the right moment to pitch Jack on her new plan for employment now that Ella was in kindergarten: converting their dining room into a film studio so she could start offering her services to Etsy Moms, Pinterest Moms, Instamoms, bloggers, vloggers, and YouTubers. All the -loggers, -Tubers, and social media lifestyle influencers she knew in her gut lived within the nooks and crannies of the Village of Primm.

But no. Streaks of washable glitter glue shone in the morning light down the dog's back. A yellow construction paper smiley face was stuck to Struggle's hind leg like a *kick me* sign—only not quite *kick me*, more like *love me, pet me, give me a treat*. And therein lay the problem. Struggle was lovable but as of late had become Ella's canine craft project. Ella decorating the dog while the dog wagged her tail, just as happy as could be. The result? A family dog more bejeweled than the Miss Universe Pageant, more bedazzled than a celebrity contestant on *RuPaul's Drag Race.*

Last week, Ella tried turning Struggle into Rarity, the white fashionista unicorn on the *My Little Pony: Friendship Is Magic* television series she loved, unloading half her dad's Gold Bond Medicated Body Powder all over the dog in the master bedroom. Feeling itchy, no doubt, the dog shook like crazy. Clouds of powdery white dust filled the air, the carpet, Holly's bed, and four piles of folded laundry on top of it. Ella screamed, started crying, white powder in her eyes and mouth. So yeah. That was fun. (Not.) And then, as Holly was in the middle of trying to clean up, the doorbell rang. Down the stairs Holly went to find the UPS man, an exquisite specimen of a man, on her front porch needing a signature for a package—Holly covered head to toe in what she was sure looked like a controlled substance.

Today? Ella was heck bent on turning Struggle into Twilight Sparkle, her favorite *My Little Pony* pony, but it was proving difficult to turn a chocolate Labrador into a purple horse with your mom in the house. Despite the very clear admonition from Holly that "dogs are not for bedazzling," Ella managed to unload pale-purple Crayola glitter glue with silver sparkles down Struggle's back before slipping that tutu around Struggle's neck, thrilled to be capturing the shock of pink in Twilight Sparkle's mane. Holly's lesson in all this? Never turn your back on a determined five-year-old. Especially when there was a family dog to decorate.

"Struggle, come," Holly yelled. "Struggle, sit!"

But the darn dog didn't listen.

Setting her coffee and *Primm Gazette* down, she marched onto the grass because surely there had to be *someone* on Petunia Lane who hadn't yet witnessed Holly fail at dogmomhood.

Maybe it was her film degree, her love of movies, or her sense that life could so easily transfer to the screen, but Holly could imagine what they must be saying about her as clearly as if the gossip were written as snippets of dialogue in a screenplay. It would look something like this:

SCENE 1 — EXT. NEIGHBORHOOD — MAILBOX —
MORNING

    Stand by on the set.
    Stand by to roll tape.
    Roll tape.

               FIRST NEIGHBOR
The mom at #12 Petunia Lane? One word:
hot mess.

              SECOND NEIGHBOR
Can't even control her own dog.

THIRD NEIGHBOR
Didn't she sniper crawl out of a PTA
meeting the first week of school?

FOURTH NEIGHBOR
Yep. She's the one. Probably moved
here from Southern Lakes.

Holly tried, "Treat! Get your treat, Struggle!" But nope. Nothing. Nothing but constant, incessant barking at a suave silver-haired man two doors down now pointing his *Primm Gazette* straight at the dog like a silken-bathrobed magician harnessing a rolled newspaper as a wand—presumably channeling the fates above to hurry up and decide the outcome of this meeting, because if they didn't, through an act of free will, Houston Bonneville-Cranbarrie would surely be looking to whack Struggle on the snout with his coupon-stuffed newspaper, and by golly, if that happened, that—more than the barking dog—would send Holly running. What Struggle was doing was rude and alarming and unneighborly, sure, yes, of course. And Holly felt bad about it. It was Holly's fault for accidentally letting the dog out, et cetera and so on, but c'mon. Struggle was harmless. She was just saying hello.

In a singsongy voice, Holly tried, "Come 'ere, Struggle, good girl . . ."

But it was more than that, should Houston whack Struggle on the snout. Struggle was family. Holly's family. And though Holly loved being a part of her new community—the Petunia enclave and the broader Village of Primm she'd lived in for about a month—and though Holly cared deeply (in theory, at least) for her fellow man, Holly, like most members of a community, felt fiercely protective of her particular family. Struggle was Holly's tribe. Struggle slept in Holly's cave at night. *Because hey, sometimes your dog gets out. But don't whack her with a newspaper. Don't you dare whack a member of my family on the snout. I don't give a flip if we're neighbors.*

Holly was aware a neighbor was watching while watering his grass and that the couple out for a walk and in complete control of their leashed Goldendoodle had also stopped to watch, instructing their pooch to sit at their feet. Which, of course, it did—first command. Yay for the Goldendoodle. Nay for the Labrador.

"Why'd you let her out?" asked Jack, appearing with Ella on the front porch, a look of concern on his face, hands wringing in that nervous "Jack" way he did when things were about to invert and go sideways.

"I didn't 'let her out.' She got out." Holly bristled. "Fix the hole in the back fence," she said over her shoulder toward Jack, aware Maeve Bling had stepped onto her porch, arms folded across her chest, feisty Pomeranian at her feet. Holly suspected another Petunia Enclave Homeowners Association "Hello Note" would be taped to her mailbox by lunchtime. *Why the heck does shrimp like this always happen to me?*

Holly wanted relaxed. Holly wanted normal. Holly wanted Primm. Maybe Maeve Bling carried Hello Notes in her back pocket. She probably slept with them beneath her pillow.

~

HELLO NOTE—Taped to Holly's Mailbox Last Week

Friendly reminder trashcans shouldn't remain at the curb after rubbish has been removed. I watched a strong wind knock your empty trashcan into the middle of the street. A second wind weaponized the can, sliding it toward the Patels' mailbox like a torpedo!

—Maeve Bling

~

Holly knew she shouldn't care this was happening before a live audience, and yet, she did care. *Shake it off,* she told herself, feeling the heat rise on the back of her neck. Sparkly purple dogs roamed the streets wearing hot-pink tutus all the time, right? None of this implied *her* home was chaotic or discombobulated. You should never judge a family from the distance of next door. You couldn't possibly know what was going on from that far away.

Holly traveled up the hill toward the entrance to Petunia Lane, the length of two wide-expanse, manicured front yards, cursing the wet grass beneath her bare feet before reaching Houston's exposed aggregate driveway, only to be welcomed with: "That dog will be the death of me," newspaper wand pointed straight at Holly.

"I'm so sorry," said Holly. "Truly. It won't happen again."

She took two steps toward her dog, and her dog took two steps back, maintaining an equal distance between them, as if they were magnets whose wrong ends repelled each other.

"I caught her digging holes in my backyard. Three holes!" he said, holding up three fingers. "She pooped on my lawn, you know. Maeve!" Houston waved toward Maeve Bling.

"Please leave her out of it," said Holly. "I've only lived here a month. Can you cut me some slack? We apologized about the holes. We offered to fill them," she reminded him. "And hey," she added, hoping to lighten the mood, "Struggle found an 1895 Indian Head penny." Shouldn't he be thanking her? Her dog found buried treasure.

"Struggle, sit," she said in a calm but authoritative voice. She expected to be ignored, but what the flock. The dog sat. Holly, afraid to make one false move, approached the dog, slowly stretching her hand out, thinking if she could just grab hold of that tutu . . .

Moving closer and closer, on the count of five, she planned to snatch the tutu, pull Struggle toward her, and then, because she couldn't grab her by the collar because she wasn't *wearing* a collar, Holly figured she'd have to overwhelm Struggle somehow with an Olympic-gold wrestling move. Maybe swing a leg over Struggle's back so she could heave her into her arms and then carry her home.

Count of five, four . . .

"Staaaaay," she said.

Three . . . two . . .

One! Holly leaped at the dog, seizing the tutu, pulling the dog toward her before slinging a leg across Struggle's back, not hurting her but straddling her as if she were riding a bull in a rodeo. Then *hooyah!* Holly ninja-wrapped both of her arms around Struggle's belly, hoisting her dog from the grass, bear-hugging her the entire time.

Problem was, Struggle wasn't having any of it.

Now off the ground in Holly's arms, Struggle reared her head back, began twisting, flipping, flopping, smearing pale-purple glitter glue all over Holly. Bodies contorting, Holly and dog clamoring, a spiraling ball of tutu and sparkles. Holly didn't mean to, but she dropped the flailing, squirming dog on the grass. More like the dog dropped her, trying to escape.

Struggle quickly righted herself; then Jack whistled from the porch, one of those two-fingered, tongue-pushed-back, earsplitting whistles. Struggle ran straight to him. *Why didn't Jack do that before?* Ella opened the door, and like magic, Struggle ran inside the house, followed by Ella and Jack—leaving Holly smeared groin to neck in glitter glue, still clutching the tutu, feeling tumbled and spun out, like she'd just survived a ride in a laundry machine set to spin cycle.

Show over, the couple with the Goldendoodle resumed their walk. The neighbor across the street returned to his watering. Even Maeve Bling left her porch to step inside.

"I give up," said Holly, so frustrated she didn't know what to do with herself.

She saw a minivan pull up to her curb and park, and then the driver waved. *Shanequa? With Talia?* Holly was so stunned she didn't wave back.

"What time is it?" she asked Houston.

"Ten o'clock?" he guessed.

"No! They're early," she cried. "Our playdate was supposed to be at twelve—my house is a wreck."

Holly ran to greet the minivan, reaching the driver-side window with a "Hey, Shanequa" and a smile, sensing Shanequa was probably right about the time, and Holly had gotten it wrong.

Shanequa signaled through the window she needed to make a quick phone call before coming inside with Talia.

"Yes, of course," said Holly, two thumbs up. "I'll wait inside."

Off she went, half walking, half running toward the house, eventually closing the door behind her and leaning her back against it while assessing the condition of her home. A download of panic settled in her body. This was Shanequa and Talia's first visit to Holly's house. Her first time hosting a playdate in her new home. Where had the morning gone? Why hadn't she cleaned the night before?

Jack was upstairs washing Struggle—she could hear the water running. Taking matters into her own hands, Holly snatched a laundry basket, then tossed out-of-place items inside, before setting the basket on a folding table in the garage, where two *other* laundry baskets filled with random stuff sat—there from the *last* time she cleaned the house in a hurry. Panic baskets, she called them, sitting on a panic table where all items she'd deal with later were kept.

She slipped shoes on, doused two paper towels with lemon-scented floor cleaner, then stepped onto the paper towels and skied toward the kitchen table to load all the breakfast dishes onto a cookie sheet before skiing to the dishwasher to set the cookie sheet and everything on top of it inside. Later, she would load things properly, because now was the time to whip open a clean trash bag and slide the pile of clutter from the kitchen counter into it before swinging the bag and its contents onto the floor of the pantry. Closed doors hid everything. Possible titles for a book about her style of cleaning could include *The Life-Changing Magic of Panic Baskets* or maybe *"Oh, Crap! They're Here!"* or simply *Clean Enough: The Holly Banks Method.*

As Holly cleaned, Ella sort of jumped about, not really helping, more like clapping her hands while cheering, "Go, Mommy, go!" before springing into frenzied quasi–jumping jacks beside the couch piled high with stuffed animals on one end, a load of laundry in need of folding on the other.

She rushed upstairs, bursting into the bathroom, where Jack was shampooing Struggle in the claw-foot tub. After stripping free of her gooey purple shirt and yoga pants, tossing everything into the bathtub with the dog, she tugged a clean pair of jeans on before pulling a shirt over her head. "Shanequa's here."

"I'll make coffee," he said. "I want you to try a small batch of Honduran beans I roasted in the backyard using a popcorn popper."

"Oh, jeez," she said, then planted a kiss on his lips, grateful to be married to someone who studied coffee for a hobby.

She hurried back to the front door just as the doorbell rang. She opened it with a smile, finding Shanequa and Talia smiling back.

"Welcome," she said, hoping to convey a sense of calm-on-the-surface despite feeling hot-mess-so-stressed underneath. They were either on time or two hours early. But then, what did it matter? Clean house or not, they were here now. "Come in."

2

Ever since Saturday morning's playdate with Shanequa and Talia, Holly had struggled to shake feelings of complete incompetence where kindergarten playdate snacks were concerned. It was a gamble figuring out what to serve at your first-ever playdate in your new home, with new friends, in a new town, but Holly thought apple juice with saltine crackers and cheese would be a safe bet: no nuts and nothing too sugary. There was nothing *wrong* with her snacks. They were perfectly *good* snacks. Except Shanequa surprised her by bringing a twelve-cup cupcake tin filled to the brim with bite-size finger snacks for the girls. Adorable, colorful mounds of strawberries, blueberries, and kiwi sat where muffin batter would have been poured. Two cups were piled high with salty offerings: pretzel sticks and Goldfish crackers. There were cucumber slices, apple slices, baby carrots, and blocks of cheddar cheese. Not to mention the dips in pink, white, and toffee colors that sweetened the offering, all the more interesting for dunking things in— pink strawberry yogurt, white ranch dressing, and toffee-colored melted caramel. "I hope you don't mind the sugary caramel," Shanequa had said, showing *her* cards: she, too, worried what another mother might think about serving sugar-infused food to children. Holly lived in the Petunia enclave, known for its density of Foodie Moms, though Holly was certainly not one of them. Should Holly have been surprised to receive a muffin pan of food that looked like an artist's palette of paint colors? Presumably, no. Shanequa lived in the Dillydally enclave, known for its density of creatives.

It was now Monday morning, and though it was a total waste of money but sensing Ella's kindergarten teacher, Miss Bently, might judge her if she didn't, Holly tucked a snack pack of baby carrots inside Ella's cloth lunch bag. She knew Ella would never eat them, nor would she eat the apple sitting like deadweight at the bottom of the bag. The carrots would come back slimy at the end of the day, but the apple? Holly kept that sucker inside Ella's bag the entire week, instructing Ella if she didn't eat the apple or the carrots, she should at least unpack them and leave them in plain view of Miss Bently during lunchtime. "It's complicated," Holly told Ella when Ella protested the carrots and apple inside her lunch bag. *How do you explain the complexities, the nuance, the vulnerability a mother feels when something as primal as her feeding her child is in view of others with strong opinions about the matter?*

It was only a few weeks into the school year, and at least three handouts had already traveled home in the backpack. And hey, Holly understood—those flyers were insightful, valuable public service announcements. But news flash—Holly didn't have the option of slicing cherry tomatoes on top of romaine and thinking there was a snowball's chance in Miami Ella would eat it—Ella wouldn't eat salad no matter *how much* ranch dressing Holly dumped on top. The most exotic thing Ella ate beyond beige-colored carbs, carbs, and more carbs was cauliflower cheese—also beige but at least a vegetable. On the "expert's" list of suggested foods for Holly to pack? Lima beans (slug pillows according to Ella), lentils, tofu, and tuna fish. *Pah! Right.* Tapioca pudding? That texture was so whack even adults wouldn't eat it. Holly had nothing against omega-3s, tempeh, or plant-based nutrition. Families whose kids would eat it without Armageddon-level temper tantrums could have at it, but Holly was mom to a picky eater. Being made to feel slack and uninformed when she wasn't made Holly a bit angsty every time she packed Ella a "ready to learn" lunch. That Monday morning she'd just finished packing it when Greta rolled in, wearing the same earthy black dress for the second time that week.

"Where've you been?" Holly asked her mother, watching as Greta set her ukulele on the kitchen table to free her curly gray hair from a U-clip and a pair of crisscrossed amber chopsticks. Holly wished she had inherited some of her mother's naturally curly hair, but nope. Her sister, Sadie, insisted on being born a few years ahead of Holly, so she got first dibs and took all of it. *Typical.*

After taking a seat, Greta swung her foot onto the table to unlace her black ankle-high military boot.

"I seriously don't know how you do that," said Holly. "How are you so flexible? I'm not flexible."

"You're doing it again," said Greta.

"Doing what?"

"Comparing yourself with others."

"It's hard not to," said Holly, knowing she needed to stop but not knowing how. "You passed sixty, and you're practically slapping yourself in the forehead with your own foot."

"I feel like my heart is beating fast. Have you checked on Charlotte?" asked Greta, glancing to the cat doula birthing plan taped to Holly's refrigerator for the pregnant stray Greta had taken in. Part of that plan was Holly's checking on Charlotte at the top and bottom of every hour, a perfect example of a point Holly so frequently made: *Who's the parent and who's the child?* The cat was Greta's responsibility. Not Holly's. Full clumps of fur missing from her back and hind legs, Charlotte so inspired Greta she'd blown a chunk of cash she'd borrowed from Holly and Jack on an online cat doula certification. Now in the corner of Holly's dining room was Charlotte lounging comfortably on a pillow inside a moving box with the words *maternity ward* stenciled on the side by Ella. Also painted by Ella: baby kitties, rainbows, a painted stick figure of Ella wearing her new glasses and smiling. The other morning, Holly came down to find Struggle asleep beside Charlotte's box. Charlotte would never let on she was warming to Struggle, but they all suspected she was.

Dining rooms weren't ideal for birthing kittens. Holly knew that, but she didn't have a mudroom, and the garage was out of sight, out of mind, so where else would you put a pregnant cat? And besides, no one ever stepped foot in that room except for Holly. She used it to collect things she needed to purge since the move—like that baking thing-amajig Greta bought because she thought Ella might want to concoct a four-layer checkerboard Bundt cake someday. Ella was five years old. When Greta handed Holly the twelve-by-twelve box it came in, Holly was like: *Where the flock am I going to store this?* and then carted it from their old home in Boulder City, Colorado, to their new home in the Village of Primm. Well, no more. Holly was purging, getting organized. Just last week, she received an Enclave Alert about home organizing from Penelope.

Penelope Pratt
Feathered Nest Realty

—ENCLAVE ALERT—

At Feathered Nest Realty, we believe in getting down and dirty with our clients.

GOT MUD? SEND PHOTOS!

With heavy rain in the forecast, it's no wonder the minds of homeowners shift from climate change to the ever-important issue of mudroom organization. Send us YOUR best tips for managing mudroom mayhem and you might win a copper boot tray from the Feathered Nest Home Collection.

NO MUDROOM? NO PROBLEM.

Create one by claiming a small bench as your mudroom. Add storage underneath, a chalkboard above, and a few hooks for hanging items and *presto!* a place to dump life's many necessities.

ORGANIZE YOUR NEST WITH FEATHERED NEST

Call today to book your appointment with an in-house Feathered Nest professional organizer. Remember! Organizing is like therapy. It's not just about your stuff. It's also about *you*.

~

"What happened here?" Greta pointed to a pile of clutter strewed across Holly's kitchen table. "Looks like a desk threw up."

Ha! *Desk.* Holly didn't have a desk. She had a countertop next to the refrigerator; ran a family from a launchpad only twelve inches wide. Launchpad: a term Holly picked up from Penelope's Enclave Alerts, though Holly wasn't sure if she was using it correctly. *Is a launchpad a desk?*

On the counter slash desk slash launchpad were pens, pencils, and papers, yes, but also the vintage pilot goggles Greta wore on her forehead because she thought they made her look like Snoopy dressed as the Red Baron, and a single cuff link because Jack had lost the other one but felt certain it would show up, so would Holly hold this one for a little while? Like that was her responsibility? Why did every single solitary thing in that house somehow fall under Holly's jurisdiction? Was *anyone* responsible for their own stuff?

Holly loved her family. Super loved them! Really, she did.

A ziplock bag of batteries in random sizes, no one knowing if they were good or bad, sat beside a flashlight in case the power went out, but Holly had checked the flashlight and knew it needed size C. But of course, the ziplock didn't have size C. Why would the ziplock have size C? The pile of batteries, papers, and personal stuff stood an easy six inches high, and it was an eternal battle keeping things from sliding off the counter. Whenever Holly added something, she'd have to shift the center of gravity till everything was leaning against the side of the refrigerator. *Do other people live like this?*

"Big changes are coming around here. Big!" Holly counted on her fingers. "Moving boxes are all unpacked. That's one. Ella's settled in school. That's two. And Jack's good with work. Three. Therefore, I'm getting organized," she announced. "It's time. And Penelope's helping me—already booked. I'm converting this entire house into a family-thriving success *machine*. I was up all night researching."

"Pinterest again?"

"Also, mommy blogs and influencer sites," said Holly, drawing a smiley face and a *love Mom xoxo* on Ella's napkin before tucking it into her lunch bag. "And I'm getting a job. Or at least, I'm starting one. A whole business—a new business. It'll be great. I think." She almost felt dizzy saying it. "Caleb's picking me up, and we're going to talk to Penelope about it after I get Ella on the bus. I'm hoping Penelope will be my first client."

Greta lifted a flyer from the pile, the laugh lines at the corners of her eyes growing tighter as she squinted to read the notes Holly had scrawled in the top corner. "And this?" She held it up. "You're putting the house on the Village of Primm Enclave Tour?"

"I was thinking about it."

"Does Jack know?"

"I'm not putting the *entire* house on the tour," said Holly, moving swiftly to the refrigerator for the white grape juice. "I was thinking I'd add the living room. That way, people take three steps inside the house, they look, then bam. They're gone. And I get credit for helping rebuild the Topiary Park by putting my house on the tour."

The plan was brilliant. Get traffic into the house to see the living room but then also have a fully functioning film studio in operation in the dining room and hopefully get word out she was available for hire. The ol' bait and switch, but hey!—she had an unused film degree and bills to pay, so she figured a home-based photography and film studio was her best shot—pun intended. She set the juice on the island to pinch the top button of her shirt with her fingers, before pulling a few times at the neckline to fan herself. "Is it getting hot in here?"

"Oh, it'll get hot all right," said Greta. "But hey, I'm game."

"No." Holly pointed. "You're not game. Because we're finding you an apartment."

Greta's unannounced "visit" the first week of September had somehow shape-shifted into her living with them. But that arrangement had a deadline of a month from now because Holly intuitively knew her mother would eventually do something utterly bizarre like start collecting pizza boxes or grow pot plants and overstay her welcome.

Struggle wandered into the kitchen with a yellow belt from Ella's bathrobe tied to her collar because Ella didn't trust her mom to keep the dog inside, which was a bit harsh, as far as Holly was concerned, and she did wonder: Why the bathrobe tie? Why not a leash? Holly would have preferred to see a defeated look on Struggle's face after Saturday morning's frolic to Houston's, but to Holly's chagrin, Struggle still appeared quite pleased with herself, so the joke was on Holly. Maeve Bling didn't think it was funny.

~

HELLO NOTE—Taped to Holly's Mailbox

The Petunia enclave is not a dog park. Friendly reminder front doors and doors to backyard gates should remain closed and leash laws obeyed. After 15,000 years of domestication, there's no reason for a dog to be wandering around leashless.

—Maeve Bling

~

"And what have we here?" asked Greta, reaching down to rub Struggle behind the ears.

"That," said Holly, "is a dog that's learned how to turn the water on in my bathroom. She rolled in something, so I had to give her another bath, and when I was drying her off, she wiggled away from me and trotted over to stick her snout between the bathtub water spigot and the wall. Then she pushed the cold-water handle with her nose and—*bam!*—turned the water on full blast and started lapping it up."

"Smart dog," said Greta.

"Stupid dog! I love Struggle, but that's a freestanding claw-foot tub—and it's small and shallow. There's no overflow valve on that thing. She'd have that thing flooding the bathroom in ten minutes," said Holly, pouring a thermos of juice for Ella's lunch. "Ella covered her in art supplies the other morning, and then she got out and terrorized poor Houston again." Holly stopped midpour. "Why is she so obsessed with his yard? It's weird." She looked at Struggle, who twitched her eyebrows, then looked away, broadcasting her dog guilt. "I swear she understands English."

Holly left the kitchen to shout up the steps for Ella. "Ella Bella Cinderella! Bus stop. Let's go!" Bus 13 was due in fifteen minutes, and Holly didn't want to miss it. There was a two-hour school delay that morning, which meant Holly's meeting with Penelope had been rescheduled to ten. Her plan was to get Ella on the bus at 9:40 and then hop in Caleb's car so they could practice their pitch on the ride to Feathered Nest Realty. *Where is Caleb? He should be here by now.*

She reached for her lipstick, then applied a pinkish-reddish color whose name she googled the day she bought it because she didn't know what it was: amaranth. A plant family that included the love-lies-bleeding plant, which made her rethink entirely that song by Elton John. Love-lies-bleeding was a much better name for lip color than amaranth, but maybe it had too many letters and wouldn't fit on the sticker at the bottom of the tube. A tiny drip of water, so tiny Holly hardly noticed it at all, fell from the foyer ceiling onto Holly's head. She brushed it off without ever looking up, performing a check in the mirror: hair "swooshed," as Ella liked to say; white shirt; relaxed but professional pants. Accessories? Thin belt; new shoes; Relexi's Fortune & Fate cuff bracelet in gold for love, luck, and serendipity, purchased because Holly hoped to be receiving those things shortly. She would, wouldn't she? Yes, she decided. She would. It said so on the bracelet.

"I'm going to start bullet journaling too," she told Greta. "Shanequa's helping me get everything set up: my index, my future log . . ."

"Bullet journaling? Sounds criminal."

"More like—life changing. I'm investing big-time," said Holly, anxious to get started. "I think this is the answer I've been waiting for."

"*That's* the answer you've been waiting for? Bullet journaling?" asked Greta. "You don't want to know the meaning of life or what happens when you die or whether cereal is soup?"

"Of course I want to know if cereal is soup," said Holly, feeling defensive.

"And what about the hair on your head?" Greta pointed.

"What about it?" asked Holly with a quick check in the mirror.

"Ever wonder why it grows faster than the hair on your arms?"

"Mom, stop. I want to get organized," said Holly. "I told you that. And besides, I'm going through a thing right now, and I think bullet journaling will help."

"What thing?" said Greta. "You mean like—a crisis?"

"Maybe," said Holly, thinking about it. "Although, no, maybe not a *crisis*."

"You mean like the time you told your classmates you were spending summer break in Hollywood because producers of *The Simpsons* called to announce they were writing you in as 'Ruby,' Lisa's friend from band camp?"

"Not this again," said Holly, folding her arms across her chest, settling in.

"But then, that summer, when friends from school saw you on the high dive at the swimming pool and they hollered up, asking you why you weren't in Hollywood recording *Simpsons* episodes as a voice actor, you didn't have an answer, so you pretended you *lost* your voice and, for some bizarre reason, chose that moment to run the length of the diving board while grabbing hold of your own throat with both hands, like someone was trying to choke you as you ran."

"Will you stop? I panicked. Big deal," said Holly.

"Oh! And then you jumped. Legs scissor kicking as you took flight. It was magnificent," said Greta. "Until you launched into an explanation on the way down using nothing but hand gestures and face twitching—your mouth forming exaggerated shapes as you explained why Ruby was cut from the episode. It was like watching someone on fire play a quick game of charades while free-falling from an airplane. No—a *mime* artist getting tased."

"Are you finished?"

"And then—and then—" said Greta between bouts of laughter, "you stayed underwater for so long two lifeguards dove in after you."

"*Mom.* I stayed under because I was trying to hide," said Holly. The memory of those poor lifeguards . . . she felt so bad. The way she made angry faces as they approached her underwater because she didn't want to be dragged to the surface, where she'd have to face her friends. She tried escaping by swimming away, but one of the lifeguards grabbed her by the ankle, and the other grabbed her torso, the three of them popping up like buoys in the deep end, gasping for breath in front of an audience of at least fifty faces staring back at them.

"I'm trying to figure out what I want to be when I grow up," Holly said, chin up. She knew what she wanted to be—what she wanted to do—she just wasn't sure her plans would pan out. It was hard going from stay-at-home mom to entrepreneur overnight. Especially when money was tight. She felt a certain pressure.

"And you think bullet journaling will help?" asked Greta, one eyebrow up.

"Imagine having a personal life coach in a journal. It's for busy people with a million things to do," said Holly, not knowing much about bullet journaling—yet. She knew a little by stalking the bullet journaling influencers online. They made it look so easy. Like anyone could do it, right? "It's for people with official-looking pens and nifty handwriting and goals and habits they want to track."

"Like you," said Greta.

"Yes, like me," said Holly. "I have goals . . ."

"And habits."

"Mom. Do you want to know what it is or not?" Holly waited. "Fine. I'll tell you. It's a journal with pages covered in dots—those are the bullets. And they're all spaced a half centimeter apart."

"Sounds like a blast," said Greta. "I was thinking I might count a box of toothpicks."

"Don't make fun."

"No, really. I think it's great. We can take you to Applebee's and set you loose on a kiddie place mat. Do bullet journals have calendars?"

"Absolutely," said Holly. "All kinds of calendars!"

"Do me a favor? Check the calendar and let me know if there's a day mattresses are *not* on sale?"

"You're ridiculous. Bullet journaling is the latest and greatest. Ella!" yelled Holly up the stairs. "Let's go!"

Ella, in socks, began bumping her way down the steps.

"Careful, honey. Don't slip," said Holly. "Teeth brushed? Where are your shoes?"

Ella pointed over Holly's shoulder to the coatrack with the screw loose. Her shoes hung high on the rack like a set of antlers on a deer head cocked to one side.

"Hi, Gammy!" said Ella, swooshing her feet across the foyer using the exaggerated steps of a long-distance skier. Arriving at her grand-mother, she wrapped her arms around Greta's waist as Greta bent to push Ella's auburn hair off her forehead, where she then planted a kiss. Ella was wearing a big white T-shirt with seven magical ponies: Twilight Sparkle, Pinkie Pie, Shutterfly, Applejack, Rarity, Fluttershy, and Rainbow Dash. Crazy that Holly knew that. She'd be hard pressed to name all nine Supreme Court justices, but *My Little Pony*? Nailed it. The T-shirt hit Ella midthigh over sparkly lavender leggings and orange socks.

Ella beamed. "I'm marrying the letter *Q*!"

"Aren't you a little young to be getting married?" Greta asked Ella.

Miss Bently had emailed with the news Ella's name had been picked out of a hat to be the letter *U* in the Q&U Wedding at school. A boy in Ella's class would be the letter *Q*. So, yay! Let the games begin. The Banks family had a wedding in their future. It had all begun the way many things began in Holly's new life as a new school mom. With a cryptic email that led to a misunderstanding:

21

EMAIL—Time Received: 4:15 p.m.

> TO: Holly Banks
> FROM: Miss Bently, Primm Academy
> SUBJECT: PA PPRRA & PA PRRA
>
> At Primm Academy, two Kindergarten reading assessments are given in preparation for First Grade. The Primm Academy Pre-Reading Reading Assessment (PA PRRA), and the Primm Academy Pre-Pre-Reading Reading Assessment (PA PPRRA).
>
> At this time, a conference is requested to discuss Ella's performance on the PA PPRRA.
>
> P.S. Ella is U!

~

Me? Never mind the confusing acronyms, was she suggesting Ella's performance on the reading assessment was somehow inherited? Holly had wondered, not realizing Miss Bently's postscript was referring to Ella's selection as the bride in the Q&U Wedding.

Never quite understanding why school correspondence was so often directed only at her, Holly added Jack to the email and responded with:

EMAIL—Time Sent: 4:37 p.m.

> TO: Miss Bently, Primm Academy
> FROM: Holly Banks
> CC: Jack Banks
> RE: SUBJECT: PA PPRRA & PA PRRA

I am eager to discuss Ella's performance on the PA PRRA. When might you be able to meet, and can you give a short description of the problem?

P.S. When you said: Ella is U—were you suggesting it's genetic?

~

A few moments later, Miss Bently responded with:

EMAIL—Time Received: 4:46 p.m.

TO: Holly Banks
FROM: Miss Bently, Primm Academy
CC: Jack Banks
RE: RE: SUBJECT: PA PPRRA & PA PRRA

A meeting is required to discuss Ella's performance on the PA PPRRA, not the PA PRRA. The PA PPRRA is administered at the start of the school year (hence, pre-pre-reading). The PA PRRA is administered in the Spring (known simply as, pre-reading).

Regarding the PA PPRRA, it appears that although Ella knows her letters and has a beginner-level awareness of their sounds, she is often confused when letters are presented in a sequence.

P.S. I wouldn't consider the union of letters to be *genetic*. Cultural, maybe?

~

Ella passing the Pre-Pre-Reading Assessment was something Holly intended to add to her bullet journal, brush lettering the *Pre-Pre*, block lettering the rest. Shanequa said she'd show her how.

"Let's go, let's go, let's go," urged Holly, worried they'd miss the bus. She took Ella by the hand, pulling her from her embrace with Greta. "Mom, will you get her backpack?"

Grabbing Ella's shoes from the coatrack, Holly couldn't help but think about Iraq, Qatar, and even Iqaluit, the capital of Nunavut, a Canadian territory. *U* didn't follow *Q* in any of those words. In Greenland, there was a town named Qaqortoq, and that had three naked *Q*s. Oh, but, as Jack said, *Leave it alone, Holly*. Because the wedding ceremony was meant to teach the kids in Ella's kindergarten class an important spelling lesson, and yet, Holly took issue with what that lesson taught. Miss Bently wanted the kids to know the letter *U* ALWAYS followed the letter *Q*. Stress placed on the word *always*. And you couldn't say that because that wasn't true.

Holly and Greta were avid Scrabble players and, as such, had study sheets with Scrabble-approved words written in capital letters, so they knew a whole host of words that started with *Q* and didn't have a single *U* in them. Take QI, for instance: the life energy believed in Chinese philosophy to be inherent in all things. And then there was QAT: leaves you could chew like tobacco or make into tea. Chew enough qat and you might get high. But, oh, your teeth might fall out, and your heart might attack you. And then there was MBAQANGA. South African dance music with Zulu roots. Play MBAQANGA on a Scrabble board, and you'd probably win the game. Not to mention, a marriage where the *U* always followed the *Q* was almost like saying the wife always followed the husband, and that was certainly not true. Holly and Jack were equal partners.

Holly checked the time. Seven minutes. Maybe five. You never knew with Bus 13.

"Mom? Ella's backpack?" Holly urged, missed-bus PTSD setting in. She lifted Ella's chin to focus her daughter's attention, then slid her glasses off her face to clean them with the bottom of Ella's shirt. "You good?" Holly asked, sliding them back on, ensuring Ella had a clear view.

"I'm good." Ella nodded, calling for Struggle, then taking hold of the end of her bathrobe tie. "You know how last night you said ketchup was tomatoes? How do you get the tomato into the bottle?"

"Hmm?" said Holly, distracted by the time. "You just press it in."

"Through the hole? In the bottle?" Ella was always so suspicious. It was as if she sensed Holly might not be telling her the whole truth half the time.

"Um-hmm. That's right," said Holly, kneeling down to open up Ella's shoe and slip it on her foot. "You just press the tomato through the hole." She felt a bit hypocritical engaging in half truths about tomatoes. Especially after taking issue with Miss Bently's *Q* and *U* spelling lesson.

"What about cows?" Ella asked, her hand digging into Holly's shoulder as Holly worked to get the shoes on. "They're bigger than tomatoes. Is that why the milk container is bigger than the ketchup?"

"Can this wait till after school?"

"If chickens are inside the eggs, are the cows inside the milk?"

"*What?*"

Holly shook it off, directing both Ella and Struggle toward the porch.

Through the door, then down the porch steps, Ella ran with Struggle toward a box of sidewalk chalk at the foot of the driveway while clinging tight to the bathrobe belt knotted around Struggle's collar.

"Don't let go!" Holly yelled.

"I'm a big girl," reminded Ella as she ran. She stopped when she arrived to tie Struggle to the mailbox post.

Just in case, Holly went outside so she could monitor.

"Mom? Are you coming?" called Holly.

Almost immediately, Holly noticed Houston sitting on his front porch overlooking his expansive front yard. According to Penelope, Houston's house was the original house on Petunia Lane. Petunia, as it turned out, was a person—Houston's grandmother, Petunia Bonneville, who married Clive Cranbarrie—the marriage that created the famed Bonneville-Cranbarrie name. Famed because both family names were so sullied that no one could fathom what the blending of the two would produce. What wasn't Houston's five-acre property became the Petunia enclave.

Greta caught up with Holly on the sidewalk, waving at Houston as if she were a beauty queen perched in the back seat of a convertible, fingers and thumb positioned like a Barbie doll's. She whispered while keeping a celebrity smile plastered to her face, "I heard he has a prescription."

"Stop waving like that. You look thirsty." Holly gave her own slight wave toward Houston. "And how do you know if he has a prescription?"

"Rumors."

"You've lived in Primm two weeks. How are you hearing rumors?" asked Holly as Houston stood from his chair. "Great. Now he's waving. And wow. Such enthusiasm."

"He's showing his gusto. I have that effect on men."

"That's so gross," said Holly, pulling Greta's arm down, glad they were out of earshot of Ella. "Stop waving."

"Relax, Holly. The world is swiping right."

"What are you talking about?"

"I started a profile." Greta shrugged.

"A profile?" *A profile?* "On what?"

"A dating app."

"You can't date." *That's ridiculous.*

"You're not the boss of me."

"You think this is funny? You're not bringing guys home. Not when you're living in my house." *She can't date. She can't.* "Mom. I have a child. No," said Holly, stress level rising. "No way. Absolutely not."

For Holly, there was real life and there was life imagined as it would play out on the big screen. Often, the one she imagined was way better than the one she was living. But in this case, they both felt ridiculous.

SCENE 1 — INT. HOUSE — FAMILY ROOM — EVENING

    Stand by on the set.
    Stand by to roll tape.
    Roll tape.

                HOLLY
    (walking in on her mom kissing a guy)

    You can't date. Not in my house.

                GRETA
        (standing to leave)

    Fine. I'll use the driveway.

                HOLLY
    You're not dating!

"Holly? Hello?" said Greta, tugging on her arm, snapping her fingers in front of Holly's face. "Focus. You're a million miles away."

"Hmm? Oh, sorry," said Holly, shaking free of her imagination: her Walter Mitty tendency to momentarily lose herself in a brief, fantastical thought. Did other filmmakers do this? Slip so easily into the world of film?

Pulling Holly firmly back into reality, Greta pointed to something in the sky beyond Houston's. "What is that?"

It looked like a black dot, a blur of something Holly couldn't quite make out because it was surrounded by morning sun. It wasn't a bird. It was something human made. Not a drone. It was an aircraft of some sort and still a good distance away, but Holly could tell it wasn't flying right. It was bouncing, flying a bit topsy turvy: up, then sideways a bit, then dipping down.

"Ella, honey? Let's go inside," said Holly, running to the foot of the driveway, where Ella was busy drawing flowers with sidewalk chalk. She swooped Ella into her arms before running with her toward the porch. "Everything's all right, honey. Don't be scared," she said. "I just want you on the porch right now." Holly yelled behind her, "Struggle. Come!"

Struggle, loosely tied, pulled free of the mailbox to follow Holly, Ella's yellow bathrobe tie still fixed to her collar.

Whatever it was—that thing in the sky? It was headed straight for Holly's house.

3

Safe on the porch, tucked amid a landscape of small but well-appointed homes marked with lush, HOA-approved curb appeal—densely carpeted lawns composed of prized, custom-grown sod; tall fescue mixed with heavily irrigated Kentucky bluegrass because (according to Jack) zoysia plugs took too long to grow—Holly realized that yes, something up there, off in the distance, was headed their way.

Like a shadow emerging from the sunlight, the blurry dot was getting closer and closer and clearer and clearer as it swelled in size, took shape, and made noise. *Bzzzzz.* Like a lawn mower. A flying—something. *What is that?* thought Holly. A UFO? A pterodactyl?

In film school, Holly learned to shoot straight into the sun, exploiting light and lens flare to produce veiled and ghosted shots. She could take a subject, like a person or a . . . *thing* flying over there above and beyond the magnolias, douse it with penetrating light till you felt there was nothing *but* light. But this wasn't just light, and it was getting bigger and bigger.

Greta was quiet, but she, too, bent over the railing, looking the way Holly was.

Struggle, fur like a mohawk down her back, growled, deep and continuous beside Ella, who was now drawing on the porch floor with chalk.

The spot in the sky appeared unpredictable in the way it was flying, bouncing about, swooping up, swooping down, tipping to the side, correcting itself, then starting the pattern over again.

"Ella, go inside," said Holly.

The unidentified flying object was getting closer. A private airplane of some sort? A Cessna? But no, Cessnas were bigger. This was more like a golf cart, but with wings. It was odd. About a hundred and fifty yards away. Then a buck twenty-five. Houston left his chair to step inside his house.

"Ella—inside," said Holly.

"I wasn't finished drawing my daffy dillies," said Ella with a stomp of her foot.

Greta picked her up, rushing inside with her, leaving Holly on the porch with Struggle.

Now the object was low enough to clip the tops of the distant magnolias upon approach, and Holly could see it was indeed a lightweight aircraft of some sort. Something with a vibe that screamed *amateur enthusiast*. It appeared homemade, like a flying contraption someone built in their garage, and it kept dipping downward as it came into view. It had legit hang glider wings—the kind people used to run off dunes or fly high above a boat while tethered to a rope—and attached below the glider wings was a giant two-seater baby stroller with a person sitting in it. No protection that Holly could make out, no windshield of any kind. Just a stroller set into an aluminum frame of support beams and bars. A flying baby-stroller saucer. A baby-stroller spacecraft. Something. Holly figured there must be an engine of some sort attached to the back of the stroller because the noise sounded like a souped-up lawn mower: *bzzzzzzz. Bzzzzzzz. BZZZZZZZ.*

Baby strollers should keep to the ground so fit moms have something to run behind. Baby strollers don't FLY. *No one's ever seen a flying baby stroller.* And yet, there one was, headed straight for Holly's house, presumably in an attempt to use Petunia Lane as a landing strip. Would it fit? It would fit. The width between wingtips wasn't much.

Twenty-five yards now.

Holly had a huge oak tree with sprawling branches to the left of her front porch. If that thing didn't stop in time, it would hit the tree. It was happening . . . in like—aw, hell-o. It was happening *now*: in front of Holly, in *her* front yard.

From the aircraft came the cry of the pilot: "INCOMING!"

It dipped and turned, this way and that. Holly worried the glider might make a sharp left and head straight for her—her back now plastered against the siding of her house. Struggle, barking furiously, backed up toward the door.

Fifteen yards, then ten, then—"TAKE COVER!"

Ka-pitz.

Ka-putz.

Ka-pertz.

Followed by *ka-chhhhhhhhhhhhhhh* as the plane crash-landed, slashing everything in its path. The plane's back end, caught up in a violent whiplashing—arse dragging, snagging, zigzagging its way across Holly's lawn—ripped a new one through the carpeted, HOA-approved grass. It whipped and rolled, coming to a jagged stop.

Whatthe

frrrrrruck

just

happened.

Holly's heart was pounding. Struggle, barking. She took hold of the yellow bathrobe tie, muttering, "Oh, no. You're not slipping away from me now, Struggle."

Dressed head to toe in a flight suit with a black scarf and goggles on his face, the pilot appeared shaken but okay. The propeller blades had ground down and dug in as the plane bounced about, making Holly now certain her curb appeal would never survive the flogging.

Her first thought was for the pilot's safety, yes, yes, of course, but also: a flying baby stroller falling from the sky, crash-landing the entire length and width of her front yard a month before the opening of the Village of Primm Enclave Tour? *Is there no end to my bad luck?*

Holly considered the possibility lightning might strike at any minute, or she might win the lottery but lose the ticket, or a shark might bite her. Wholly aware a plane had just Mayday'd an unlikely descent across her front lawn, Holly worried all this might be a sign the stars *weren't* aligned in her favor, that her fate in the Village of Primm was forever doomed. Was everything about to come crashing down?

4

Holly, with wits hardly intact, rushed toward the pilot. Mixing with the buzzing noise of the aircraft's engine was the sound of Struggle's insistent barking. The pilot killed the engine, and all the buzzing ground to a halt, leaving only the racket of Struggle barking with such frenzied confusion you'd think a mailman had landed delivering cats and squirrels. Holly's first words were the most obvious. She almost cringed hearing herself say them: "Are you okay?"

"I'm good!" said the pilot, flashing two thumbs up.

That voice. It sounded familiar. The pilot removed his goggles, his identity revealed: "Caleb!" said Holly. "Good gravy, no. No, no, no. What are you doing? This is *insane*. You were supposed to pick me up in your Subaru. We have to be at Penelope's in like—twenty minutes."

Was it wise or foolish to go into business with someone as obsessed with tech gadgets as Caleb? This recent stunt suggested it was the latter. Caleb was a cable guy for Primm Cable by day, moonlighting the same way Holly hoped to as a filmmaker. He was the one who told her about the Wilhelm Klaus Film Festival coming to Primm in October. A film festival you could enter and win prize money from. He was the one who hooked her up with a spy camera during Ella's first week of kindergarten to help her get started with her own entry. However, that hadn't quite panned out the way Holly had hoped. And now, he was the one falling from the sky into her front yard?

She surveyed the damage inflicted by the propeller when landing: deep crevices, violent fissures, rifts and splits gouged into the Kentucky bluegrass, hacksawed openings in the skin of the lawn so brutal it would take buckets of money and weeks to recover. "Look at my lawn," she said. "You Kentucky'd my bluegrass. You know how much sod costs? You're fixing this." She pointed. "You are. Not me." Jack was going to freak. They didn't have time for this. They didn't have money for this. Resod the front yard in mid-September? Did grass even grow in September?

"Think of the competitive advantage," he said, climbing out of his seat. "With aircraft, the sky's the limit. Aerial footage is the wave of the future, Holly. And you and me? We're the only gig in town with manned aircraft."

"You have a drone. You hit me with it two weeks ago capturing footage of the Topiary Park."

"Everyone has drones," he said. "But on this beauty, we can mount ten cameras—of all shapes and sizes. And you can capture special footage from the passenger seat."

"I'm not riding shotgun in that thing. No way. And my *daughter* was at the bus stop," said Holly. "Someone could have gotten hurt. Jeez, Caleb."

"Nah." He brushed her off. "You're overreacting. The odds of dying in a plane crash are one in eleven million."

"Odd that you should know that."

"What could go wrong?" He shrugged, reaching up to give a jovial slap to one of the wings.

It was a two-seater but wasn't a baby stroller attached to hang glider wings as she initially thought. It was a legit hobby aircraft, seats and parts made by a company that configured these things.

"These things are totally safe," Caleb said. "Top speed is only fifty-five knots. Max."

"No idea what that means," said Holly, watching that sly Maeve Bling peek out from behind a curtain, poking her nose against a downstairs window. *Mind your own business, Bling! It's just an airplane,* Holly wanted to shout. Although, Holly had to admit, all of this was a bit bizarre. She waved, and Bling's face disappeared from view.

"Fifty-five knots is about sixty-three miles per hour. And that's at top speed, level flight," said Caleb. "What are you afraid of?"

She raised an eyebrow. She hated flying, preferred the ground with tangible things around her, things she could touch like dirt, grass, trees. Not sky. Not wide-open sky. *Of all the creatures ever to populate the earth (the total number forever uncertain), there's a reason only a few species were built to fly unaided. Leave the sky to them.*

"It's an ultralight aircraft with foldable wings," he continued. "But don't worry—it's extremely portable. You can tow it behind a car. Her name's *Henny Penny.*"

"I can see that," said Holly, eyeing the words painted beneath one of the dark-beige wings. "Henny Penny, like Chicken Little? The chicken in the folktale who runs around telling everyone the sky is falling? You don't find it at all ironic to name an airplane that?"

"Nope," said Caleb with no apologies. And apparently, no sense of foreboding either.

"Sit, Struggle," Holly said as Ella's bus rolled up, air brakes making that distinctive *ppssss* sound as they exhaled. All the kids rushed to the windows to gawk at the contraption in Ella's yard. Holly kept hold of Struggle's bathrobe tie as she turned, expecting they'd still be inside but finding Ella behind her, on the sidewalk, backpack on back, holding Greta's hand.

"Is this ours?" asked Ella, with an excited smile.

"Definitely not," said Holly as Greta volunteered to copilot.

Greta was absurdly excited. "I've got goggles!" she told Caleb.

And Caleb said, "I've got a sport pilot's license!" Though everyone knew he was talking to Holly. "I was hoping Holly would be my copilot."

"That'll never happen." Holly waved at the bus driver. "We're coming!" To Caleb she griped, "Flying is noisy. I'm afraid of heights. And you don't serve snacks."

"I can serve snacks," said Caleb. "What do you want? Pretzels?"

"Right," said Holly. "Like I'd sell out for a bag of pretzels."

Greta said, "She'd fly all day long if you set a bucket of Nutella on her lap."

"Mom. Enough." Holly dropped the end of Struggle's bathrobe tie in the grass to lift Ella and give her a great big hug and kiss. Setting her back on the ground, Holly told her, "Cauliflower cheese for dinner tonight."

"Yay!" said Ella, taking off to run with Greta to catch the bus as Caleb leaned into the ultralight to finish shutting down and fuss with his belongings.

Worried about getting to Feathered Nest by ten, Holly checked the time, walking a few steps until she had a clear view around the ultralight to wave once more to Ella as she climbed the bus steps. "I love you, Ella Bella! Have a great day!" said Holly, so distracted by the destruction of her lawn and getting Ella on the bus that she didn't notice Struggle's silent, sneaky departure from where she once sat. "We're going to be late," Holly told Caleb.

"I think we should take your car."

"Ya think?"

"Do you think Rosie will like it?" he asked, chasing Holly up the porch steps like a schoolboy experiencing his first crush. "Ever since you introduced us at the Cherry Festival on The Lawn, I can't stop thinking about her. She's the prettiest woman in Primm. She tutors kids at the Village of Primm library. Did you know she's a literacy specialist? That's so hot."

A literacy specialist? Hot? Holly stopped to say something, then decided to leave it alone. "Wait here," she told him, leaving him at the front door as she walked into the kitchen, nervous about the meeting with Penelope and shaken by the events of the last ten minutes.

"Holly?" he said, as she walked the length of the foyer, never looking back to see him holding his hand out, catching a single barely there drip as it dropped from the ceiling. "I think you've got a leak."

Holly went straight to the kitchen pantry with a quick grab of a spoon on the way, stepped inside, then closed the door and dipped her spoon into a jar of Nutella, the surface of the hazelnut spread shiny like a pool or a looking glass. So rich, so creamy, so perfectly everything. No way in hell-o kitty would she *ever* fly around in a baby stroller. *No way, not gonna do it.* Then—*whoops!*—the pantry door opened, and Holly jumped, metal spoon tinging her teeth.

"See?" said Greta to Caleb while pointing at Holly. "Add in-flight Nutella, and she'll fly with you."

"Mom!" Holly stomped, scrambling to close the jar. She pushed past them, chucking the licked spoon into the sink. "Caleb, let's go. We're late."

She snatched her keys from the counter, Caleb running after her through the front door and toward the driveway. Bus long gone, Holly noticed Maeve Bling's front door opening, Bling stepping onto her porch to have a look-see. Holly waved—"Hey there, Maeve!"—as she slid into the driver's seat. *Who drives off moments after an aircraft lands in their front yard? The neighbors must think I'm nuts.* "I've got a bad feeling about all of this," she said, backing down her driveway to drive up the hill and past Houston's, still not realizing that Struggle, out for a gleeful adventure on a beautiful September morning, was hightailing it through the neighborhood in the opposite direction.

Holly and Caleb fell silent as they left Petunia enclave, tucked a safe distance from the Topiary Park and the devastation that recently befell the Village of Primm's primary tourist attraction. A few turns later, everywhere they looked was a stark reminder of what had happened.

"For the record, Plume's a peahen," Holly told Caleb. "At least she was." Technically, she was a topiary peacock with long, colorful plumage made of plants. Built as a peacock, she was referred to by everyone as female, which drove Holly crazy because males were peacocks. Females were peahens. Although, now she wasn't a peahen or a peacock. She was skeletal remains, nothing but a twenty-five-foot-tall, forty-foot-long topiary wire frame standing spent and empty on a herringbone-brick courtyard at the entrance to the now-defunct topiary petting zoo, once filled with gigantic plant animals you could touch but not climb: Mother Goose, the Three Little Pigs, horses lined up for a steeplechase, a turkey, butterflies, and more. In one devastating night, it had all gone up in smoke, and every single solitary topiary in the Village of Primm Topiary Park Petting Zoo lost its life. All over Primm, all topiaries were ordered destroyed to prevent any further damage caused by the chilli thrips, an invasive species of flying insect shipped to Primm in a scheme to commit insurance fraud.

"Weren't you raised in Primm? Is it true tourism dollars from the Topiary Park fund the village?" Holly asked Caleb.

"Yup. Without tourism, the mom-and-pops are put at risk. Small businesses are the heart and soul of Primm. All of the shops that border The Lawn could be affected."

"Do you agree with Penelope?" she asked. "All that talk about the risk to property values in Primm?" Holly and Jack had sunk everything they had into a house they could barely afford so Ella could attend Primm Academy. If something happened that caused them to sell—a job loss or transfer—even if they lost only 5 percent of their home's value, when you added real estate fees to sell their home, there was a real possibility they'd hand over the keys still owing the bank.

"Unfortunately, yeah," Caleb acknowledged, his face somber as he looked out the car window. Not only had he grown up in Primm, but he also worked days with Primm Cable, so he'd been inside most of the homes and knew the homeowners. "I do think property values would tank."

"Tank?" Holly said quickly, her words like a counterpunch to Caleb's. She needed to tamp down her panic, so she tried again, clearing her throat to say it more softly. "Tank?"

"Think about it." He shrugged. "No right-minded homebuyer would touch a Village of Primm home with a ten-foot pole any more than someone in need of a good night's sleep would stay in a hotel room riddled with bedbugs. I feel bad for residents in the Peloton and Blythe enclaves. If anyone has reason to be angry about what happened, it's them."

Peloton and Blythe, with their close proximity to the Topiary Park, were hit especially hard when the Topiary Park Petting Zoo burned to the ground. It wasn't *just* the burning of the town's tourist attraction and primary source of tax revenue that hurt surrounding enclaves. In the days following the bonfires, the invasive little buggers that *hadn't* caught fire had managed to "hop leaf" and were now chewing gaping, unsightly holes into ivy and English boxwoods—both popular choices for bushes and ground cover in home landscaping across the Village of Primm. The thing that had everyone concerned now was the effectiveness of the CBD-420 spray the Topiary Park concocted and whether the all-natural insecticide was actually *killing* the bugs like it was supposed to or, worse, giving the drugged-out little buggers a bad case of the munchies.

"Now people are trying to drown the bugs," said Caleb, pointing out Holly's front windshield to a homeowner drenching his bushes with a garden hose. "They're stressing the water tower."

"What water tower?" she asked, figuring she should know, but having lived here less than a month, she didn't.

"There's a water tower that feeds both towns," explained Caleb. "It's on the line between the Village of Primm and Southern Lakes, and it's old and needs repairs. Every year there's talk of building a new one, but the two towns never agree on who pays for what."

As Holly drove, she noticed Caleb falling further and further into reflection. "Can you imagine? The bugs come, kill the topiaries; then we stress an old water tower with overconsumption, and soon we won't have the tax revenue to fix the situation because tourism is down?" He shook his head. "I hope the Enclave Tour does what Penelope thinks it'll do."

"And what is that?" asked Holly, suspecting she already knew but wanting to confirm.

"Rebuild the topiaries. Lift everyone's spirits. Remind them Primm is home, and home's worth fighting for." His eyes were kind and hopeful and reflected his good heart.

Holly hadn't enjoyed Ella's first week of kindergarten one bit. Competitive moms, at times petty, but in the end? All that volunteering helped produce a powerhouse school. Holly respected that. She complained that her neighbors obsessed about their yards but was thankful. Her view out her window was made better by their effort. The residents of Primm invested in Primm. What was worth fighting for? Community. Primm was high maintenance, but Primm had heart.

"I'm sure it will be a huge success," said Holly. Penelope was a Realtor with the mind of a city planner. A parade-of-homes "enclave tour" was right up her alley.

"Let's hope so," he added.

Holly pulled into Feathered Nest Realty. She killed the engine, checked her reflection in the rearview mirror. "Same game plan?" she asked, wanting to confirm before entering Feathered Nest. "We go in and do what we said we were going to do?"

"Yup," said Caleb, apparently believing a flight suit was as good as a business suit, because he climbed out of Holly's car without taking it off.

She knew in her heart and hoped she wouldn't be proven wrong that no one, except maybe two or three people in the entire Village of Primm, knew about her involvement in the chilli thrip infestation. Jack, yes. And Mary-Margaret St. James, who was wrapped up in it far more than Holly, considering it was her husband who brought the pests to Primm in the first place. But Penelope? Did she know of Holly's involvement? The verdict was still out on that.

So yeah, as Holly left her vehicle and made her way with Caleb toward Feathered Nest, she wondered if Penelope knew about her unintended role in the spreading of the chilli thrips. No doubt, as a descendent of one of the founding families of Primm, Penelope harbored a few secrets of her own. *Let's see how secrets deal with secrets,* thought Holly. *Let's see if, perhaps, two secretive people can strike a deal and work together to rebuild what is broken.*

5

As Holly and Caleb crossed the threshold into the world of Feathered Nest Realty, Penelope met them at the door, and like a shot, the three were off and running. Holly attempted small talk while trying not to stare stupidly and openmouthed at the impossibly gorgeous carpet beneath her feet. *Stunning, that carpet. Handwoven?* Feathered Nest was both a real estate office and a home-lifestyle boutique. No wonder Holly felt this way every time she entered the office. Oil paintings, a new addition, now lined the entry, presenting Primm as a place of great ease and luxury. A paradise, a place of abundance, where all your dreams came true. The allure, the promise, the *marketing* behind Primm were fueled by Penelope Pratt, ninth-generation Primmer, master marketer, architect of community. She created the ambience inside Feathered Nest Realty that posited: *You, too, can live a perfect life . . . if . . . you live* here.

"I'm sorry we're a few minutes late," Holly began. "Strangest thing," she said with a backward glance at Caleb, "I was walking Ella to the bus stop, and then I looked up and saw something flying, headed straight for my house." This was a good excuse for being late, right? A plane crash-landing in the front yard? "Lo and behold, it was Caleb."

"That's right. Me. Piloting an ultralight aircraft," Caleb piped in. "Imagine the aerial footage, Penelope. If you work with us, we can provide a bird's-eye view of Primm! And when I say 'bird's eye,' I mean bird's eye—the ultralight is named *Henny Penny*."

"You mean, like Chicken Little?" asked Penelope. "The folktale?"

"That's the one!" Caleb winked at Holly.

"You don't find that ironic?" asked Penelope with a quick look at Holly. Penelope waved him off, then kept walking. "Plume, Henny Penny. This town is full of birds."

Of all the real estate agents in the tritown area of Menander, Southern Lakes, and the Village of Primm, including the dueling resort towns of Quixotic and DooLittle, none surpassed Penelope in sales and pocket listings. Pocket listings, Penelope often said, helped shape the Village of Primm into what it was today: charming enclaves run by stellar homeowner's associations populated by carefully matched families.

Holly two-stepped to keep up with Penelope, deciding to "fake it till you make it" by channeling Diane Keaton, an actress she loved and studied when she was a film major in college, the Diane Keaton who played J. C. Wiatt in the 1987 film *Baby Boom*. Holly still felt Keaton should have won Best Actress for that movie. The Nancy Meyers writing was brilliant, the film keenly articulated, still wholly relevant, and Keaton blew the plight of motherhood in the workplace wide open with that role. So yeah, Diane Keaton as J. C. Wiatt. That was what Holly was hoping to channel as she walked the carpeted plank toward Penelope's office.

Holly copped a glance over her shoulder at a chandelier made of golden twigs forming a brilliant metal nest above dangling fat-bellied glass birds—it was a beautiful chandelier, and she found herself wishing it hung in the foyer inside her home.

"Stunning chandelier," said Penelope, top in sales, trained to notice what others were noticing.

"It is," said Holly. "Feathered Nest has a beautiful collection." Throughout the offices, chandeliers available for purchase hung in all shapes and sizes. Bright, sparkling constellations you could hang indoors to remind yourself the sky was the limit.

"Well, maybe it will be yours someday."

Is now the time to ask how much it costs?

"Catch," said Penelope, stopping at a garment rack filled with aprons outside her office.

Holly caught the apron Penelope tossed her way: a sweet, skirted apron with a pastoral scene of yellow birds perched on branches. No, not yellow. *Buttercream.*

"Chickadee's perch," said Penelope, pointing to the birds on the apron. "Do you solve crossword puzzles?"

"Yes, I do. I love crossword puzzles," said Holly.

"Well, that apron is a crossword puzzle clue."

"How so?" asked Holly. "It's an apron."

"It's part of a village-wide puzzle," Penelope explained. "In life, answers are often hidden in plain sight."

Holly inspected the apron. "Hidden in plain sight?"

"Now *that* sounds like a clue," said Caleb.

"Watch," said Penelope. "Chickadee's perch," she said, pointing to the birds on the skirt of the apron before taking the apron from Holly's hands to spread the apron ties. "You think it's just a pretty apron. And it is. But it's also a crossword puzzle clue. See?" She pointed to the embroidered words on one of the tails of the apron:

DOWN

NUMBER 10. CHICKADEE'S PERCH (FOUR LETTERS)

"That's the question," said Penelope. She pointed to the word *twig* embroidered on the other apron tail. "And that's the answer. Twig." She smiled. "There are crossword puzzle clues and answers all over Primm"—she nodded toward the garment rack—"and those aprons—available for sale here at Feathered Nest Realty—are part of it. Mitch

& Lucy Creamery has a clue; Primm Paper has a clue. It's all about the sales, Holly—that's the name of the game. We have to raise money to rebuild the Topiary Park. We have to. So we designed a crossword puzzle you can solve using the Enclave Tour app with pieces of the puzzle hidden in plain sight. Oh, sure, you can solve the puzzle without buying anything, but isn't it fun to link puzzle clues to merchandise available only in Primm?"

"A crossword puzzle coming to life," said Holly, sharing her thoughts.

"That's right," said Penelope. "We're selling aprons, bullet journals, lavender candles." She counted on her fingers.

"Lavender? Not lilac?" asked Holly.

"No, why?"

"Just wondering."

"We're selling all sorts of things. In our beloved, bug-infested Village of Primm, an important principle is at play: *consumer spending drives the economy.* It's that simple. The Enclave Tour sells the lifestyle, the merchandise supports local businesses, and everything is wrapped up in a tidy little bow and connected with a puzzle. A crossword puzzle. Inside the app. And also outside. Across the Village of Primm."

"Dang," said Caleb. "That's impressive."

"I agree," said Holly, wowed by Penelope's ability to pivot so quickly after the destruction of the Topiary Park. She was like a thought leader and ringmaster rolled into one. "You should run for political office."

"Don't tempt me," said Penelope, the lift of her eyebrow implying she might. She pinched Holly's sleeve, using it to pull her inside her office while asking Caleb to wait outside. "My apologies, Caleb, but there's something urgent I need to speak with Holly about before our meeting." She swooshed closed the double glass doors, leaving Caleb on the other side. To Holly, she asked, "Are you joining the Enclave Tour?"

"Yes, I'll be touring," said Holly.

"No," said Penelope. "Are you showing?"

"Well, I don't know." She had thought about it. She even told Greta she was thinking about it. And she sensed she probably *should* show her home after all that had happened. She *should* do whatever possible to help rebuild Primm. "I'm hardly unpacked," she began, using the same excuse she'd given Mary-Margaret the first week of school when she had asked Holly to volunteer for the PTA. "I need to paint. Hang curtains." Maybe buy a new couch? Definitely buy a new couch.

"I can help with the house," said Penelope. "You know that. You've already signed an engagement letter for home organization services. Homes are my specialty, and Feathered Nest has offered professional organizing and staging services for years. I'm happy to help. You can keep the apron. I have something more pressing to speak to you about." She pulled Holly a few feet from the door before leaning in to deliver what concerned her. "Mary-Margaret is hiding."

"In plain sight?"

"No. She's *in* hiding. We have to do something."

"Whoa, whoa, whoa. Do not involve me," said Holly. "Absolutely not. I don't want to have *anything* to do with Mary-Margaret St. James." If Mary-Margaret St. James, the PTA president and woman who nearly broke Holly during her first week in Primm, was a crossword puzzle clue, Holly's answer would be: AVOID.

"Mary-Margaret's in an 'undisclosed location.' She's in a 'secret bunker,'" said Penelope, using her fingers to create quotation marks in the air when she said *undisclosed location* and *secret bunker*.

"Are you speaking crossword puzzle?"

"What? No," said Penelope. "I'm just talking."

"Well then," replied Holly, using her fingers to throw the quotation marks right back, "this is not 'my problem.' And I know this might sound rude, but I 'don't care' if she's 'in hiding.'"

Caleb, standing a few feet away with only a glass door between them, motioned to Holly as if to say: *What? What's going on?*

"Penelope," Holly began, hoping to pivot the conversation, "Caleb and I were hoping to speak with you about the job we proposed? Mind if he comes in?"

"Mary-Margaret's situation is serious," Penelope continued, folding her arms across her chest. Penelope had a stake in the game: Mary-Margaret was her cousin. They had a shared family legacy, had reputations to protect. "She won't come out until you have a meeting with her."

Me? said Holly. "What does she want with me? She made my first week in Primm a living nightmare. She bullied me. She tricked me into being on the PTA. Why in the world does Reese Witherspoon's pink-bubble-gum-chewing evil twin want to talk to me? No. I'm not getting involved. I can't do this again. I can't."

"You have to."

"I don't want to."

"But I need you," said Penelope. "Primm needs you."

"Why? I mean, fine. I mean, no. I mean—" *Ugh!* Holly struggled with her conscience. Those dang chilli thrips. "Where is she?"

"How shall I put this?" Penelope's voice trailed off as she contemplated options. "She's locked herself—barricaded, more like it . . ."

"Go on."

"She made me promise not to tell anyone her location," explained Penelope. "But we have to bust her out, Holly. You and me. With a crowbar."

"Crowbar?" *Is she for real?* "I really don't know, Penelope. I want to help, but after all that's happened, I think I should keep my distance."

"I've tried everything! She's dug in deep. If we add more homes to the tour, we'll sell more tickets, but no one wants to put their private home on public display. I keep asking, but everyone's like: *Nope.* I need Mary-Margaret to rally the troops. You know how persistent she can be. She'll chase someone to the ends of the earth to get them to do what she wants them to do. Help me, Holly. You're my only hope."

Did she seriously just say that to a film school major? Holly imagined Penelope morphing into Princess Leia, huge Cinnabons on both sides of her head.

"Um . . ." Holly tapped a finger against her cheek, acting as if she were considering it, when in fact, she wasn't. Not anymore. "I'm sorry, but I'm busy that day." Holly averted her eyes, looking anywhere but at Penelope, eyes landing on the chandelier above Penelope's desk. "Mind if I ask? What kind of chandelier is that?"

"Big Bang Bubble. Calista Weaver, designer. She won Singapore last year. And last month, in Paris, the Je Veux Jouer competition. She won that too."

"Step aside, Dale Chihuly," said Holly. The chandelier in the hallway was more Holly's speed, but this one was exquisite.

"She apprenticed beneath an accomplished glass sculptor in Primm." The tone of Penelope's voice was—*off*. Something was amiss. *Does she not like Calista Weaver?* Penelope traced the slope of her thin nose with a finger, as if thinking. Not about the big bang but about something bigger, more important.

The chandelier appeared to Holly like a cosmic explosion of art and life traveling through time and space to land here, in Penelope's office, above Penelope's thick glass desk, hanging from Penelope's high-gloss ceiling. A remarkable splendor in gold-speckled, iridescent peacock-green glass, its reflection was mirrored in the ceiling paint's ultraglossy, ultrablue, shiny, pearlescent finish like the sky reflected in a clear mountain lake.

"It's stunning, almost . . ." Holly searched for the right word, thinking a slight change of topic would lighten the pensive look on Penelope's face. "*Bewitching*, the way the chandelier throws light across your ceiling."

"Ha! Yes, well, the glass sculptor certainly found Calista Weaver enchanting. But thank you. The ceiling paint was polished so smooth no bumps of paint show through," Penelope added, eyes joining Holly's as they both looked up toward the heavens inside Penelope's office.

"Penelope?" said Holly, both of them fully aware of Caleb, still standing behind glass, wishing to be included.

"Hmm?"

"Can we talk about that job now?"

"Actually, no," said Penelope. She folded her arms across her chest and tapped her foot, thinking. Thinking, thinking. *About what?* Finally, she asked, "You don't find it odd those chilli thrips spread across the Village of Primm?"

So there it was. Penelope knew about Holly's involvement in the destruction of Primm. Mary-Margaret must have told her. How Holly had inadvertently helped to spread the little buggers all over Primm, never realizing she was doing so at the time, because how was she to know the bug smuggler used the same rental car the week before she did?

"Fine. Where is she?" Holly said at last. "Where's Mary-Margaret?"

"Does Jack have a toolbox? A chain saw?" Penelope asked. "Or maybe a forklift?"

"Are you serious?"

"Okay, fine. Forget the forklift. So here it is," said Penelope, leaning in, her eyes laser focused on Holly. "Mary-Margaret . . ."

"Go on."

"She's . . ."

"What?"

"Well, you see, she's . . ."

"Penelope, come on, just tell me."

"She's in a she shed."

"Beg your pardon?"

"She's shut herself inside the St. James she shed, and she won't come out."

"Goodness," said Holly. "Say that ten times fast."

"She's shut herself inside the St. James she shed—"

"I was kidding!"

"I think she's depressed," Penelope added. "She's been humbled, disgraced after what happened, and her marriage is falling apart. My Love—excuse me." She corrected herself to call him by his real name and not *My Love*, the nickname Mary-Margaret used so often it had stuck. "*Michael* is facing jail time—as you know."

Ouch. That stung. Holly felt terrible about her involvement in the matter, but it was his actions that led to all of this—not Holly's. She was just there at the end.

"Only you have the power to convince her to come out," said Penelope.

"Well, I'm sorry. I don't believe that. I can't believe that," said Holly. She pointed. "You're her cousin." *You convinced me to buy an overpriced home with no storage. You can't get your cousin out of a she shed?*

"Trust me. I've done everything I can. She explicitly mentioned you. Maybe she wants to apologize. I don't know." She picked at something beneath her fingernail and then added, "If you want to know the truth, I'm a bit perturbed."

"At me?" asked Holly, feeling uncomfortable since learning Penelope did, in fact, know about her accidental involvement in the chilli thrip incident.

"At both of you. Okay, okay. Michael St. James, most of all. But yes, I'm a bit frustrated by her refusal to come out and face what's been done and your reluctance to help me get her out of there. Do you have any idea how hard I've worked to build this town? And now, because of a bug smuggled in from overseas, I have to throw an Enclave Tour to save it?"

"I thought I was coming here to talk about a job," said Holly, feeling, in part, responsible for what had happened, sure. But also a bit hoodwinked by Penelope.

"I need Mary-Margaret to convince others to put their private homes on public display," said Penelope, laying it on the line. "Without you, that'll never happen, so the way I see it? The fate of the Enclave Tour is in your hands. Once we save Primm, then we can discuss that job."

6

"What'd she say?" asked Caleb as they left Feathered Nest, their meeting with Penelope cut short once Penelope got what she wanted. "Did we get the job?"

"Who knows. I think so," said Holly, hopping in her Suburban, then tossing the chickadee's perch apron in the back seat before fastening her seat belt.

Caleb pulled his phone out and tapped icons to check social media.

"Which ones are you on?" asked Holly, watching him move effortlessly through multiple platforms.

"All of them. Have to be," he said. "Aren't you?"

"Oh, yeah, of course," she said. Duh. "I'm on all of them too. Don't friend me. I'll friend you."

She checked her own phone and found a text from Greta asking her to call home, then a Penelope Pratt Enclave Alert already sent to the residents of Primm. She clicked the link inside Penelope's text and found this:

Penelope Pratt
Feathered Nest Realty

—ENCLAVE ALERT—

THE STATE OF PLUME

Horticulturists at the Topiary Park report estimates to repair damaged, post-bonfire wireframes for all of the Topiary Park Petting Zoo animals have been received. The costs are steep, with repairs to Plume totaling as much as all of the other topiary animals combined.

It's not easy repairing a twenty-five-foot-tall peacock with a forty-foot tail spread made of double-epoxy-powder-coated, rust-resistant, handcrafted wire strong enough to hold hundreds of pounds of plant material, but it's well worth it, and I know—the Village of Primm is up to the task. We have to be. If the Topiary Park goes under, we all know who'll be knocking on our doors wanting to buy the property. BOXMART. Imagine a parking lot where our children used to play.

THERE'S NO PLACE LIKE HOME

Unless, of course, it's other people's homes!

In the Village of Primm, private homes are on public display in next month's Village of Primm "Enclave Tour" benefiting the Topiary Park Petting Zoo.

In the aftermath of the bug infestation that caused the apocalyptic collapse of the village's number one tourist destination, homeowners associations in the following twelve enclaves recently hit a homerun by honing in and driving home the importance of community by signing up to place their neighborhoods on the "drive-thru" portion of the tour.

Drive-thru Enclaves:

Ballyhoo	Dillydally	Parallax
Blythe	Gilman Clear	Peloton
Castle Drum Tower	Hobnob	Petunia
Chum	Hopscotch	Pram

In another stunning display of "go big or go home," four enclaves from the above list have already achieved platinum status by submitting four homes from their enclave to the Enclave Tour Map.

PLATINUM STATUS (four homes on tour): Blythe, Castle Drum Tower, Hopscotch, and Peloton

GOLD STATUS (three homes on tour): Ballyhoo and Hobnob

SILVER STATUS (two homes on tour): Dillydally and Parallax

BRONZE STATUS (one home on tour): Gilman Clear

ALUMINUM FOIL STATUS (no homes on tour): Chum, Petunia, and Pram

At Feathered Nest Realty, we believe charity begins at home.

To add your home to the Village of Primm Enclave Tour, text "LIGHTS.ARE.ON" to NO.ONES.HOME.

~

The speed limit in the center of town dropped to a slow crawl as Holly and Caleb passed a shop owner ripping a patch of dead ivy from the side of his store. "It was so pretty there, trailing up and around the shop door and windows," said Holly, remembering their conversation on the way to Feathered Nest, a knuckle of tension forming in her chest.

Out of nowhere, Caleb announced, "I submitted a second entry to the Wilhelm Klaus Film Festival."

"Another one?" *Ouch.* "That's great, Caleb. Wow. You're really prolific." She glanced over to get a good long look at him, to see what someone chasing their dreams looked like. She had yet to see the word she most longed to see—*FIN*, French for "the end"—at the end of any of her films, because she hadn't yet reached "the end." Of anything. "I'm happy for you."

"Yeah, well, fingers crossed—that's a lot of prize money."

"Are you happy?" she asked. "With the outcome?"

"You mean, do I wish I had more time to work on it? Yeah, sure. Of course. But a deadline's a deadline."

"I suppose," she replied, her voice trailing off.

"I've been meaning to ask you about Rosie."

Here we go. Holly smiled. "You're really into her, aren't you?"

"I want to ask her out, but our lives don't intersect. I know she works in the school office, but I don't have any kids, so why would I go there? And even if I did find a reason to see her at the school, I don't want to ask her out when she's at work." He let out a long, slow exhale. "Can you help?"

"You want me to play matchmaker?"

"Really? Aw, thanks. That would be awesome."

"I didn't say I would," she stressed. "I was just clarifying."

"Do you think she likes me?"

"How would I know? I was with the two of you for, like, two seconds. Why didn't you ask for her phone number?"

"I know! I'm such an idiot." He dropped a fist onto the top of her dashboard. "Ugh! I've asked myself that question every day since meeting her. I was just so nervous," he confessed.

"What's happening over there?" Holly pointed to a crowd of people gathering on The Lawn beside the South Gazebo. And then, "Wait a second . . ." She slowed to a stop, before shifting her car into park to have a closer look at the dog panting at the foot of a man Holly didn't recognize. "Is that Struggle?" And yup, finding something she didn't know she'd lost, she saw it was Struggle, yellow belt that belonged to Ella's bathrobe still attached to her collar. "Park the car," she told Caleb, getting out to run toward the commotion. "That's my dog!" she hollered, one arm up as if hailing a taxi. "That's my dog!"

But the man, holding an object in the air, was busy shouting, "He found it! The dog found it!"—drawing a crowd of onlookers, not just from the area around the South Gazebo, enclave flags circling its roofline, but from the shop sidewalks flanking the east and west borders of The Lawn. At least twenty or thirty people gathered around. Maybe more. But why? And how in the world did Struggle end up in the center of town?

"That's my dog," said Holly, pushing through the crowd, repeating, "Excuse me, excuse me, excuse me," before reaching Struggle, who immediately jumped on her, paws on chest, sloppy kisses on Holly's neck. "Thank you so much," Holly said to the man. "My apologies. I'm so sorry." Reaching her hand out, expecting the man to hand over the reins, she asked, "Where'd you find her?"

But he didn't hand over the reins. He tightened his grip on Ella's yellow bathrobe tie.

"I'll take it from here," Holly assured him. "The leash, please? This is my dog." *Who is this guy?* She sized him up: dark hair, olive skin, with a full head of hair and wire-rimmed glasses. Midfifties? An air of earnestness about him, he seemed harmless, but was he? *I can take him,* thought Holly, shoulders back, chin up, rolling up on her toes a bit to claim more space, hoping to appear taller, bigger, more authoritative. She pointed beyond his shoulder toward nothing in particular. "Whoa! What's that over there?"

When he turned to look, Holly reached over to snatch hold of the bathrobe tie, yanking it from his hand. *Ha!*

"Hey!" the man whined, realizing he'd been duped.

"This is *my* dog," she told him. "My dog."

"Then you're responsible for the holes dug around the compass rose?" he asked.

"Umm . . ." *What holes? Oh, Struggle, what have you done?* She glanced left where he pointed, toward the area where she first saw the inlaid compass rose in the grass near the North Gazebo. Weirdly, the metal compass inset didn't point north. As if someone had taken the whole town and spun it like the wheel in the Milton Bradley Game of Life board game, only the Village of Primm, once it had stopped spinning, landed crooked and cockeyed. Not quite lined up. As far as Holly could tell, it had always been that way. Another odd thing about the Village of Primm.

"I've already called the media," the man informed her.

"The media? Because a dog dug a few holes?" *What is it with this town?* Holly looked at Struggle, then toward a guy holding a Frisbee, as if to say: *This is insane. Am I right?* Would this happen in Southern Lakes? No. It wouldn't. Holly's theory—the uppitier society got, the more dogs were asked to conform.

In the man's hand was a flat, circular piece of metal crusted with dirt—a dial or a disc of some sort. It looked to Holly like a CD, only slightly smaller, not as smooth, and clearly very old. She was about to ask what it was, but from across The Lawn ran a woman in a green suit and heels, reaching behind her back to fasten equipment to her waist-line, a cameraman trailing a few feet behind her—VOP News. Holly knew because she spotted the bright-white sticker affixed to one side of the camera broadcasting the logo—a camera topiary. As the reporter and cameraman neared, the crowd gathered around, pulling close, as if realizing a cameo on camera would require staking a position behind the action.

The reporter arrived, breathless but able to swing her back to the crowd to face the camera with her auburn hair and fierce, green, I'm-on-local-TV eyes. With a thin body and controlled posture, she had long, sleek hair polished with timeless finger waves reminiscent of the 1920s—s-shaped auburn waves, probably created with a flat iron, duck-bill clips, and a lot of hair spray. Someone in hair and makeup knew what to do with this Irish beauty fresh out of broadcast journalism college.

"Eliza Adalee, star reporter, VOP News, reporting *live* from the South Gazebo, where a *dog* has just uncovered a *clue* to a decades-old mystery." She paused, whispering, "One, two, three," and then added,

"THIS is your top-of-the-hour news hour brought to you at the bottom of the hour and sponsored by . . . Village of Primm's Cup! 'Because you don't need alcohol to make bad decisions.' Cut!" she said, holding a smile until the cameraman swung the camera from his shoulder to signal they were off the air.

Probably midtwenties, she flashed Holly a small-town, big-aspirations smile that proved the orthodontics her parents invested in ten or twelve years ago might yet pay dividends. "Is this your dog?" she asked.

"It is," said Holly. "But I have no clue what's happening right now, so I think I'll take my dog and go home. Thank you." She turned to leave, relieved she was dressed in the outfit she wore to Feathered Nest Realty, a huge improvement after getting caught carpooling Ella to school while wearing pink piggy pajama bottoms a few weeks ago—which then made the paper, considering she'd also rear-ended the school bus parked in front of her.

"Hold on—" the man interrupted. He stepped forward to say, "Miss Adalee, thank you for coming. I'm Frank Mauro, the town cartographer, Francis Mauro's son? I took over Mappamundi when he passed. Our shop is in The Quiet next to the clockmaker's cottage." He pointed across The Lawn, making a hopping gesture with his hand as if hopping up and over the roofs of the stores that lined The Lawn and into the section of Primm known as "The Quiet," where a group of older establishments sat biding their time in a world rumbling toward the future. "Like my father and grandfather before him," he said, "I make maps, sell maps, collect maps. Our specialty is medieval maps and mapmaking instruments. *Mappa* in medieval Latin means 'cloth' or 'chart,' and *mundi* means 'of the world.' I'm an expert on the history of mapmaking, from the clay tablets of Mesopotamia to today's GPS. The name's Frank," he said again, assuming a posture that made Holly wonder why he thought any of this mattered. "Mauro. M-a-u-r-o." Not that Eliza Adalee was writing any of this down. Maybe television crews had this effect on people? "I'm the one who called the station," the cartographer named Frank said, reaching out to shake Eliza Adalee's hand.

"I have to go," said Holly. "Goodbye."

"This dog"—Mauro pointed to Struggle—"is a wonder dog!"

"Oh?" Holly turned around. "How so?" she said. "She dug something up. She's a dog. That's what dogs do."

Mauro continued, "This is the dog residents in Primm *and* Southern Lakes have been waiting for. This dog"—emphasis on *dog*—"this *dog* is better than any metal detector. Now, I know Axel Farah and his crew of treasure hunters will disagree, but this dog"—emphasis again on the word *dog*—"found this! So, ha! Take *that*, Axel Farah." Fist pump. "Booyah!" He thrust the disc above his head, acting as if the dog had just unearthed the Holy Grail. It looked like a dial of some sort—the innards of a grandfather clock. Big deal.

"We're here! Cameras off, stop the presses. Hold up," came the sound of a man's voice approaching from behind the crowd. He pressed through the center of the crowd, joining Holly, Eliza Adalee, and Mauro. "Podcast division of Radio SOLA from Southern Lakes," the man said, reaching out to shake Holly's hand, a Zoom H6 six-track portable recorder at his hip. "Are you the owner of the dog?"

Eliza pressed in, focusing all her attention on Holly. "VOP News, here. We're going live with the story in four minutes. Can you tell me where the dog was trained? Did he attend search and rescue school?"

"What? No," said Holly. "Dog can't find her own collar."

"What is the dog's name?" asked the Radio SOLA podcast guy.

"Exactly how many holes did the dog dig before finding it?" Eliza wanted to know.

"Well . . . I don't know exactly," said Holly, glancing in the direction of the inlaid compass. She could see piles of dirt where Struggle kicked the soil out. Should Holly kick it all back in? First Caleb, and now this. Not a good day for lawns. "I have to go," she announced, attempting to walk straight through the crowd, hoping to part everyone as she went, giving her a clear shot toward the shops at Pip's Corner, where behind Primm Paper, Caleb should be waiting with her red Suburban.

"Don't leave!" pleaded Eliza, rushing after her. "This is newsworthy. Breaking news. Your dog is making headlines."

"No comment," said Holly over her shoulder. *They can't interview me against my will. None of this is our concern,* she kept telling herself, not wanting to call any more attention to Struggle for fear they'd get a call from animal control.

"Would you be willing to loan your dog out to hunt for the remaining pieces?" the Radio SOLA podcaster shouted.

"Pieces?" muttered Holly. "What pieces? I don't even know what that thing is or why it's important." She kept walking, more swiftly now. With a glance back, she realized they were being chased. The VOP News cameraman was still shooting, the camera steadied on his shoulder. Radio SOLA not far behind, turning the dials. And then came the cartographer, Frank Mauro, holding whatever that thing was, as the crowd of onlookers followed behind him.

She picked up the pace, able to create a somewhat reasonable distance between herself and everyone else, but then, *bam!* Holly stepped in a hole, knees buckling as she fell to the ground with an *oof!*

"Mother trucker!" said Holly, arse in the air. She managed to hold tight to the belt attached to Struggle's collar. After she climbed to her feet, a scan of her surroundings confirmed almost everyone on The Lawn was watching. "Oh, Struggle," she muttered, getting out of there as fast as she could. "Now what have you done?"

Struggle's legs kept up with Holly, but her eyes looked like they needed a nap. Her tongue hung out of the side of her mouth as she panted, giving Holly the impression she was smiling, thrilled, utterly thrilled by the mayhem she had created in the town square. Holly loved Struggle. Super loved Struggle. But good gravy, she didn't want this kind of attention.

7

Later that night, with dinner on their laps and the local news on TV, Holly, Jack, Ella, and Greta watched as Eliza Adalee told viewing audiences, "A peculiar thing happened in the Village of Primm. A wayward dog named Muggles unearthed a valuable artifact."

"Muggles?" snarled Ella, fork clanking against her bowl as she set it down. "Her name's not Muggles."

"And she's not wayward," scoffed Holly, with a glance toward Jack. "Wayward? Jack, that's bad. I was on camera with Struggle," she said, concerned about the optics. They were new in Primm. Having a dog with a bad reputation could morph into all kinds of trouble. "Dang it, Struggle." She stretched her foot out to pet Struggle on the back with her toes. Struggle twitched her eyebrows and let out a long, slow exhale, giving Holly the impression she, too, was worried about her wayward reputation.

As far as Holly and Greta could piece together, Struggle had slipped away toward the co-op gardens on the cul-de-sac and through the side yard of a house that led to a common area beside an easement that eventually led to a park that led to this, and then that, and then, yeah. Somehow, Struggle ended up in town. Why she chose the inlaid compass as a spot to start digging eluded everyone. Although, no one knew quite why she was fixated on digging in Houston's yard either.

They were watching a segment shot for the evening news. Having had the afternoon to scoop the story, Eliza Adalee, now in a spiffy new outfit, spoke while walking toward the holes Struggle dug. "For decades, an astrolabe once used for land survey during the early days of Primm's settlement has been missing and presumed stolen from the Land Survey Records Department. Today's discovery by the dog is sending shock waves through the Village of Primm and neighboring Southern Lakes, as important boundary notations along the border of both towns were inscribed on the back of three plates belonging to the astrolabe. These special plates are known in the astrolabe community as tympanums or tympana." She slowed her pronunciation to educate her viewers: "Tim-pan-um. These disc-like tympanums fit inside the casing of the still-missing planispheric astrolabe."

"Planispheric astro what?" asked Jack, scooting an ottoman over with his foot so he could eat with legs extended. *That ottoman needs to be retired,* thought Holly. Torn at the top and frayed around the edges with a crooked leg that kept buckling—it was time. A month into a new home, everything stood out to Holly. "Whatever that astro thing is," said Jack, "looks like Struggle found hidden treasure. I wonder if there's a reward?"

Struggle stayed at Holly's feet but lifted her head to watch Greta's cat wander into the room. Charlotte, purring, stopped to rub a cheek against Greta's leg. "Well, I don't know about you," said Greta, "but I want to know more about the astrolabe community. Sounds eccentric!" She reached down to lift Charlotte onto her lap.

From Eliza: "Frank Mauro, Village of Primm cartographer, explains."

"Astrolabes operate using celestial bodies for navigation, geography, surveying, timekeeping, as well as the study of astronomy and astrology," said Frank, taking the mic from Eliza's hand.

Astrology? How interesting, thought Holly, keeping her thoughts to herself.

"It works like this," said Frank. "The coordinates of the celestial bodies are engraved on the tympanums, essentially converting a sphere, like the sun or a planet, into a flat surface—the tympanum, or more simply, the *disc*. Because coordinates for celestial objects depend on where you're located on earth, these *tympanum discs* are created for specific latitudes and locations, making the missing discs not only valuable for the survey notations engraved on the back, but because there are no known discs specific to this area still in existence."

Eliza grabbed her mic, stepping in front of Frank to begin walking again.

"According to sources," said Eliza, making her way toward the mounds of dirt Struggle had kicked out, "engravings on the discs were most likely made during the late eighteenth century, when this area was still being established. The discs in question contain the earliest known notations of a land survey along a five-mile strip of land bordering the two towns that would later become known as Southern Lakes and the Village of Primm."

"I would have filmed the shot differently," Holly announced, knowing no one would respond for fear she'd elaborate. "What's with all the walking?"

"The missing astrolabe and discs are important because the Land Survey Records Department was once shared by both towns, and the fire of 1941 destroyed most of the original maps and survey documents, which were, of course, made of paper," explained Eliza, arriving at the inlaid compass where Struggle had made the discovery. "Without the astrolabe and the inscriptions carved on the back of the three discs, what has long been considered the oldest record of one of the most valuable pieces of real estate in either town remains in question."

"Oh, Lordy. Pandora's box," said Greta, setting her glass on an end table without a coaster. Not that it mattered. Holly didn't own end tables nice enough for coasters. But she would. She had two sets of alabaster coasters "tucked away" in an online shopping cart, just waiting for her to hit purchase.

More from Eliza: "It is believed as many as thirty separate discs were created during the earliest days of Primm's settlement. Thankfully, twenty-seven were left behind during the theft, suggesting the targeting of these three discs, along with the body of the astrolabe itself, was a deliberate act. For some reason, someone, or perhaps a group of people, wanted to conceal what was inscribed on those discs."

"The dog dug something up. So what? Beyond that, this has nothing to do with us," declared Holly, not wanting her family dragged into any trouble, but sure, her interest in the matter might be building. An astrolabe? A land dispute between rival towns? This was getting juicy. "I'm sure it will all blow over."

"Tell that to the astrolabe community," said Greta. "This'll put 'em on the map."

The camera cut to Frank Mauro. "Christopher Columbus used dead reckoning to navigate but also used celestial navigation to determine latitude using a quadrant and an astrolabe. Thomas Jefferson's astrolabe is on view in his home at Monticello." He went on and on as Greta exhaled, closing her eyes to take a break from something.

"Mom? Are you okay?" asked Holly.

"No, I'm not. I want this guy to stop talking," said Greta, pointing at the television. She fell backward in her chair, letting out a long, slow snore before popping back up. "Can we watch HGTV?"

"I'm serious. You seem easily winded lately."

"I have a question," said Ella, raising her hand as if she were in school. "Why doesn't the glue stick to the inside of the glue bottle?"

Ella looked at Jack, who tried to explain as Holly asked Greta in a hushed voice, "Is it your heart?"

"My heart's fine," said Greta, waving her off as if her question were ridiculous.

"Lungs? Maybe you need a chest x-ray."

"Nope. Don't need an x-ray."

"Arthritis? Osteoporosis. You're not moving around like you typically do. I haven't seen you do yoga in a week. Does your back hurt?"

"Holly, I'm fine."

"You know what I think?" said Jack, pointing at Greta with his fork. *Oh, boy. Here we go,* thought Holly. She knew that smirk on Jack's face. "I think she's suffering from an enlarged prostate."

Eliza cut Frank Mauro's lesson about the astrolabe short, encouraging viewers to stay tuned for more coverage of Muggles, the Astrolabe Dog, but Frank wasn't about to surrender his moment in the spotlight. He leaned into the camera shot and grabbed hold of the microphone. Eliza pulled back, hard, the two wrestling for control over the mic. "Stop by Mappamundi in The Quiet for a live demonstration!" yelled Frank. "I have astrolabes, mariners' sextants, compasses, survey equipment, and navigational artifacts you wouldn't believe!"

"Oh, yeah. Now that guy's definitely a member of the astrolabe community," said Greta.

"You should join them," said Jack with a playful wink. "I'm sure the astrolabe community could use a ukulele-playing cat doula."

Finishing Eliza's segment, a shot of Holly's back as she scurried with Struggle away from reporters, and then, *bam!*—she was caught on camera stepping in a hole, her knees buckling as she fell to the ground with a "mother trucker!"

"Whoa!" said Jack, trying not to laugh. "You didn't tell me *that.*"

"Seriously, Jack? I could have gotten hurt," said Holly, though she had to admit it was kinda funny.

She grabbed the remote to switch to a show about a couple downsizing their life to live off-grid in a tiny home. After watching a few minutes, Holly asked Jack, "Would you ever do that? Live in an off-grid tiny home?" She understood the appeal. Understood why these shows were captivating audiences.

"Give up what we have for a life like that?" he said, pausing to look thoughtfully around the family room. She knew his answer. He was thinking about the creature comforts of home. The indoor heating and cooling that flipped on with a switch. The roof over their heads. The lock on the door. Jack was a provider. He appreciated sound shelter for his family. He'd never give up the life they had for a life like that—no way. "In a heartbeat," he said. "I'd sell this house so fast your head would spin." He went back to eating his dinner. "Find me a buyer."

"Find you a buyer? You're joking," said Holly.

"No, actually. I'm not," he said matter-of-factly.

"But that's insane. You'd drop everything? You'd give up all of this?"

"Moment's notice. Say the word." He stabbed a few green beans onto his fork. One rolled away, so he chased it across his plate with his fork.

"I thought you liked living in the Village of Primm. Ella goes to a blue-ribbon school." They'd been over this before. "We're living the dream, Jack."

"None of this was my dream," he said. "If it were my dream, I'd live in someone's garage and have a gig roasting my own coffee."

"Okay, wow. That's a low blow," she said, lowering her voice so Ella wouldn't hear. "Seriously, Jack? Stop with the nostalgia. You're reminding me of every movie ever made with the word *bachelor* in it."

"I don't want to make you mad, Holly." He shrugged. "But I didn't want any of this. You wanted it. The house is way too expensive for what we've got. Heck, Primm is expensive. I'm working my tail off just to keep up."

"And what, *that* looks better to you?" She pointed to the TV, to a man in Wyoming walking a donkey to a riverbed to fetch the day's water. A light snow was falling, so the man blew into his mittened hands to keep warm. "When was that guy's last shower?" she asked. "He can't shower till he fetches water and then boils it on a fire." *What the flock, Jack. You'd rather dig a hole for an outhouse than pay a mortgage for a house*

67

in the suburbs? Our house has toilets! "I'm sorry you feel that way," she muttered. "I'm sorry *that* looks better to you than *this*."

"You asked."

"Is everything okay at work?"

"Sure, why?"

"Just checking." She moved away from him, settling into the corner of the couch, pulling her phone out to give herself something to do. She opened a text message from Shanequa sent earlier that day.

SHANEQUA: Talia tells me Ella is the bride in the Q&U Wedding? Did she mention she asked Talia to go wedding gown shopping with her?

Wedding gown shopping? This better not be getting out of hand. Holly lowered her phone to look at Ella. She had read the flyer that came home in Ella's backpack, traded two more emails with Miss Bently about the matter. Miss Bently didn't mention a wedding gown.

"Ella, what are you wearing to the Q&U?" asked Holly. "Need a costume?"

"Wang."

"Excuse me?"

"Vera Wang," said Ella with complete innocence. Like, duh. Of course she'd wear Wang. "The lady who makes dresses?"

"Um, no," said Holly. "Hold up." Was the Letter U turning into a bridezilla? *Not if I can help it.* "You're five. How do you know Vera Wang?"

A text came in from Penelope.

PENELOPE: You never told me your dog was trained for search and rescue!

HOLLY: This whole thing is a fluke. Some random act by a dog I can't explain.

PENELOPE: Well, I think it's more than that. I'm beginning to believe there are no coincidences in this life. Just look at you! Newly moved to the Village of Primm and now so involved in its inner workings.

"Ella?" said Holly. "After supper, we have to finish that 'Words That Start with *CH*' worksheet. Then we're cleaning your room, and you're taking a bath. And speaking of cleaning rooms," she announced, "we're all getting organized. It's a new day at the Banks house. And Jack"—*Ef you for saying you'd rather fetch water with a donkey*—"we're painting the living and dining room. I'll do the painting. But I need you to build the bookshelves we talked about." *You look like the manly type. You want to live off-grid? Start by building some bookshelves—then let's see how you feel about building a log cabin.* She paused, considering everything she knew about him. He wouldn't get to Wyoming with his donkey and forgo living in a log cabin for a yurt, would he? *Please tell me I didn't marry a yurt man. Furniture placement sucks when you live in a circle.*

Ella raised her hand as if she were in school, waiting politely for someone to call on her.

"Yes, Ella?" said Holly, pretending to be Miss Bently. "You have a question?"

"What's a bridal registry?"

"What? No," said Holly. "Absolutely not."

Someone knocked at the front door. It was an aggressive knock, a knock that said: *Open. NOW.* Jack got up to answer it with Holly and Struggle close behind. It was Houston and, behind Houston, the foreboding presence of *Henny Penny* and the implied promise the sky could fall at any minute.

"I came as fast as I could," said Houston, looking from Jack to Holly. "I heard the dog uncovered a piece of the missing astrolabe." As he stepped over the threshold, Struggle let out a low, rumbling growl. "My grandfather, Clive Cranbarrie, was implicated in the fire," he explained. "People think he started it, but in the end, charges were never filed. The stress made Grandma Petunia sick. She never recovered and later died in the back bedroom of the house."

"Goodness," said Holly, thinking she'd never look at Houston's house the same way again. "I'm so sorry."

"How fast can the dog uncover the remaining pieces?" he asked, appearing quite troubled by the matter. "I want this to go quickly. I don't want to drag the Bonneville-Cranbarrie name through any more mud."

8

After Monday's excitement, Tuesday had come and gone, and the time was now approaching one o'clock Wednesday morning. Upstairs, everyone was asleep. Downstairs, Holly was snuggled on the family room couch with Struggle, thumbing through channels in search of something to watch. Her tossing and turning had been keeping Jack awake the night before critical meetings were set to begin at work. Clients at Jack's firm were facing federal charges for tax evasion, and Jack, if all went well, would likely be promoted for his role in protecting the firm. Fingers crossed he'd also earn a sizable bonus by month's end. Not that Holly was eyeing a Kinnersley sofa or anything.

One of the clients up for discussion was Michael St. James—"My Love," as his now-estranged wife, Mary-Margaret, used to call him. Holly assumed the name My Love went up in smoke the night Plume did. Could you blame Mary-Margaret? That man destroyed beautiful, iconic topiaries—killed the spirit of Primm by attacking the beauty that lay at the heart of the community. And he caused his own wife to fall from grace and social standing—a devastating blow when you're "ninth generation" and live in a town as small as the Village of Primm. Good gravy, she was holed up in a she shed when typically she'd be strutting the halls of Primm Academy, full of confidence, slaying everything and everyone in sight as president of the PTA.

Holly opened her laptop and searched through her history, clicking onto a particular website, then scrolling to the bottom, where the words *FREE! FREE! FREE!* blinked in red letters around a box inviting her to ask a psychic a *FREE! FREE! FREE!* question. She had tried replying to the last email received from the site, but her email had bounced back, so she placed a check mark in the reCAPTCHA box, then waited for a random generator run by a computer to spit out an assignment that would allow her to prove to the computer she wasn't a computer. As she waited, she imagined her future, arguing with a toaster equipped with artificial intelligence. *Are* you *a toaster?* the toaster would ask. Then Holly would have to somehow prove to the toaster she wasn't a toaster before the toaster would toast her toast.

After passing a series of reCAPTCHA walls—boxes filled with photos of fire hydrants, motorcycles, intersections, and storefronts—she typed her *FREE! FREE! FREE!* question inside a box.

> Does Psychic Betty still work here? I need to talk to her. Tell her it's me, Holly Banks.

She submitted her email address, then hit send, before setting her laptop aside to watch Netflix. After a short while, she checked her email.

∿

EMAIL—Time Received: 1:23 a.m.

> TO: Holly Banks
> FROM: Psychic Betty, Psychic Hotline Network
> SUBJECT: Your FREE "Ask the Psychic" Question
>
> Welcome back, Holly Banks. How R U? I missed U. Question: Ever tire of the abbreviations? I do.

Everyone is ROTFL, but I'm not laughing out LOL. I'm worried about the future of language. Can I buy a vowel?

From this moment forwardeth, I have decided to bringeth backeth the old language. (YOLO!) If thee wants me to speaketh today's English and stopeth with all of this, I shall have to chargeth thee two dollars.

I accepteth Zelle, Stripe, Venmo, PayPal, and BitCoin. Thee decideth.

Clicketh HERE to ask another question.

Clicketh HERE for coupons to Dizzy's Seafood.

~

Holly clicked "here" to ask another question, and a new reCAPTCHA appeared, asking her to count how many letter *Y*s were shown in a series of license plates. Some of the *Y*s looked like *V*s because the plates were turned every which way. It took a solid minute of her life to complete the assignment. reCAPTCHA complete, she typed her question inside the box.

TWO DOLLARS??? That's such a rip-off! You should pay *me* two dollars to readeth througheth that cr@p. I've missed you, too, Psychic Betty. It's been two weeks since our last correspondence, and so much has happened. Remember that woman I couldn't figure out? Mary-Margaret St. James? I thought I reached a place where I could keep her at a distance, but Penelope says she's depressed and is asking to meet with me in her she shed. I said I would, but the truth is: I'm scared. That woman is T.O.X. toxic.

And can we take this conversation off the website now? This little box is creeping me out, and the reCAPTCHAs are excessively time-consuming. I had to solve four sets of questions using a grid of photos that were either blurry, too far away, or could qualify as either a right or wrong answer. Storefronts? Some of them looked like houses to me. Upside-down license plates? WHY. Or rather, Y, or even V. It was confusing. I felt like a test rat in some futuristic autonomous-car-driving-deep-learning-neural-network-AI-your-robot-vacuum-cleaner-isn't-simply-following-you-it's-STALKING-you world. Are bots getting smarter than humans? You know we'll never be able to dial that stuff back. Tell reCAPTCHA to dumb it down. If the future is now, it's freaking me out.

~

EMAIL—Time Received: 1:53 a.m.

> TO: Holly Banks
> FROM: Psychic Betty, Psychic Hotline Network
> SUBJECT: Are You Smarter than a reCAPTCHA?

It's the Digital Era, so it's no wonder humans are feeling disconnected and alone in the universe. reCAPTCHA technology tests our humanity and texting changes our language. What's next? GPS-assisted holographic street signs? Cars that drive themselves? Oh, wait.

And yes, Holly. We can move off the Psychic Hotline Network website and into an email exchange. It would be my pleasure to resume services as your personal online psychic. The cost of each email is one dollar. Zelle, Stripe, Venmo, PayPal, BitCoin, but also, Susan B. Anthony and Sacagawea.

And now, an answer to your question.

You mentioned a lot had *happened* in two weeks, but I suspect your underlying question is whether things have *changed*.

First, I wouldn't measure time by the hands of the clock, nor by the days on the calendar, but by the gloriously textured landscape of the cosmos. You might *think* two weeks is too soon for a person or relationship to change—but that's simply not so.

Consider the Moon, which rules feelings, emotions, and intuition. It travels halfway around the Earth every two weeks. Not only is that a great distance to travel, but it does so while "changing faces" as it travels—two weeks marking the distance between opposing states. For example, a new moon "beginning" and a full moon "ending" or "completion."

Don't believe celestial bodies have the power to influence life on Earth? Try telling *that* to the ocean. You think the tides and water levels are acting according to their own free will? HA! The Sun and Moon are playing tug-of-war with a massive body of water that covers 71% of the Earth's surface. How's that for celestial interference?

Holly, as far as your relationship with Mary-Margaret goes, I suspect you'll safely navigate your next steps if you point your inner compass toward the heavens. If I've learned anything over the years, it's this: The universe, with its infinite wisdom, holds endless possibilities.

Try to stay balanced.

And remember, there are two halves to every whole.

Which is doubly so at Dizzy's Seafood!

Half-price options include half-platters of half-fried catfish coupled with half-platters of oysters on the half shell. Served daily with a half dozen shrimp at half-past the hour. Drink like a fish and chase your half-price half-platter with your favorite beverage, served in a glass that's either half-empty or half-full. You decide.

At Dizzy's Seafood, saving money is like shooting fish in a barrel. Bring your better half and split that half-price half-platter 50/50.

Click HERE to order a lunar calendar.

Click HERE to answer the Dizzy's Seafood Question of the Month: Tartar Sauce? Or Cocktail?

~

EMAIL—Time Sent: 2:01 a.m.

TO: Psychic Betty, Psychic Hotline Network
FROM: Holly Banks
SUBJECT: Celestial Thoughts

Hey there, friend. It's so nice to be back in touch. I've missed you.

9

Wednesday morning, Holly opened her door to the sight of *Henny Penny. Ugh! Caleb.* It had been two days already. Once Ella was on the bus and Holly back inside, she phoned Caleb.

"Seriously, Caleb? No more excuses—I want *Henny Penny* off my lawn." She poured herself a cup of coffee before returning with a spoonful of Nutella to the foyer, where her front door stood ajar.

"I know, I know," he began. "Sorry. My buddy Nathan told me he was picking it up yesterday. I'll call him again."

"He better come soon, because it needs to go—you're lucky I haven't gotten in trouble with the HOA yet," she told him, checking to see if a Hello Note had been taped to her mailbox since she last looked. Thankfully, no. Maybe Bling needed to check the bylaws. "Did you see the article that ran yesterday about Struggle in the *Primm Gazette*? They didn't have a photo of Struggle, so they sent someone out to take a photo of my house," she said. "And now *your* ultralight aircraft is causing speculation about *my* family that I didn't want and hadn't asked for."

What do we know about the Banks family, newly moved to the Village of Primm? the article had asked. Holly didn't want the media asking probing questions about her family. She certainly didn't want them *speculating* about them either. Maybe she *should* take questions from the press. At least then she could control some of the content that was being released. She did wonder why the reporter from the *Primm Gazette* didn't know *Henny Penny* belonged to Caleb. You could see a thing like that flying overhead. "How long have you been flying *Henny Penny*?" she asked.

"That was my first flight over Primm," he admitted. "I bought it from a hobby-aircraft dealer in Menander. That's where I did all of my flight training. And I guess, technically, I'm not supposed to fly over congested areas, but I figure, what's Officer Knapp going to do? Pull me over and write me a ticket? I'm in the air, for Pete's sake."

Great. So that confirmed it: the optics surrounding *Henny Penny* were questionable too. First flight over Primm, and he landed in *her* yard? No wonder people wondered. The village was home to some peculiar residents. Was she becoming one of *them*? "Well, if Nathan's not here by this afternoon, I'm finding my own person to tow it. You're lucky we're not asking you to pay for repairs to the yard," she pointed out. "Don't make me pay for a tow truck."

"Okay, okay. I'll call him when we hang up."

When Holly and Caleb had returned home after finding Struggle in town with Frank Mauro, they learned Greta—when she couldn't reach Holly by phone—had called Jack home from work to help search for Struggle. As Holly suspected, Jack had been quite miffed to find that an ultralight had ripped its way across his yard. Thank goodness the damage was limited to their yard and hadn't also torn up the neighbor's lawn, but now, with their lawn as the "eyesore next door," Jack would surely start grumbling about where to buy zoysia plugs in September. He was a bit terse with Caleb at first but then relaxed a bit and started asking questions, intrigued by *Henny Penny* and the world of ultralight and microlight aircraft. *Let's hope Jack doesn't pick it up as a hobby,* Holly had thought at the time. *Please, Jack, no.*

"Are you looking forward to our first flight?" asked Caleb. "Let's shoot some B-roll—aerial shots of all the enclaves."

"That's *definitely* not happening," said Holly. She nearly wet her pants on a ropes course Jack brought her to when they were dating. She caused such a backup on the course that a lanky teenager who kept saying "hey, lady" had to coach her down a rope ladder because she wouldn't let go of the tree trunk on the third platform.

"Aw, come on. You're letting your fears hold you back. Live a little," nudged Caleb.

"I live a little. I'm collaborating with you, aren't I?"

"Kick it up a notch," he challenged. "Live a lot."

Like the time she was six and tried to "fly" from the edge of a dock onto a giant floating party raft? No, thank you. Sadie had loaded her up with multiple arm floaties until Holly stood erect, arms out like an airplane. The plan was to yell *timber* the moment she was airborne, hoping to impress the older kids as she landed among them on the raft.

Everyone cheering her on, Holly had taken off running from a patch of dirt, down the length of the dock like an aircraft or an albatross picking up speed down a runway. With target in sight and arms flapping wildly, a few feet before liftoff she stepped in a puddle—legs slipping out from beneath her. She fell backward, tailbone nailing a gap between two planks of wood, head landing next, hard. Arms with yellow inflatables still extended by her sides—Holly clenched her butt cheeks, trying to contain the pain, letting loose an anguished cry that split a hole through the middle of the clouds above her. She had to carry a doughnut pillow for three months. Either her mom or her dad or Sadie or the teachers at school had to lift her by the armpits to get her off a chair without her experiencing excruciating pain. Early proof bad things happened when you tried to fly.

"We can take off from the field beside the Clock Tower Labyrinth," he added. "Bring Ella. She can watch her mom do something brave."

Holly felt something fall on her head. A drop. *Of what?* she wondered, looking up, noticing for the first time a stain on the ceiling and two thin cracks where the ceiling met the walls. "I have to go," she told

Caleb. "I need to get ready for something." She was meeting Penelope at noon outside of Mary-Margaret's she shed.

"Oh, hey. Get this. Rosie's sister, Olivia, owns the bookstore. Duh. I don't know why I didn't make that connection before. I installed their dad's media room for Primm Cable. Anyway, I bought a book of poetry from Olivia and tucked one of my business cards inside it for Rosie. Olivia said she'd give it to her. Do you think she'll call? Women like poetry, right? That's better than sending her a card that says *roses are red, violets are blue* or something else like that. I wanted to go big. Send a message. I wanted it to say: *Here. You can have a whole* book *about poetry.*"

"Oh, Caleb. That's super nice. I'm sure she'll love it," said Holly, eyes on the stain on the ceiling. "I didn't know you read poetry."

"I don't. Why. Was I supposed to read it first?" he asked. "The whole book?"

"I mean, maybe?" said Holly. "Were the poems about love?"

"I don't know. I just asked where the poetry section was, and then I grabbed one off the shelf."

Oh, jeez.

"I wanted her to know the ball's in her court. She can call me if she wants to. I hope she'll call. Do you think she'll call?"

"I'm sure she'll call."

"You know what I really want? Don't laugh."

"I won't laugh," Holly said. "Promise."

"I want to breathe deep the scent of Rosie's skin."

"Ew, yuck!"

"You said you wouldn't laugh."

"'Breathe deep the scent of Rosie's skin'? I don't want to imagine that."

"I'm not talking about *that*," he said, "although, that would be nice . . . I'm talking about our first hug. The first moment she's in my arms, and I have a chance to be that close to her. I bet she smells nice."

Holly thought about it, remembering the time she barged into the school office moments after Rosie had applied perfume. At the time, she thought she smelled either gardenia or rose. "I'm sure the time will come when you find out for yourself. If I did know, I wouldn't tell you. That's the sort of thing a man should find out for himself. You have to earn it."

"I want to earn it."

"I know you do," she said. "And I'm sure you will."

They said goodbye, then hung up.

~

Holly freed the Wilhelm Klaus Film Festival flyer Caleb had given her two weeks ago from its spot beneath a thumbtack on her bulletin board.

Wilhelm Klaus Three-Minute Film Festival
Win $10,000 and dinner with THE Wilhelm Klaus
Germany's most celebrated filmmaker
Any Genre | Any Style | Any Technology | Any Level | Any Age
www.WilhelmKlaus.com/three-minutes-to-personal-glory/

After logging onto the festival site to check submission requirements and deadlines, she learned the last *possible* moment to submit was as a "late entry" by midnight on Friday, the weekend of the Enclave Tour—three and a half weeks from now.

When she was in film school, she made a ninety-second stop-motion compilation of Audrey Hepburn movies, from *Dutch in Seven Lessons* to *Always*, including a paper cutout of Audrey eating a danish and drinking tea while staring longingly into a Tiffany & Company window filled with chandeliers in *Breakfast at Tiffany's*. Maybe a stop-motion like that would make a good entry for the Wilhelm Klaus? An Audrey-esque character peeking in windows during an Enclave Tour made of homes cut from decorative papers? If the stop-motion didn't place for any prizes in the Wilhelm, at the very least, she could use it locally to promote her skills as a filmmaker. Or maybe it would become the first entry in a portfolio of her professional work post–film school. She imagined cute little cutout letters walking their crooked little selves across the screen to form the name of the film studio she planned to launch: *HOLLY BANKS PRODUCTIONS.*

How great would it be to have birds or paper airplanes folded from the pages of a novel usher onto the screen all the letters in HOLLY BANKS PRODUCTIONS until the letters were fully assembled and floating in the air? And then, how great would it be to layer those letters onto a backdrop she shot of the clear blue skies over Primm—wispy white clouds, charming enclaves below? Not a still, static photograph of the sky as a backdrop, but a moving film sequence that she herself had shot while flying with Caleb in *Henny Penny.* Hmm. Could she do it? Fly with Caleb to capture footage of the sky? She remembered watching an old-timey airplane fly over the Cherry Festival on The Lawn, pulling a long, lettered sign behind it. She remembered noticing the fluffy white contrails left by the plane—how they looked like dash marks. And she remembered wondering, if those dash marks had been set into dialogue, what would they say?

Shifting gears from the film she wanted to create for the Wilhelm Klaus Film Festival to the production company she hoped would pay the bills, she spread a few sheets of paper on the kitchen table, then labeled each with the name of a social media platform. She knew there was business to be had in the Village of Primm and surrounding communities. There had to be.

Take Collette, for example. In August, Holly and Jack bought the house they now lived in from Collette and her husband. Collette still lived in Primm but now lived in Dillydally, an enclave *filled* with artists and crafty people. Collette had gained a gazillion followers on Pinterest after uploading pin after pin of "seasons" on the front porch that was once hers (but was now Holly's). Not to mention the step-by-step how-to pins Collette uploaded showing Pinterest enthusiasts *her* method for throwing two separate but simultaneous birthday parties at a swimming pool for her son and daughter. Party themes? Sharks and mermaids. "*Sharks and mermaids?* Sounds like a bloodbath," Holly told Jack the day she discovered Collette's pin. Collette's how-to-decorate-around-the-family-room-TV series? Not "surround sound" but "surround stuff." Those how-to pins were so popular they scored Collette a write-up in her sorority alumnae magazine—college-football edition. Special feature? Collette, poised and pretty, standing beside her wide screen holding an impeccably crafted stadium cake with tiny fondant fans cheering miniature football players hunched on the line of scrimmage waiting for the quarterback to call *Hike!* Though Holly still thought of her as "Pinterest Collette"—she was that good on the platform—Holly sensed an edge to Collette and her online profile. Her smile was picture perfect, but her eyes? Holly saw in them that telltale show, that under-lying frenetic energy that always underscored unrealistic pursuits of perfection. Collette was quintessentially Primm, but behind the scenes, Holly suspected there might be cracks in the facade. Perhaps Holly's services would help take the pressure off Collette. Or, since Collette was clearly a social media influencer, maybe they could collaborate on a project?

Holly opened accounts for Holly Banks Productions on all the major platforms, scrolling through similar businesses on social media to see how everyone else was marketing their services online—and ugh. Everyone was *way* ahead of her.

"Oh, hey," she said as Greta walked through the room. "You good?"

"Just checking on Charlotte." Greta looked at Holly's screen. "Scrolling mindlessly through social media again?"

"Everything is so—perfect. Look at this film studio in LA. Filled with light and bamboo plants. Says here they like serving their clients caviar and crème fraîche on toasted brioche. Who are these people?

Were they born perfect? And this one in Chicago, green screens on all four walls, the ceiling, and the floor. Look at that square footage—penthouse suite. I don't have a penthouse suite. I have a dining room with a pregnant cat in the corner."

"You're doing it again."

"Research?"

"Comparing yourself to others."

"I want to be successful."

"Then stop scrolling and start working."

"I am working."

"No," said Greta. "You're scrolling."

Holly knew she had the skill to produce high-quality content for her clients—she had graduated near the top of her class before setting everything aside to start a family. Still, there lingered a nagging doubt when it came to marketing a business in a town where she was still a newcomer. Why would #socialmedia #influencers want to hire *her*, Holly Banks? Never mind the public humiliation that had already occurred during her short time in Primm—getting busted for sneaking out of a PTA meeting, rear-ending a bus in front of an apple brigade of moms, puking Mary-Margaret's peckled peanut butter cookies at the Scrap & Swap Fund-Raiser. If moments like those, coupled with Struggle running loose and digging up decades-old village mysteries, kept happening, Holly's #momlife might appear to some as the "before" picture in a before-and-after comparison. Who was Holly to pitch herself as a personal-branding photographer and film crew? At the moment, *Holly's* "personal brand" could use a makeover. Not only that, she felt like an imposter. For the longest time, she had openly complained about social media. Never quite appreciating the many ways social media built community and kept people connected, helped businesses with little to no budget compete with the big guns, and hey, social media was fun. So now? After all that pooh-poohing and complaining about chasing likes, comments, and subscribes? She was wrapping a company around it? To that, Holly would say: Yes. Yes, she was. And proud of it. Even if her personal brand needed a makeover. Even if she felt like an imposter.

Maybe none of this mattered. Maybe she was overthinking it.

Either way, Holly knew this: she had both the talent and the desire to get back into film, she had bills to pay, and she hoped to design a workday that fit inside Ella's schedule. This was her best idea. And she was going for it.

10

Leaving Petunia en route to Mary-Margaret's she shed, Holly snatched a Hello Note from Maeve Bling off her mailbox. This note was photo-copied, a relief for Holly, as it meant she wasn't the only one to receive it.

~

HELLO NOTE—Taped to Holly's Mailbox

Whoopsie! We missed you. Important decisions need to be made regarding our neighborhood's participation in the Village of Primm Enclave Tour. We're slated for either front door or mailbox decor. Feathered Nest Realty is producing a calendar of the twelve enclaves, our month is June, and the photo will be a composite of either doors or mailboxes from our enclave. Which are we decorating, and what's our theme? Please attend HOA meetings. A simple majority was needed to meet quorum, but because we lacked quorum, a final vote could not be taken.

—Maeve Bling

~

Holly drove toward the famed Hopscotch Hill, where Primm's most prominent homes were located. A small playground and dog park marked the transition from winding streets to an older road lined with sugar maples, leaves blazing with golden fall color. The road was perfectly curved, eventually leading to a gate that began the ascent up the hill. Exactly twelve homes roosted on that hill, and none of them had postal numbers. Instead, names were given long ago, so addressing a letter to Penelope meant no *number 2* or *10* or *420* but *Tryst on Hopscotch Hill*, the name given to the home where the Pratt family lived.

PENELOPE PRATT
TRYST ON HOPSCOTCH HILL
VILLAGE OF PRIMM

Penelope lived next door to Mary-Margaret St. James. Two cousins, side by side in separate homes, each as grand as the other, perched like birds on a gilded branch overlooking the Village of Primm. It wasn't easy parallel parking in front of Penelope's with a G-Class Mercedes you didn't want to hit parked behind you. As Holly was maneuvering into her spot, she received a brief tap on her window from none other than Collette offering a smile and a friendly wave. Collette then hurried off, down the cobblestone walk and toward her car, which she drove off, apparently having left Penelope to speak alone with the man in the G-Class. Now what did Collette need with Penelope? Was she selling her home in Dillydally?

"Right this way," chimed Penelope, meeting Holly at her Suburban as the driver of the G-Class pulled his car out of his space and onto Hopscotch to drive away. Holly knew the driver of the G-Class as a client of Jack's. Not one of the clients under investigation, although Holly had thought so at the time, just a client from an investor group that recently purchased the local vineyard and had shown interest in buying the Stone House and Glass Studio property.

Holly mentioned, "I just saw Collette. Is she selling again?"

"Collette's always selling," said Penelope. "Oh, hey. Guess what? I was just confirming the vineyard as sponsors of three crossword puzzle clues. They're offering wine tastings in the vineyard with a view of the Stone House and Glass Studio."

<u>DOWN</u>
NUMBER 6. HALF-FULL OR HALF-EMPTY (FIVE LETTERS)

<u>ACROSS</u>
NUMBER 8. BRANCHED HANGING LIGHT (TEN LETTERS)
NUMBER 9. YOU CAN SKIP ONE ON A LAKE (FIVE LETTERS)

"Congratulations," said Holly, thinking, *Sign me up!* She'd love to bring Jack to a wine tasting at the vineyard with a view of the Stone House and Glass Studio.

They proceeded up the gentle, rolling hill that was Mary-Margaret's front yard, using the serpentine bluestone walk that wandered up and through the property along a lengthened grove of bigleaf magnolias, sugar maples, and pignut hickories. How many hilltop acres did Mary-Margaret own? Three? Four? Five? This was prime, "old money" real estate. The kind that made you wonder if family treasure had ever been buried, then long forgotten.

Not that size mattered as far as she sheds were concerned—Holly would have been thrilled with a three-foot-by-three-foot shed with a chair in the middle so long as she got to decorate it and call it her own. Mary-Margaret's was about half the size of a one-car garage but looked nothing like a garage and was, instead, of the quaint, gabled-roof variety, more "luxury coastal cottage" than anything else.

Upon approach, a tiny front porch with a lushly cushioned swinging love seat with pillows made from vintage fabrics greeted them. On the seat cushion: cherry blossoms. On the center throw pillow: an old gray goose on finely woven pink chinoiserie. Flanking both ends of the love seat: throw pillows made of French-farmhouse grain sacks. Opposite the love seat, the bluestone patio curved to create an alcove large enough for a cozy wrought iron café table and four matching chairs, all painted bright white with playfully fringed pink chair cushions stuffed with down feathers. Someone—a professional—had designed this place. How anyone could call this a shed was beyond Holly. Even the pinks in the landscaping matched the pinks on the love seat and café table. Come spring, the white walls of the shed would match the white blossoms on the dogwoods. The door and shutters were stained an espresso brown that matched the colors of the trees, their trunks stretching up like architectural columns. It was charming, a wonderland, complementing Mary-Margaret's stately home and gardens, appearing as if it had always been there.

The closer they got, the more they lowered their voices, as if sneaking up on Mary-Margaret were somehow the answer. Penelope grabbed Holly by the sleeve to pull her behind a shade-loving French hydrangea still bursting in mid-September with ball-shaped white clusters.

"What is she, a hobbit now?" whispered Holly to Penelope.

"Shhh, no. Of course not. That's her lair," said Penelope. "Don't be silly."

"Lair? *I'm* not the one being silly. *She* is," said Holly, pointing toward the she shed. "Who's getting her kids to school every morning?"

"She gets her kids to school, but then I watch her walk up here in her pink bathrobe carrying a tray of tea and some food every morning. Avocado toast. Muesli with berries and yogurt. I'm telling you, Holly, she's not getting dressed, and she doesn't come out all day. I think she's depressed. Principal Hayes told me she resigned her post as president of the PTA."

"What? No, that's not possible." That surprised Holly. That *really* surprised her. Holly was a reluctant member of the PTA executive board—secretary. Long story. And now, Penelope was telling her the president had resigned? How could Holly not know this?

"It hasn't been announced. I told Hayes you were coming to talk some sense into her."

"Me? Don't tell him that," said Holly.

"Oh, Holly. Everyone knows you're new in town. You're the only one who doesn't have a history with Mary-Margaret. Or at least, your history with her is a short one. An itty-bitty history—only one week, so what's the damage?"

"A lot of damage!" said Holly. "That woman made my life a living nightmare. And she gave me a *stupid* nickname—Lavender. Said the scent of fabric softener inspired her. The whole thing was ridiculous." Traumatizing and ridiculous. Maybe she should leave. Maybe this was a mistake. She turned to go.

"You promised," Penelope reminded, pulling Holly by the sleeve to keep her on task.

"Fine, but after this, I want to talk about the job Caleb and I came to your office to discuss."

"Any thoughts about adding your home to the Enclave Tour?"

"Is this a bribe?" asked Holly.

"People hire me to negotiate."

Both bent slightly at the waist to peer around the hydrangeas to spy on Mary-Margaret in the shed. That's when Holly spotted it. Above the door, a sign written in scrolly letters. "She named her she shed?" asked Holly, pointing to the sign.

"Well, duh. This *is* Hopscotch."

"You don't find that funny? I mean, come on," said Holly. "The sign says 'That's What She Said.'"

"So?"

"So she's holed up in a 'That's What She Said' she shed?" Holly covered her mouth, tried not to laugh. "I know she's a narcissist, but is she at all self-aware? Even just a little?" She began to laugh, taking an elbow to the ribs from Penelope.

"Stop that!" Penelope hissed. "This is serious. Listen to me. You have to get inside That's What She Said. Make her feel special. Elevate her. Tell her she's needed."

"Can't we just yank her out? Knock on the door, and when she opens it, we grab her and pull her onto the lawn?"

Penelope considered it for a moment. "You mean, like, tackle her?"

Holly shrugged, looking down at the Bill's Pizza sweatshirt she was wearing. "I suppose we could use my sweatshirt and toss it over her head to blind her."

"What if she makes a run for it?"

"With a sweatshirt over her head?" Holly imagined Mary-Margaret attempting to flee the scene in a silken bathrobe, pizza sweatshirt over her head. "I suppose I could dive for the ankles, wrap my arms around, and try tripping her?"

"Come on, Holly. Focus."

"You're the one who suggested a forklift," Holly reminded her as they stepped out from behind the bushes and approached the shed.

A few steps later, "Mary-Margaret?" Penelope asked with a rap of her knuckles on the door. "Anybody home?" No response. "Come on, Mary-Margaret, I know you're in there. I can smell cupcakes." They waited. "It's your favorite cousin. And I'm with Holly Banks." Penelope gave Holly a thumbs-up, as if to imply the very mention of Holly's name would pull Mary-Margaret from hiding. But nope. Nothing. Penelope signaled to Holly to say something.

"The Village of Primm needs you, Mary-Margaret," said Holly, trying to sound authentic, wondering *how in the world* events in her life had brought her to this. She could think of a thousand things she'd rather be doing. Cleaning the lint tray, taking Ella to the grocery store when Ella was tired, getting crushed in a mammogram machine . . .

"More, more," whispered Penelope. "Say something to flatter her. Butter her up."

"I like your she shed," Holly offered.

Thin fingers from the inside lifted the metal mail slot, and through the crack came Mary-Margaret's tiny voice, like a peep, or a wounded mouse. "Oh, sure. That's what she said." And then, with that, the mail slot slammed closed.

Contact! Elated, Holly and Penelope high-fived.

"Go on Go on," Penelope urged Holly.

Holly bent until her face was level with the mail slot. "Mary-Margaret?" she tried. "Can I come in?"

Mary-Margaret slipped her fingers out, lifting the mail slot once again. "Umm . . . ," said the tiny, defeated voice. "No?" Mail slot slamming shut.

"Aw, come on, why not? It'll just take a minute. Penelope said you wanted to talk to me," said Holly, looking up at Penelope.

"Keep going," she whispered to Holly, knocking on the door again. "Mary-Margaret? Let us in. Please? We've come to talk to you about the Enclave Tour. The Village of Primm needs you. I need you."

Silence. Not a peep from inside. And then, signs of life. They could hear Mary-Margaret bustling about. Holly tried peeking through the window beside her, through a crack in the pulled shade and drawn curtains.

"What is she doing?" Penelope asked, pressing her face closer to the door.

"I don't know," said Holly. "She's making so much noise. Is she moving furniture?"

"She must be cleaning."

"Cleaning?"

"Sure," said Penelope. "Don't you clean when people visit?"

Holly lifted the mail slot, both she and Penelope now on their knees, catching a glimpse of Mary-Margaret setting dishes on a tray, fluffing pillows, dusting.

"Who keeps a feather duster in a she shed?" Holly wanted to know.

With no warning, the door snapped open, and into its frame stepped Mary-Margaret St. James, dressed head to toe in her signature pink. She looked done up and coiffed like a celebrity housewife from one of those reality shows on TV. Pink hair ribbon pulling blonde hair from her face, pink bathrobe scattered with red poppies at the bottom. She peered down at Holly and Penelope, caught spying, still on their knees.

"Hip! Hip!" offered Holly. Something Mary-Margaret often said to convey she felt the hooray in her heart.

"Thank you," said Mary-Margaret, chin held high, maintaining her composure. "I like your sweatshirt. I wish we had a Bill's Pizza in Primm, but we don't."

"Oh. Well," offered Holly, with a glance toward the logo on her chest from a pizza shop near her previous home in Colorado, "maybe you will someday. If you're lucky."

"Yes," said Mary-Margaret. "If we're lucky. Until then, we must endure Primm's award-winning brick-oven pizzas at Gourmet Pie on The Lawn. I like the gluten-free Savory Pie with brie and arugula," she added. "With pine nuts. Not only tasty but stunning on Instagram." Holly and Penelope climbed to their feet. "You've come to ask me a question?" Mary-Margaret lifted a hand to check the position of her hair tie. Finding everything in place, she looked at Holly, then at Penelope. "Well?" She blinked. Mary-Margaret knew she had something good behind that door.

"Can we come in?" asked Penelope.

She sheds were like unicorns, thought Holly. You saw them in magazines and on Pinterest, but whoever saw one in person? Not Holly. She'd never seen one. She waited with eager anticipation, thinking

Penelope should ask Mary-Margaret to add the That's What She Said she shed to the Enclave Tour. Holly would pay money to see it.

"Very well," said Mary-Margaret, pushing the door the remaining few feet till it stood ajar. She took a step back, inviting them inside.

Penelope entered first. Holly followed, impressed to find That's What She Said was temperature controlled by a unit designed for auxiliary spaces. The air inside was fragrant, a small pink candle burning on a tiny gilded table beside a daybed that doubled as a sitting area with oversize custom throw pillows and a linen bed skirt that brushed the floor with whipstitched box pleats. Penelope took a seat on the daybed. On the wall behind Penelope was a collection of portraits of women, the frames arranged like a family tree. Perhaps the lineage of women on Mary-Margaret's tree?

"Wow," Holly said, a bit breathless as she took it all in. She looked up, spun around. "This is truly beautiful, Mary-Margaret."

"Hip, hip," said Mary-Margaret, delicate hand patting twice on her chest. "You look exhausted, Holly. Have you been sleeping well? Would you like to have a seat?"

"Yes, please," said Holly, not exhausted and not taking the bait. She identified where she would sit—on a hammock chair hanging from the rafters. She reached for the crocheted edge of the hammock, attempting to steady it. Bending at the waist, she jutted her butt out, then took a step backward, attempting to sit in the swinging chair—willing her tush to land at the center of the hammock. No such luck. The hammock swung back, landing Holly butt first on the braided area rug.

"Goodness," giggled a wide-eyed Mary-Margaret.

Holly got up to try again, this time grabbing hold of the ropes that led to the eyebolt in the rafters. No doubt Mary-Margaret was spellbound by the possibility things could go south at any moment at Holly's expense. *Penelope* wasn't interested in watching Holly sit in the hammock. More interesting to her was watching *Mary-Margaret* watch Holly attempt to sit in the hammock. Now, why was Penelope so keen on observing Mary-Margaret observing someone else? Did triangles offer more information than straight lines?

Holly steadied the hammock, slowly lowering herself, before taking a careful, deliberate seat. Once planted, she took a moment to admire the hammock's tassels and finishes. This was Holly's first she shed. She was savoring it.

"Mayan artisans from the Yucatán Peninsula made that seat," Mary-Margaret informed her. "The Maya preferred hammocks—for sleeping in, for sitting in. They believed hammocks felt like a mother's warm embrace."

Holly felt the warm embrace, all right. She felt it all over her body. She leaned back, the hammock providing cozy but firm support as it swung slightly, hugging her tuchus. "Heaven," she said, not caring that she might be gushing. She wished she had a blanket and a free afternoon to sleep the day away in the hammock. She understood why Mary-Margaret dug in. The birds chirping outside the window led Holly to imagine herself waking from a dream in a she shed the way feathered friends woke Cinderella at the start of the Disney animated classic. What was that song Cinderella sang upon waking? "A Dream Is a Wish Your Heart Makes"? If Holly were Mary-Margaret, if she had a she shed like the That's What She Said she shed, she wouldn't come out either.

Above them, hanging from a pewter chain, was a crystal teardrop chandelier. *Ugh!* Holly wanted one so bad. She wanted a chandelier. In her foyer. Preferably, the chandelier with the gilded nest and glass birds she saw in the hallway at Feathered Nest. And she wanted this hammock chair. And that daybed. And the candle, the gilded table, and the wooden hutch behind Mary-Margaret. And the small mason jars filled with fresh flowers from the garden, perched prettily on Mary-Margaret's she shed window ledge. And that cupcake, sitting beside the teacup and saucer on Mary-Margaret's tray, expertly piped with swiss meringue buttercream and then topped with a pink edible sugar pearl. Holly thought she might jump up and eat it. Shove it in her mouth and then chase it with a swig of whatever was in that teacup. She wanted it. All of it. Every inch of the she shed, every perfectly articulated detail, every crumb from that there cupcake. Holly . . . wanted it all.

Penelope shifted her attention to Holly as Holly continued to canvass every nook and cranny of Mary-Margaret's she shed. "Almost everything you see here can be purchased in the shops on The Lawn," said Penelope, with an eye toward Mary-Margaret. "Homeowners with homes to show will stimulate the local economy, buying items in preparation. And tour goers, after touring beautiful interiors, will want the same for their homes, which should, in turn, stimulate the local economy."

The knowing glance Penelope exchanged with Mary-Margaret caused Holly to wonder if the plot to visit the she shed was a plot to convince Mary-Margaret to get back in the game or a plot to convince Holly to get *in* the game. Buy in. Become Primm. Or at least go into debt trying.

"I get it now," Holly said to Penelope. "I understand. The Enclave Tour—it's devilishly brilliant. It's not just about ticket sales to rebuild the topiaries or raise the confidence of the village post–chilli thrip infestation. It's about envy and desire. Keeping up with the Joneses."

Wanting more than you have, thought Holly. *Often, more than you can afford.*

That was what Primm did best—dangle all the things. Pretty things, things other people had. The Village of Primm Enclave Tour was illuminating the plight of the consumer, disguising it, wrapping it in a pretty little bow. *Compare yourself to others. What they have and what you do not. Work, earn, spend. Work, earn, spend.* It was a vicious cycle.

"No, no, Holly." Penelope shook a finger. "It's more than that. Far more than that. Sure, we need to help local businesses stay afloat while tourism is down during the rebuilding of the Topiary Park."

"A noble pursuit," said Mary-Margaret. "I see nothing wrong with that."

Penelope continued. "If tourists aren't coming to town to stimulate the local economy, then, sure, we need to convince the residents to stimulate the local economy until tourism returns. We need to work together. I know you'll hear me touting an important principle is at play in our beloved, bug-infested, postapocalyptic Village of Primm: *Consumer spending drives the economy.* It may *seem* that simple, and I know it sounds shallow and harsh, but trust me, it goes deeper than that. There's a higher ideal beneath all of this." She looked at Mary-Margaret, and in an instant, the two became one: Penelope, telling Mary-Margaret a story she already knew. A story, Holly suspected, their families knew and had lived through the generations. "What has meaning? What matters?" asked Penelope. "This village is on life support. I don't want to give up, pull up stakes, and fold. Nor do I want to sell and lose anything. There's true beauty here. Artistry, character, community. Fighting for what makes Primm Primm means fighting to preserve an enduring legacy for our children."

Penelope turned to Holly and said, "You're new in town. You don't realize it, but you bring fresh life to the village. You're a leader, Holly. I've been watching."

"Me?"

"Yes, you," said Penelope. "You immediately made your mark."

"I thought so too," said Mary-Margaret. Falling quiet after admitting it.

That relentless pursuit during the first week of school—was Mary-Margaret testing Holly? Penelope giving Holly a yellow T-shirt to wear when the entire room had worn pink. Was she marking Holly? Signaling to Mary-Margaret: *Her. She's the one.*

"I hit a school bus," Holly announced, wanting to sting Mary-Margaret. She was there. It was her fault.

Mary-Margaret shot a quick, shameful glance toward her own hands, folded across her lap. Holly could sense Mary-Margaret felt bad about what happened. The way she'd pursued Holly, relentlessly hounding her to volunteer when what Holly needed most was a few weeks to get acclimated to her new surroundings.

"I think the three of us would make a great team," said Penelope. "Maybe not now. Not after the rough start you two had. But someday."

"What? No," said Holly, shaking her head. Trying *really* hard not to squirm. "I mean. Thank you? But . . . no. Absolutely not." She stared straight at Mary-Margaret. "That'll never happen."

"Like I said, probably not now . . . but someday," said Penelope. The three sat quietly for a moment before Penelope added, "Mary-Margaret, you wanted to speak to Holly? Well, here she is, so speak your piece. And when you're through, get inside your *actual* home and get dressed. You and I have work to do." To Holly, she said, "Thank you for meeting with Mary-Margaret. I look forward to learning more about what you and Caleb have to offer Feathered Nest Realty."

And with that, Penelope lifted from the daybed to face the portraits of women framed and hanging on the wall. A moment later, she turned, then left, leaving Holly alone with Mary-Margaret.

"Thank you for meeting with me," said Mary-Margaret, the earnest look on her face appearing genuine. "I'm embarrassed by my husband. Ashamed, really. I never meant for that to happen. I love the topiaries. I love Plume—I do. I wish I could tell the whole world I'm sorry."

"The whole world?" asked Holly. "Isn't that a bit much?"

"You're probably right," acknowledged Mary-Margaret. "I suppose the Village of Primm would suffice." To Mary-Margaret, the Village of Primm and the world were probably one and the same. Mary-Margaret, with a tiny tear forming at the corner of her eye, added, "I'm horrified the chilli thrips have taken so much from this community. And I'm sorry for what I did to you during the first week of school."

"It's okay," said Holly, certain the three would never be a team but warming to the idea she and Mary-Margaret might be able to move past their many indiscretions—provided Mary-Margaret changed many of her ways. After all, as Online Psychic Betty recently pointed out, the moon, which ruled motherhood, intuition, and emotion, covered great distances in two short weeks. From the full moon to the new.

Holly took a moment to consider their situation—where they'd been and why they became what they had become to one another. Mary-Margaret had made mistakes *for sure*, but then, so had Holly— the chilli thrip infestation had taught them both that. Curiouser still, thought Holly, was where they might go together in the future. If this relationship took a step forward, assuming Mary-Margaret was truly sorry and made a concerted effort to change her ways, where might that lead?

"I forgive you, Mary-Margaret," said Holly. *Because why not? Why hold grudges? Grudges are like supergluing your forehead to a tree. You're not hurting the person you're grudging against. They've moved on. But you? You're stuck there. And eventually, that tree will move on too. It'll grow, taking you and your forehead right along with it.*

"Well then. I suppose you've given me no choice," said Mary-Margaret, now standing, a towering pink pillar over Holly's seated position in the hammock. "Since I'm a charitable person, and you've come all this way to offer me your forgiveness, who am I to refuse?" She extended her hand as a peace offering.

"What? No, no, no," said Holly. *She isn't turning this around on me. Is she?* "Let's be clear. I haven't 'come all this way.' You invited me. And *I'm* not offering you my forgiveness. *You're* offering me your apology."

"And I accept." Mary-Margaret smiled brightly. "Holly Banks, you're forgiven. Hip! Hip!"

"What? No. That's not what happened." Holly shook her head. "You can't announce that I'm forgiven. I never apologized. You apologized." She tried pulling herself up and out of the hammock chair, but it kept swinging her around. "Don't turn this around," she kept saying as she tried climbing to an upright position, wanting to regain her footing and meet Mary-Margaret face to face. "You're manipulating the conversation. That's not what happened."

11

"You should have seen it, Jack—an honest-to-goodness she shed!" said Holly, using hands-free to talk with Jack on speaker as she passed the gate at the foot of Hopscotch Hill before driving beneath the golden leaves on the tree-lined circular road, then past the dog park. "Can we do that?" she begged. "Let's do that, Jack. Let's convert a shed into something amazing."

"We don't have a shed," he reminded her, home sick from work that day. "If we had a shed," he reasoned, "I'd put the lawn mower, the rake, the ladders, and probably all of the camping equipment that's now in the crawl space inside the shed. Sheds are for storage, and we don't have any."

"Okay, fine. But don't you ever want to get away from it all?" she asked. "And I'm not talking about living off-grid. I'm talking about our actual life. In Primm on Petunia Lane. Don't you wish you had a refuge of comfort—your own little piece of heaven?"

"All the time. But Holly, there's no shed. It doesn't exist."

"I'd paint the inside blue. Not blue, blue. More like *blue*. A soft Twitter blue with bright-white trim. No. Maybe fern green. Or maybe not a color at all. Maybe just white. And why am I not surprised Mary-Margaret has a she shed," she added. "She probably inherited the house she lives in, so of course she'd have money to build a she shed. I doubt she even has a mortgage."

"I'm going out on a limb here, but I'm thinking that's none of your business?"

"Why are you so angry all of a sudden?"

"I'm not angry," he said.

She wondered if his response had anything to do with the financials at the St. James residence in light of the scandal Michael "My Love" St. James now found himself in. "It wasn't your fault," she told Jack. "You did nothing wrong."

He didn't respond.

"Jack, you're the good guy in all of this."

"I know."

She heard him exhale.

"I'm sorry, Holly, but I'm really not in the mood to talk about it right now."

"Has he been arrested?"

"That's up to the feds, not us. I'm sure it's coming, but it's probably too soon."

"Where is he?" she asked. As far as she knew, he wasn't in Primm.

"Can we change the subject?"

"Fine. I'm just saying I suspect there are she sheds all over Primm." Maybe she'd drive around that afternoon looking for them. Conduct a she shed search. "I'm sure Collette has a shed now that she's in Dillydally—all of those artists? You *know* they have sheds. That's probably why she moved."

"No one sells a house to buy a shed."

"Sure they do. You watch tiny-house, off-the-grid shows."

"Fair enough. But Holly?"

"Hmm?"

"We don't have a shed."

"Oh, but we could! I looked online. They sell kits. We can pick one up cheap."

"No, actually, we can't," said Jack. "The kind of shed you'd need to use it year-round would cost thousands of dollars."

"I'm not suggesting we go out and buy one tomorrow," she countered, "but maybe next year? If we save up? Maybe I'll get a she shed—a cheap one, don't worry—I'm talking small. Super small. And then you can man cave the garage."

"I have to go. I have a conference call."

"From home? I thought you were sick."

No response.

"Oh, come on. Dream with me," she said. "Why not have one itsy-bitsy moment of fantasy? You're always so practical."

"We haven't gotten over the hump of the move yet," he reminded her. "You need four new tires, and I've got a crack in my windshield. The lawn is trashed thanks to Caleb, and the upstairs bathroom needs to be addressed. I think it's causing stress fractures in the ceiling by the front door because there's two huge cracks on the outer edges of the foyer ceiling where the ceiling meets the walls. We talked about this the other night. Do you have any idea what that's going to cost? We might have to rip up the bathroom tile and open the floors and ceiling just to fix the plumbing."

"It can't be that bad," said Holly. "Let's spackle the cracks, then slap a quick coat of paint on the ceiling." Jack was a worrywart. Always overreacting. Although, it was concerning that the stain was spreading a bit and the cracks were seeming to deepen and stretch. "So, I guess now's a bad time to tell you I'm thinking about adding our home to the Village of Primm Enclave Tour?"

"Why in the world would you subject us to *that*?"

"I'm not *subjecting* you. You can take Ella and get out of the house when it's happening. I don't know . . . I thought it would be fun. And it's for a good cause."

"You can climb Mount Everest, but you'll never reach the summit of your own desires," he warned.

"That's stupid."

"You're climbing."

"No, I'm not," she said, about to turn onto Petunia Lane. "Don't say that."

"Why do you care what people think?"

"I don't."

"When was the last time you were online?"

She didn't tell him this, but about ten minutes ago. Before starting her car to pull away from Hopscotch. "Yesterday sometime? Day before? I can't remember."

"I know you, Holly. Having our house in a parade of homes will take hold of you."

"Wanna bet?"

"Sure. What's your wager?"

"She shed versus man cave. If I pull this off, we start saving for a she shed to be installed sometime this year. If I don't pull it off, all of that money goes into a man cave for you in the garage. Deal?" she said, thinking the moment she got inside the house she'd make him shake on it.

"Deal," he said. "Although I'd rather cash out of the Village of Primm and into an off-the-grid tiny home on Lake DooLittle than bother with a man cave in the garage that's tied to a mortgage."

"I know. I know. Jeez. Stop saying that."

Points made, they said goodbye, then hung up.

Birds chased each other beyond Holly's window as she pulled onto Petunia Lane. She loved the humble yet stately "village" charm of the Petunia enclave. Hammond lantern lampposts with sign brackets identifying each home by number, white Saint Andrews mail posts with black mailboxes and white lettering identifying house numbers and either Petunia Lane, Petunia Loop, or Petunia Knoll.

Right away, Holly spotted Houston Bonneville-Cranbarrie dressed in jeans, loafers, and a blue button-down shirt unbuttoned one button too low. He waved, signaling for her to stop beside his mailbox, where he stood talking with Greta. Holly could see Struggle was along for the conversation, secured by a leash in Greta's hand. Greta's new friend from across the street, Aahna Patel, was with them.

Holly rolled her window down, hit by the muskiness of Houston's cologne, trying hard not to stare at the silvering chest hair poking out of his shirt. He wore a silver chain with a Saint Christopher's medal on it, and Holly supposed that maybe, *maybe* he was attractive for a man slightly older than her mother. Maybe. Greta was dressed in her usual garb: flowy, hippie-looking dress, those goofy Red Baron goggles on her forehead. And Mrs. Patel appeared just as sweet as she did the day Greta flagged her down in her yard to ask if Primm had any casinos nearby. An odd question to ask when you first met someone, but the two seemed to connect somehow and were now showing signs of a budding friendship—though Holly doubted Aahna hit the slots. And her mother, a card-carrying member of GA, had better not.

"Well, hello," said Holly, appraising the situation between her mother and Mr. Houston Bonneville-Cranbarrie from two doors up, aware her mom had mentioned—how'd she put it?—the world was swiping right.

"Don't mind us," said Greta. "We're swapping slow cooker recipes and planning a takedown at next month's Scrabble tournaments."

"Is that so," said Holly, aware little would thrill her mother more than playing TAKEDOWN on a triple word score. She watched as Greta slipped her arm beneath Houston's, resting her hand on his forearm as if they were about to walk somewhere together. Perhaps that was what they were about to do when Holly drove up? Take a stroll down Petunia Lane?

Houston reached over, resting his hand on Greta's, the gold wedding band he wore in plain sight of everyone—including Greta if she were paying any attention. It was on his right hand, but still. Holly would be asking Greta about *that* the first chance she got.

"We've been admiring your lawn ornament," said Houston, smiling, nodding toward *Henny Penny*, still perched in Holly's yard.

"Yeah, well, say goodbye because someone's on their way to pick it up now," said Holly, not wanting to verbally shut Houston down but rather to show her dismay at having *aircraft* parked on her front lawn in a neighborhood with an active HOA.

It must have been odd for Houston, witnessing the first-ever plane landing on Petunia, but it wouldn't have been possible were it not for the open space above their yards and the yard that sat between them. With most of the homes sitting on quarter-acre lots, Holly wondered if he ever calculated how many could fit in his front yard alone, which was massive. He had explained the other night that upon Grandma Petunia's death and then, later, Grandpa Clive's death, he and his brother, Boris, inherited the family estate, promptly selling the land surrounding their home to a developer, a deal brokered by Penelope, one of her first. What wasn't Houston's home and the five acres surrounding it became the Petunia enclave. Houston's brother, Boris, now floating on a yacht somewhere, poured his fortune into creating CranBran BranMan ManMuffins™, sold in shops across town. Houston kept the family home. And if Grandpa Clive was indeed the thief everyone assumed he was (those were Houston's words), then Holly suspected Houston was probably still sitting on his fortune: a house chock full of paintings and jewelry won by Clive while playing poker. Houston said he loved his grandpa, but his ways were often suspect and always left Houston feeling mildly anxious.

"I've been wondering why that young man didn't simply turn it around and fly it out of here," said Houston.

Holly shrugged. "He told me he couldn't lift off from that spot. I think the plan is to tow it to the field beside the Clock Tower Labyrinth."

"Oh, sure," said Houston. "That makes sense. That's where the hot-air balloons take off."

"Mom, do you want me to take Struggle home?" offered Holly.

"Would you?" said Greta, opening the back door of Holly's car so Struggle could jump inside. "I'll be at Houston's for a while. We're meeting some friends from town."

Oh? Well, aren't you the social butterfly, thought Holly.

She said her goodbyes and then shifted her Suburban into neutral, rolling the rest of the way down the hill and into her driveway as Struggle panted and whined, anxious about something beyond the window.

As Holly climbed out of her car with a hold on Struggle's leash, *wouldn't you know it?*—Maeve Bling was crossing the street, headed straight for Holly's mailbox, feisty Pomeranian tucked beneath her arm. *Seriously? Ugh.* Holly moved quickly toward her mailbox, then read the note Maeve Bling handed to her.

~

HELLO NOTE

Effective immediately, the Petunia Enclave HOA has ruled front lawns may NOT be used as heliports. Kindly remove your aircraft.

—Maeve Bling

~

"We held an emergency HOA meeting last night to discuss regulation of drones and aircraft within a residential area," Maeve informed her, petting her Pom on his head. "It's our feeling that although we may move to drone use for home security in coming years, it is not desirable for anyone to have an aircraft parked on someone's front lawn. Kindly remove it."

"Yes, I know. But you see, this isn't my aircraft," explained Holly, taking a few steps onto the grass to put some distance between Struggle and the Pomeranian. "It belongs to a friend of mine, and he's sending a tow truck this afternoon."

The farther Holly moved onto the grass, the more Maeve's dog grumbled, lifting his upper lip, flashing teeny tiny needlelike teeth at Struggle.

Holly shortened her grip on Struggle's leash to keep the two from interacting. *Dogs are supposed to be leashed at all times,* thought Holly, eyeing the jerking, lunging movements Maeve's dog was making. *Should I bring that up?*

"Maeve?" she said instead. "I'm new to the Village of Primm. Could you cut me a break? And I'm new to the Petunia enclave, so I'll admit"—Maeve's dog continued with the long, slow growl—"I haven't read the HOA bylaws yet." What authority did Maeve have anyhow? she wondered. What exactly could a homeowner's association *do* to a homeowner? Take your house? Have you arrested? She didn't *own* the ultralight. This wasn't her fault. And she was actively pursuing the person who did own it to have it removed from her property. *Come on, Caleb. Hurry up with that tow truck.*

Maeve held a commanding presence, though she didn't engage. Her dog, on the other hand, a nippy Pomeranian, apparently *did* want to engage—eyes fixed like lasers on Struggle.

Struggle, though her tail was wagging, began a low, slow grumble.

"No," whispered Holly. "Not now, Struggle. Shhh." She wanted to tell Struggle: *One false move, and you* won't *be attending your birthday party next month, no matter how long or how hard Ella worked to plan it.* Why? Because Holly didn't know what kind of woman Maeve Bling was. For all Holly knew, Bling would file a complaint with animal control or take some other action, and before long, Struggle would be shipped off to Kalamazoo or Timbuktu or Elbow, Saskatchewan, even though—*no, absolutely not*—Holly would never let that happen. But it did worry her. What was Maeve capable of? Did anyone ever know what an overzealous neighbor was capable of?

Struggle pounced downward with her paws in a ready position to play with the Pomeranian.

"I think we should both go inside," said Holly to Maeve. Holly moved farther onto the grass and away from the Pom, even though, eyes happy, ears flopping about, there wasn't a speck of agitation in Struggle's bark; more like her bark was friendly banter between friends—tail wagging, hips swinging from side to side. Struggle appeared quite thrilled to be making friends with the dog from across the street. But then—*bang!*—out shot the Pom from Bling's arms, springing to the ground like a fuzzy orange ball shot from a Nerf Gun Blaster. Spry Pomeranian. Struggle bolted and ran the other way—moving so quickly and with such rock-solid determination the leash ripped from Holly's hand.

That Pomeranian didn't want to play. He was in full attack mode: a whizzing red-orange fireball now hauling butt so fast toward Struggle you couldn't see his wee little legs as they scrambled through the blades of grass. Tiny slip of a snout, set of teeth bared—savage, beastly growl.

Struggle, clearly the beta to the alpha Pom, looped circles around *Henny Penny* as Holly hightailed it toward the ultralight with Maeve Bling hightailing it behind her. But it was Jack who arrived first, appearing on the front porch and able to intercept the running dogs before either Holly or Maeve did. *Where'd he come from all of a sudden?* From beneath a wing of the ultralight, Jack kicked his leg into the early stages of the dogfight, trying to divide the dogs and break up the fighting currently underway.

"Stop it! Stop it!" shrieked Maeve, arriving to tug at Jack's arm. "Get your hands off my dog."

But Jack stood his ground, leg extended, pivoting when necessary to keep the dogs separated. He leaned in to snatch Struggle by the collar. Maeve's Pomeranian was so whipped up in a fury you couldn't pinpoint the dog's face amid the violent puffball of fur lashing about. After some effort, Jack did manage to hook his fingers under the Pom's collar.

"Take your dog!" he snapped toward Maeve as both dogs reared up on hind legs—not because Jack was pulling their necks upright but because both dogs elected to stand, hoping to establish dominance with one another. Holly noticed Struggle's tongue lolling out of the corner of her mouth. It looked to Holly like Struggle was smiling. Wagging her tail. Sure, it may have started as play, then moved to conflict, but for Struggle, it was ending as play. Frolicking fun. Struggle thought she was making a new friend. Having another adventure. Oh, but Maeve's dog—not so much. Maeve's dog had lost it. *Maeve's* dog was a fighting dog.

"Mildred! Get your dog!" ordered Jack.

Holly winced. *Mildred? No, Jack. That's not her name.*

Maeve scooped her Pom into her arms, freeing Jack to take two steps back, still holding Struggle by the collar. Everyone—the dogs, Holly, Jack, and Maeve—caught their breath, taking stock.

Holly leaned toward Jack. "Her name is Maeve."

"What?" Jack looked at Holly as if he had no clue what she was talking about. "Who is?"

"She is." Holly pointed.

"Your dog," seethed Bling with a finger stabbing the air toward Holly, Pomeranian in her arms all jacked and twisting, flipping, yipping. "Your dog attacked my dog!"

"You're joking, right?" said Holly, still clutching the Hello Note. "Because that's insane."

Jack moved swiftly and silently to bring Struggle inside the house, never saying another word to Maeve. Holly knew what he was thinking. Holly knew what he wanted to say.

"My husband's pant leg is torn." Holly leaned in. "And I think I saw blood."

"Your dog started it," snapped Maeve, trying desperately to keep hold of her manic Pom.

"Your dog was in *my* dog's front yard, and *your* dog lunged at mine," said Holly. So she got a Hello Note for the plane. Big freaking deal. This time, it wasn't Struggle that ran into someone else's yard to stir up trouble. It was Maeve's dog. "*Your* dog should be leashed!" said Holly. "*My* dog was on *my* property. I should write *you* a Hello Note."

Too wrapped up in a tizzy to think of anything to say, eyes opened wide, Maeve stomped her foot before taking her leave in a pout, marching around the tail of the ultralight and through Holly's grass, clutching her Pom.

Greta yelled from Houston's mailbox, "That's right, Maeve! And you can take your Hello Notes and stick them up your—" Houston covered her mouth, blocking the expletive.

Holly added, "If I see teeny tiny shark bites on Jack's ankle—I'm calling animal control!"

And then, from the top of the hill at the entrance to Petunia Lane, in drove Caleb's buddy Nathan, there to remove *Henny Penny* from Holly's front yard. *Finally.* Maybe her luck was changing. On second thought, she'd better not jinx it.

12

Penelope Pratt
Feathered Nest Realty

—ENCLAVE ALERT—

THOUGHT YOU WERE HOME FREE? THINK AGAIN!

Thanks to the inspiring work of Mary-Margaret St. James, homeowners in both Ballyhoo and Hobnob have joined the Village of Primm Enclave Tour, lifting those enclaves from Gold Status with three homes, to Platinum Status with four homes, joining Blythe, Castle Drum Tower, Hopscotch, and Peloton at the top of the heap.

Sigh.

Unfortunately, with the exception of Petunia, climbing from Aluminum Foil with zero homes to Bronze with one home on tour, the following enclaves haven't budged from their current positions:

Dillydally and Parallax—still at Silver with two homes on tour

Gilman Clear—holding at Bronze with one

Chum and Pram—with no homes on tour, covered in aluminum foil like suppertime leftovers.

At Feathered Nest Realty, we believe home is where the heart is. So rip your heart out and add it to the Tour by texting "EAT. YOUR.HEART.OUT" to WHY.THAT'S.SO.GROSS.

THE STATE OF PLUME

Happy to report Plume is ready to roll! Structural engineers attached wheels to her feet, giving Topiary Park horticulturists the option of wheeling her from the courtyard to the planting shed—where she awaits replanting. One problem: she's still completely naked, all plant material burned in the fire.

13

On a Saturday afternoon with Struggle sleeping on the floor and Charlotte licking her paws while splayed across a chair, Holly sat with her laptop, facing a blank page. She had exactly three weeks to complete her entry and upload it to the Wilhelm Klaus website as a late entry.

Opening scene—it was just a rough draft. *Annnnnd* go.

—WILHELM KLAUS FILM FESTIVAL ENTRY—

FADE IN:

SCENE 1 — INT. "FEATHERED NEST REALTY" —
MORNING

> PENELOPE PRATT flits about Feathered Nest
> Realty, beelike, symbolizing the hive,
> hard work, and the cross-pollination of
> community building through the sharing
> of private homelife.

Holly took a sip of her coffee to give herself time to think. Facing a blank page after being disconnected from her creative life for so long was difficult, but she needed to push forward. She thought, for starters, she could fictionalize recent events and see where it led. Lots of people were discovering, reinventing, and reconnecting with themselves. She was no different. She just needed time to get her creative groove back. True, she wasn't sure where any of this would take her, but it wouldn't hurt to try.

Think, think, think.

She planned to write rough notes, creating a three-act script with nine scenes, and had already decided to work in stop-motion, using her iPhone and tripod to manipulate paper cutouts while shooting thirty frames per second. She was thinking paper cutouts à la Lauren Child, the children's author and illustrator who created Charlie and Lola. Holly hoped to blend the aesthetics of Lauren Child with the tone and longing felt by Audrey Hepburn's Holly Golightly character in the opening scene of *Breakfast at Tiffany's*.

Holly selected a few colored pencils, then sketched Penelope with black hair pulled into a bun at the nape of her neck, standing long and lean in one of her trademark buttercream-yellow pantsuits. She sketched a tote the color of a caramel latte, imagining ways she could joint Penelope's arms as separate paper pieces at the shoulders, elbows, and wrists, so she could then move her body parts, piece by piece, threading an arm through the strap of the tote and then animating her jointed paper legs until they walked across the screen. She wouldn't use this exact sketch, nor would she use the script she was now tapping into her computer. These were thoughts, she told herself—impressions, ideas, a safe place to create.

So, back to brainstorming she went in hopes a script would emerge.

SCENE 2 — INT. "FEATHERED NEST REALTY" —
CONTINUOUS

> Penelope greets a series of sales asso-
> ciates. FIRST SALES ASSOCIATE, female,
> models an apron from the Feathered Nest
> Collection. SECOND SALES ASSOCIATE,
> male, presents a choice of two scented
> candles on a silver platter: one li-
> lac, the other lavender. THIRD SALES
> ASSOCIATE, male, displays tabletop to-
> piaries in bright-white cachepots, the
> words *Welcome to the Village of Primm*
> emblazoned on the front.

Holly stared at her screen, sensing that the reckless abandon she could so easily tap during her film school days had left her. She felt rusty and out of practice. Had motherhood zapped it out of her? She began again, deciding not to worry about the formatting conventions in scriptwriting. All of that could be handled during final editing.

SCENE 3 — EXT. "FEATHERED NEST REALTY" — CONTINUOUS

> Penelope pushes through glass doors to
> the sidewalk beyond, where she strikes
> a pose, placing a hand on a real es-
> tate sign, the words *Village of Primm*
> *Enclave Tour* scrolled in proud, gilded
> lettering.

> Shielding her eyes, she looks up to
> follow an unidentified flying object — a
> plane of some sort, except not a com-
> mercial plane, more like a hobbyist's

```
hang glider with an engine attached to
a double-wide jogging stroller — moving
across the clear blue skies over Primm.
```

That ugly voice in Holly's head reared up to yell: *This sucks! You suck, Holly Banks. You have no talent.* Maybe this was a mistake. Maybe she shouldn't make a go of it and instead apply for a traditional job, a safe job, a job that didn't ask her to take a risk or put herself "out there."

She shook the thoughts from her head, telling herself she was just scared. *Coward.*

But then she wondered—why did she call herself a coward? *Seriously?* WTHeck. Why slap a negative label on yourself in a moment of weakness or the moments following tinges of self-doubt? And where did the self-doubt come from in the first place? Fear? Holly wondered if there was an order to this line of thinking: first fear, then self-doubt, then name-calling? Because if there was, ef that. She needed to stop. Break the cycle of negative thinking.

And what was she afraid of? Why not try? Why not grab life by the ball bearings? If a script she wrote made it to the finals, she'd land a grant to produce it. She could buy equipment, hire actors, build props. She could live in Primm and be Ella's mom and Jack's wife, but more than that—she could produce the first of many short films, create the beginnings of a portfolio. The Village of Primm could be her muse; its residents, her cast of characters. It was worth a shot, right? If she didn't win, if she scored last place, at least she could say she had *done* something. *Just write. Write anything. You can always edit later.*

```
SCENE 4 — EXT. AIRCRAFT — CONTINUOUS


From the point of view of the PILOT,
Penelope grows smaller and smaller
below.
```

In FULL FRAME, as CREDITS ROLL during OPENING SCORE, pilot and aircraft,
surrounded by fanciful birds delight-
ing in flight, capture sweeping views of
the Village of Primm as quaint neighborhood enclaves pass below. Charming
slate rooftops, bright-white gaze-
bos, autumn leaves beginning to color.
Primm, an idyllic waterside tourist
town, is waking to a sunny day.

FOLLOW SHOT zooms in on a single BIRD
who cuts away, departing from the pilot, aircraft, and other birds to de-
scend toward a white house with black
shutters. Alighting first on a "12
Petunia Lane" mailbox, the bird flies
to a welcome mat on the porch before
flying away and off camera the moment
the front door opens and a woman appears, fetching a newspaper from her
porch. A chocolate Labrador wearing a
hot-pink tutu pushes past her, running
down the porch steps and toward the
neighbor's yard.

Someone knocked on Holly's front door, interrupting her thoughts.
She hit save, closed her laptop, then left the kitchen table to answer it,
deciding on the way the main character in the film she was creating
would be named Audrey. Only five more scenes to write, and she'd
have her nine-scene script completed. Or at least, a rough draft of a
nine-scene script. Editing would come later, and a lot would be decided

during filming. How long did she have? Three weeks? And that was as a late entry.

"Yes?" said Holly, opening the door to a sudden flash of a photographer's camera.

"Ms. Banks, what can you tell us about the training of your canine?" a reporter from the *Southern Lakes Daily Dose* tabloid asked, offering Holly his business card. "Did you move to the Village of Primm to uncover its secrets?"

Holly was completely befuddled. Of course she hadn't. They'd moved to the Village of Primm for Jack's job. *Secrets?* Why did he ask that?

"Are you a treasure hunter? Do you deal exclusively with navigational devices, or are you also a part of the antiquities ring that operates from Primm?" the reporter wanted to know, shoving a phone set to record in Holly's face.

This was nuts. "No," said Holly. "I'm not involved in any of that." *Go away.* She moved to close the door, but the reporter stuck his foot out, absorbing the brunt of the door Holly was attempting to shut.

"Ms. Banks, can you share the dog's schedule with the press? When will the dog reconvene the search? Do you intend to use the airplane to fly the dog through the skies over Primm?"

She pushed her toes against his, sliding his foot from her doorjamb.

"If the property beneath the water tower belongs to Southern Lakes, and the Village of Primm is declared dry because of *your* dog's discovery, are you prepared to make a statement either to or on behalf of residents in the Village of Primm?"

"We're not involved!" Holly pressed the door closed, then locked it. *Oh, Struggle. What have you done?* She shivered, unnerved the reporter had the audacity to knock, unannounced, on her front door like that. Holly loved movies and film but didn't love the media and the anxiety they provoked. Two industries using cameras for entirely different purposes.

Had she moved to the village to uncover Primm's secrets? *What secrets?* She knew a circle of nefarious characters had operated in plain sight, which had led to the chilli thrip infestation and destruction of the Topiary Park, and she knew the town had history, but my goodness, thought Holly, besides the current issues with the astrolabe, how many secrets and mysteries could one town have?

"Mom?" she called out, grateful Ella was out of the house with Jack so she could get some distraction-free work done on the stop-motion. "Do you have this morning's paper?"

Greta descended the steps carrying the *Primm Gazette* and a smoothie. "What is all that?" She pointed to a small bench beside the coatrack at the front door.

"Ta-da! This," announced Holly, "is our new mudroom!" She waved an arm across the display as if she were a game show host unveiling a prize package, stopping midwave to admire the corkboard she'd hung above a bench she'd bought at the Drunken Plaid Gift Shoppe in town. Next to the corkboard, she had hammered a hook into the wall to hold a dog leash. "See? It even has a basket underneath."

Struggle walked over to greet Greta, tail wagging.

"Doesn't the door bang into it?" asked Greta.

"No, of course not," said Holly. Although, it was a bit cramped. "I'm seizing control."

"Of what? People when they walk through the door?"

"I'm controlling *items* as they cross the threshold. Mail, keys, shoes, Ella's backpack, and school papers," explained Holly. "According to Penelope, organized homes have a system of controlling the ins and outs of daily life."

"According to Penelope."

"What's wrong with wanting an organized home?"

"Holly, your mudroom is so cluttered it's a booby trap."

"You look nice," said Holly, admiring how her mom's bohemian necklace tucked amid a flowy gray-blue shirt atop black leggings and bare feet gave her mom that down-to-earth "spiritual vibe" that reso-nated so fully with her personality. Her curly gray hair was twisted into a messy bun, then skewered with those lacquered amber-colored chop-sticks her mom so often wore. "Are you going somewhere?"

"I swiped right." Greta flashed Holly a devilish smile. "He's pick-ing me up in about fifteen minutes. Early dinner, late night." She winked.

"I know you divorced Dad when I was in elementary school, but it still feels like you're cheating on him. Is that weird?"

"This might surprise you, but when I was still in Nevada, your dad and I matched on a dating app."

"You're joking."

"Nope. We met for dinner."

"What? That's insane."

"Actually, it was quite nice," said Greta, drifting off into thought until a wistful smile appeared. "But then, that's a story for another day."

Holly knew from growing up that when her mother said, "That's a story for another day," the conversation was over. "Fine," she said. Not knowing what else to do or say, she took the paper from Greta, then snapped open the front page.

"Those the holes Struggle dug?" said Greta. "They're still making front-page news."

"I don't believe it."

"Why would I lie?"

"Not that. This," said Holly, finger poking the front page. "Treasure-hunting teams arriving in Primm?" So that was what the reporter had just asked about. "That can't be good." She read further, learning the teams were equipped with metal detectors and electronic pinpointers. "Says here some of the teams were invited by Merchant Meek." How was he involved in all of this? Merchant Meek Hopscotch III was Mary-Margaret's grandfather and Penelope's great uncle. Holly wondered what *they* would think about all of this. Hmm. Maybe they were used to this sort of thing. Maybe what others thought was eccentric was perfectly normal to them.

She followed Greta into the kitchen, thumbing through the rest of the paper as she walked, finding Penelope's first official teaser for the crossword puzzle intended to sell merchandise and stimulate the local economy.

<u>ACROSS</u>
NUMBER 3. TYPESETTER'S DOT (SIX LETTERS)

Zero? No. That was four letters. *Comma?* Couldn't be. That was five letters and not a dot. *Period?* Was that it? Typesetter's dot. Hmm . . . maybe the answer was kept at the letterpress cottage in The Quiet? She folded the *Primm Gazette*, setting it on the kitchen table to pick up a printed copy of the Enclave Tour guidelines. With furrowed brow and a pensive tone in her voice, Holly told Greta, "I have a name for the company I'm starting. Holly Banks Productions."

"Oh, it'll be a production, all right," said Greta. "But hey, I'm game. Can I help?"

"Ha ha," Holly said sarcastically. She added, "No, but thank you. And it's official. Number twelve Petunia Lane is on the Enclave Tour. I hit send yesterday, entering the living room, and then I sat down and made a huge things-to-do list."

"Oh, Lordy," said Greta. "You're going to regret that decision."

"It's only one weekend," said Holly, wondering why everyone seemed to doubt her when she told them her plans. "Judging Friday night, tour on Saturday, awards on Sunday."

Greta sat down to fiddle with her ukulele. "Does Jack know?"

"I've told him my plans. We made a bet. If I pull it off, we save for a she shed."

"And if you don't?"

"He bet a man cave in the garage for him against a she shed in the backyard for me, but then he immediately said he'd rather cash out of Primm and live in an off-the-grid tiny home on Lake DooLittle. I'm a little worried," said Holly.

"About what? Nuclear proliferation? Getting hit by an asteroid?" Greta positioned her fingers on her ukulele before starting to strum. "Looking stupid when you dance?"

"I know how to dance," said Holly. "I'm a good dancer."

"Worried the gum you swallowed years ago is still in your stomach?" Greta moved her fingers across the frets. "Worried you're missing out on life because you have too much wax in your ears?"

"You're not listening."

"What?"

"I'm worried about money. If I don't buy the right equipment, I can't start a film studio." Holly had stayed up late, researching camera equipment and taking measurements of the living room and dining room. She filled no fewer than seven shopping carts across different camera-equipment and film-supply websites but then chickened out before clicking purchase, knowing she'd have to patch together credit cards to get what she needed. "I hate that I have to spend money to make money. I think I need a small business loan."

"Seems reasonable," said Greta, attaching a chromatic tuner to the headstock of her ukulele and then plucking the fourth string. "People do it all the time."

"I picked this up from the Village of Primm Credit Union." Holly showed Greta the application. "I figured—credit unions are set up to invest in local businesses. Their website even said so. And all of the camera equipment I buy should serve as collateral, so it's not like I'm asking for an unsecured loan."

"I think you should go for it."

"Am I wrong to also want to finance living room furniture? Because I'm thinking I'll use both the living room and the dining room to conduct business."

"Give it a shot. The worst they can do is say no," said Greta. And then, intuiting Holly's discomfort, she asked, "What are you so worried about?"

"You really want to know?"

"I wouldn't have asked."

"I'm worried I might fail," said Holly, placing a hand on her stomach. "And every time I think about it, my stomach twists into a thousand tight, tiny knots."

"That's because your gut is full of nerves."

"Oh, okay. Sure. Nerves in your digestive system." *That can't be true,* thought Holly. "Is that true? Or is this part of your yoga meditation stuff?"

"Your brain has the largest concentration of nerves in your body, but your gut has the second largest. And get this," said Greta, "many of your nerve connections are shared by both the digestive tract and the brain, so thinking can absolutely affect the gut."

"Really? You're joking. Are you serious?"

"Of course I'm serious. When you get anxious, you release hormones and chemicals, and they often wind up in your gut, upsetting digestion. You should be careful. You can screw up your digestive flora. You can also decrease your production of antibodies." The look on Greta's face implied she was serious, but her expression was hard to read. One moment, she appeared relaxed and chatty. A moment later, her lips pinched, and her fingers froze on the strings as if a thought had occurred to her—a worry, a concern, something—then she tucked it deep, setting it aside. "Holly, if your gut gets unbalanced because of your thinking, you could end up with all sorts of issues."

"Stress is a normal part of life. You can't avoid it," said Holly.

"I agree. Believe me, I agree. But if you're not managing your stress and it's upsetting your stomach, you should do something about it."

"Like what? Eat Nutella? I can't stop my thinking." *Trust me*, thought Holly, *if I could, I would.*

"You can become more aware of your thoughts," Greta offered. "Maybe if you're aware of them"—she strummed a catchy tune—"you can work to change them. Do this. When a bad thought comes, notice it. Say, *Hi, bad thought. I see you. You can go now.*" She smiled. "And then you—*whoosh!*—let it float on by."

The doorbell rang. Thinking it might be the media again, Holly moved to answer it.

"Actually, that's for me," said Greta, handing Holly the ukulele so she could slip her bare feet into a pair of shoes. "Hot date, remember?"

When Greta reached the front door, Holly leaned, attempting to catch a glimpse of the man picking her mom up. And ugh, it was Houston.

"Don't wait up," said Greta. And then, "Oh! Houston, step inside a minute. Show Holly your ring." Greta held the door open for him to enter.

"Mom, that's really not necessary," said Holly, joining them, embarrassed Greta was calling her out over her concern about Houston's ring. Never in Holly's wildest imagination did she think Greta would make such a public statement over it. On second thought, Greta was Greta. Nothing she did surprised Holly anymore. "Hello, Houston. How are you?" said Holly. It felt odd carrying on a conversation with someone taking her mom out.

"Show her the inscription," said Greta. "She doesn't believe that's your grandfather's ring."

"No need. Really," said Holly to Houston. "It's none of my business."

"Oh, it's no problem," he insisted, pulling the ring from his right hand to show Holly the words engraved on the inside. "The more people who know about this, the better. See? It says: *Clive and Petunia, 1898.* That's the year they were married. And over here, it says: *Penumbra Over Primm.* Grandpa Clive had that engraved after the 1941 fire. In autumn. October, actually. I have the receipt for the Penumbra Over Primm engraving in a safety-deposit box in Menander to prove when he did it. My grandfather always told me, 'Autumn is the season to hunt for buried treasure.' He said look for a clue hidden in plain sight. I never knew what he meant by it, but during his dying days, even with his memory slipping—and his memory did slip; that's what got him in the end—he said it so much I never forgot it. I always got the sense he *knew* as his memory was slipping and that there was *one* essential memory—information he wanted to give me but couldn't. Anyway, autumn's the season."

Of all the questions Holly could be asking, the one she asked was the one that popped up first. "Why Menander?"

"Neutral territory. Any disputes between the Village of Primm and Southern Lakes tend to be settled in Menander."

Before Holly could ask why someone implicated in a fire would place a cryptic engraving inside their wedding band, Greta shut down the conversation with, "See? I told you he's not married. Satisfied?"

"I apologize if any of this has offended you," Holly said to Houston.

"Not at all," he said. "It's perfectly understandable." Offering his arm, he asked Greta, "Shall we?"

"We shall!" Greta took his arm and walked with him down the porch steps. "Don't wait up," she told Holly.

As Holly closed her front door, she tried to recall—*penumbra*—wasn't that a ring of light around a shadow?

14

A few hours later, Jack came through the front door carrying Ella, who was sound asleep in his arms after spending most of Saturday afternoon at a soccer skills camp. Jack, first day on the job as coach of the Bubble Gummers, appeared utterly exhausted after herding Ella's team through the various skills stations.

"That was insane," he whispered, eyes wide open in a state of prolonged disbelief. Holly helped him lay Ella down on the family room couch—pillow, blanket, and, of course, Struggle on the floor beside the couch with Charlotte at Ella's feet. Struggle's snout rested beside Ella's head, almost poking her in the ear. "Soccer balls getting kicked every which way," said Jack. "I kept having to duck and dodge and throw my body in front of balls to block kids from getting hurt. Kindergartners screaming and squealing in high-pitched voices and all that complaining and someone having to go potty every twenty minutes. Total chaos. And get this—besides the team mom, Malik and I were the only dads in charge of nineteen five-year-old girls. Nineteen! And they kept asking questions. 'Why is your hair like that on top?' 'Chicken nuggets: dinosaur shaped or plain?' Oh! And get this. One girl wanted to know why *people* don't have tails like animals do. Tails!"

"I take it you had fun?" Holly teased, pulling a blanket over Ella.

He followed her into the kitchen. "I'm ripping out the three boxwoods from the side yard tomorrow."

"Thrips?"

"I'm afraid so."

"I wish there was something someone could do."

"They're trying," said Jack. "Everyone's trying."

She was eager to fill him in on all that she'd gotten accomplished that afternoon. On the kitchen table: a small business loan app with supporting documents attached, a pile of paper body parts for the stop-motion she was working on, and the guidelines for Penelope's Enclave Tour. "Think you can build those bookshelves in the living room this weekend?"

"Why? What's the emergency?" he asked, pulling a coffee beer from the refrigerator and then reading the label. "Java-infused oatmeal stout. Want one?"

"No thanks," she said, wondering if now was the best time to tell him. "We're on the Enclave Tour."

"Oh, jeez."

She watched him open the beer. "Why are you looking at me like that?"

"I'm not."

"I really don't think it'll be *that* big of a deal," she told him. "Five hours on Saturday with judging Friday night, and I'll do all of the work. You can take Ella out of the house Friday night, and she'll probably have a soccer game on Saturday. The awards ceremony is Sunday, but I don't have to go to it. I know I won't be winning any awards—that's not why I'm doing this."

"Great. There goes another one of my weekends," he griped.

"What's your deal? Are you in a bad mood?"

"Holly, I have a headache. I'm exhausted. I just spent five hours with nineteen kindergartners tugging at my shirt all day long." He opened the refrigerator again and then closed it in a way that said: *There's nothing to eat in this house.*

"Shhh. Don't close that so loud." She nodded toward Ella, then walked toward the foyer, waving for him to follow her.

"Do we have any aspirin?"

"Of course we have aspirin." Once inside the living room, she said, "You promised you'd build bookshelves when we bought the house. You said it was easy."

"Fine. I'll do it," he conceded. "Add it to the list."

"Will you stop? You're acting like it's the apocalypse. I'm the one doing everything for the Enclave Tour."

"You're the one who signed us up."

She folded her arms across her chest.

"Is that all you need?" he asked. "Some bookshelves?"

"Yes. Thank you," she told him. "I'll do all of the painting, but I need you to move the dining room table and chairs to the garage. And move the old living room furniture to the driveway for donation pickup."

"Hold up," he said, his hands signaling time-out. "What's wrong with the living room furniture?"

"Seriously? You're asking? Look around, Jack. It's awful. Dingy old couch? A lamp we picked up on Craigslist? Nothing matches. It's all thrown together. Half the stuff in our house is hand-me-downs from the house Sadie owned before the home she owns now." She pointed to the bare, open window. "So glad I took down the curtains my mom made from that bedsheet—jabot? Ha! What a nightmare. We just need a few pieces. A few. Like, a couch and some end tables." Why did he seem so overwhelmed all of a sudden? "And maybe two chairs. I really think it's time, Jack. We're grown-ups. I want a grown-up space. And it's not like we go on expensive vacations. We can do this. We can finance it over forty-eight months with no interest if we pay it off in four years."

"And the dining room furniture? What's happening in the dining room?"

"I'm going back to work," she told him. "In the dining room. When Ella's at school."

"Doing what?"

It was a fair question. "I'm opening a film studio."

"You're shooting movies now? When did that happen?"

Okaaaaay. She stiffened. But also a fair question.

"I'm providing social media and video production services for businesses in Primm." Saying it out loud to someone who was born a skeptic made her wonder if the concept was even viable. "And I might have Penelope as a client. Caleb and I are hoping to start shooting her real estate listings."

"Hoping," he reminded her.

"We have aircraft. Which is much better than drones," she pointed out.

"And you're going to fly in that thing," he said. It wasn't a question. It was a statement.

"Maybe . . ."

"Can I watch?"

"Stop."

"A film studio. You mean, like, cameras and lighting?" he asked, his eyes looking over her shoulder and into the dining room as if he was trying to imagine it. "But—you hate social media."

She knew he'd bring that up. "I never *hated* it. I just complained about it." Probably because she never felt good at it. "But I don't hate it anymore. Not if it'll make us some money," she said, hoping to win him over. "But yes, I'll need the whole kit and caboodle. Camera, lights. I'll need a light table for still shots. Maybe a few backdrops. I'm thinking I can do some commercial photography to help local shops bring their inventory online. As inventory turns over, I'll enjoy repeat photography business. Jack, tourism is down. I can help brick-and-mortar businesses build their online presence. That's a good thing. I'll be giving back. Making a difference." She tried to get a read on him, but when she couldn't, she just kept talking. "A DSLR-and-mirror camera, a fifteen-millimeter-rod shoulder-mount rig, quick-release camera plate, V-lock shoulder support with dual handgrips." It was fresh on her mind after spending the afternoon itemizing everything on her small business loan application. Consumer spending drove the economy. So did investment in small businesses. "Maybe a large C-shaped support arm and top handle? I don't know." Why wasn't he saying anything? Was he freaking out? "I haven't decided yet," she added. What was he thinking? Why that look on his face? "Jack? Everything okay?"

"What?"

"Say something."

He was acting—off. Something. She turned around to look with him toward the ceiling of the dining room. "I can do everything," she assured him. "All I'll need from you is to install lighting. That's not such a big deal. Right?"

He exhaled. Loudly. But other than that, he didn't say anything. He just stood there. Why wasn't he excited for her? Why wasn't he acknowledging all the hard work she had done? All the research? The entrepreneurial drive? Was he worried about money? Worried about losing another weekend of time? "I can pay for it with a small business loan. I've already filled out the application with Primm Credit Union— very favorable terms. I was hoping to discuss it with you tonight and maybe apply for it Monday morning."

She probably should have discussed it with him first, but he was a details guy. He liked to see the numbers. She typically collected all the information she could before presenting things to him. That's how they worked. That's how it had always been. She'd never apply for the loan without having him on board.

"And hey," she said, reaching over to give him a friendly whack on the side of his arm. "Soon you'll be getting that bonus," she mused, trying to keep things light. But truthfully, she was curious about the bonus. Jack was so tight lipped these days she felt like she didn't know what was going on. Was it coming? *When* would it come, and how much would it be?

He didn't respond. He *was* getting a bonus. Right? Because it was that time of year. Fiscal year ended in July. Bonuses were paid in October. They counted on it. It was part of the package that brought them from his firm's office in Boulder City to the Village of Primm. Take a reduced salary, learn to live on less, then hope for a lucrative year for the firm and enjoy a portion of the proceeds. It was a gamble, but if all went well, the payoff would be enough to knock out the credit cards with a little left over.

"Jack?" She waved a hand across his line of sight. "Hello? Are you okay?"

"What?"

"You're not saying anything."

"What do you want me to say?"

"I don't know," she admitted. "Maybe say: *Hey, Holly. That's really great. I'm excited you're reconnecting with your art.*" She waited for his response. He had told her to reconnect with her art—on the porch, that first week of kindergarten. "We'll have two incomes," she reminded him, holding two fingers up. But again, silence. *Seriously?* "Hello?"

"What?"

"What's the deal with you? Why aren't you saying anything?"

All that hard work she did. All that planning. She'd been waiting for him to get home all day so she could share it with him. This was a big deal to her. It was important. She felt knots forming in her stomach—nerves in her digestive tract, whatever. Maybe she should have consulted him first. This was his house too. But really? No one used the dining room.

Finally, "I don't know," he said. "A business loan? *And* a furniture loan? What if now isn't the right time to stage a dining room as a film studio? What if we have to sell the house?"

"Why would we have to sell the house?" asked Holly, taken aback.

He shrugged. Looked away.

"Is there something you're not telling me?"

"No, of course not," he said.

"Then why did you say that?"

"I don't know. Is it weird to have a film studio in a dining room?"

"Where else am I going to put it?" she asked. In the mudroom? The mudroom *bench*? "Fine. Let's say I don't stage a film studio to make money from the one room in the house no one in this family uses except the pregnant cat. Where am I supposed to get a job with a film degree? There isn't a film industry in Primm unless I create one. I mean, well, sure, Wilhelm Klaus is coming. But that's because Primm is a tourist destination. At least, it was. If that doesn't turn around, Wilhelm Klaus will probably never come back. This might be my only shot." She'd love to be up and running by the time Klaus came to town. Maximize the opportunity. Be ready, should luck or fortune come her way. Time was ticking. Time was always ticking. Years wasted between film school and this moment. She waited for a response from Jack. When there wasn't any, she added, "So what do you suggest, Jack? Hmm? Do you want me to work?"

He said nothing.

"Jack?" she asked—she insisted.

"What?"

"How am I supposed to work around Ella's schedule if I don't start my own business and control my hours? Oh, perfect," she said, imagining herself in an interview. "I tell them I can work at nine after Ella's on the bus, but that I'll have to be home by two to get her off the bus. And I'll need summers off and two weeks at Christmas. Oh! And every school holiday and every delayed school opening? Let me guess. It'll be *me* who's delayed getting to work on time—not you. And if Ella gets sick, it'll be *me* taking off and risking losing my job because I'm sure *you* would *never* consider *your* job to be the job jeopardized in the name of childcare."

"Holly, jeez," he said with both arms up and an angry, defensive look on his face. "Settle down."

"No. Don't you dare say that." She pointed, ready to spit venom. "I'm not 'settling down.' That's insulting, Jack. I'm not a child. I have a huge hole in my résumé—years without employment because of my sacrifice for this family—so don't tell me to 'settle down.'"

"Sacrifice?"

"That's right. Sacrifice." She took a step closer to him. "You don't get to own that word. You're not the only person sacrificing for this family. I sacrifice. I sacrifice a lot. Every day."

If Greta returned to Nevada, they'd need to find an after-school babysitter or maybe look at day care. Holly thought about these things. They all factored into her plans to go back to work. She knew she had options, and day care was a great option. Millions of families figured it out, but right now? At this particular moment in time, Holly wanted to try working from home before moving to a formal nine-to-five. Why not try? Why wasn't he excited for her?

"Holly, you don't have a hole in your résumé. You're raising a *child*," he said. Emphasis on *child*. "You know there's nothing more important than that."

"Then you do it."

"Where is this coming from?" he asked. "You never cared about your résumé before."

"Of course I did. I knew what I was giving up to stay home with Ella."

"Then why are you yelling at me?"

"I'm not yelling at *you*," she said. "God! This is all so frustrating. Jack, it's a big deal *to me*. If I don't do something, one year will roll into the next, and before you know it, I'll have a ten-year hole in my résumé." No profit sharing or long-term incentive, no 401(k). None of the things that he enjoyed and was building. And sure, she wouldn't have some of those things if she owned her own business, but still. The further she drifted into stay-at-home motherhood, the further she drifted from the financial security she'd have if she had stayed working. What if something happened to Jack? "Forget it," she said, dismissing him with a wave of her hand before either of them said something they'd regret. She turned to walk away.

"Did I do something wrong?" he asked. And then, "I am getting a bonus. I'll be bringing more money home."

"It's not that," she said, feeling defeated. Feeling sad.

"Because I'm really sorry it's not enough for you." He sounded bitter.

"What the—" She turned around. "I never said anything like that, and you know it."

He sounded—condescending, defensive, something. She didn't know what. She wanted to tell him this wasn't about *him*. It was about *her*. Reconnecting with what she loved—film. Connecting with other women when they became her clients. She was new in town. She wanted to meet people. Make friends. If she could do film, she'd shine a little. She was good at it. And she missed it.

"Holly?"

"What?"

Never mind the fact Ella had started kindergarten, leaving Holly home alone all day, contemplating next steps. She'd known the transition back to work was coming, but she hadn't expected she'd have to *negotiate*. "I'm an autonomous, active agent in control of my own destiny," she reminded him.

"I never said you weren't."

"I don't need your permission."

"You think I have choices?" he asked.

"Excuse me?" She wanted this conversation over. Dead end into a brick wall.

And he must have sensed it. "Forget it," he said.

"Fine," she said with a shrug. Big deal. So what?

"Fine."

"Fine," she said again. *Because I don't care.*

"Okay, then. Jeez." He rolled his eyes. Like all of this was her fault. Like she was the one who was overreacting. "Forget I said anything."

"Okay, I will," she told him, folding her arms across her chest.

"Fine."

"What do I care?" she said, afraid she might cry. "I don't care."

She left him to go upstairs, stepping hard on each step. *Ef him,* she thought on her way up. She'd start a business with or without his support. *Ef you, Jack.* What the ef was that? All she was trying to do was fit a job around something she loved—around the people she loved. Was that so wrong? She entered their bedroom, closed the door, and locked it.

It wasn't that she regretted staying home with Ella all these years—she didn't. She loved Ella desperately. It was just—she worried about her own future. Worried the job market might pass her by while her résumé grew old and stale. Industry trends would come and go. The business of film and storytelling would evolve without her. Not to mention technology in her field. If she didn't keep up, then what? In the short time she'd lived in Primm, she had watched Caleb move effortlessly from drones to aircraft. He was fearless. Tried things.

With her back pressed against her bedroom door, she slid down until she was sitting on the floor.

It was wonderful, and she was grateful, but there was a cost to stay-at-home motherhood. Jack was secure in his career. Holly didn't *have* a career. She didn't even have a *job*, let alone a career. Was she wrong to feel this way? They'd met in college—so why was it that *his* degree mattered and was being applied to the workplace, but when she tried to do something with *hers*, it was met with less belief it was even viable? Was it because *her* degree was in the arts and his was in business? Did he think she couldn't make money in film? Was that it? Because ef him for not believing in her. All that did was heighten her own self-doubt, and she was just beginning to believe in herself again.

She closed her eyes, felt tears welling up, and decided she didn't give a crap if she cried, because she was frustrated. Of course she could try to get a job in town, but she wanted this one. This one had meaning. And she had so carefully crafted it so that no one in the family would be impacted by *Mom*—heaven forbid—going back to *work*.

So ef that and ef you, Jack.

15

EMAIL—Time Sent: 12:21 a.m.

TO: Psychic Betty, Psychic Hotline Network
FROM: Holly Banks
SUBJECT: I'm so angry right now!

Hi Psychic Betty.

As you can see in the subject line of my email: I'M
SO ANGRY RIGHT NOW!

What does the cosmos say about fighting with your
husband?

Jack's a Virgo.

I'm a Cancer.

Are all Virgos A-holes or just my husband?

~

EMAIL—Time Received: 12:52 a.m.

TO: Holly Banks
FROM: Psychic Betty, Psychic Hotline Network
SUBJECT: Cosmic Perspectives on Marriage

Virgos are not A-holes. Your husband might be an A-hole (I don't know, I've never met him), but if he is, it's not because he's a Virgo. Virgos are lovely people.

Using the constellations as our guide, Virgo is the virgin. Cancer is the crab. So YOUR marriage is a virgin with crabs. I see it playing out something like this:

Virgos, ruled by Mercury, can be meticulous and detail-oriented and often overanalyze. They are drawn to practical perfection, which can make it difficult for emotional Cancers, ruled by the Moon, to understand.

Usually, when touchy, vulnerable Cancers share their feelings or ideas with someone, they expect to be loved, hugged, and agreed with. Virgos, who like to serve and seek order, have a strong desire to do whatever it takes to provide and care for those they love. A Virgo who is unable to do this may retreat inward until they've organized thoughts, sorted details, and can present, with clarity, their view on the matter.

For Cancers, the crab, who live within their shells, home is where the heart is, so any stress or anger within a Cancer's home is especially upsetting to these sensitive nurturers who always seek security, but are easily hurt, especially by those they love and whose opinions they value.

To illustrate, consider this item from the Dizzy's Seafood menu:

Crab cakes, pan-grilled in brown butter and seasoned with Dizzy Spice—served with a salad and a side of roasted spaghetti squash.

You, a Cancer, might think: Yum! Comfort food. Here I am, sitting inside Dizzy's Seafood, feeling cozy and comfy, about to eat something I will love and feel nourished by. Though it is a bit freaky to be eating myself.

Always punctual, your husband, a Virgo, will surely be keeping tabs on the staff at Dizzy's Seafood, checking his watch throughout the meal. Faced with this menu item, he will most likely needle down to the essentials, thinking: *Spaghetti squash?* So which is it? Spaghetti? Or squash?

Did you know? There are many fish in the sea. Turns out, they're also in the sky! Whet your astro appetite at Dizzy's Seafood where—of course—we serve crabs. We serve everyone!

Click HERE to read a star-studded list of fishy constellations.

Click HERE to save money on crab legs during Dizzy's Sidewalk Sale.

(Get it? Crabs? Sidewalk?)

Click HERE to have crab jokes explained to you.

16

Holly opened her eyes, seeing first the ceiling of her family room, feeling next a tight knot of anxiety beneath her sternum. *What time is it?* She rolled toward the edge of the couch, reaching to pull her phone from its spot on the floor next to her laptop. *Two o'clock?* She'd fallen asleep after trading emails with Online Psychic Betty and bookmarking phonic-awareness resources for Ella: letter-sounds worksheets, coloring pages, and a reading-readiness manual for parents she intended to print the next morning. Holly heard footsteps, so she sat up to find Greta slipping into the kitchen in her bathrobe. "Mom? What are you doing up so late?"

Greta held a finger up, signaling she wanted to check on Charlotte.

When Greta returned, Holly asked, "What's going on? It's two o'clock in the morning."

"Can't sleep." Greta shrugged. "I'm good by day, but at night? I'm always lying on the worry side of the bed." Feet covered in mismatched socks, she shuffled toward Holly before plopping down in her favorite chair. "Fall asleep on the couch again?"

"Bad habit," admitted Holly. "Mom, are you feeling okay?"

Greta fiddled with a string that had broken free from her gray jersey-knit bathrobe. Finally, "I'm fine, Holly. You worry too much."

"Mom, I love you. Of course I worry. Is everything okay back home? Have you talked with Sadie?"

Greta's surprise visit, which had started during Ella's first week of kindergarten, was a bit suspect. Greta *said* she was coming to check on Holly and because she missed Ella, but Greta had recently run into a few issues with unpaid markers at the casinos in Vegas. Jack and Holly had bailed her out more than once, as the markers came due within thirty days and, like any line of credit, needed to be settled. The lighting was dim in the family room, coming from a lamp at the opposite end of the couch. Holly thought she saw glistening in Greta's eyes, so she reached over to take hold of one of Greta's hands. "Mom, what's wrong?"

Head hung low, Greta shrugged. "I'm lonely."

Lonely? "Oh, Mom, don't say that. You have us. You have Ella and Charlotte. They need you. I need you." *Don't tell me you're lonely. Please. I couldn't bear it.* The walls of the family room, with their newly hung family photos and framed artwork from Ella, suddenly felt closed in, small, and constricted. There were no pictures of Greta. Anywhere. Holly hadn't meant for that to happen and, truthfully, hadn't noticed until that moment. Not that a framed photo would fix loneliness, but still.

"I'll be fine," said Greta, offering Holly her best-effort smile.

Struggle, from the floor, let out a long, slow dog sigh. Like she knew what they were discussing and could feel what they were feeling.

"Do you want to go back home? With Sadie?" asked Holly.

"And leave Ella?" said Greta. "That would break my heart. But yes, I sometimes do think I'd be better back home."

"I understand," said Holly. And she did, though her situation was a bit different. She was thinking about "leaving" Ella for work after being home with her for five years. Different, but similar. Even if Holly did work from home and Ella wasn't in day care, there'd be adjustments. Moments where Ella would be asked to leave Mommy alone so she could get her work done. Whoever said *Mother knows best* might have been doing moms a disservice, because often, they didn't know what was best. Holly certainly didn't.

"You know what? I'm fine," Greta declared all of a sudden. "Far better than the people I've been hanging out with."

"What people?" asked Holly. "Houston?"

"I do enjoy our coffees. And he's a great Scrabble player."

"Definitely not my first choice," grumbled Holly, though it could be worse.

"We sit together at the funeral home."

"Wait, what?" Holly sat upright. Reached to turn the other lamp on, illuminating their conversation. "What do you mean, you're sitting at the funeral home?" *What kind of a date is that?*

Greta's shoulders looked thin and frail. "It's kinda nice," she said, twisting a lock of her curly gray hair. "Houston's family goes way back. He knows everyone in town. And he's friendly with the owner of the funeral home, so if, ummm . . ." She searched for the right word. "If a *client* arrives and the funeral director suspects the client will have low attendance, Houston and I asked them to give us a call. On those days, we move our coffee conversation from Primm's Coffee Joe to the funeral home, where we meet up with Javina, Lottie, Ruth, Henry, and Darnell."

"Who are these people? I've never heard these names before."

"My friends. The funeral home has great seating." Her eyes brightened. "Very comfortable. None of us want any of the clients to be alone."

"*Clients?* Mom, I'm shocked. I'm sorry, but I am." Holly didn't know what to think. "Are you doing this to spend time with Houston?"

"He's a nice man, but no. I've gone by myself when he was busy. I sometimes sit by the casket and play songs for the person on my ukulele," said Greta, presumably thinking this would somehow reassure Holly. It didn't.

"Is it a calling? Like, philanthropy or something?" asked Holly, vaguely aware that when Greta would leave her apartment in Nevada to visit them in Boulder City, there was a church in Boulder City that had a committee of volunteers that baked casseroles and such for parishioners holding funeral services at the church. They'd put out a spread of food in the church basement to ease the burden and embrace the family of the deceased. "Mom, I haven't gone church shopping yet. And I know I should, but I was so focused on unpacking." Was that it? Was that what her mom needed? "We can go this weekend. We can find a church for you to connect with."

"Don't worry about that, Holly. I can find my own way."

"Well, I don't like the thought of you sitting beside someone's casket."

"Why not?"

"I don't know. It sounds morbid. Depressing."

"Well, it's not," said Greta. "Although, I suppose it's contagious."

"Mom!"

Greta laughed. "I'm kidding! Sort of."

Holly didn't like this line of thinking. Not one bit. "Could that be what's making you lonely?"

"Definitely not. It makes me feel grateful for the life I have. And it's the right thing to do. It's the *kind* thing to do. I like thinking I might be bringing a smile to the person who's moving on. I imagine them looking down, smiling, and thinking: *Wow, will you look at that!*"

"Or maybe they're looking down and thinking, *Who are these people?* Mom, what's happening with you? Is there something you're not telling me? What does Sadie know? Does Dad know?"

Greta waved her off. "Your father's busy with his own life. Do not bother him with this."

Holly knew she'd say that. Her parents were friends now but better divorced than married. They just needed the length of Holly's childhood to figure themselves out.

"There is something," said Greta. "Remember Atticus from my apartment complex?"

"Sure. Maintenance man? Helped you hide Charlotte from apartment management so you wouldn't have to pay a pet deposit?"

"That's the one. He forwarded a certified letter from a casino. I have ten days to respond—actually, now I have three days to respond, or they're contacting the Bad Check Unit of the Clark County District Attorney's Office."

Oh, jeez. Holly reached over to rest her hand on her mother's knee. She wanted to yell, scream—something. Wanted to take this opportunity to express how *very angry* all of this made her, but Holly sensed a different response was warranted this time. Maybe a compassionate response. "What do you need?" asked Holly, and then, because she knew it all boiled down to this: "How much?"

"Four hundred thirty-five dollars and fifty cents."

Holly brought her hands to her face, covering it, letting the number sink in. "Mom," she said, not sure where to begin. "Jack's explained all of this to you—more than once. If you don't reply to these certified letters within the ten days they give you, the district attorney will issue a warrant for your arrest, so you can't ignore it because you feel bad about it. And they can arrest you here, in another state, and then extradite you to Nevada. You understand this, correct?"

Greta nodded.

"And you understand bad check crimes in Nevada are considered to be a type of fraud. A conviction like that on your record can affect everything. Employment, housing."

Greta nodded. She understood. She knew all of this. *Then why does she keep doing it?*

Holly watched as her mother's face turned from anxious to overwhelmed to just plain sad. "Why, Mom?" asked Holly.

"I don't know," she whispered, shaking her head. "It just happens. One minute I'm lucky; the next minute I'm not. I feel jinxed. Like I can't catch a break no matter what I do."

"Stop." Holly held her hand up to signal she needed her mom to stop feeling she was a hopeless voyager following a path destined to fail. "This isn't a matter of luck or fortune or fate. You aren't destined to lose at the slots or blackjack. You have the power to act on your own behalf. You have options. You can go into the casino or not. It's that simple." At least, Holly hoped it was. With addiction, it was more complicated.

With both of them pausing to consider their last exchange, Holly's gaze wandered off beyond Greta and toward the kitchen and, for some reason, focused on a pile of clutter on the kitchen table. Then the clutter on the counter by the refrigerator. Then the laundry basket of unfolded clothes at the entrance to the family room. Then the lamp that needed a new shade on the floor next to the pantry. Then the supplies she'd gathered to rewire a painting she wanted hung in the living room. They were unpacked, but they were a far cry from settled. Still, the things she needed to do around the house were less difficult to think about, and maybe, at the moment, her brain needed a break.

"It's late," she said.

Greta nodded. "I'm sorry, Holly. I am."

"Is this it? Are there any more certified letters?"

"This is it."

"I'll call Sadie in the morning. Between the two of us, we'll get this taken care of tomorrow. But you are paying us back, and we're finding a GA group nearby, and I think you should stay in Primm for a while. I don't think it's good for you to be in Nevada."

Greta nodded. She agreed.

"I'll need you to help with Ella. I'm going back to work." She glanced around the family room at the three stacks of folded clothes on the floor by the TV. At her laptop on the floor, at Ella's collection of *My Little Pony* toys positioned across the hearth, at the massive box of

Goldfish crackers on the table beside the plant that needed watering or it might die. She could have this place cleaned in ten or fifteen minutes but was too tired to do anything at the moment.

She waited for Greta to get her glass of water, and then, once Greta had said good night and headed up the stairs to go back to sleep, Holly slipped a spoon from the utensil drawer and enjoyed one small spoonful of Nutella before heading to bed. The Nutella was, as always, smooth and creamy and lifted her spirits ever so slightly. When she was finished, as she was screwing the Nutella cap back on the jar, it occurred to her that what she probably needed most at this juncture in her life was a little faith that everything would turn out okay. Between her and Jack. With going back to work. With her mom. With Ella learning to read. With all of it. Faith—with a little courage and a whole lot of patience tossed in.

17

"What am I doing here?" muttered Holly, marching across the open field beside the Clock Tower Labyrinth, Ella in her arms, sitting at her hip, wearing a sweatshirt and tutu over sparkly purple leggings and boots. "I must be crazy."

"You can do it!" cried Ella, using both hands to slap Holly on the cheeks.

"Ow!" Holly recoiled. "Ella, honey, that hurt."

Greta told Ella, "Go easy on your mom, shortcake. She's staring fear in the face."

"Sorry," said Ella, reaching up to pop Holly on the head before kicking both legs into Holly, cheering, "Giddy-up, Mommy! Giddy-up!"

"Ella! Will you stop?" said Holly. *Jeez.* The randomness of a five-year-old. Holly asked Greta, "Why is she doing this?"

"Beats me. Maybe she's nervous," said Greta, winded. "Actually, will *you* stop?" In a linen tunic over pants blazing with psychedelic flowers, she bent to place her hands on her knees, trying to catch her breath midway up the hill.

Holly spotted Caleb across the field, waving both arms over his head while standing next to *Henny Penny.* It wasn't that steep of a slope. Holly didn't know why her mother was having so much difficulty. "You need to see a doctor," said Holly.

"Well, duh—why do you think I joined a dating site?"

Holly had parked in the side gravel lot like Caleb had told her. Now they were crossing an empty, open field where hot-air balloons took off. Trees sloped up the hill toward the orchards on the other side of Pip's Mountain. The "runway" was in plain view (if that was what you wanted to call it). So was the eventual ledge they'd lift off from, flying first over a few acres of boxwoods that formed the Clock Tower Labyrinth on the hillside below. Tall bushes shaped into an elaborate walking path. A maze of sorts. Made entirely of bushes.

"I really don't want to do this," whined Holly. "Why am I doing this?"

It seemed Greta knew why. "You're facing your fear of flying. But why now? That's what I'm wondering."

"Yeah, me too," agreed Holly. Why now? Why this moment? Holly had been afraid of flying her entire life. Should she tell them she'd called Caleb because she was so *freaking* pissed at Jack? Because *of* Jack—questioning her plans to start a business in their dining room. Starting a business took courage. Submitting her first film to a film contest took courage. Flying took courage. If she could fly, surely she could do those other things, right? "I'm capturing live footage of the clear blue skies over Primm," Holly said, once they started walking again. To Ella, she said, "When you grow up, I hope you never let anyone tell you you can't capture footage of the sky."

"Really, Holly?" asked Greta. "What's that about? Nobody ever said that to you . . ."

As they approached *Henny Penny*, a tight ball of anxiety formed in Holly's chest.

"How are you doing? You good? You okay?" asked Caleb.

"I'm fine," she said. *No, I'm not.* "Let's get this over with." *I want to go home.* "How long will this take? How high will we fly? When will it end?" *I'm scared.* And then, finally, "AIRPLANE?" she blurted. "What am I doing?" She took a few steps back.

"Relax," he said. "It's not an airplane. It's an ultralight hobby aircraft. They come in kits people build in their garage."

"Exactly!" said Holly, thinking she should leave right now.

He said, "That alone should tell you how low tech and safe this is. In the States, they're not even considered as aircraft. They're considered vehicles. And one-seaters don't even require a pilot's license. You think the FAA would allow that if it wasn't safe?"

"You can do it, Mommy. Be brave," said Ella. "You're a filmer!"

"If you want," said Caleb, "Ella and Greta can run beside us as we're taxiing down the runway."

"Really?" said Holly. Wow. Now *that* felt better.

"There will come a point where we'll go faster than they can run, but in these conditions"—he looked around—"with this headwind, not by much."

"How fast will we be going?" Holly wanted to know. "As fast as a horse can run?"

"Slower. More like a gallop. And when we're up, you'll feel like you're gently gliding—motoring just above the treetops. Trust me. These wings can support those two seats, no problem. And we won't be that high up. Holly, you got this."

"Life's short," said Greta. "Conquer your fears in this life so you don't carry them over into the next."

"Be brave, Mommy," said Ella. The look in her eyes spoke volumes to Holly. How many times had Holly told Ella to be brave? Most recently? On the first day of school when Ella didn't want to get out of Holly's car.

"Okay, fine. Let's do it," Holly announced, setting Ella on the ground beside her, knowing if she didn't get this over with—and fast—she'd change her mind and chicken out. "Give Mommy a kiss," she said, bending down, showing Ella a brave face despite seriously feeling she might throw up.

"We'll wait over here," said Greta, handing Holly the camera.

"Aw, come on. You don't want to run beside me?"

"Yeah, no," said Greta, taking Ella by the hand before walking off to sit in the grass.

Holly turned to confront the contraption as Caleb set a helmet on her head. He tapped it into place before buckling it beneath her chin. "I thought we'd taxi down the runway toward our starting point so you'd have the chance to get used to what it feels like while we're still on the ground. It'll feel like driving in a bumpy, lightweight golf cart. We're going to drive down there." He pointed across the field. "And then we'll turn around and get into position before taxiing back down the runway, retracing our steps while picking up speed, and then we'll lift off over there." He nodded toward the place where the runway disappeared because the ground sloped down a hill toward the Clock Tower Labyrinth below.

"Well, I'm not very happy about this," she griped, handing him her camera so she could step into an impossibly huge flight suit. "No matter how safe you say it is. Good gravy, this flight suit is heavy. It's like a bulletproof vest. What's this made out of?" The outer fabric was woven so tight it felt puncture-proof. Despite bunching the sleeves as much as she could, she could barely poke her fingers out. "What size is this? Buffalo?"

He zipped her up. Checked the straps on her helmet. "Men's extralong. I bought it surplus on eBay."

"There's so much fuzzy lining in here I feel like a marshmallow. This is huge. I look like I'm six hundred pounds. Shouldn't I be wearing something my size? Maybe we should cancel." She waddled after him toward *Henny Penny*, crotch of the suit a foot below hers, pant legs bunched like a shar-pei puppy.

He gestured for her to climb in.

"On second thought, I don't want to do this. No. You can't make me." She backed up a few steps, folded her arms across her chest in protest—at least, she tried to; the flight suit got in the way.

"I thought you wanted sky footage?" he reminded her. "Do you want *me* to shoot it for you?"

"Ugh! Fine." She stomped, before climbing into the passenger seat and then climbing back out again.

Caleb laughed. "Are you getting in or not?"

"Stop rushing me!" she snapped. "You're always rushing me." She closed her eyes.

"What are you doing?"

"Nothing. I'm just taking a minute." Eventually, she opened them, then climbed in. "I really don't want to do this." *This is so stupid.* "I can't believe you're making me do this."

Walking around to climb into the pilot's seat beside Holly, Caleb said, "I'm not making you. You called me."

And she had. The other night. To prove to herself she could do it.

He set her camera on her lap and started the engine: *bzzzzzzz. Bzzzzzzz. BZZZZZZZ!*

"What do I do now?" She felt like she was screaming from the seat of a freakishly loud lawn mower. She pushed her sleeves up, before attempting to buckle her seat belt without causing the camera to slide off her lap. "How'm I supposed to film with this stupid suit on!" she yelled, flapping the sleeves around. "What if I drop the camera?"

"What?"

"What if I drop the camera?" To prevent panic from setting in, she reminded herself of the shot she wanted to capture of the skies over Primm. How that one shot could be used for so much. Potentially, for the opening and closing of a portfolio of stop-motions she was hoping to create with "Holly Banks Productions" featured. Sure, she could buy stock footage or ask Caleb to shoot it for her, but that wouldn't be the same. She was a filmmaker. Filmmakers took their own shots.

"At takeoff? With this headwind? And these wings?" he said, tethering her camera to a carabiner, assuring her it would stay inside the plane should Holly drop it. "Leaving the ground in something this light won't

154

need much speed at all, and we're using the drop-off at the end of the runway, so we'll be instantly airborne at that point."

"Instantly airborne?" Somehow that didn't sound so good. "Where's my parachute? Shouldn't I have a parachute? *Where's my parachute?*" she cried, looking around, starting to lose it.

"Bye, Mommmmmy!" she could hear Ella yell above the sounds of the motor as Caleb turned *Henny Penny* around to drive across the grass toward the start of the runway. Holly waved as she passed Ella, plastering an "I'll be just fine!" smile on her face so Ella wouldn't worry. At this point, Holly reminded herself, she hadn't left the ground yet.

Bumping along, trying not to notice the swiftly moving tree line to her right or the ominous *Henny Penny* painted above her on the glider wing, she closed her eyes, using as inspiration the memory of the old-timey airplane flying over the Cherry Festival just a few weeks ago: the fluffy white contrails left by the plane—how they looked like dash marks. Many, many times since seeing those markings in the sky, Holly had wondered: If those dash marks had been set into dialogue, what would they say? Today, she imagined they'd say *AIEEEEE!*—the comic book and gaming standard for someone shrieking in fear. If this was the "driving" part, the "getting used to what it felt like" part, she didn't like it one bit.

They reached the start of the runway, Caleb driving a large circle on the ground until *Henny Penny* was completely turned around and in position to begin their official taxi down the runway. The taxi that would end with Holly's leaving the surface of the earth.

"Welp, looks like we're cleared for takeoff!" Caleb said. "Here. Put these on." He handed her a pair of goggles.

"Cleared for takeoff? Cleared for takeoff? Who cleared us?" said Holly, looking every which way, feeling she might pee her pants at any moment. "There's no one here." Where was traffic control? Shouldn't there be people waving orange flags or something? This wasn't an airport. It was a field. It was a mutha fricking *field*. "You never showed me your license." She stabbed a finger in his direction. "How do I know you're telling me the truth? How do I know you're not lying to me?"

Shouting above the noise, pointing to the goggles in her hand, "Put 'em on!" he said with a laugh. Presumably, because she was snarling at him from beneath a wacky-jack helmet while wearing a flight suit six sizes too big. *Dang you, Caleb. eBay surplus.*

They were still sitting there, not yet headed down the runway, and yet, she was sweating, contemplating the length of the runway, the ledge at the apogee that awaited her—no. Not ledge. More like—cliff. Deadly drop-off. She didn't know what.

"I can't breathe!" she told him, grasping at the neckline of her flight suit. She started gagging. *Henny Penny's* propeller whirling circles behind them, ready to roll, making it feel as if the whole contraption was vibrating—because it was. "Let me out," she whined like a baby in a baby stroller about to take flight. "Let me out!"

"I thought you said you wanted to do this," he yelled, trying not to laugh as she hung her head back and *really* started to cry—eyes closed, mouth held open in anguish.

Above the noise, amid the terror: "Ugh! Yes," she wailed, not caring what she looked like. "Do it." Face crumpled up. Heart pounding. "Just—do it. Ugh!" More crying. More wailing. *"Damn you, Jaaaaaaack!"*

"Because we haven't gone anywhere . . . ," he pointed out. "We're just sitting here."

"Go. Just—go." She waved onward.

"Umm, okay." He shrugged, then reached over to tug the goggles down and across her helmet, until they sat across her face, lopsided and cockeyed.

As Caleb accelerated and they started rumbling down the runway— *bzzzzzzz. Bzzzzzzz. BZZZZZZZ!*—she tried mustering courage, she did, wrapping her fingers around an aluminum bar that helped frame the cockpit. Squeezing tight, bumping, bumping, bumping, roaring past Greta and Ella—*"Bye, Mommmmmy!"*—Holly, scared spitless, felt close to becoming that woman in the comic book shrieking *AIEEEEE!*

"You'll be fine!" said Caleb, keeping his focus straight ahead as *Henny Penny* sped down the runway: faster, faster, headed toward the ledge, until—*whoosh*! The ground dropped off below. Liftoff.

"Ou, gwaud. Help meeeeee!" She let loose with an anguished cry as the ground fell away beneath her. Holly Banks, full of angst, hand still clasping the camera. She opened her eyes the moment they left the runway and took flight. Over the ledge and flying now—*Henny Penny* was four, maybe five feet off the ground, headed straight for Clock Tower Labyrinth. Holly's heart pounding. They continued to climb, reaching heights of nearly seven, possibly eight feet in the air as the fear overcame her. Had Jack been standing below, she would have been flying two feet above his head. Two feet!

"I can't take it anymore!" she cried, too afraid to close her eyes.

They were flying over the length of the Clock Tower Labyrinth— green, six-foot-tall boxwood hedges—Holly bearing witness to the gaping holes left by the chilli thrips.

Panic seized her as the aircraft continued to ascend: eight feet, then nine.

"I can't do it," she told him, looking out over the rows of box-woods below. Helmet on head, flight suit huge. Goggles cockamamie and askew. "I'm not brave!"

"Sure you are!"

She clutched hold of his arm, sleeves of the giant suit getting in the way, snapping free of her seat belt.

"What are you doing?" yelled Caleb. "Are you jumping?"

Holly, a giant, fat marshmallow wrapped inside a puncture-proof flight suit, sprang sideways, letting out an *AIEEEEE!*, then free-falling three or four feet before belly flopping into a bush.

18

Penelope Pratt
Feathered Nest Realty

—ENCLAVE ALERT—

CHILLI THRIPS AREN'T THE ONLY THINGS WITHERING ON THE VINE

Let it be known that on the eve of the Enclave Tour, standing six feet in height and rivaling those of the Kentucky Derby in both pomp and pageantry, "Enclave Ribbon Awards" will be installed at *every* entrance of *every* enclave throughout the Village of Primm.

Unfortunately, there has been zero movement since our last report and many enclaves risk receiving short, stubby ribbons in dull, lifeless colors—or worse—no ribbon at all!

Unsure of your position within the community? Consult this friendly guide.

PLATINUM (awarded 6-foot "platinum glory" ribbons at every entrance): Ballyhoo, Blythe, Castle Drum Tower, Hobnob, Hopscotch, and Peloton

GOLD (granted 3-foot "good job" ribbons at every entrance): no one

SILVER (given 1-foot "meh" ribbons at every entrance): Dillydally and Parallax

BRONZE (no ribbon—just a flag that says "enter"): Gilman Clear and Petunia

ALUMINUM FOIL (no ribbon and no flag—just a bearded smelly guy wearing a headset holding a sign with the word "participation" scratched out): Chum and Pram

Parting thoughts from Feathered Nest Realty, organizers of the Village of Primm Enclave Tour:

1. Dillydally, please rally.
2. Parallax, don't stop now—you've come so far!
3. Gilman Clear, maybe it's time to throw a Hail Mary pass.
4. Knock, knock. Who's there? Petunia. Petunia who? Petunia and me, you're sorta letting everyone down.
5. Chum, fish or cut bait.
6. Pram, you're kinda throwing your toys out.

The fate of our beloved plant animals is in your hands. The rebuilding of the Topiary Park Petting Zoo depends on YOU. Add your home to the Village of Primm Enclave Tour by texting "ALL.TALK" to NO.TROUSERS.

THE STATE OF PLUME

Judging by the current state of the Enclave Tour? Nothing but sadness.

19

Running errands on a Monday morning, Holly walked around Pip's Corner from the back parking lot, spotting a man whose uniform implied he might be a groundskeeper for the Village of Primm municipal department. She didn't have Struggle with her, but he must have recognized her, having watched her fall into a hole on television, because he was signaling for her to come over.

"I had half a mind to send you a bill to cover the cost of landscape repair," he told her, pointing toward the compass rose, "but who am I to fine the owner of the town's most celebrated dog?"

"Ha!" she said with a roll of her eyes. "Tell that to my HOA. My dog gets out almost every other day to bark at the neighbor."

"I heard," he said, amused.

"Oh? How so?"

"Maeve Bling. She called municipal services."

"Are you kidding me?" said Holly. *That twitch.* "Seriously?"

"HOAs have power," he said. "I've worked in the Village of Primm municipal department for thirty-five years. We're responsible for the library, parks and recreation, community water systems, sewers, snow removal, signage." He counted on his fingers. "Parking, roads, public transportation. Police. Fire department. Emergency medical services. You'd be surprised by the calls we receive in a week."

"I bet I would," said Holly. "Treasure hunters?" she asked, pointing to a group of people spread out across The Lawn waving metal detectors across the grass.

"Yup."

The Lawn was expansive enough to host at least ten or twelve treasure-hunting teams, a few wearing jackets, the words *MEEK ENTERPRISES* across the back. "Everyone's concerned about that water tower, huh?" she said.

"Oh, sure. But that's not why they're here," he said. "Merchant Meek caught wind of the value of astrolabes. Do you have any idea how rare astrolabes are?"

"Not really." Holly shrugged. *I mean, sure, I figured they were worth* something. *If you're into that sort of thing.*

"A few years back, a sixteenth-century astrolabe was found and returned to a Swedish museum. True story," he said. "Want to know how much that astrolabe was worth?"

"How much?" she asked, assuming he'd say they were worth hundreds of dollars. She gave it a stab. "A thousand bucks? Maybe twenty-five hundred?" The astrolabe stolen and assumed scattered across Primm had to be worth something to attract this sort of attention. "Five thousand," she guessed. "Final answer."

"Try seven hundred and fifty thousand dollars."

Her jaw dropped. "Excuse me?"

"You heard it. Three-quarters of a million dollars."

"Whoa. I had no idea," said Holly. This added a whole new layer to the frenzy surrounding Struggle's discovery. No wonder the media hounded her. "Do you think the Village of Primm astrolabe is worth that much?"

"Probably not *that* much. It's not as old. Whether it's found and put back together or not, I think this little adventure is great. The whole town is united. We needed something to take our minds off things."

He pointed toward the South Gazebo. "Those folks in those chairs over there? Most of them are from Southern Lakes with a few from Menander. Everyone's speculating. Placing bets. Does the Village of Primm own the land beneath the water tower? Or does Southern Lakes?" He cocked his head to the side, jutting his chin out so he could scratch the whiskers on his neck. "I put a work order in to subdivide The Lawn using a grid system and some twine. It's peaceful right now, but if someone finds another disc, it'll be go time. People get strange when money's involved."

"Will you excuse me for a moment?" she said, stepping aside to check her phone for a text and finding the one she was hoping for. A text from Jack.

JACK: Go ahead with everything.
HOLLY: The furniture loan or the small business loan?
JACK: Both.
HOLLY: Are you joking or serious?
JACK: Serious.

"Yes!" she whispered, so excited. *Woot!* It was happening. It was really happening. A film studio! A dedicated space to call her own. She pinched her arm to confirm she wasn't dreaming. She suspected it was the itemized list she had left on the kitchen table that had done the trick. Jack was a Virgo, ruled by Mercury. He liked details, especially around transactions. And so what if she was receiving marital advice from an online psychic named Betty—why not? Who cared? It was cheaper than marriage counseling.

HOLLY: I love you. Thanks, Jack. It'll be great, I promise.
JACK: Is there room for a commercial coffee roaster in your studio?
HOLLY: Are you joking or serious?

She waited . . . but got no response. She tried again.

HOLLY: Joking or serious?
JACK: Neither.

She stared at her phone for a minute, not sure how to respond.

He wasn't serious, and yet, he wasn't joking?

"I'm sorry," Holly said to the man from the municipal department. "You were saying?"

"Oh, don't worry about me," he said. "I was just going to point out whichever town ends up owning the water tower will hold power over the other town for years to come. One town setting water prices for the other town?" He shook his head. "That can't be good. When one town is declared the owner, the other town will immediately be declared dry and will be at the mercy of the wet town." He shook his head. "Humans are always fighting for resources. Money, gold, oil. Food and water. I hope for your sake Primm is declared the winner."

"Oh, boy."

"Yup." He nodded toward the treasure hunters. "They don't know what they're doing. No one does. The only thing that's made a dent in this decades-old issue between the two towns is your dog. What if you took your dog out for a walk around The Lawn? See what happens?"

Holly spotted Eliza Adalee and a VOP cameraman miking up down The Lawn toward the North Gazebo, where a tent was set up to shelter metal detectors. "Do me a favor," Holly asked the groundskeeper. "Don't tell anyone you saw me here?"

"Oh, sure," he said. Scratching his neck whiskers. "Your secret's safe with me." He gave Holly a wink. "I have a chocolate Lab too. Coco. She sleeps at the foot of my bed."

20

Holly peeked inside Primm Paper's triple-bay window, trimmed in wood and painted bright white, seeing a triangular swallowtail paper pennant displaying the letters *P.R.I.M.M. P.A.P.E.R.* strung across the window like a clothesline over a Heidelberg windmill letterpress. She spotted Katie at the register, wrapping a customer's package beneath a waterfall chandelier made of what appeared to be translucent white capiz seashells cascading from a gold frame. Holly wondered yet again why everyone seemed to have a chandelier but her.

Here goes nothing . . .

As she pushed through a heavy black door with the words *PRIMM PAPER* and a bee etched into the glass, she had the distinct impression she was crossing a threshold, forever leaving her dumpy old world of nothing-special paper and entering a world of elegant living amid high-end stationery. A world that said: *Of course stationery matters in a digital world. Stationery is an analog reflection of you.*

Bzzt. She felt her phone vibrate in her pocket. A text from Mary-Margaret.

MARY-MARGARET: Where are you?
HOLLY: Picking up a BuJo Kit from Primm Paper.

MARY-MARGARET: Good for you. Consumer spending drives the economy! So important in light of all that's happened to our quiet little village. I'm working with Penelope now.

HOLLY: So I heard.

MARY-MARGARET: Ready for your visit from a Feathered Nest professional organizer? Also, now that you're on the Enclave Tour, it's probably time a member of the Enclave Tour Committee paid a visit. How about Wednesday? Day after tomorrow?

HOLLY: Sure. What time were you thinking?

MARY-MARGARET: Wonderful. Tomorrow it is. I mean Wednesday.

HOLLY: Wait. Today's Monday. Which day are you talking about— Tuesday or Wednesday? And what time?

MARY-MARGARET: Tomorrow—Wednesday.

HOLLY: Tomorrow is Tuesday.

MARY-MARGARET: I have good news and bad news. Which one do you want to hear first?

HOLLY: I want to hear the date first. The time second.

MARY-MARGARET: Fine. Good news first. I've been on a recruiting mission all over town. The bad news? We've hit a wall. Only six of the twelve enclaves have met quota. In fact, you're the only home in the Petunia enclave listed on Penelope's tour. Any insights as to why homeowners are so reluctant to help elevate their enclaves to Platinum Status?

HOLLY: I don't know. Do their HOAs suck? Maybe they're bitter.

She slid her phone into her pocket. But then, on second thought, she pulled it back out.

HOLLY: What time tomorrow? Or were you talking about Wednesday?

MARY-MARGARET: Thursday.

"May I help you?" Katie asked.

"Oh, yes. Please. I called earlier? I'm here for my BuJo tool kit," said Holly, hardly able to contain her excitement. *BuJo!* Such a cute term.

Just saying it made Holly feel she was part of the "in" crowd. Things were looking up. Things were definitely looking up!

"Name, please?" said Katie.

"Holly Banks."

She wondered if Katie remembered her from the Scrap & Swap Fund-Raiser at Ella's school. She assumed she didn't, based on how she was acting. Holly, standing in the front third of the corner shop, knew the back of the shop housed Katie's artist studio, where Shanequa and Katie gathered to film YouTube videos. Holly leaned, trying to catch a glimpse of the lighting setup in Katie's studio.

"Follow me." Katie smiled, leaving the counter to lead Holly to a wall of custom-built wood bookshelves with glass shelving, where two substantially deep drawers were positioned at the base, easily opened along heavyweight metal tracks. *Dang it,* thought Holly. She wanted a bookshelf as beautiful as that and with storage underneath. They'd be perfect in her home—a home desperately in need of storage.

From a drawer, Katie retrieved a package marked with Holly's name, and the two returned to the register. "Everyone is clamoring to get their hands on these kits before the online class starts," said Katie. "I think you're buying the last one."

"Online class?" asked Holly.

"I'm starting a series," said Katie. "Trying to expand my business beyond foot traffic. The destruction of the Topiary Park has me realizing I need to catch a wider audience. Maybe sell BuJo kits to people in faraway places."

"I see. Do you need help with video production? Photographing product for e-commerce?"

"I do, actually," said Katie. "Yes."

"Oh, goodness," said Holly, patting her pockets, digging deep into her tote for business cards she knew darn well didn't exist, but she pretended they did. "I seem to have forgotten my business cards. I'm Holly Banks of Holly Banks Productions." She extended her hand. "I work in film and video production. I specialize in boosting the social media presence of small business owners. Perhaps I can help?"

"Wow. Yes. Most definitely," said Katie. "Oh, but I'm a bit busy at the moment. Can we set an appointment to meet when the shop is closed?"

"Yes, of course. I'll touch base later in the week to establish a time that's best for you." *Ha! Take that, Jack. Customer number two. First Penelope, well, hopefully Penelope, and now Katie.*

"Wonderful. Thank you so much," said Katie, readying Holly's items to be rung up, explaining how she was hoping to divide her online classes to suit bullet journalers, who typically fell into different types: the artist, the tracker, the early bird, and the planner. Katie asked, Did Holly know which one she was?

"Who, me?" said Holly, not quite sure. "I've never actually bullet journaled before. I mean, I've been practicing using regular paper, but this is all new to me."

"How wonderful," said Katie, her eyes bright, cheeks soft and pink. "This BuJo kit is a great place to start."

Holly spotted a sign taped to Katie's register.

ACROSS
NUMBER 3. TYPESETTER'S DOT (SIX LETTERS)

"Bullet!" she said, pointing to the clue. "Is that right? I saw this clue in the *Primm Gazette* the other day. I thought it was *period*." Holly wagged her head a bit as if saying, *Duh, silly me.* "What was I thinking?"

"It's perfectly all right," said Katie with a wink. "The first few people through the door thought the same thing."

"Is the merchandise out yet?"

"We're supposed to wait until the app goes live, but for you, I'm happy to make the exception." She pulled a box of small, four-by-six bullet journals from beneath the counter. Kraft paper covers, the words

VILLAGE OF PRIMM and *PRIMM PAPER* in black ink on each front and inside each journal, about ten stapled pages lined with bullet marks. "It's a bullet journal cut slightly larger than four-by-six photographs so if you want to incorporate photos, you can slip them right in. When the crossword puzzle is officially launched, I'll be selling these for a dollar with any store purchase, but for you, I'm happy to tuck one inside your bag. Oh, but shhhh," she said with a playful smile. "Let's keep this between you and me."

"Yes, of course," said Holly. "Between you and me." She took the four-by-six bullet journal from Katie, finding an almost empty crossword puzzle printed on the back. The only clue listed beneath the puzzle was the clue for Katie's shop. The only answer inside the puzzle—*BULLET*—was filled in as Number 3 Across.

Shanequa entered the store, waving at Holly. "Sorry I'm late." She beamed, clearly excited to be introducing Holly to the world of bullet journaling. Almost too excited. Shanequa was the type whose spirit came alive around paper. "Hey, Katie," she said, walking confidently behind the counter to give Katie a hug. "Are those the new Staedtler pigment liner sketch pens?"

"Sure are," said Katie. "Eight widths. Point oh five, point one, point three, point five, point seven. And then there's one, one point two, and chisel tip."

What the hell-o kitty are they talking about? How many widths did one bullet journaler need? They were talking pen tips, right?

Katie began ringing up the items in Holly's BuJo kit, a combination of scanning bar codes and hand-keying prices depending on the item. When the bar code didn't work (as it so often did not), click, click, Katie's fingernail tapped the totals until *cha-ching!*—Holly became the proud owner of a 249-page, medium A5, dotted, hardcover black Leuchtturm1917 bullet journal along with something called a "planner accessories bundle." *Cha-ching!*

Next up? The pens . . . iBayam fineliner pens. *Cha-ching!* Twenty-pack Staedtler triplus fineliners. A package of Faber-Castell Pitt Manga pens in four sizes. *Cha-ching! Cha-ching!*

"So how's it going?" asked Shanequa, walking around to join Holly on the other side of the counter as Holly eyed the subtotal creeping awfully close to sixty dollars.

"Great! Just great," said Holly, feeling pensive about the rising costs but intuiting she should convey some excitement. "I can't *wait* to get started!" She supposed there were worse things to spend her money on, like trampolines (someone could get hurt) or in-app purchases. *Dryer sheets!* Sadie said dryer sheets were laden with chemicals.

"Do you want to get the girls together soon? I was thinking an ice cream at Mitch & Lucy Creamery might be fun," said Shanequa.

"Absolutely. Let's do it. Ella loves that place."

"Talia tells me Ella's excited about the wedding?"

"She is," said Holly, reminded she had a meeting with Miss Bently about Ella flunking the pre-pre-reading thing. She felt a tinge of worry. What if this was the start of learning difficulties for Ella at school? *Nah. You're overreacting,* she told herself. *Ella's in kindergarten. No one's paying attention to these things at this age. Right? It's too soon. She's five.*

Shanequa said, "They staged a bridal portrait near the swing set during recess."

"Beg your pardon?" said Holly, pulling her attention from the ever-changing subtotal on Katie's register. "Who did? Miss Bently?" She'd never mentioned photos.

"No, I think the girls dreamed it up themselves. Apparently, there's a whole crew of them. They call themselves 'the Bridal Party,' and they're spending all of their time during recess living out the life of a bride getting married—with your daughter at the center."

"My daughter? You mean—she's the ringleader? Ella's never even been to a wedding. She wouldn't know the first thing about it."

"I don't sense she's driving the narrative," said Shanequa, "but rather, she *is* the narrative."

Oh, jeez.

Shanequa reached for a stack of blue paper samples from a basket, so Holly reached for a stack of white, each paper swatch labeled by its specific color and neatly trimmed to three by three inches. She fanned the stack a moment, eyeing Shanequa, wondering what Shanequa was thinking.

"Should I get involved?" asked Holly.

"I don't know." Shanequa traded the blue stack for red. "Let's get them to Mitch & Lucy Creamery and do a deep dive. Maybe with ice cream they'll spill it, and we'll get all of the details in one download."

"Smart."

"Yeah, well. Talia's youngest of four. I've picked up a few tricks along the way."

Holding a stack of paper swatches, Holly figured, if she were the one ordering a wedding invitation or baby announcement or personal stationery from this stack, she doubted she'd have the will to decide. Simply white, snow white, snowy day, chalk white, white diamond, white glass, china white. There had to be forty or fifty swatches of . . . *white*. Paper white, decorator's white. Why so many options? Green was no different. Holly flipped through the green stack: forest green, hunter green, lettuce green, emerald green, alligator green, lime green, evergreen, frog. Why was life so complicated? Why did *everything* always seem to get so complicated? Based on the items Katie was ringing up, the same was true for bullet journaling, apparently. *How did we get from a one-pen, one-journal world—to where we are today? Did the dots make us do it?*

"I never realized getting organized required so many pens!" Holly said with a cheerful smile toward Katie, her eyes checking the subtotal. "A pen's a pen, right? I mean, they all look the same to me," she admitted, hoping to find a polite way out of this.

"If you keep your receipt and the package isn't open," said Katie, standing amid a livelihood made of papers and pens, "you can always return what you don't use. Do you want to put everything back and just get a journal and pen?"

Holly sensed the defeat beneath Katie's offer. Defeat of a sale she probably needed as a small business owner. Beside Katie's register was a Plexiglas donation box dedicated to the replanting of Plume. The donation box was brimming with cash.

Holly eyed the supplies on the counter, intuiting she *could* bullet journal with no more than a journal and pen. For that matter, she didn't need to be in Primm Paper at all. She could take her wallet and go home, grab a pen from the coffee can next to her kitchen phone and some dumb ole spiral notebook, and *presto!*—begin bullet journaling her way toward a more productive life. *You can bullet journal without buying all of this stuff, right?* Oh, but this was Katie's shop, and Katie was standing before her—so sweet and so lovely—*and* Katie was a potential client.

"Oh, no. I want it all!" Holly said, reassuring Katie she was there to spend. "But I am wondering, is the Liechtenstein the only bullet journal on the market?"

Shanequa coughed. After clearing her throat, she whispered, "Liechtenstein is a country in Europe."

"Oh, right," said Holly, feeling herself blush. "Yes, of course." She wished she could coerce one of them into pronouncing *Leuchtturm* for her. Was it German? Probably German. She glanced at the word again, trying, "Letch-t-t-turm? Hmm." She tried again: "Luck term." And why was there no space between the word and the date? Was 1917 even a date—or was it something else, like the number of dots on the page?

Without flinching, Katie said "Leuchtturm" as Shanequa nodded. Just like that: *Loi-sh-turm.*

Aw, come on. There had to be a time in their lives when neither of them knew how to pronounce it, right? Why not admit it?

"*Leuchtturm* is German for 'lighthouse,'" said Katie. "But, no. This isn't your only option. You have plenty of options."

"Ha! Plenty of options. Why'm I not surprised?" Holly quipped, thinking, *simply white, snow white, evergreen, frog.* If Jack were here and this were coffee, there'd be Arabica and Robusta, broadly speaking, but also Criollo, Sumatra, Bogor Prada, Pluma Hidalgo . . .

"Are you thinking you might like to return it? I can delete it from your purchase," Katie offered.

"Me? Oh, no. Let's keep it." Holly reasoned, *There's an upcharge for things you can't pronounce.* And besides, Leuchtturm1917 had numbers attached, implying vintage, like a fine wine. "Please," said Holly, signaling Katie to continue ringing up. "I want it all."

Tombow "Fude" Fudenosuke pens in both soft and hard tip. From the register: Click, click. *Cha-ching!* Rulers, pencils, stencils for making circles and squares and rectangles. *Cha-ching!* Katie kept ringing items; the subtotal kept growing. Holly could buy a lamp for the living room with this money. Maybe two lamps. Not to mention she was taking out a business loan—what was she doing buying *pens*? "Stop!" said Holly, hands up in partial surrender. "I mean—I'm good," she said, taking control, leaving a few items on the counter. "Thank you." She smiled sweetly. "Thank you so much."

"That'll be one hundred thirty-seven dollars," said Katie.

What the FROCK. Holly gulped, trying to hide her shock. *One hundred thirty-seven dollars? For polka dots on paper?* "Yes, of course," she said sweetly, digging deep inside her bag to retrieve her wallet, hoping Katie would, indeed, become a client of Holly Banks Productions. *And hey,* she reminded herself with a quick glance toward Plume's name on the Plexiglas donation box, *consumer spending stimulates the economy.*

With a chipper smile once she had bagged all Holly's supplies and taken her money, "Here you go," said Katie. "And let's set an appointment. I want to learn more about Holly Banks Productions. Welcome to bullet journaling!"

"You're going to love it," said Shanequa. "Soon, you'll be following hashtags on Instagram and searching for design layouts for daily logs, monthly logs, and habit trackers. You'll start future logging, rapid logging, migrating, and threading. Incorporating tabs and washi tape and creating double-dutch doors and custom bullets . . ."

Rapid logging? Threading?

"You've entered a whole new world," said Shanequa, reaching over to rest a hand on Holly's arm. "Trust me. This is only the beginning."

~

Later that day, with a cup of vanilla hazelnut coffee and her BuJo kit spread out in front of her, Holly turned to the first page of her Leuchtturm1917, thinking she'd "officially" start "officially" bullet journaling by writing something "official." Like her name.

:: ~~Holly~~ :: HOLLYB ::

Ugh! What the heck. She tried again, this time forming the letters with a light pencil and then tracing over the pencil marks with her Tombow "Fude" Fudenosuke brush pen. *Food-NOS-kay.* (She looked it up.)

Concentrating this time, she produced this:

:: HOLLY :: BANKS :: PRODUCTIONS ::

It wasn't future logging or double-dutch doors or some other such thing, but Holly thought it was beautiful. And she felt proud to be starting something new. Not just bullet journaling but Holly Banks Productions. She felt courageous and brave treading into uncharted waters despite difficult pronunciations and terms she didn't understand. Adventurers exploring new worlds often met with languages they didn't understand.

And to think, it only cost $137 and a mere ten minutes (okay, maybe twelve) to write three simple words. Two of which were her own name.

Holly smiled, enjoying her coffee, remembering what Greta had said when Holly announced she was launching Holly Banks Productions: *Oh, it'll be a production, all right.*

21

Holly picked up supplies for painting the living room, dining room, and foyer, but as she was unloading everything from her Suburban, a car pulled up. *Not again.* She rolled her eyes, thinking it might be the media, relieved Ella was still at school and Jack was home sick from work again—which was surprising, considering all that was going on with the firm. As Jack said, people didn't schedule when they got sick. Still, if it were the media, maybe she'd let Jack deal with this one. He didn't seem all that sick.

The man from the car approached Holly, offering his hand for her to shake. "Holly Banks?" he began, sweeping his baseball cap off his head in a show of respect. *He must come from good stock,* thought Holly, *a man raised right by his momma.* "My name's Thom."

He seemed kind. His leathery skin clean shaven. He wore a navy North Face vest, unzipped halfway over a plaid flannel shirt. His jeans showed wear in all the right places, but his boots gave him away; he was an outsider. From somewhere out west—Colorado, Nevada, Montana. Maybe a large ranch. Certainly not from around here.

"No comment," said Holly. She dipped her head into her trunk, pulling the last of the paint cans out before slamming it shut. Cans in hand, she headed toward her front door.

"I just flew in from Nevada," he said. "Your neighbor Houston reached out to me. He said your dog made an important discovery?"

"No comment," she said again, reaching her porch steps. *Wait. Why is Houston contacting someone on our behalf?* "Houston called you?"

"I bet you wish this whole thing would go away," he said.

"Yes, actually. I do." What she didn't say, what she felt, was that she didn't like the attention. Didn't like feeling out of control. It embarrassed her that her dog misbehaved. That she was giving everyone the impression she was a screwup. She had a business to start. A house to show in less than three weeks. She wanted to feel respected. If every time she appeared in town, something chaotic happened, who'd want to do business with her? "I've had a run of bad luck since moving to the Village of Primm."

"That's the problem with luck," he offered. "Everyone's quick to label it as good or bad. What if it's neither good nor bad? What if it just *is*? The bad luck you perceive is happening to you could be good luck for someone else."

"Point taken," she said.

And it was worth considering. Maybe, if you asked the universe, luck wasn't a thing at all. Maybe things just *were* and didn't exist with value judgments placed on them. When Holly left home late and found herself stuck in traffic, she'd often wonder, Was it bad luck she was late and now stuck in traffic or good luck? Had Holly left on time and been five minutes farther down the road, it might have been *her* car that was in the accident now holding everyone up.

At some point in her past, maybe in college during ethics class, she remembered discussing luck and a dropped twenty-dollar bill. If she dropped a twenty-dollar bill and kept walking but then realized she'd dropped it and returned to retrieve it, was she unlucky, lucky, or both? If she was unlucky while dropping it but then lucky while finding it, did the good and bad luck cancel each other out? Was luck even at play, or was this just some random act that corrected itself? And what if there were two twenty-dollar bills, each dropped at separate times by two separate people, and the bill Holly retrieved was never hers at all; it had, in fact, belonged to the other person now on *their* way to retrieve it? What then? Could Holly still claim to be lucky if she replaced the missing twenty-dollar bill if the bill she found was not rightfully hers? What then? Was karma now at play? Did she now have bad karma because she took what didn't belong to her and interfered with someone else's opportunity for luck? What if the person looking for their dropped twenty-dollar bill had been Jack, and he had intended to use the money to take a cab to meet Holly for their first date, but because he never found the money, he never took the cab, and they never met? The possible scenarios were endless.

That was the problem with value judgments applied to luck—labeling luck as something good or bad. Because you never knew. It could all be some random, disconnected series of actions, provoking turns of events you never intended, and you had no way of ultimately knowing if they were meaningless or life changing.

"I think you have a very special dog," Thom said, interrupting Holly's thoughts. "I think she has a special talent."

"Talent?" said Holly. "She doesn't have talent. The dog doesn't listen. All she wants to do is play."

"Maybe there's a reason she does what she does. Maybe she's driven to do it. Maybe it's her destiny."

"To do what? Run away? Dig holes? Torture poor Houston?" Holly shook her head no. "I believe they all go to heaven, but dogs don't have a *destiny* per se."

"Why not?" He shrugged.

"Heck, I don't even know if *people* have a destiny," she told him.

There can't be anything preordained for the life of a chocolate Labrador, can there? They're born. They eat. They sleep. She thought back to the day they adopted Struggle. It did seem like Struggle *knew* she was meant to go home with them. Did dogs know something humans didn't? Could animals tap another sense of knowing?

"May I speak with you and your husband? Together?" said the man named Thom. "I think you'll both be interested to hear what I have to say."

Holly considered this last question and then told him, "Wait here," leaving him on the sidewalk to fetch Jack from inside.

"Jack?" she hollered, setting the paint cans down beside the mudroom bench. Ever since Holly had established a "mudroom" inside the front door, the foyer had sure become cluttered. She kept moving things around, but nothing seemed to work. Maybe the mudroom bench needed to move.

"Oh, hey," he said, eating an apple, leaving the kitchen to join her in the foyer.

"What happened there?" She pointed to the haphazard construction site happening to the wall between the living room and dining room. It wasn't bookshelves. Instead, the doorway between the living room and dining room had been widened by a whopping four feet or more. Demoed trim and drywall sat in a pile. Three jagged edges were cut into the wall, the left side, right side, and top of the doorway. She cocked her head to get a glimpse inside the dining room, and good gravy, the windows from the living room were now flooding the once-dark dining room with more light.

"You said you wished the opening between the two rooms was wider, so I widened it," he said. "Now there's hardly any wall left. It's all doorway. So instead of two separate rooms, it'll function like one big one." He searched her eyes for approval.

"You must be feeling better. I thought you were sick," she said, taking it all in. She knew what this was about: this was his way of saying he was sorry about their fight the other night without actually saying *I'm sorry*. Jack's way of showing he supported her pursuing her dreams of becoming a filmmaker? Knock a wall down.

"I love you," she said, wrapping her arms around his neck before kissing him.

"I think the rooms look bigger."

"Huge improvement. Thank you," she said, taking his hand to walk with him toward the door. "There's a man outside wanting to talk to you."

After a few minutes of talking to Thom on the front lawn, Jack invited him inside for a cup of coffee. The three sat at the kitchen table as Struggle warmed to their visitor from Nevada before leaving to lie down beside her water bowl.

"An ore dog," Jack clarified, setting a cup of coffee in front of Thom.

"That's right," said Thom, lifting his mug in thanks toward Jack. "Ore dogs are working dogs specially trained to find mineral deposits just below the surface of the ground. From what Houston tells me, your dog may have a nose for minerals. I suspect she smelled the buried piece of the astrolabe before she began digging based on the proximity of the dug holes and the fact that she was drawn to the metal compass inlaid in the grass."

"Interesting," said Holly, tapping the outside of her mug with her fingers, thinking he seemed deep and thoughtful. The kind of guy you'd want around a campfire. There was something about him that made her feel the pace of things should be slower. As if the second hand on a clock should move like the arms of a sloth. She took a sip, intuiting it would be rude to ask the guy to speed it up a bit.

"Back in the day, blacksmiths used ore dogs to search for iron ore the smiths could smelt into an ax. A walk through the woods with one of these dogs is a sight to behold. One minute they're frolicking; the next minute they're pouncing about in a pile of leaves as if trying to stomp on a mouse burrowed beneath. But!" Thom lifted a finger for emphasis. "It's not a mouse. These dogs are detecting mineral ores. Sulfide ores, that sort of thing. There's a specific aroma these dogs can be trained to detect."

"So what does this mean?" said Holly with an eye toward Jack.

"Are you saying these dogs can prospect for gold? Silver?" asked Jack.

Thom acknowledged Jack was on the right track by nodding his head a few times before saying, "A few decades ago, these dogs were trained in greater numbers to search for nickel for the steel industry. The major players in ore dog training were Sweden"—he counted on his fingers—"Finland, and Russia. But then the steel industry went belly-up, so most ore dog training programs folded. But the dogs can still do what they do, and I suspect your dog comes by it naturally."

"And, so . . . what?" said Holly. What did this man want? Did he want Struggle? Because he wasn't getting her. Struggle was their dog. Struggle was Ella's best friend.

"Mind if I . . . ?" Thom motioned toward his car outside. "I want to show you something. I'll be right back," he said, taking his leave, presumably to retrieve something from his car.

Holly leaned back in her chair, following the sight of him till he disappeared out the front door. "What does this mean, Jack?" She felt panicked. "Does that guy want Struggle? He's not getting Struggle."

"He doesn't want Struggle. At least, I don't think so." Jack called Struggle to his side. "What have you been up to, ole girl? Hmm?" he asked Struggle. To Holly he said, "We have a wonder dog. Maybe I'll get into treasure hunting."

"What, so you can be gone all day and then come home to tell us you found a coin from the Roman Empire? Don't be ridiculous. The Roman Empire was across the pond. Waste of time," said Holly.

"Unless," said Jack, "I take Struggle on the road or we pack up this place in Primm and head back to Boulder City or Alaska to prospect for gold."

"That's insane."

"Off-grid tiny house," said Jack. "Or a she shed." He winked. "If that's what you want to call it. Or we can move in with your sister in Nevada. History books make you think the gold rush is a thing of the past, but Nevada's on their fourth gold boom."

"How do you know this?" asked Holly. Although, it wasn't *that* odd that Jack would know this. With family in Nevada, the topic had come up a few times whenever someone felt lucky or mentioned playing the lottery. Gold was big business. Big dreams. People talked.

Thom returned with a sack of rocks. Nothing out of the ordinary, they appeared to be just some dumb old rocks. He pulled one from the pouch. Offered it to Struggle, who went absolutely mad for it. "See? She smells it. I knew it!" Thom dumped the bag of rocks on the kitchen floor, letting Struggle smell around in it. A few moments later, Struggle picked up a rock and stood looking at Thom, tail wagging.

"How'd she do that?" asked Holly. "Is this a joke? Are they that easy to train?"

"It takes more work than this. We're in a controlled environment. She'd have to train in the field to become really good, but I think your dog is special." Thom looked at Jack and then at Holly. "I really do."

"What do you know about the area around Elko, Nevada?" Jack asked Thom.

What the . . . , thought Holly. *Elko?*

Impressed with the question, Thom said, "They're looking at pulling seven billion dollars in gold out of the ground over the next decade."

"You don't say," said Jack, nodding, thinking.

"This has *nothing* to do with us," Holly reminded him.

"Most of the gold mined in the United States comes from Nevada—upward of seventy, eighty percent," said Thom. "If Nevada were a country, it would be the world's fifth-largest producer."

"So now what?" asked Jack.

"*Now what?* As in, next steps?" Holly shot a mean look at Jack. "No." *You're not giving our dog away. You're not.* "Excuse me," said Holly, taking Struggle by the collar to lead her out of the kitchen and to her bedroom upstairs, where she closed Struggle inside the master bathroom. Leaving her in the bedroom meant she'd rumple the window blinds, poking her snout through to bark at things beyond the window, or she'd nuisance bark at the closed bedroom door until someone came and got her. Somehow, closing her in the bathroom prevented these things from happening. Typically, Struggle would surrender almost immediately and flop down on the bathroom floor to take a nap.

Holly returned to hear Thom telling Jack, "Most ore dog training schools are in Scandinavia, but if you're wanting to build her skills, I can train her in Nevada to search for all sorts of sulfide ore. Zinc, nickel, copper. Some dogs can even find oxide ore."

"Arsenian pyrite?" asked Jack.

Holly shot a look at Jack. *What are you talking about?* "Time-out," she said, wishing she had removed Struggle from the conversation before Thom had the chance to show her his rocks. "End of discussion, fellas. The dog's not going to Nevada or Sweden or anywhere else." Holly spoke directly to Jack when she said, "And she's not getting trained to search for gold, silver, or unicorn glitter, for that matter. Nope. Not gonna happen." She walked with her coffee to set her mug in the kitchen sink. "My apologies, Thom. But this is a family dog. I'm sorry we can't help you further."

No one spoke for a few moments, until Thom said, "Oh, I'm not wanting to take her back to Nevada. I'm just here for a week or two. Houston hired me."

"Houston?" said both Holly and Jack at the same time. Thom had told Holly in the front yard he was in Primm because Houston had called to tell him about their dog. But to learn Houston had *hired* him?

"Why? To do what?" Holly wanted to know.

"To clear his family name," said Thom. "To right a wrong. I understand he told you about his grandfather, Clive Cranbarrie?"

He had. The night Struggle and Holly were on television. The night it all went down. According to Houston, his grandfather almost did time in jail for arson after being implicated for starting the fire at the Land Survey Records Department. There was speculation in both towns that Clive had something to hide. That he'd taken an unusual interest in the land along the banks of the tributary that now divided the Village of Primm and Southern Lakes.

"Is this about ownership rights beneath the water tower?" asked Holly. "You're worried about water?"

"Not exactly," said Thom, "although Houston tells me that's probably the story line the media will go with. There's more. A lot more."

"This is about the astrolabe," said Holly, with a glance at Jack. She returned her focus to Thom, telling him, "I heard an astrolabe like the one that's missing in Primm was turned in to a museum and was valued at close to a million dollars because it was from the sixteenth century. Are they really that rare?" The whole thing seemed crazy to Holly. "I never even *heard* of an astrolabe until last week."

"Well, I don't know much about astrolabes," said Thom, "but sure, I imagine an original astrolabe from the sixteenth century *would* fetch a pretty penny. I'm here because of your dog. And I feel you have a right to know—" He paused, almost as if he needed a moment to decide whether he should say what he was about to say. After a prolonged moment, he said, "I'm here because Clive Cranbarrie was a well-known gold prospector. Back in the day."

"Are you saying there's gold in Primm?" asked Jack, taking a moment to digest everything.

Gold? In Nevada, sure. But Primm?

"Interesting the topic of gold would come up with Penelope running around hoping consumer spending drives the economy," muttered Holly. And that guy from the municipal department mentioning humans always fighting for resources. Gold, oil, water . . .

Thom explained, "All I'm saying is that Clive Cranbarrie was a gold prospector, and I arrived in Primm yesterday and spent all day looking at the land around the water tower. That's a gold-bearing creek if I've ever seen one."

"But Primm is nowhere near Nevada," said Holly. "The only gold you'd find in Primm is wedding bands, and the diamonds attached are more valuable."

"You'd be surprised. This area of the country was quite active back in the day."

"How can you tell?" asked Jack.

"Why are you asking?" Holly said to Jack, sensing something odd. "You're not becoming a *gold* prospector. That's ridiculous. No." She shook her head. "No way."

"It helps to know gold geology and how to look at land differently," said Thom. "There's a lot more to it than this, but for example, red soils are typically an indicator of iron-rich soils, which could be an indicator that gold is present . . ."

He continued, on and on, as Jack listened intently. Holly was listening, too, until her eye caught something on the family room TV. Over Jack's shoulder was a woman in a YouTube video performing a coffee cupping session using an SCA Coffee Taster's Flavor Wheel. Holly noticed a pad of paper and a pen on the couch. Had Jack been taking notes?

Holly picked up in the middle of what Thom was saying: ". . . the land around the water tower borders a body of water. Now, most people walk directly to the water, never pausing to look at the land formation around the water. And often, gold is found hundreds of yards from a water source in an area known as a dry gulch, which could have formed after years and years of soil erosion."

"So what do you want from us?" asked Holly, cutting to the chase. "You want to take our dog out to search for gold or for the two missing discs and the astrolabe?"

"In this case, despite the real possibility there are gold deposits to be found, and despite the fact that I typically train dogs for these sorts of things, it's the two missing pieces of the astrolabe that I care about," said Thom. "That's what I've been hired for."

"Then why bring up the gold and Clive's past?" asked Holly.

But before Thom could answer, Jack asked, "Is Houston hoping you'll find the astrolabe so he can cash in on it before the treasure hunters find it?"

"That would be nice," said Thom. "But I think he has something else in mind."

"Surely you don't care who owns the land beneath the water tower," said Holly, speaking to Thom. "You're from Nevada. Why would you care about water in the Village of Primm?"

"I don't. Houston reached out to me. Beyond my wages, I don't have a stake in any of this. But yes, finding the missing astrolabe pieces so that land ownership is established *does* matter to Houston."

"Why?" asked Holly. "Because of Clive's past? Because there might be gold deposits?"

"I've said all I'm able to say," said Thom. "You'll have to talk to Houston for the rest of the story."

"Then why are you here and not Houston?" asked Holly. She looked at Jack. "You'd think Houston would have at least come with him."

"This was my stipulation," said Thom. "You're the owners of the dog. I told Houston I needed to meet with you first, alone, before I agreed to sign anything with him."

He looked at Jack, presumably because he sensed Jack would be easier to convince than Holly. "I'd like to work with your dog. I think it would take one week, two max, to find the remaining discs. Then all of this goes away, and everyone leaves you alone."

"But there are treasure hunters with metal detectors on The Lawn right now," said Holly.

"Let 'em look," said Thom, unfazed. "Metal detectors can't hold a candle to what a properly trained dog can do. I believe Struggle can do it faster and more efficient."

"Absolutely not," Holly insisted. "You're not taking our dog. I'm sorry. No." *What do we know about this man? What if he's a con artist? Some gold-prospecting crackhead here to steal Struggle?*

As if intuiting her thoughts, Thom pulled a series of folded papers from his pocket. "Take a look at these. A list of references. My photo ID. My website. Two newspaper articles about my work. Do some research. Make some phone calls. If I check out, call me. And while you're at it, call Houston. He's expecting to hear from you." He stood to leave. "But know this: if what Houston told me is correct, this is the kind of town that won't let something like this go. And if I were Houston, knowing what I know, I'd want to get to the bottom of this too."

Neither Jack nor Holly responded. There was too much to figure out. This was all so strange. *I bet Houston wants to mine for gold,* thought Holly. *So then why not mine for gold? Why worry about the discs proving ownership to the land? Why not skip that step?*

Thom extended his hand to Jack and then to Holly. "I'm staying in a hotel one town over." He pulled a business card and pen from his pocket, scribbling his mobile number, the name of his hotel, and his room number. "If you change your mind or want to speak further, give a ring. What I'm proposing is this: I work with Struggle for one week. Two, max. The astrolabe pieces get found, the mystery gets solved, and all of this goes away." He looked at Jack. "And, there's something in it for you. Two weeks with me, and that dog will have some serious skills."

Holly glared at Jack. *You're not becoming a gold prospector!*

Thom took his hat from the kitchen table and nodded toward Jack. "Thank you for the coffee. You know where to find me." And with that, he turned to leave, walking down the hall toward the front door, leaving Holly and Jack dumbfounded in the kitchen.

Holly rushed after him and caught him at the front door.

"You can make this all go away?" she said.

"I can," said Thom, now standing on her front porch.

"You can take Struggle, find the two missing discs, hand them over to the authorities so property rights are determined, and all of this will go away?" she clarified. "As far as my family and I are concerned, the attention will end, and we can go back to living a normal life?"

"Yes." He nodded. "I believe so."

Maybe her luck was changing. Maybe the stars were beginning to line up in her favor. Was it good luck a man named Thom stood before her or bad luck?

Provided his references checked out, she was about to give him tentative permission to work with Struggle, when he said, pointing to the ceiling above her head, "You might want to get that fixed."

Holly glanced up, seeing for the first time bubbles hanging from the drywall on the ceiling. The stain that began a week ago had darkened substantially, practically overnight, appearing now as something ominous overhead, like a menacing shadow or a storm cloud. She reached for the umbrella propped against the mudroom bench, poking a few bubbles with its tip. "Why is it doing that?" she asked, pressing the tenderness of the ceiling. "That's so crazy."

"I wouldn't do that if I were you," said Thom.

But then—*whoa!* A swath of drywall the width of her shoulders gave way, falling onto her head like a slice of bread soaked in milk.

"Jack!" she shouted, half-bent and covering her head, too stunned to do anything else as water poured down on her, drenching her from head to toe as if someone had upended a bucket with her name on it.

With Jack rushing toward her, Thom reached in, grabbing her by the arm to pull her onto the porch beside him. And then, just as suddenly as it had started—it stopped. The deluge over. Water now streaming in as a thin line, an almost invisible cord flowing quietly from the ceiling before announcing itself as it splashed onto the hardwood floor.

"What in the world?" said Holly, soaking wet, bits of soggy drywall in her hair, on her shoulders, on her shirt, on the floor in front of her. She said to Jack, "I think the sky is falling."

And then everyone, Holly, Jack, and Thom, peered into the two-foot hole in their tiny foyer ceiling to the now-exposed wooden studs and the bathroom flooring above that, realizing the dog they heard barking was directly overhead.

"No!" cried Holly, hands over her mouth. Struggle must have tucked her snout between the wall and the knobs on the claw-foot tub again. Only this time, Struggle had succeeded in flooding the bathroom floor. "Is that even possible?" she asked Jack. "That kind of damage in such a short period of time?"

"Easy. It's called shoddy construction, deferred maintenance, and a dog that's either too stupid or too smart," griped Jack. *"Argh!"* he yelled, giving a swift kick to a piece of fallen drywall. "I *knew* I should have fixed it the moment I thought there might be an issue."

"Jack—go," Holly urged as she made her way to the kitchen to get towels and pots. "Struggle can't fall through, can she?"

"Doubt it. The bathroom floor and subfloor are still intact." Jack hoofed it up the stairs, skipping a few on the way up to get Struggle and stop the flow of water. "Must be the pipes. That's what you call new damage on top of old," he shouted down.

Thom helped Holly sop up the water and position the pots. "Good luck, bad luck, or dumb luck?" she asked him.

"Is this multiple choice? D. None of the above."

"What are you? A Stoic? Some sort of dog-training, gold-mining philosopher?"

He shrugged.

"Because to me, it feels like the universe is kicking us when we're down." She looked up, as if through the clouds and into the heavens, where saturated subflooring met with leaky plumbing and wet floor joists.

"Those two-by-eights are spaced way too far apart," Thom said, taking a closer look. "And shouldn't there be a support beam up there?"

22

Later that day, Holly texted Penelope.

HOLLY: Have a moment?

PENELOPE: Sure!

HOLLY: Soooo . . . we're not sure, but we're thinking our foyer used to be a two-story foyer? But someone might have "closed" the foyer to expand the master bathroom into that space? We're thinking this was done without proper structural support . . . and . . . the plumbing install on the claw-foot bathtub that's now in that space probably wasn't installed properly . . .

PENELOPE: WHAT??? Oh, no. Holly, I had no idea.

HOLLY: I'm thinking this work was done without a permit or a proper building inspection? Not sure why our home inspector didn't pick this up . . .

PENELOPE: Neither am I. I'll call him. Although, I'm not sure what anyone can do at this point.

HOLLY: I thought you might say that. Also, we had an overflow event that's complicating matters. Accelerating the damage, you might say. The moisture is weakening the subflooring.

PENELOPE: I'm so sorry.

HOLLY: We've called a contractor to assess.

PENELOPE: Smart.

HOLLY: ANYWAY. I'm afraid our home won't be ready to accommodate crowds. Therefore, I have to withdraw #12 Petunia Lane from the Enclave Tour.

PENELOPE: I completely understand.

HOLLY: I hope this isn't too much trouble.

PENELOPE: Not at all. We're running all of this through an app. It's an easy fix. I'll make the update in the next twenty minutes.

HOLLY: Oh, good. Thank you. My apologies.

PENELOPE: None needed. I'm so sorry to hear this news.

A few minutes later . . .

PENELOPE: Regarding your request for home organizing services from Feathered Nest Realty, do you want to cancel, and I'll refund your deposit, or continue with services?

HOLLY: Let's continue. I see them as separate issues. Even though I can't be on tour, I'm recently unpacked from a move and I think a few hours would help me figure out a few storage-related issues with the new home.

PENELOPE: On second thought, I am refunding your deposit and it would be my pleasure to provide professional organizing services at no cost after what you've experienced.

HOLLY: Thank you, Penelope, but not necessary.

PENELOPE: I insist. Please let me do this, Holly. It's the least I can do.

23

The following day, Tuesday, at the narrow, pale-speckled Formica countertop that stretched the width of the floor-to-ceiling window of Mitch & Lucy Creamery on Pip's Corner, Ella and Talia sat, both girls enjoying double-decker ice cream cones. With seat cushions wrapped in pink laminate, the barstools were so tall the seats stood at almost Ella and Talia's height.

"Are you good? All set?" Holly asked Ella, planting a kiss on the top of her head before stepping back to talk with Shanequa. Ella moved her body to avoid her mother's touch, a nonverbal response that said to Holly: *I got this, Mom. Don't worry about me. I'm a big girl.*

"So what happened?" whispered Shanequa, using her straw to stir the milkshake in her hand.

Holly drew a deep breath, the smell of sweetness and dairy in the air wafting through her nostrils, sitting uncomfortably in her stomach. "We met with a guy from Nevada who trains ore dogs. He's offering to take Struggle out to hunt for the two missing discs."

"Ore dogs?"

"I know, right? I had never heard of them either. They're prospecting dogs. They can smell mineral deposits below the surface of the ground."

"The towns are going to love that," said Shanequa. "Has Eliza Adalee caught wind of it?"

"I don't think so. I suspect if she knew, she would have shoved a microphone in my face by now."

From their view through the words *Got Pretzel Cone?* on the Mitch & Lucy Creamery window, they could see a team of treasure hunters swinging metal detectors over the grass on The Lawn, *MEEK ENTERPRISES* plain as day across the backs of their jackets. "The ore dog guy said he thought Struggle would find them quickly."

"An anonymous donor has posted an award," said Shanequa. "Five thousand dollars to anyone who finds a disc."

"Is there a reward for finding the astrolabe?"

"Ten grand."

"Interesting," said Holly, suspecting that the astrolabe and discs were worth more than most people realized. Maybe they were not as valuable as the one turned in to the museum, but surely they were worth a lot more than the rewards posted. She wondered if Merchant Meek had posted the rewards. Or maybe Houston? Maybe she and Jack should ask for a cut of anything Struggle found. Might help pay for the repairs to the house.

Talia said something to make Ella laugh, Ella leaning back on her stool to such an extent that Holly had to reach over to stop her from leaning too far and possibly falling to the polished concrete floor. What was it with motherhood? That awful feeling tragedy could strike at any moment, and your child might get hurt.

At Mitch & Lucy's, everywhere you looked, pale-gray-and-white striped walls with framed photos of comical dogs and cats eating ice cream in the most unlikely of places stared back at you. On top of the Eiffel Tower, in a gondola. The biggest photo of all, the one above the register near the door, was of a pudgy English bulldog (Mitch?), riding a skateboard while sporting sunglasses. Wind-whipped, drooping jowls, a bouquet of balloons tied to his collar. If it was Mitch, Mitch was balancing a banana split on his back, skateboarding down a board-walk past a bathing beauty beneath a beach umbrella—a cat. A skinny, completely hairless, bikini-clad white sphynx with a pink nose drinking a root beer float through a tall lime-green straw sticking out of an enormous scalloped carnival glass. Maybe Lucy?

"So then," Holly continued, "as I was walking the guy to the door, a giant piece of drywall fell on my head."

"Whoa. Were you hurt?" Shanequa tucked a few napkins on the counter beneath the girls' ice creams as Gary-Gee set up his stool and speaker in a back corner of Mitch & Lucy's, readying himself to start strumming a few tunes on his guitar.

"No, just stunned. Struggle stuck her snout between the wall and the bathtub faucet upstairs and turned the water on while we were talking with the ore guy in the kitchen."

"You didn't hear the water running?"

"The TV was on. Jack had been watching programming about coffee roasting."

"He's really into that, isn't he?" Shanequa slid a chair out to sit down. "I've never had a cup of coffee made from beans someone roasted in their backyard using a popcorn machine. That was amazing. I told Malik about it. He wants to learn more."

"Oh, believe me. They've already talked about it when they were with the Bubble Gummers at soccer skills camp," said Holly. Both of them shared a moment to laugh about the disastrous time their husbands were having outnumbered by five-year-old girls as Gary-Gee began strumming, opening his show to an ice cream–eating audience of less than fifteen with a zippy rendition of "Zip-a-Dee-Doo-Dah."

"Malik said one of the girls grew bored of soccer and suggested the team play hide-and-seek instead, so a bunch of them began running around in circles, trying to figure out where to hide on a wide-open soccer field."

"You know they're never going to learn all of those names," said Holly. "One of the Bubble Gummers came to practice wearing kitten whiskers and meowed the entire time. Jack said at least six girls swarmed her, refusing to leave her side, declaring she was their pet. He's pretty sure it was Olivia, because every time he called her name, she'd answer by licking her wrist."

Ella, feet dangling, took a swipe with her tongue across a scoop of mint chocolate chip, which was packed into Mitch & Lucy's signature pretzel cone. The cone, thin and pointed, was gluten-free and lightly salted on the outside, designed that way to enhance the rich flavors of the hand-churned ice cream. Intending to go into the ice cream business, Mitch & Lucy Creamery had found itself a distributor of proprietary pretzel cones, made with a secret recipe and shipped from their website.

On the wall behind Shanequa, Holly noticed an Enclave Tour crossword puzzle clue written on a chalkboard. In bold, colorful lettering were the words:

ACROSS
NUMBER 11. TWISTED TREAT (SEVEN LETTERS)

"What do you suppose the merchandise is?" Holly asked Shanequa.

"Oh, I already know," she said. "I asked when I was paying for Talia's ice cream. They're known for their *Got Pretzel Cone?* merch: T-shirts, bumper stickers, ceramic ice cream bowls. For this, they're releasing limited edition T-shirts that read: *Got [Twisted Treat] Cone?*"

Ella shifted in her seat, chomping down on the top of her ice cream. "Ella, careful," said Holly. "You're going to knock the top scoop off." To Shanequa she said, "These barstools are freakishly tall."

"Agree. When Malik and I bring the kids here, we usually sit at a booth."

"I'm so sorry. Let's move," offered Holly, hoping Ella's insistence they sit at the window hadn't inadvertently put Shanequa in the uncomfortable position of having to hoist her five-year-old onto a stool her same height. *How rude of me.*

"It's fine," said Shanequa, waving the situation off. "Back to the drywall."

"So now we have a contractor coming out, and truthfully, it's not looking good. I swear there should be a support beam or something beneath that claw-foot. Claw-foots are heavy. Once the drywall fell from the foyer ceiling and we got a look inside the ceiling to what was beneath the master bathroom floor—I don't know. The whole thing looks shoddy. The dog trainer thinks someone closed up a two-story foyer to expand the bathroom upstairs. Jack agrees."

"You know who closed up the foyer, don't you?" asked Shanequa. "Collette. Her husband did it before selling the house to compete with homes with better master baths."

"You're joking."

Collette's *husband* closed the foyer ceiling and then placed a *bathtub* on top of it?

"He thinks he's a contractor. He thinks he's a grill master, too, but I swear his dry-rub short ribs stayed with me way too long."

"I'm not sure which I feel more: Shock? Or anger?" said Holly. She paused a moment to consider her options, thinking shock definitely won out but that anger would soon follow. "Jack keeps talking about cashing out and downsizing. Do you ever think about downsizing?"

"Never. If I mentioned downsizing to Malik, I'd end up in a house with no room for craft supplies. So, nope. Not gonna happen. With four kids, having a creative outlet is the only thing keeping me sane. I need my stash," she proclaimed. "My stash keeps me happy."

"What's really frustrating," said Holly, "is that I was hoping to use the Enclave Tour to promote the new business. Now it feels like I'm missing the opportunity to launch to a live audience. Had I been on the Enclave Tour, people would be coming to me, walking through the living room and seeing the film studio in the dining room plain as day. It's so depressing. That would have been the perfect way to launch. Free media, word of mouth. We can't even use our front door now because of the upstairs bathroom. We come and go through the garage because Jack propped up a bunch of two-by-fours to support the ceiling while we wait for a contractor to come by. Hold up," said Holly, taking a moment to weigh her options. "What if . . . instead of new living room furniture . . . I bought a she shed, put the shed on the Enclave Tour, and ran Holly Banks Productions out of it?"

"I think it's a great idea. What's not to love about a she shed?"

"Exactly," said Holly, warming to the idea. *Yes. This could work. This could work quite nicely.* "You can serve caviar and crème fraîche on toasted brioche in a she shed."

"I'd eat it."

"Can I ask you something? You have an online presence. Do you ever look around at what others are doing online and think you're not doing enough?"

"All the time," said Shanequa. "Although, I'm starting to think success is a process."

"Hmm. I'd agree with that," said Holly, thinking much of what she was doing at the moment for Holly Banks Productions was all process work—maybe she should relax and stop being so hard on herself.

"Katie and I were talking about this last night. She's really interested in working with you. Remember, Holly: Everyone you see online? They're in the same process as you are, but everyone goes about that process differently."

"Well, I don't know about process, but I sure see a lot of results. Facebook posts, tutorial videos, Instagram live videos, online courses. I keep thinking: Do these people sleep?"

"Ha! Sure, they sleep," said Shanequa. "Katie wants to develop online courses. I'm thinking the first time anyone designs an online course, they take a ton of time figuring out how to do it. I have to believe the second course is easier to produce than the first. And the third? Even easier. The result is the same—online course. But the process? I suspect the top producers online are masters of process."

"Interesting."

"Focus on the process, and the result will take care of itself."

"Good point," said Holly, rethinking everything. Maybe she should stop comparing herself to others. Stop focusing on other people's results. It was so much healthier to focus on the process—the doing of. *And you know what?* thought Holly. *That might be the bull's-eye in the marketing plan. Shoot straight into the client's process. Make the process easier and more streamlined—more and better results for everyone.*

Ella tapped on Holly's arm, telling her, "Chloe wants to be my bridesmaid."

"Bridesmaid?" said Holly. "I didn't think bridesmaids were included."

"They're not," said Talia. "She's collecting them on the playground."

"Whoa, whoa, whoa. Hold up," said Holly with a look toward Shanequa. *Collecting bridesmaids?* "Ella, no. Absolutely not. Miss Bently is in charge. You're not in charge."

"Chloe said if I'm the bride, then I'm in charge." Ella licked the top scoop.

"Ella's in charge," Talia told her mom with a thumb toward Ella.

"Shhh. Honey, no. She's not," Shanequa told her daughter, with a light touch to Talia's arm.

"Lick on the side, Ella, so it doesn't drip." Holly tucked a napkin into Ella's collar. "And I hate to tell you, but Chloe's wrong. You don't make the rules. Miss Bently makes the rules."

"But I already told Chloe she could be my bridesmaid," said Ella, coming up from her most recent lick with ice cream on her nose. She was clutching the cone so tight Holly half expected it to crush under the force of Ella's fist. "And after that is Talia. What's that called?"

"What's what called?" asked Holly.

"The one that goes first. Next to the bride," said Ella. With no reasonable explanation Holly could find, Ella took that moment to swing her head back and then swing it forward, taking a wild chomp out of the top scoop.

"Ella—stop," said Holly with a hand to her back again. *No sudden moves, please. You might fall.* She wiped Ella's chin. "You mean maid of honor?"

"That's it." Ella smiled, lips covered in ice cream. "Good, Mommy. That's Talia because Talia's my best friend." To Talia, she said, "You're the maiden honor." Ella and Talia smiled at each other, tucking in close to giggle as, over their heads, Holly and Shanequa exchanged concerned glances.

"And then Chloe can be next," Talia said. "After me, who comes first. And then Ava after Chloe. In a line." She drew a line on the countertop as Gary-Gee switched tunes and started singing "Five Little Ducks."

"And Isabelle," Ella told Talia, taking another lick. "And Mia." Another lick. "And Rashmi and Mary-Caroline."

"You can't invite girls to be your bridesmaids, Ella," said Holly. "That's not what this is about. This is about the letter *Q* and the letter *U* forming new words. Words like *quilt* and *quack* and—*quote*." She tried to think of another.

"*Quarter?*" Shanequa offered.

"*Quarter.*" Holly nodded. "Words like that."

"Then why have a wedding?" Talia wanted to know as Ella tried sticking her tongue between the two scoops.

"Don't do that, Ella. You're going to knock the top scoop off." Holly opened a few napkins, creating a patchwork tablecloth on the counter, but Ella persisted. "Ella—stop licking like that. This isn't a game."

But Ella wasn't listening. Or maybe she was, but she was choosing to ignore her mom. Either way, she stiffened the end of her tongue and began wiggling it between the two scoops. *Why? Why is she doing that? Why do five-year-olds do anything they do?*

"Seriously, Ella? Stop," said Holly, showing her frustration. She didn't *mean* to show her frustration. It came out that way. What she *wanted* to say was: *Freaking listen to me and stop acting like a bridezilla in front of Shanequa.*

"Hailey and Addison? They're my flower girls." Ella held up two fingers. Touched the tips of them to Holly's cheeks. "Addison has baskets."

"Two baskets," added Talia. "One for her and one for Hailey."

Shanequa kept gently telling Talia to *shh*. As if this were a family matter. A Banks family matter.

"Ella, stop. You're not having flower girls. Now, that's enough," said Holly, assuming she'd be getting a call from the school soon. She sensed it. She could feel it in her bones. "And don't push the ice cream that way, or the top scoop is going to fall off."

Was the groom giving the wedding any thought? Was his mom concerned, as Holly was becoming about Ella? Did Q's mom have to tell him: *Whoa, whoa, whoa. Slow down there, Q.* No, Holly decided. Q's mom wasn't.

Holly checked the time. "I need to get Ella home to my mom soon. I have a meeting with Miss Bently about her pre-reading test."

"The PPP AAA RRR thing?" asked Shanequa.

"Yup," said Holly. "That's the one."

24

Knowing she was headed to Primm Academy for a teacher conference about Ella's pre-pre-reading results and knowing she'd *also* be paying a quick visit to the Primm Academy school office—Holly had kind of sort of told Caleb he could meet her there, and they'd somehow conjure up an excuse for him to see and hopefully talk to Rosie.

"I smell good, don't I?" asked Caleb, hopping out of his beaten-up old Subaru to meet Holly at her Suburban in the back lot of the school. He leaned in so she could smell his neck. "How do I look? Do I look good?"

"You look the way you always look," said Holly, eyeing his pocketed khaki cargo pants, boots, and black T-shirt. "If you're trying to impress her, you should dress up."

"Ah, nah," said an anguished Caleb, grabbing the sides of his head. "I screwed up."

"You look fine," said Holly, taking pity on him, deciding it wouldn't help his confidence if she told him his cologne was *way* too strong. "Come on—let's go."

After a winding walk along the sidewalks and then through the heavy front doors of Primm Academy, Holly grabbed the handle to open the door that led to the school office, then noticed Caleb standing absolutely frozen a few feet away, a look of utter dismay on his face.

"What should I say?" he asked, the mere thought of seeing Rosie again causing him to seize up. "Should I go in and say, *Oh, hey,* like I'm super relaxed and surprised to be bumping into her, or should I say something like, *Wow, that's a pretty shirt?*"

Holly softened. He'd annoyed her at times and caused trouble for her by landing *Henny Penny* on her lawn—one could say if he hadn't done that, Struggle wouldn't have gotten loose and might not have made the discovery she'd made that was now rocking village life and placing unwanted attention on Holly and her family—but oh em gee. She'd never seen a guy so smitten with a woman before. "Caleb, breathe. She's a human being like you."

"You go in first," he said. "I'll wait out here."

"What? No," said Holly. "That's so unnatural. What am I supposed to do, make up some excuse for her to come out here? She probably can't leave the front counter." Holly thought about it a minute. "You know what? You shouldn't be asking her out when she's at work anyway, so the pressure's off. Just come inside and smile. Act normal. I'll help with the conversation. I'm sure it will be fine. Just be yourself."

"You're right." He nodded, releasing a nervous laugh. A laugh so strange and awkward it seemed almost heinous.

"What? No. Don't laugh like that in front of Rosie."

"Got it. You're right," he assured her. "I won't. Good plan, I got it. Right." He gave Holly a thumbs-up, then pressed smooth the front of his T-shirt. "Okay, I'm ready. No, I'm not!" Checked his hair. "Okay. Ready."

"You sure?" She turned the knob, and together they entered the school office. Holly, making her way to the counter. Caleb, hanging back by the door.

As expected, she found Rosie McClure behind the counter, sitting in a chair applying lipstick in a vintage handheld mirror. Holly had always admired the 1940s vibe Rosie often wore, but Rosie's signature feature was most definitely her lips. Her lips were the lips a World War ll soldier in a foxhole in war-torn Europe would remember. Rosie today was the woman of that era, blouses with squared shoulders, hemlines that rose to the knee because fabric was rationed after Order L-85 was put into place by the government, restricting fabric yardage to only one and three-fourths yards of fabric per garment. Rosie had lips like the *Palicourea elata*, a tropical plant native to the rain forests of Central and South America, a plant locals called "hot lips" because of the plant's distinctive red bracts that resembled a woman's lips while puckered.

Maybe Caleb was out of his league with this one.

Caleb with his round, boyish face, spiked hair, black T-shirt, and cargo pants. He played Dungeons & Dragons, liked spy equipment, and had a hobby ultralight aircraft. He was a gadget geek. Owned multiple sets of essentially the same outfit—an outfit he wore because it made him feel legit, like he was a bona fide filmmaker.

Maybe the complexity of Rosie's beauty was what captivated him.

Her pouty lips said *kiss me*, but her hair, tied sweetly with a ribbon at the base of her neck, said *send me flowers*. Holly could see she was wearing her signature freshwater pearls beneath the opening of a pale dress, the dress's thin, lightweight fabric giving the impression she was wearing a garment made from the delicate petals of a flower. Her dress, the color of soft pink moving toward a peachy coral, matched her lips and freshwater pearls. Rosie was a sight to behold.

"Hi, Rosie!" said Holly, keeping it chipper, keeping her arm low and by her side so Rosie wouldn't see her signaling to Caleb to join her at the counter. "I'm here for a conference with Miss Bently?"

Stiff as a board, like a wooden soldier in the *Nutcracker Ballet*, Caleb moved mechanically, first pressing the door closed. Then pivoting. Then jutting a leg out to take one exaggerated step toward the counter, before arriving by Holly's side as if his body had snapped into place. She nudged him, muttering, "You okay?"

He made a noise through closed lips, "Um-hum," nodding in the affirmative.

"Stop staring."

"I can't help it," he said, a ventriloquist speaking through a smile that showed all his teeth.

Rosie stood from her chair to glide toward the counter, never taking her eyes off Caleb until she needed to speak to Holly. "Hello, Ms. Banks," she said to Holly with another quick, flirty glance at Caleb. "Introduce me to your friend." She smiled at Caleb, awaiting Holly's introduction.

Caleb's shoulders dropped.

No! That's so unfair. Holly closed her eyes. Her heart broke for Caleb. "Rosie, you remember Caleb," she said. "I introduced you at the Cherry Festival on The Lawn."

With a look of confusion on her face, "Oh?" said Rosie, offering him her hand. "I'm sorry—we met at the Cherry Festival?"

Caleb didn't move. Didn't take her hand. Didn't—anything. He stared straight ahead, standing upright as if made of wood. Poor Caleb had been pining over a woman who didn't remember meeting him. His impression on *her* was nothing like the impression she had made on him.

Rosie's hand still offered, Holly used her leg to give Caleb a discreet nudge. *Say something, Caleb. Shake her hand.*

He pulled his hand out, banging it on the ledge of the counter before reaching hers. He grabbed hold, gave her hand a rough shake, and then dropped it as fast as he could, as if her hand were a lizard covered in spots or a smelly kitchen sponge past its prime and crawling with bacteria.

Caleb, what are you doing?

The twitch in Rosie's eyebrows showed her confusion. The handshake Caleb had given was awkward, borderline rude, and very, very strange.

Through the windows behind Rosie, in the curved bus lane in front of the school, Holly spotted a large brown vehicle pulling up to the curb. *Oh, no. No!* The UPS man. Rosie's crush. The reason, no doubt, Rosie had been applying lipstick. *Think of something, quick!*

"Caleb is a filmmaker," Holly told Rosie, hoping to jog her memory. Rosie seemed so impressed by this when Holly first introduced them. "He has entries in the Wilhelm Klaus Film Festival coming next month to Primm. Don'tcha, Caleb. Caleb, tell Rosie about your work as a filmmaker." Holly glanced at Caleb, still stiff as a board in Rosie's presence. Holly nudged him. When that didn't snap him out of it, she elbowed him in the ribs. Hard.

"Dungeons and Dragons," he offered.

Both Holly and Rosie waited for what would follow, but nothing did. Holly knew his entry in the Wilhelm Klaus had something to do with Dungeons & Dragons, but Caleb had fumbled the second half of his own sentence.

Holly watched through the window as the UPS man approached the front doors of the school. *No. He can't come in.* If the UPS man pushed his way into the room, there'd be no chance for Caleb to recover.

"Caleb filmed a documentary at a Dungeons and Dragons convention using a pinhole camera and mic setup," said Holly, though beyond that, she knew nothing about the film. "Groundbreaking. And he's entered it in the Wilhelm Klaus. It'll probably win a huge prize. It's one of the best documentary films I've ever seen." Holly nodded toward Caleb. "Huge prize. Isn't that right, Caleb?"

Holly could hear the UPS man outside the door to the school office.

"Caleb?" Holly said louder, hoping to pull the words out of him. "Tell Rosie how much you love poetry."

"That was you?" Rosie brightened. "Thank you. I didn't realize there were so many poems written about birds."

"Birds?" said Holly, with a quick glance at Caleb. *Birds?*

That moment would have been the perfect moment for Caleb to speak, but it was too late. The door opened, and in walked Primm's heartthrob—the UPS man. Longish dark hair, dark, smoky eyes, olive skin, jawline as rugged as the Alaskan coastline. Tight brown uniform, biceps bulging from a short-sleeved shirt. He carried a large, heavy box and a device for collecting signatures. Rosie straightened her back and fixed her hair, assuming a flirty position from behind the counter.

"I'll sign!" volunteered Holly. "I'll sign for the package." She grabbed the electronic signature device from the UPS man's hand and scrawled her signature. "There you go! All done." She grabbed the package from his arms and hoisted it on the counter. "Thank you," she said to the UPS man, pressing her hand against his chest as if pushing him out to sea and away from the counter. "Buh-bye. Have a great day!" She whooshed him off, but as he was taking his leave, he winked at Rosie, tipping an imaginary hat before grasping the door handle to make his exit. "Nice truck," Holly added, waving bye-bye. "Still running. Better go jump inside!"

With the UPS man out of the picture, Holly, returning her attention to Rosie and Caleb, said, "Well. I see that's done. So . . ." *Are either of them going to speak?* "Bird poetry, huh? I hear that's really gaining traction in poetry circles."

Caleb stood dejected, head hung low. Rosie didn't remember meeting him at the Cherry Festival on The Lawn. And now, he was just outdone by a manly man in a big brown truck.

"Shall we go?" said Holly to Caleb. "I'll walk you to the door. Out we go," she added, taking hold of Caleb's arm to yank his wooden-soldier self toward the door. "I'll be back in a moment, Rosie. I'm just saying goodbye to Caleb. You're friends with Miss Bently," she added. "Are you attending the Q&U Wedding? Caleb is going. He's a friend of the bride."

She grabbed the door handle, swung the door open, and pushed Caleb into the corridor beyond the office. Then she closed the door, leaving just her and Rosie in the front office. "You know who he is," she said. "How could you do that to the poor guy?"

"I'm sorry!" Rosie looked devastated. "I don't know why I just did that."

"He bought you a book of poetry."

"I know. And I love birds. I'm such an idiot. Why did I just do that?"

"This is none of my business, Rosie, but if you want to find a great guy, you need to pay better attention. Sometimes things are hidden in plain sight. Sometimes a great guy is standing right in front of you."

"You're right—I think that's my problem."

Holly swung open the door, stepping into the corridor with Caleb. "Good gravy, Caleb. What happened in there?"

"I don't know." He grabbed his head with both hands. "I froze up."

Through the windows, the UPS man revved up his brown truck and then pulled away from the curb. Holly knew Rosie crushed on the UPS man, but she wondered if Caleb knew. Did he notice the effect the UPS man had on Rosie?

Turned out Caleb had noticed. He confirmed Holly's suspicion by saying, "I don't stand a chance with a girl like that. She likes guys in uniform. And that guy drives a big truck."

"A truck? *Pssht*. Who wants a ride in a truck when you could fly in an airplane? You're a far better catch."

"Thanks." He shrugged, looking down at his feet.

"But bird poetry?" The quizzical look on Holly's face said it all. "What were you *thinking*?"

25

EMAIL—Time Sent: 9:40 p.m.

TO: Miss Bently, Primm Academy
FROM: Holly Banks
CC: Jack Banks
SUBJECT: Today's Conference

Thank you for meeting with me this afternoon to discuss Ella's performance on the Primm Academy Pre-Pre-Reading Reading Assessment. As you can imagine, I left today's conference a bit alarmed.

May I ask? Exactly how many children in your classroom are meeting expectations? I suppose you can't disclose this information. Consider it a rhetorical question.

I ask because I've just completed quite a few hours of online research and am beginning to wonder if it's *Primm Academy* that's a few steps ahead of what is typically expected of children one month into kindergarten.

P.S. Ella mentioned needing a wedding dress? I forgot to ask. Is this for real? A wedding dress?

∼

EMAIL—Time Sent: 10:01 p.m.

TO: Miss Bently, Primm Academy
FROM: Holly Banks
CC: Jack Banks
SUBJECT: WHOA! WHAT THE HECK?

Me again.

I just googled Q&U Wedding and WOW I had no idea it was a thing. Wedding cake? Table decorations? Party favors???

Of course, I don't want to duplicate efforts . . . am I to assume the groom's parents are also contributing?

26

Thursday morning, in the kitchen with Ella eating breakfast, Holly heard a knock at the door.

"Ella?" she asked. "Where's Struggle?"

Half-awake, Ella rested her head against her arm, which was stretched across the table. "I don't know," she said, yawning, closing her eyes.

Holly set the gallon of milk on the counter, walking toward the front door for what she assumed might be Houston or Thom. Or maybe Maeve Bling or someone else holding Struggle by the collar, returning her home. It wouldn't be the media this early, would it?

She slid past the temporary support structures Jack had installed to secure the upstairs bathroom before opening the door, ready to offer her best excuse. "I'm so sorry—I—" But then she stopped, realizing Struggle, coming from somewhere inside the house, had just squeezed past the support beams and was now standing behind her, tail wagging. Maybe Struggle had been with Charlotte in the dining room? To the two women standing on her front porch, Holly said, "Mary-Margaret? Penelope? What are you doing here?" She checked her watch. Didn't they have kids to get to school?

"Surprise!" sang Mary-Margaret, clapping with excitement.

"Ready to get started?" Penelope asked.

"Started? On what? Organizing? Now?" said Holly, panicked, slight tightening in her chest. What time was it? She knew she'd told Penelope she was still interested in services, but today? Right now?

Mary-Margaret extended her hand to shake Holly's. "Feathered Nest professional organizers," she announced. "At your service."

"Actually, technically," said Penelope, correcting Mary-Margaret, "I'm the one certified by a national organization to provide home staging and professional organizing services. Mary-Margaret is here as part of the newly formed Enclave Tour Task Force."

Mary-Margaret nodded. "Task force. That's me."

"But my house isn't on the Enclave Tour anymore." Holly looked at Mary-Margaret. "So why are you here?"

"I'm in *training* as a professional organizer!" said Mary-Margaret with a smile that showed all her teeth.

Oh, jeez, thought Holly. God help the homeowners. She caught a glimpse of a tiny wad of pink gum at the back of Mary-Margaret's teeth.

"After this visit for home organizing, we're starting home visits for the Enclave Tour," explained Penelope.

"We drove together," Mary-Margaret added, thumb pointing over her shoulder at the Feathered Nest Realty car parked at the curb.

"Is now a good time?" asked Penelope.

"Um, actually, no," said Holly. *On what planet would anyone let a professional organizer into their house with no notice? Is this how it's done?* "I'm about to get my daughter on the bus. Can we set an appointment for later today or tomorrow? And why aren't you at your houses getting your families ready for school?"

"We made special arrangements," said Penelope.

"For you," said Mary-Margaret. "Oh! But don't feel bad for turning us away after we've come all the way to your doorstep to help you. I mean, if you *want* to feel bad, go ahead. Who am I to stop you?"

Penelope explained, "Surprise visits help me to best assess the needs of my client. When clients know I'm coming, they tend to straighten

212

up and even organize before I arrive, and that helps no one. If we can see how you live and function within your home, we can better develop a plan that suits your family's particular needs. Do you really want to reschedule? We're happy to—if this isn't a good time."

"Only *you* can determine if it's a good time," coached Mary-Margaret. "She's a certified professional organizer, and I'm on a task force, but you're in control, Holly, so don't feel pressured. *I* think it's a great time," she said, consulting with Penelope, "but the decision is up to you . . . so, which is it? Is it a great time or a good time for us to come in?" After waiting for Holly's response but receiving nothing, she continued. "Because I want you to know I'm perfectly okay if you say it's a good time. If that's your comfort level, we can step right in and get started. This is your home, Holly. You're in control."

"What are you doing?" Holly asked Mary-Margaret. "You're supposed to be working on your friendship skills."

"I am working on them," Mary-Margaret whined, baby blues appearing both eager and forlorn. "Why, am I messing up?" She looked at Penelope, who agreed with Holly. "I'm messing up, aren't I? But I was giving you a choice."

Holly's first, second, and third instincts were to reschedule. The house was a mess, and Ella needed to get to school, but, "Sure," she said, not wanting to admit defeat by turning them away. Holly had grown. Holly was secure. "Why not." Maybe Penelope was right. It probably did make the most sense for a professional organizer to see how you really lived. "Wait here," she instructed, closing the door, leaving them both on her front porch.

With Struggle hot on her trail, Holly rushed to the kitchen, where she whispered frantically to Ella, who was sitting at the table, hung over a bowl of cereal, "Quick! The professional organizers are here." She wasn't sure why, exactly, she was whispering. She supposed it felt natural, given the heated circumstances.

"Who?" asked Ella, wide eyed, hair still not brushed, shoes nowhere to be found. Struggle stood fully alert, thrilled the morning had taken this decidedly exciting turn.

How do you explain a professional organizer to a five-year-old? "They're like—fairy godmothers," said Holly. "From that 'Bibbidi-Bobbidi-Boo' song. It's like that. They wave magic wands, and *presto!*—socks are sorted, matched, and put away." Distracted, she spun around to quickly assess. "But first, we have to clean up. Like those mice and birds in *Cinderella*. You always clean before a fairy godmother arrives." That wasn't quite how the movie went, but close enough.

Like a hawk or a seagull or a pigeon in the park, Ella scrambled to stand on her chair. *"Squawk!"* she screeched, arms fluttering by her sides. She flung herself from her chair, landing with both feet on the floor, then flapped her wings across the kitchen, swooping down on a stack of clutter next to the refrigerator, clenching everything to her itty-bitty chest as she rushed, waist bent, toward the dishwasher.

"Ella—stop," said Holly, Struggle barking.

Opening the dishwasher with one hand, Ella attempted to shove everything inside—papers, bills, stapler—but at five, she couldn't manage, debris slipping from her grip, sliding all over the floor. "Noooo!" Ella wailed, head falling back, frustration overcoming her as her tiny shoulders shook, and she began to cry.

"Honey, it's okay," said Holly, stepping into the mess to pick Ella up to console her. "Thank you, sweetie. You were doing a great job. You were helping Mommy." Holly kissed Ella's cheek, smoothed her hair, rocking her side to side as Struggle kept trying but failing to lick Ella's moving feet. *What have I done? What kind of an example am I setting for my child? The Life-Changing Magic of Panic Baskets?* No. That wasn't the book Holly wanted placed on Ella's shelf. She looked around the kitchen at the dirty dishes on the counter, the laundry basket in the family room. The clutter. *Ef it—it's morning.* And then—*ef that. Doesn't matter what time it is. This is life. This is MY life. Life is messy—MY life is messy.* That was the book Holly wanted placed on Ella's shelf. The life-changing magic of knowing life was messy and being good with it. The doorbell rang.

"Ella, are you okay, sweetie?" She gave her a kiss.

Ella nodded, wiggling down from Holly's arms. "I'm good."

"Great," said Holly as she finished setting her down. Ella returned to her cereal bowl, and Holly gathered everything from the floor before placing it back on the counter. "I love you," she told Ella on the way to the front door. "You're a big help to Mommy. Thank you."

With a check on the time, "Come in! Penelope. Mary-Margaret. Come in," she said in her calmest, most welcoming voice, knowing both needed to slip past the support structure and should probably enter through the garage instead. Penelope took one long look up as she passed the support structure, Holly signaling to her they could talk about it later. Struggle by her side, Holly led them to the kitchen. "Ella was just finishing her cereal. Right on schedule!" piped Holly. "Right on schedule."

Ella set her spoon in her bowl, eyeing them with suspicion. Holly was sure Ella was sizing them up, deciding whether these women were indeed fairy godmothers.

"Mind if we take a quick peek?" asked Penelope, pointing to a kitchen cabinet. "And don't worry, Holly. All of this is so we can establish a course of action."

"To spark joy," said Mary-Margaret.

To spark joy, thought Holly.

"Oh, sure, sure. Go right ahead!" Holly said, flinching as the rubber lid to a casserole dish fell from an upper cabinet the moment Penelope opened it.

So her cabinets were a tad crowded. Big deal. It wasn't Holly's fault. The two-door, twenty-four-inch-wide cabinets above her counters were built with twelve-inch depths. Everyone knew nine by thirteen was the most popular size of casserole dish. Add the handles, and the dish

215

length you were dealing with was more like nine by fourteen. Putting this simple, commonly used dish away meant Holly had to open one side of the cabinet and then attempt to turn the dish crooked and sideways just to fit it into place. Never mind the stack of nested dishes that had to come *down* from the cabinet to rest a moment on the counter while the nine-by-thirteen was wrestled into place. By the time Holly got *those* back into the cabinet, the rubber lids that would undoubtedly start falling out always angered her. So she'd toss them into the cabinet like Frisbees—F.U. Frisbees, like the kind used by the moms in the F.U. Frisbee tournaments Holly had recently learned about. Was it *her* fault her cabinets were dangerous to open? No wonder most people hated their kitchens. There was never enough room.

Not wanting to witness another thing fall on anyone's head, Holly snatched the brush from the kitchen table and began brushing Ella's hair. She announced, "Oh! Will you look at the time! Out the door, Ella. Scoot! Scoot! Scoot! We have a bus to catch!" Holly slipped the cereal bowl and its unfinished puddle of milk out from in front of Ella. "Let's brush your teeth, sweetie," Holly urged. "Come on!"

"I'm too tired," whined Ella, head held like it was a bowling ball rolling backward off her shoulders. It was awful trying to get a five-year-old through breakfast and onto the bus with two women standing in her kitchen quietly passing judgment. Neither Penelope nor Mary-Margaret spoke—which had to be hard for Mary-Margaret, but maybe Penelope had told her she needed to keep her thoughts to herself if she was going to continue training her. Clipboards pressed to their chests, Penelope opened cabinet doors while Mary-Margaret took notes. What were they writing down? It wasn't weird Jack kept his vitamin bottles in the plate cabinet. Was it?

Holly scooped Ella into her arms, then carried her to the hall bath. "Open up!" Holly said in a singsongy voice, attempting to tuck Ella's electric toothbrush into her mouth while feeling the heat of Penelope and Mary-Margaret a few feet away. "Time to brush!" And then, quieter, "Come on, Ella. Please? Open your mouth. We have a bus to catch."

Stubborn, Ella clamped her lips together, shaking her head no.

Maybe what Ella wanted in front of Penelope and Mary-Margaret was to look like a big girl and brush her teeth all by herself. "Fine, Ella," said Holly, setting the readied toothbrush on the counter. "You do it. I'll grab your backpack and meet you at the front door."

Holly closed the bathroom door, leaving Ella alone inside. She retrieved Ella's backpack from a kitchen chair, then walked to the front door to wait patiently for Ella to emerge from the bathroom. She waited. And waited. But nothing. No Ella. "Ella? How's it going, honey? You just about finished?"

Why had she let them inside? What a stupid decision. Next time a professional organizer showed up at her door unannounced, Holly would reschedule. To heck with rolling with the punches. That never worked. "Ella Bella Cinderella," said Holly, using her sweetest voice. "Walk to the front door, please. We need to get to the driveway."

Still nothing. Holly slid past the support structures holding the ceiling up and then marched to the hall bath and knocked on the door. "Ella? Let me in."

Ella opened the door—alarming Holly because Ella had opened the door by leaning backward from a kneeling position on the counter. Having climbed from her stool onto the counter, Ella was now standing on her knees, licking her reflection in the mirror. Fearing she might fall, Holly grabbed hold of Ella's waist. "What are you doing? You're supposed to be brushing your teeth."

"I'm trying to lick my eyes, but all I can lick is my tongue," said Ella, licking sloppy circles all over the mirror. Meanwhile, her electric toothbrush lay vibrating on the counter.

Having a closer look, Holly realized Ella was right. No matter where she moved her tongue on the mirror, if she lived the rest of her life trying to lick her eyes, she would only ever make contact with the tip of her tongue.

"Climb down from here, Ella," Holly coached, helping her off the counter.

"Who are those mean ladies?" asked Ella on the way down.

"They're not mean, honey. They're here to help. Now will you *please* help Mommy?" Holly placed both of her hands in prayer position. "We need to clean your teeth."

"More cleaning?"

"More cleaning," said Holly, "but we have to hurry. The bus is coming."

"Got it," said Ella, big smile for Holly. She snatched her toothbrush, lifted the lid on the toilet seat, and then tossed it in the water and closed the lid. "Ta-da! Just like you, Mommy."

"Ella, noooo—" Holly lifted the lid to find a jumpy toothbrush bouncing and splashing around the bowl like a windup pool toy. She dropped the lid, hearing a continuous *zzzzz, ba-bump-ump-ump!* from inside.

"Everything okay?" Mary-Margaret asked, tapping on the bathroom door. "I heard a bang."

"We're fine!"—*zzzzz, ba-bump-ump-ump!*—hollered Holly. "All good." *Zzzzz, ba-bump-ump-ump!*

"We're cleaning!" yelled Ella, bouncy, springing up from her stool to get another look at her reflection in the mirror. She stuck her tongue out, leaning in, trying to lick her eyes.

"All righty then," from Mary-Margaret. "We'll be out here if you need anything . . ."

Holly lifted the lid—toothbrush flipping, flopping, splattering about. *Ugh!* She closed the lid. *Should I flush?* Whoooosh! She flushed, emptying the water from the bowl, leaving the toothbrush banging loudly against the porcelain. She grabbed a hand towel to cover her hand, then reached in to grab the toothbrush before the water began refilling the bowl. *Blech. So gross.* She switched the toothbrush off and dropped it and the towel into the trash can before rigorously washing her hands with soap, telling Ella, "Electric toothbrushes aren't cheap. *Don't* do that again." Bye-bye, expensive toothbrush. Bye-bye, hand towel.

Hands clean, she grabbed the tube of toothpaste. "Lick your eyes, Ella," she said, taking the opportunity to squeeze a drop of paste on Ella's outstretched tongue as she tried licking her eyes in the mirror. She scooped Ella from the counter and onto her hip. "Lick your teeth, Ella. Your actual teeth." After handing her a cup of water, she leaned Ella over the sink. "Now spit. We have a bus to catch."

Before heading to the bus, Holly popped her head into the kitchen.

"Mary-Margaret and Penelope, I want your help. I know I asked for your help. But right now? I'm feeling a little bit out of control. Maybe because you've surprised me—if you told me you were coming, I forgot to write it down. Anyway. I don't know. But if you wouldn't mind, please join me on the front porch until I get Ella on the school bus, and then the three of us can reenter the house and have a cup of coffee before beginning. Agreed?"

Penelope glanced at Mary-Margaret before telling Holly, "Yes, of course."

"Thank you," said Holly, proud to be maintaining control when Mary-Margaret was around. Sending them home or rescheduling might have ended Holly's discomfort, but Holly decided that wasn't an option. It was hard asking for help, but the unpacking, the clutter, the lack of storage—all of that needed to get resolved. It was time. Panic baskets? *Clean Enough: The Holly Banks Method?* Ella had tossed a toothbrush in the toilet. She learned that from Holly. No more. Or at least, less.

~

After Ella caught the bus, they all had coffee, and Penelope explained how things typically proceeded during a home organization audit. The reason she suggested beginning in the kitchen: it was the easiest to declutter and organize because people rarely harbored emotional attachments to kitchen items. Coloring books, on the other hand . . .

"I searched 'organizing coloring books,'" said Holly a little while later, "but everything I found online was for storing *new* coloring books or coloring books currently in use." She hoisted an oversize plastic tub onto the kitchen table.

"They're complete?" asked Penelope, a look of either concern or confusion on her face. "Finished? No more pages to color?"

"Completely finished. Every last page," said Holly, proud, excited to share. "Would you like to see one?" She handed Penelope a Disney's *Frozen* coloring book, Elsa and Anna on the cover, then leaned over to relive the pages as Penelope thumbed through. Holly laughed, pointing. "We wore *at least* eight white crayons to the nub finishing that coloring book. Ha!" She shook her head, remembering. "Snow. So much snow! Everything was frozen," Holly explained.

"So I see," said Penelope, looking up from the coloring book, eyeing Mary-Margaret, who shrugged, offering Penelope this advice: "Let us not think of this client as hopeless. Instead, let us bring hope to this hopeless client."

"What are you talking about?" said Holly. "Organized in this tub are all of Ella's completed coloring books. All of them. And each one was numbered—*by me*, in Sharpie marker." *How do you like me now?* "I cataloged Ella's first-ever coloring book to her most recent. And! I put the date below the number documenting Ella's age when she started it and when she finished it. Look." To prove it, she pointed to a 2.3–2.5 in the top-right corner. "Two years, three months old all the way to two years, five months old. How is that not organized? In fact," she pointed out, "you could say the Banks family coloring books are *colorganized.*

Ha!" She winked at Penelope before getting serious: "You can use that in an Enclave Alert if you want to."

"Or not," said Mary-Margaret. She shook her pretty little head toward Penelope while whispering, "No one does this."

"They might," said Holly. "If someone explained it to them." It was brilliant. Pinterestworthy. Short-tutorial-on-YouTube-worthy, right?

Holly flipped to the most recent, number 62, cataloged about a month ago, pausing to flip through it, feeling a slight pang in her heart as she realized just how *big* Ella was becoming. *So big!* And how truly advanced her coloring. It seemed to happen overnight. Once a master scribbler—that chubby little hand of hers at two and three using the flailing movement of her hand and wrist to annihilate a picture—and now? She was a freaking Picasso! Some pictures still a bit askew, but *holy moly, look at that control.*

"Look at this," said Holly, opening number 62 to show them a spread. "See how far she's come since this?" She opened number 48, then number 20. "Isn't that amazing? It's like a scrapbook or photo album, but art. You can retrace her steps. Watch her growing up. And sure, they're not *photographs*, but almost. *I* can see Ella in these drawings. I was with her. *I* can see her in the waxy Crayola colors of tickle me pink, sky blue, and bittersweet." It almost brought tears to her eyes—okay, it did. "I'm sorry," she apologized, realizing she was getting emotional. "But have you noticed the eight-count Crayola box has simple, pure color names like red, yellow, and blue? But by the time you—okay, I'm just going to say it—*grow up*, and you reach the one-hundred-twenty-count box, you're on to color names with meaning and history like piggy pink and lavender." At the mention of those two color names, which stirred up all sorts of memories of Ella's first week of kindergarten and the mayhem that ensued between Holly and Mary-Margaret, she shot an angry glance toward Mary-Margaret to keep her in check. *Don't say a word. And don't you dare call me Lavender.* "Anyway, I can't help but think the one-hundred-twenty-count box has grown-up, 'big girl' color names like big dip o'ruby, mauvelous, and razzmic berry. I mean, hello? What's razzmic? That's such a cool word. Deep space sparkle? Unmellow yellow? By the time you're coloring with those color names, you're talking about all sorts of things, like how tomatoes get inside ketchup bottles and why glue doesn't stick to the inside of the glue bottle." It surprised Holly just how much this was bothering her, talking about colors. Big-girl, grown-up colors. Her nose stung. She felt her eyes welling with tears. "The other day, Ella asked me if her pinkie and thumb were younger than her other fingers."

"Let's refocus. Shall we?" suggested Penelope, appraising the tub of coloring books, presumably wondering what to say next.

"I'm just so proud of the work Ella has done in these coloring books," said Holly. "Solid evidence of progress." Mary-Margaret, whose youngest, Mary-Caroline, was in Ella's class, stepped in to take a much closer look than Penelope, mother to a junior in high school who probably never colored a day in his life.

"I know exactly what you're saying, Holly," Mary-Margaret began, picking up number 56 to thumb through a few pages. "For us, the moment we coached Mary-Caroline to 'stay within the lines,' she picked it up lickety-split." She snapped her fingers. "Just like that. But what was truly miraculous was witnessing how 'staying within the boundaries of a picture' had taught Mary-Caroline visuospatial abilities. You know, architecture?"

"Architecture?" said Holly, growing concerned. She hadn't thought about visuospatial abilities. *Visuospatial abilities?* She took a closer look at a picture Ella had colored of an elephant standing on a beach ball, angry she hadn't noticed the blatant misrepresentation of physics. What kind of message had Ella received while coloring? An elephant would never stand on a beach ball.

"Geometric shapes too," Mary-Margaret was quick to point out. "Although, Mary-Caroline was way beyond the eight-count box, so she already knew circle, square . . . *quadrilateral*." She shrugged a thin, pointed shoulder, dropping number 56 back in the bin. "And so, you know me! Silly me! I just launched right into three-dimensional geometric shapes, and well, before you know it, Mary-Caroline had advanced to triangular prisms and dodecahedrons. You know what I'd suggest for you?" she asked, tapping a finger on the elephant. "Try prepositions. If Ella is coloring within the lines, point out the space *around* the lines," she overenunciated, "*above* the ball, and *below* the elephant. See if that helps."

"Helps?" said Holly, begging to differ. "Ella doesn't need help."

Penelope jumped in with, "Of course not. And these are precious coloring books, Holly. Wonderful memories of mother-and-child time spent together." She scowled at Mary-Margaret.

"Oh, I agree!" said Mary-Margaret, blinking her baby blues. "And I didn't mean to *offend*. I meant to *suggest*."

"Is that what this is?" Holly asked Penelope, rethinking the appointment she had set to get organized. Rethinking her willingness to give Mary-Margaret another chance. "I share Ella's coloring books with you, and now *she's* talking dodecahedrons?"

"I'm sorry, I'm sorry, I'm sorry!" cried Mary-Margaret, wincing. She slapped her forehead. "I did it again, didn't I?"

"Will you excuse us?" Penelope said to Mary-Margaret, pulling Holly by the arm into the foyer as Mary-Margaret called after them, "I promise I won't mention the battery Mary-Caroline built with copper wire and a potato!"

Out of earshot, "Don't listen to her," said Penelope. "She doesn't know what she's talking about."

"She's ruining my memories," said Holly. "Belittling them." Holly was so angry she could spit. "Twisting something sweet into something competitive."

"She's a narcissist," reminded Penelope. "You know that. She's utterly incapable of surviving a *moment* where someone else is in the spotlight."

"She sucks the air out of the room," cried Holly. "And honestly? I'm beginning to wonder if she even knows she's doing it."

"Don't listen to her. Tune her out. I'm sure half of what she said about Mary-Caroline was completely fabricated—my son's a junior in high school. I've been around the block a few times with this competitive crap parents do."

"Does it get easier?" asked Holly, worried Ella's flunking her pre-pre-reading test was the start of a difficult road ahead.

"Oh, trust me. It gets worse, culminating in college bumper stickers moms and dads use to 'brand' their cars and families. It's all so stupid. Let's try again, shall we?" she suggested, luring Holly back into the kitchen before saying, "I agree your colorganizing method is a good one, but I suspect you might be having a little trouble throwing sentimental things away." They stopped at the tub of coloring books on Holly's kitchen table. "This is an easy fix," Penelope announced. "I can help."

"How?" asked Holly. She had tried and failed many times to throw a coloring book away. Sometimes, it would sit in the trash can while Holly tried distracting herself, the coloring book a broken heart inside the can, only to be pulled out again by Holly before Jack or Ella or Greta threw something in on top of it.

"Close your eyes," said Mary-Margaret, slyly lifting a coloring book from the tub.

"What are you doing?" asked Holly.

"Nothing. Never mind," said Mary-Margaret, tiptoeing backward toward the trash can until she was standing in front of it, coloring book hidden behind her back.

"You know I can see you," said Holly. To Penelope, she said, "I'm not falling for that horse hockey. I know what she's doing."

"Let's just *try*," said Mary-Margaret, tucking the coloring book slowly through the lid's swinging flap until it dropped onto the trash inside the can.

"Absolutely not!" Holly charged past Mary-Margaret, slinging the lid from the trash can, letting it crash to the floor. She dove in to rescue number 57. "Don't you dare throw my coloring books away."

"*Your* coloring books?" asked Mary-Margaret, acting as if she'd just cracked the code. Some dumb, ridiculous professional organizer code. "Is this about you? Or is this about Ella?"

Penelope suggested, "Maybe we can save your favorite coloring book from each year of Ella's life?"

"Throw more than fifty-five coloring books away?" asked Holly, feeling horrible inside. She imagined them sitting in a recycling bin at the curb. Um—no. That was like throwing their time together away. To Holly, that felt like throwing Ella away. Her chubby little toddler, preschool, kindergarten hands had worked so hard to color something pretty. Ella often hummed or sang when she colored. She'd say the craziest things. "Absolutely not." Holly shook her head, clutching number 57, pressing it against her chest, surprised by her sudden onset of emotions. "I can't do it."

"Perhaps we can scan your favorite pages? Create a digital scrapbook?" Penelope tried.

But Holly didn't like that suggestion either. She wanted to keep all of them. She wanted to *add* to the collection. "Ever since Ella started kindergarten, she's given up on coloring. I mean, not *completely*. She still does it. But recently, she's started cutting back. She comes home from school tired." Holly slid the palm of her hand across the cover of the coloring book. Felt the smoothness of the cover, considered the mother hen on the cover reading a book to her baby chick. Something caught in Holly's throat when she said, "The other day, when I asked her if she wanted to color, she told me she had already colored at school." The last fully completed coloring book was number 62. Their current coloring book was number 63, and they were hardly through the first ten pages. What if they never finished? *Is this how it happens? One day, the coloring just stops?*

Mary-Margaret asked again, gentle this time. Not biting or condescending. She really wanted to know: "Is this about you? Or is this about Ella?"

"I think it's both," said Holly. Colorganizing had given her the chance to sit with Ella, lie on the floor with Ella. Record and document the precious growth and development of this amazing little girl. They played *My Little Pony* together all the time, but these coloring books—they stood as evidence. *We were here. We were together in the pages of this book. Look at us. You can SEE us.* How could she toss that out? Life was once fat, chubby crayons in red, yellow, and blue, and then, in the blink of an eye, life became razzmic berry. "I can't throw this away," she told them. "I can't throw any of them away. I can still see her. I can see her in her art." Like a photo rendered in the waxy Crayola colors of tickle me pink, sky blue, and bittersweet.

27

Holly and Jack stood at the foot of the ladder that a contractor stood on, shining a flashlight into the foyer ceiling. They both knew he was about to tell them what they'd already figured out.

"I suspect the previous homeowner converted a two-story entryway into an upstairs bathroom," he said. No surprise there. "And I think they did a pretty lousy job." Also no surprise. "There's no support."

Jack bent at the waist, resting his hands above his knees. He dropped his head in defeat, not saying a word.

"That's what we thought, but what does this mean?" Holly asked. "You're not thinking the *bathtub* could fall through the ceiling, are you?" When in fact that was *exactly* what Holly and Jack thought might happen, but sometimes it wasn't real until someone told you it was real.

"It could," said the contractor.

"Jack? Say something," said Holly, trying not to panic but finding it hard watching Jack morph from mildly alarmed to freaked out to completely defeated.

The contractor climbed down from the ladder, explaining, "They should have run crosswise support beams to hold the weight of the bathtub—especially when it's filled with water. And the plumbing? It doesn't pass muster at all. I suspect you have problems with the tub *and* the shower. The toilet base isn't caulked, and I couldn't find evidence plumber's putty was used for sealing, so nothing in that room is watertight. That's probably what started the water staining on your ceiling in the first place. Your dog just finished the job for you. Everything will need to be ripped out and replaced: the foyer, the bathroom upstairs." He climbed down from the ladder. "The bathtub looks pretty fancy to me," he said, having already been upstairs. "Maybe it was just for show. Maybe that's why they didn't take the time to install it properly. People have been known to do all sorts of things to sell a house."

"What? No," said Holly, shaking her head. "We have no reason to believe the previous homeowners did this on purpose." Because what would that mean? What did that imply? Collette was a real estate con artist? All of this was a facade? Smoke and mirrors?

"Do you know if they were flippers?" the contractor asked.

"Flippers?" said Holly, considering Collette and her *massive* following on social media. Collette's branding reminded Holly of a power couple on TV who built an empire renovating homes. In fact, Holly distinctly remembered a post Collette shared on Pinterest expressing her excitement about moving to Dillydally so she could start decorating and pinning a new house. But—she had only lived in Dillydally a month. She wasn't amping up to move again, was she? "No, I don't think they're *flippers*," she said, looking at Jack. "I mean, I don't think they're running an official *business* flipping homes. Although, that doesn't mean they aren't. Penelope did mention Collette moves a lot. And her home's on the Enclave Tour. But—she's a mom at Primm Academy. There's no way she'd try to get away with something like this."

"Then I'd say they were probably doing their best," said the contractor. "Some homeowners are do-it-yourselfers. Maybe they thought they did everything right."

"So what's the damage?" asked Jack. "What do you think it will take to fix this?"

"Depends on what you're fixing. Repairing the pipes and closing the ceiling? My guess? A few grand. Removing the tub, ripping out damaged subflooring before mold sets in—"

"Mold?" said Holly, sharp glance toward Jack.

"Building a proper support structure, running better pipes, doing the plumbing the right way, retiling the bathroom floor, reinstalling the bathtub?" The contractor stopped, appearing to calculate costs in his head. "Add trim work . . . painting. That'll run closer to ten grand."

Jack let out a sound like he was about to blow a gasket.

"But that," said the contractor, pointing with the battery end of his flashlight toward the door opening Jack had created between the living room and dining room, "that's crazy. Did they do that too? Because that's just stupid."

When Jack didn't answer, Holly asked, "Why? What's wrong with it?"

"It's not expensive to fix, but whoever did that is compromising the structure of the house. If you leave it like that, that's way worse than your bathtub issues. That's a load-bearing wall." He said it like, *Duh, anyone knows that.*

"But it's not that wide. It was only opened an additional—what, like three feet? Maybe four?" said Holly.

"Well, it needs to be fixed. It can't stay like that," he said. "You need to install a load-bearing beam, and it needs to be repaired according to code. If I were you, I'd hire a professional."

Jack opened the front door, marched down the front porch steps, and then proceeded to trek across the lawn toward the co-op gardens in the cul-de-sac. Was he mad? Distraught? Holly couldn't tell. Maybe both?

"Um, sorry," she said, surprised Jack left without saying anything.

"No problem. Hey, I get it." He shook his head as if pitying them for being in this situation. "If you want, I can prepare a quote." He lifted the hinges to close the ladder and then propped it against the wall.

"In the meantime, I can have my crew out here later today to properly secure the place and patch it up for safety. It'll look bad but be safe and functional. I wouldn't wait if I were you."

"Do it."

"Today?"

"Like, now. If you can," said Holly. They had no choice. Safety came first.

"The whole job or just securing it?"

"Right now, secure it. Make it safe and functional. I don't care what it looks like," she said. They could pore over the quote and figure out how to pay for the big repairs later.

~

Contractor gone, when Jack finally returned, Holly was watching Struggle in the backyard from the window above the kitchen sink, thinking their issues about Struggle getting loose weren't resolved; Struggle could slip through a gap in the fence in seconds flat. All she had to do was clamp her teeth onto the wire mesh and pull backward, snapping the staples off, exposing opportunities between the planks of wood in the split-rail fence.

"Hey," said Jack, joining her in the kitchen, *Primm Gazette* and some mail beneath his arm as Holly was letting Struggle back inside. "Looks like you got a letter from that guy at Mappamundi."

"Really? That's odd," said Holly, slicing open the envelope to read the letter. "He's inviting me to his shop to look at a replica of an astrolabe. Why?"

"Maybe he thinks you'd be interested."

"Should I go?"

"Why not? What do you have to lose?"

"Maybe." She let out a sigh. "I told the contractor to send a crew out today to secure both the foyer and the open wall in the living room.

They're installing a temporary header in the living room and will build a support structure beneath it. In the foyer, pretty much the same thing. That will buy us some time until they can come back to start the actual repair."

"Thank you," said Jack, taking a seat at the kitchen table.

"The house is safe to live in, but we can't use the front door." With a half-spirited laugh, she slid into a chair beside him and then admitted, "When I first signed on to the Enclave Tour, I was so concerned about Collette seeing what I had done with the place. And yet *she's* the one who enclosed a two-story foyer to expand a master bathroom? I'm so angry right now I'm almost numb."

"There's nothing we can do about it," said Jack, resigned to dealing with it. "Although, I admit my level of anger about the situation was off the charts when I walked out on that guy."

"It wasn't his fault. He was just telling us what we already knew. What I can't get over is why do *we* have to get stuck with this? Can we sue?"

"For what? How would we prove they did anything willfully wrong? They're probably do-it-yourselfers. I took out a load-bearing wall."

"True." Holly supposed he was right to let it go. They bought the house contingent upon inspection, and the house inspection didn't pick it up. Except for there being no caulk where the toilet met the floor, you couldn't say it was a problem hidden in plain sight. It was hidden within the floor and ceiling. No sense blaming the house inspector. And maybe Thom was right. Bad luck, good luck, or dumb luck, maybe the answer was "D: none of the above." It happened. Deal with it. "You know what helps me with my anger? Knowing this isn't personal. We're experiencing it, but they didn't do this *to us*," said Holly. "Bad things happen to good people all the time. What matters is how we handle it."

"Roll with the punches."

"Go with the flow." Holly fell quiet. "It still sucks." What Holly wanted to know was this: Why *did* she idolize Collette when moving into this house? Because Collette knew how to decorate? Pick pretty colors?

When Collette lived here, it was her home. Collette's home where Collette's family lived. But on the day the property transferred from the Williams family to the Banks family, Collette's home stopped being a home. It became a house. A structure. Something solid and concrete that could be described in terms of brick foundation, fiber-composite siding, windows, shutters, doors, front porch, a shoddy bathroom remodel, and a foyer improperly enclosed. A house became a home when the people living within it called it that; when they felt it. When all roads led to one place. When there was no place you'd rather be. A house was an object. A home was a place, something you felt in your heart. As Mary-Margaret would say, *Hip! Hip!*

"Oh, hey," said Jack, sliding the *Primm Gazette* toward himself upon noticing a headline. He opened the paper to full view, telling Holly, "You know that horticulturist from England? The guy who specializes in ivies and boxwoods? Says here he traveled to Primm with a representative from Neem Oil."

"Why is he traveling with someone from the oil-and-gas industry? That's odd," said Holly.

"Not oil and gas," said Jack, reading further. "Neem oil is a pesticide. Says here it's been in use as a pesticide for hundreds of years and it comes from the seeds of the neem tree. It's naturally occurring; can be formulated into dust, powder, granules, or concentrate; and it should work on the chilli thrips."

"What? No way," said Holly, walking over to read the *Gazette* over Jack's shoulder. "'In the evening, spread diatomaceous earth at the base of the plant and on the plant's leaves to desiccate the chilli thrips and their larvae. Then apply neem oil around the plant's base and on both sides of the plant's leaves.' Jack!" She gave him a high five. "Do you think this is it? Could this mean the end of the chilli thrip infestation?"

"Maybe," said Jack, almost as encouraged as Holly was. Oh, yes, please. *Please!*

She checked the time. "I have to go to the store to buy supplies for a gathering Mom's having at the house on Friday. Something she's calling a Crock-Pot Pit Stop."

"She has friends? She just got here. The only friend I have is Malik."

"Not just friends but a Scrabble study group. Haven't you noticed? She's never here. She's always out. They're gearing up for the Scrabble tournaments coming to Primm next month. Hold up. What's this?" said Holly, taking the paper from Jack to read a small box in the lower right-hand corner. "Penelope's teasing another crossword puzzle clue."

<u>DOWN</u>

NUMBER 11. NOM DE _____; PEN NAME (FIVE LETTERS)

He stood from the kitchen table to walk toward the front door.

"Jack, what's wrong?" she asked, following him into the foyer, noticing an odd look on his face, a tightness in his shoulders. He stopped beneath the hole in the ceiling, looking up. "Is everything okay?" she asked.

But he remained quiet, pensive. And then he said it. Four little words. "I lost my job."

"What?"

"I was fired. I was waiting for the right time to tell you, but none came."

"When, today?"

"A week ago."

"A *week* ago?"

He nodded. "Those important meetings? Senior VP from Human Resources flew in to escort the entire Special Projects team out the door."

"Bethanny too?" she asked, wondering if his boss—the woman responsible for their moving from Boulder City to the Village of Primm—lost her job.

"Bethanny too. All of our hard work—in the end, none of it mattered. Getting rid of us was a face-saving move for the firm." He exhaled, rubbing his temple in a way that showed his stress. "I guess I can't blame them. Everyone's trying to save their own neck."

"Wow. So that's why you've been sick? No, wait—"

"I wasn't sick."

"No. I guess you weren't," she said. She hadn't *really* questioned it while it was happening, but sure. Now that she thought about it, there hadn't been any medications lying around, no cold remedy, no thermometer. "Why didn't you tell me?" she asked. "It happened a week ago? We're supposed to be a team. Why lie about being sick?"

"I'm sorry, Holly, I've never lost a job before." He took a moment to look around their house—she presumed, to take it all in. To assess all that had happened. The ceiling above him, the wall he'd removed between the living room and dining room that was now compromising the structural integrity of their home.

"I'm your wife," she said. "We're supposed to communicate." *Oh, Jack. I'm so sorry.* She reached over to hold his hand, piecing things together. His concern over her starting her own business—that wasn't about her working from home as opposed to her working for an employer. That was about the money they'd have to spend to establish a film studio. And he'd mentioned the possibility they might have to sell the house—concerned a film studio in the dining room was a bad idea. It was a remark she'd dismissed, even felt angry about, but now, it all made sense. His frustration when she called saying she wanted a she shed. And what a ridiculous thing for her to talk about when all along, he must have sensed he was about to lose his job—and then he did. "Did they give you a package?"

"Six months of income and six months of job placement services with a professional headhunter," he said. "I think they were generous, given the circumstances."

"Okay, then," said Holly, encouraged by this. That was more than most people got. No doubt, after all that had happened with the firm, they wanted everyone to land on their feet. "We have time. We'll stay afloat for six months. No need to panic."

"Yet."

"You'll find work," she said softly. But would he? He just got fired from a firm caught up in a high-profile scandal.

"Let's hope."

The question was—when. When would he get a job? And—where? Holly didn't want to think about it, but what if this meant they'd have to leave Primm? Both fell silent for a few minutes, together in the situation but separate in thought.

"I took the house off the Enclave Tour—it's not safe," said Holly. "But maybe I should ramp up efforts to start my own business while you explore options with the headhunter."

He nodded but said nothing.

"Jack, what if I used the business loan—not to buy furniture to set the living room and dining room up as a film studio but to buy a she shed instead?"

"A she shed?" He almost sounded angry.

"Hear me out," she said. "I can't show the house. I can't bring clients inside. I can't stay on the Enclave Tour. I'm trying to launch a brand-new business in a town I just moved to a month ago. We don't have money lying around for advertising and marketing. Penelope's Enclave Tour was the perfect venue for getting a lot of free publicity— fast. So now, the question becomes: What's the best, most frugal way for me to get up and running and making money as soon as possible? I think I should stage the she shed as the film studio."

"I don't know," he said. She watched him fold his arms across his chest.

"I know it sounds like a risk, but I could be up and running in a week's time. If I try to do it here, inside the house, it would take a lot longer and cost a lot more. For one, I'll miss the Enclave Tour opportunity and all that provides, and two, it'll cost a lot more than a shed because we can't bring people inside the house until we repair all of the damage. Our bathtub might fall through the ceiling. But if I'm working in the backyard out of the she shed, I can hopefully start making some money while repairs are happening in the house and you're looking for work."

"Good point." He was buying in. Jack was buying in!

"I'm a cash-strapped new business. If I'm *not* on the tour, I'm starting at a disadvantage. I really think we should go for it. And trust me, a she shed—there's just something about it. I think it will attract *more* attention to the business than if I was set up in the dining room. Don't laugh—but a business run out of a she shed is Instagram-worthy. That's good publicity. Plus, it could be a way to add some value to the home if we did have to sell. Which I don't think we will. But maybe while you are lining up your next job, you might have a bit of extra time to help me get all the—"

"I agree," he said, nodding his head, rubbing his hands together in that "Jack" way he did when he was thinking, letting his Virgo mind consider all the options. "Yes. You should do it."

Really?

"Okay," said Holly with an exhale. *Whoa.* At that moment, what had long been Holly's dream became Holly's job. Ready or not, Holly Banks Productions was in business. No longer *planning*. Holly was *doing*. It was go time.

"I believe in you," said Jack, before averting his eyes.

"And I believe in you," she said, wanting him to know how much she loved him. "You'll find work, Jack. It'll be okay. I know it will." She stepped toward him to wrap her arms around him, the two of them beneath the hole in the ceiling. Their sky had fallen. But together, Holly and Jack would weather whatever was dealt them. They had to. They had no other choice.

"This might be a bad time," she whispered, still tucked within his embrace, "but I know the perfect chandelier to hang above our heads." She smiled, imagining the chandelier she saw in the hallway outside of Penelope's office, the one with the gilded twigs forming a bird's nest above twelve fat-bellied glass birds. Maybe she could convince Penelope to sell it to her for a good price. Hey, a girl could dream.

28

HOLLY: Any chance you need another she shed on the tour?
PENELOPE: Right now, Mary-Margaret's is the only one. Why?
HOLLY: Well . . .

29

TO: Miss Bently, Primm Academy
FROM: Holly Banks
CC: Jack Banks
SUBJECT: Reading Readiness Skills Packets

I noticed Reading Readiness Skills Packets were sent home in today's backpacks.

I'm encouraged to see many of the activities involve coloring.

I'm happy to share my Colorganizing Method with other parents if you think it would be helpful.

30

Prepping for Greta's Crock-Pot Pit Stop, Holly counted RSVPs . . . *six, seven, eight*. Eight people in total were coming; two were staff from the funeral home that Greta now counted as friends—Ruth and Henry—but also, friends Javina, Lottie, and Darnell were coming, as were Houston and Aahna Patel. Greta made eight. All of them had been told by Greta to bring family-size slow cookers and twenty bucks to pay for their portion of the groceries. On the menu? Greta's recipe for chicken-taco soup, which she pitched as the perfect meal for getting drunk while watching football. Every time Holly heard Greta say that—a part of her would stiffen, fearing Greta, who gave up drinking years ago, would take her own advice and pop a cold one while watching the Broncos.

Greta and Houston were picking up Javina and Lottie, who didn't drive, so Holly was left to double-check ingredients from the list Greta gave her, making sure all the assembly stations Greta so carefully established throughout the kitchen had the right quantity of food.

Greta said everyone would arrive promptly at 10:00 a.m. for happy hour and socializing while assembling the meal, then leave by noon to get home to plug in their slow cookers and take naps so that the taco soup would be ready by kickoff. "This is for Lottie," said Greta, setting out supplies for Bloody Marys. "Lottie's the drinker."

"Isn't it a bit early for drinking?" Holly had asked. "I mean, good gravy, Ma, it's ten o'clock in the morning. I'm not sure that qualifies as happy hour."

"Do it," Greta ordered, stabbing a finger into Holly's chest. "When you've reached our age, you answer to no one."

"Well, then," said Holly, hands up in surrender. "I see you've joined a gang."

And that was how Holly came to find herself mixing Bloody Marys at almost ten o'clock on a Friday morning, ready to welcome a gang of seniors through her patched-together foyer. She heard a knock at the door.

Struggle lifted her head to offer a half-hearted, noncommittal "woof!" as if it were an afterthought, something hardly worth exertion. Maybe Struggle knew there was no cause for concern, that whoever was on the other side of the door posed no threat? It occurred to Holly she needed to ask Jack where things stood with Thom.

Holly opened the door to Greta and Houston and a round of introductions. They weren't *supposed* to use the front door, but using the garage for everything was a pain, so everyone simply slipped past the support structures. The contractor would be here Monday to fix everything. Seventy-two more hours, and the house mayhem should be over.

"This is Javina and Lottie," Greta began, one hand covering her eye.

"Mom, are you okay?"

"I'm fine. Just a bit of eye pain."

"Eye pain?"

Greta waved her off, continuing with the introductions.

Javina, tall and lean in a khaki jumpsuit and long ivory cardigan that lengthened her silhouette, guided an older, shorter, pudgier Lottie-with-a-hat through the door. Lottie's dress skirted her ankles, and her pale-gray hat made of loosely woven sinamay shaped into a ginormous flower was perched forward and off-center on her head like a peony or dahlia staring you straight in the eye. With a crooked, swollen-knuckled, arthritic finger, Lottie touched Holly on the shoulder. "Get me a drink, will you, honey?"

"Yes, of course," said Holly, reaching to help with slow cookers as the guests entered.

"And this is Darnell," said Greta, huge smile on her face, hand still covering her eye. "He's practically a Scrabble master."

Darnell was the young one (maybe midforties?), sturdy, and with a Howie Long flattop. He carried three slow cookers stacked one on top of the other (presumably Javina's and Lottie's?). Henry and Ruth came next, then sweet Aahna, tiny, but clearly with strong arm muscles as she carried her family-size Crock-Pot almost beneath her chin.

Greta wasn't kidding. The crowd enjoyed their morning beverages—except for Ruth and Greta, who were drinking iced tea. On one of her passes through the kitchen, Holly stopped to watch Greta strumming a few tunes for everyone on her ukulele, after Houston yelled, "Free Bird!" the moment she sat down to perform. Vintage aviator goggles on her forehead holding her hair back, favorite black dress and black military boots on, her rendition of Monty Python's "Always Look on the Bright Side of Life" was a big hit—everyone laughing and singing along—but it was "City of Stars" from the movie *La La Land* that really got to Holly for some reason.

Maybe it was the sudden turn from fun and games with Greta to the serious, soulful sound Holly heard in her voice, the way her face seemed to drop, no longer happy go lucky but instead lost somewhere. Distant. Was she still feeling lonely? Holly leaned against the counter by the fridge as she watched a side of her mother she didn't often see come forward through a song that was tender and emotionally bruising. Her mom, small at five feet two inches, growing older with each passing day, head of curly gray hair, and suddenly vulnerable, exposed, almost weakened by the lyrics, the strumming, the pain in her eye she was so clearly feeling.

"Mom, are you feeling okay?" Holly asked.

Concert over, Greta set her ukulele aside, looking up briefly to deliver an odd, very peculiar look to Holly as Ruth and Henry passed around what they announced was a strategy document in sealed envelopes, pitching a meeting next week to discuss ways they could all work together as a team to—Henry's word—*annihilate* competitors in the upcoming Scrabble tournament.

Holly walked over to place her hand on the back of Greta's chair, leaning in to whisper, "Does your eye still hurt?"

"Go away," Greta whispered.

"Migraine?"

"Go back to what you were doing. I'm having a party here." Greta pushed Holly away.

"Mom."

"You're embarrassing me," said Greta.

"Oh, what. Now you're a teenager?"

Ruth announced, "EW and OK were added," referring to acceptable words recently added to the Scrabble dictionary.

"And TWERK,'" said Henry. "Don't forget TWERK."

"Do you want some aspirin?" Holly asked.

"Go." Greta pushed Holly to the side.

"Fine, I give up," said Holly, thinking her mom could be so bullheaded sometimes. "I'll be in the dining room." As she passed Houston, she muttered, "Is she okay?"

He shrugged, whispering back, "I asked. She said she has a headache."

With Charlotte somewhere in the house and Struggle on the ground at Holly's feet, she stayed out of their way, laptop, bullet journal, and printed papers in front of her on the dining room table.

She opened her laptop to review notes of the four scenes she recently wrote and later shot, picking up from the scene that had ended with a bird flying onto a welcome mat on the front porch of 12 Petunia Lane the moment "Audrey" fetched a newspaper as her tutu-clad dog ran toward the neighbor's yard. The stop-motion Holly was creating didn't have any words or dialogue, just a whimsical tune she downloaded from a royalty-free site. She began typing, capitalizing the first appearance of character names in each scene.

—WILHELM KLAUS FILM FESTIVAL ENTRY—

FADE IN:

SCENE 5 — EXT. FRONT YARD THEN VILLAGE — CONTINUOUS

    Chasing her tutu-clad DOG from the front porch, to the NEIGHBOR'S drive-way, then all the way into town, AUDREY bumps into PENELOPE, where she purchases a ticket to the Village of Primm Enclave Tour.

SCENE 6 — EXT. VILLAGE — FOLLOW SHOT

    At the close of the scene, AUDREY and DOG hail a taxi, and then drive off camera, stage right.

Scissors in hand, she sat down to finish snipping the paper houses. Next, she would work with a palette of papers meant to capture the sky at twilight, and then later, she'd manipulate the sky at nightfall in what would become her final scene. She cut twelve fat-bellied birds from opalescent paper, meant to resemble glass birds like the birds hanging from the gilded nest chandelier she saw and admired at Feathered Nest Realty. Birds—an ever-present motif in this quirky little village Holly now called home. She sighed, frustrated she didn't have actual footage of the clear blue skies over Primm.

A few Bloody Marys in, Greta and friends stopped their chatter and began assembling.

"Cover the entire floor of your slow cooker with chicken breasts," Holly could hear Greta saying, as Struggle lifted her head and pointed her snout toward the kitchen.

Holly smiled, reaching down to pet Struggle. "Is that making you hungry?" she said, then was caught by surprise when her hand knocked onto the hard bone of Struggle's head the moment Struggle sat up—alert—training all her attention toward the kitchen. "Struggle, what's wrong?" She stifled a laugh, reminded of Pal, the long-haired collie who played Lassie in six or seven MGM films. Later, in the fifth-longest-running primetime television series, the descendants of Pal played Lassie for nineteen seasons. *What is it, girl? Is Timmy in the well?* In the episode "The Well," property rights to a strip of land were called into question as a water company pursued water rights beneath Gramps's property, but neither Timmy nor Jeff, the two boy characters in the series, ever fell into a well. Ever. It didn't happen. Not on any episode.

Struggle's grumble was so soft it was almost all vibration and no sound. Holly took hold of her by the collar. "Struggle," she commanded, her voice low but authoritative, worried Struggle was calculating a quick run through the kitchen to see if she could score a piece of chicken from an unsuspecting guest. "Sit, Struggle. Stay."

She heard Houston say, "Greta? Everything okay?" as the voices in the kitchen fell quiet.

"What's going on?" said Holly, entering the kitchen holding Struggle by the collar. She looked from Henry to Houston and then to Greta—who appeared confused. As if she suddenly had no idea who any of these people were or what they were doing in her house. "Mom?"

Letting go of Struggle, who ran to Greta's side, "What's the matter?" said Holly, rushing over to help Greta sit down. She checked her forehead. She wasn't hot. "Is it your eye?" she asked, Greta's leg jumpy, her face constricted on one side, showing her pain. "Answer me. Ma?"

Struggle positioned her snout across Greta's jumpy leg, as if pressing her there, holding her steady. She began to whimper. Those sad Labrador eyes looking at Holly as if to say, *Do something, Holly. Fix it.* Struggle's eyebrows twitching.

"I don't know," said Houston when Holly looked at him. "Something just happened."

Holly rested a hand on Greta's shoulder. "Everyone's making chicken-taco soup. See?" She pointed to the people in the room. All the food, the cans of corn and black beans stacked into pyramids at an assembly station on the counter, the Bloody Marys Greta had insisted they serve before noon. "I don't understand," Holly said to Houston. To Ruth. To Henry. "Mom? Can you speak? Say something. Say anything. What's my name?"

The expression on Greta's face was cloudy.

"What's my name? Can you tell me?" Holly's voice was shaky. Should they call 911?

Lottie moved in—hat leading the way. "Greta," said Lottie, snapping her fingers. "Talk to me, home sauce. How you doing?" Lottie knelt to eye level with Greta. "I laid my chicken breasts down. They're in my slow cooker. Now what's the next step? Hmm? Can you tell me?"

Greta looked vacantly at Lottie, eyes like a dazed and distant star.

"What's happening?" Holly asked the room—asked Javina and Aahna. Henry. "Ruth? What's happening?"

Struggle whined, trying to climb onto Greta's lap.

"Struggle, stop," hushed Holly, pulling Struggle from her mom. "Mom?" It was all happening so fast—everything—happening all at once. Holly's thoughts: *Migraine? No. Something else? Something worse?*

"Greta, lift your arms," said Aahna, lifting her own to demonstrate till she was standing with both arms outstretched.

Lottie grabbed Greta's arms and held them out to the sides. "Hold them up," she ordered. "Can you hold them up?"

No, Greta couldn't. Almost immediately, her right arm dropped.

Holly glanced at Houston, trying to get a read on him. *Stroke?* Was everyone thinking stroke? "Call 911," Holly announced. "911—someone call it. *Now!*"

Her words transforming the energy in the room.

"I'm calling," said Javina, rushing to grab the phone beside the fridge.

"I'll watch for the ambulance," said Henry; then out the door he went.

"Should we move her?" asked Darnell. "Want me to move the table?"

"Yes," said Holly, nodding toward the table. "Make room." To Houston she said, "They'll need to come through the garage."

"I'm on it." Houston headed to the garage to prepare a path.

Holly tended to Greta. Aahna and Ruth began clearing items as Darnell pushed the table toward the island, providing first responders clear access to Greta when they arrived. Table moved, he joined Houston in the garage. Greta was still sitting in her chair, looking at Holly, appearing helpless, childlike, scared.

Holly knelt beside her. "It's okay, Ma," she said, trying not to cry, trying to be brave. She took hold of her hand, kissing it.

"What is the address?" Javina asked the room.

Aahna took the phone to provide the answer.

Holly reached up to touch Greta's face. "I love you, Mom. You're going to be all right, okay? Everything's going to be okay. I promise."

Why was this happening? Holly felt a sting in her nose, a shakiness about her whole being. She wanted to cry, could feel tears welling, but refused, struggling to fight it off. *Be strong,* she told herself, seeing the scared and confused look on her mother's face. *Be brave.* "I'm right here, Mom," she whispered, still kneeling beside Greta. "I'm right here."

Realizing she couldn't hold them back any longer, as tears fell, Holly tried hiding them by laying her head on her mother's lap, pressing her cheek against the top of Greta's hand—it was the only thing she could think to do. If she could, she'd lift her mom from her chair and run with her to another time and place. To a distant land—to this morning, before the pain in her eye. To yesterday, last week. To each and every moment she had questioned her mother's health. How had things gotten this far? Why didn't she put two and two together? Had she failed her? If this was a stroke—everything would change, her wild and crazy and goofy, free-spirited mom. "No," Holly whispered, leaning in to wrap her arms around Greta's waist, pressing her face against Greta's stomach. A stroke could rob her of her mobility, her speech. She'd lose yoga. Lose playing her ukulele. *This isn't fair. This isn't fair.* "I love you, Mom. You'll be fine. It's just a thing. Don't be scared. I'm not scared. I'm sorry." She nestled in further, held her mother more tightly. "Don't be scared. I got you. I got you, Momma. I won't let go."

She held fast to Greta until the ambulance arrived and EMTs entered through the garage behind Henry, Darnell, and Houston. Houston took hold of Struggle's collar, trying to comfort her as Struggle became inconsolable, crying, howling, barking as Holly stepped back so that the EMTs could tend to Greta. In moments, she was on the stretcher, headed toward the ambulance through the garage because Holly's front door had support structures and a patched hole, where earlier Holly had declared the sky had fallen. So stupid. It was drywall. Plumbing that needed fixing. *So what. Who cares?*

"Is this yours?" Ruth asked, lifting a small leather bag.

"Yes, thank you," said Holly, grabbing her bag and her phone, a bit stunned to find Charlotte sitting beside the pantry door all of a sudden. Charlotte, sitting perfectly still, her eyes narrowed, staring at Holly. "I'll see that nothing happens to her," she said to the cat, Charlotte appearing stoic, twitching her tail in that "cat" way cats did. Holly looked at everyone standing in her kitchen. At Houston, Aahna, Henry, Ruth, Javina, Lottie, and Darnell. "I'll call later."

"Go." Lottie waved. "Go!"

On Holly's way out, Struggle broke free of Houston's grip to run over. "Oh, I'm sorry, sweet girl. I don't have time." She knelt, whispering to Struggle, hoping Struggle would understand. She tucked herself close to Struggle—tears stinging Holly's eyes. She hugged Struggle, gave her a kiss, and pulled away with the distinct impression Struggle knew precisely what was going on and was telling her to *go*—take care of Greta.

Holly took one last look around her home before turning to leave, suspecting the next time she walked through her door, she'd be entering a different place, a place forever changed. She shook free of the thoughts. *You don't know what this is. This could be anything.*

She breathed deep.

So this is it.

She rushed toward the ambulance, then climbed in, grabbing hold of Greta's hand. "I got you, Momma. I got you."

31

With a stiff neck and the feeling her lower back was crooked after lying most of the night in a pullout sleeper chair, Holly woke in the wee hours of Saturday morning to adjust her pillow and take a moment to stretch, twisting at the waist and then holding that posture until she felt the muscles in her back had been given a nice long stretch. *What time is it?* she wondered, blinking toward the clock on the wall in the dimly lit hospital room. Three thirty. She didn't want to wake her mom, so she lay back down, cheek pressed against a white cotton pillowcase, legs tucked beneath a sheet and lightweight blanket. She closed her eyes, remembering the feeling of climbing into her mom's bed at night the way Ella did now whenever a dream felt too intense or something went bump in the night.

All night, she had slept facing Greta at all times, afraid if she rolled over by accident to face the windows, she might miss something—Greta trying to move or reach or get up. To Holly's mind, if her eyes were closed to catch a few hours of sleep, the least she could do was face every other part of her body in her mother's direction. That way, she could hear or sense anything Greta might need and then wake up and respond, ready to help, ready to hit the call button for a nurse or a doctor—whatever. Anything. Anything her mother needed, Holly would make happen.

Running over and over in Holly's mind were the what-if questions. What if her friends hadn't been over? What if Holly had been out and Greta was alone when it happened? Timing was everything with a stroke—and it was a stroke. Testing began in the ambulance, the results routing Greta to a specialized stroke center in Menander. A brain scan confirmed the type—ischemic—and right away, the attending physician gave Greta a thrombolytic to break up blood clots and improve her chances of recovery. What surprised Holly—but not Greta, nor Sadie when Holly had called to give her an update—was that the ischemic stroke was caused by atrial fibrillation. Greta's heart had been going haywire, and all this time, Greta never mentioned it.

"But why?" Holly had asked Sadie late last night when she had called to give her an update. "Why would she ignore something like that?"

"I don't know. Denial? She doesn't trust doctors. She dismissed it as stress. She assumed it would go away, or slow, or stop. She's old school," Sadie said. "She flat out told the cardiologist I dragged her to she thought he was overreacting. Accused him of wanting to overtreat and take all of her money."

"She doesn't have any money," grumbled Holly, acknowledging the financial mess her mom had made of her life.

"Maybe that's why she chose to ignore it."

"But why didn't *you* tell me?" Holly had asked Sadie.

"Mom said she told you."

"Well, she didn't. That's what I'm not understanding. Why wouldn't she tell me?"

A-fib made sense, now that Holly thought about it. Her shortness of breath. Her complaints that she felt her heart was beating fast. Should Holly have guessed it? How would she guess something like that? She wasn't a doctor.

"Sorry, I really got the idea you talked about it," said Sadie. "Listen, don't beat yourself up about it. Adult children the world over are caring for their parents. I'm sure Mom's not the first parent to withhold medical information from their children."

"Well, I wish she had told me," griped Holly, feelings hurt.

"She probably didn't want to bother you. I'm sure she thought she could handle it. And hey, I love her, but she doesn't always make the best decisions."

~

How quickly their lives had been turned upside down. Sadie, half a country away, would arrive later that morning to stay with Greta at Menander Medical. Sadie would never speak *these* thoughts out loud—but Holly knew what they were: Holly wasn't as capable of taking care of Greta as Sadie was. Sadie was the Big Sister. Sadie was the one with her life together.

So what did that make Holly?

"I'll take care of things," Holly had told Sadie. "Stay home."

But no. Sadie did as Sadie always did. She booked a flight, then told Holly she booked a flight. No questions asked. You didn't ask Sadie questions when things like this happened. Holly loved her sister, but Sadie was a statement. A sentence with a period at the end. Full stop. Holly was built as a question. A sentence that began with *who*, or *where*, or *why*, or in this case, *what happened*? How did it happen? Why did it happen? Greta and Sadie might have known about the A-fib, but no one had planned for an ischemic stroke. None of them knew what to do. There was no rule book. No bullet entry in the bullet journal or appointment on the calendar that read:

- On this day: Your mother will have a *:: STROKE ::*
- On this day: You will learn her *:: HEART ::* is in *:: A-FIB ::*

• On this day: They will tell you :: *BLOOD* :: pooled in her :: *HEART* :: forming a :: *CLOT* :: that blocked the flow of blood to her :: *BRAIN* ::

Still a bit sleepy, Holly watched seconds pass on the clock on the wall. The slow, steady movement of the red second hand cast against the black-and-white features of the clock called to mind how precious every second truly was. So precious clockmakers rendered it in red as if to proclaim: *Look at me. Pay attention—to me. Tick, tick, tick.*

Hard to believe it is almost October. Holly reached above her to the windowsill, where her phone had been set while charging, thinking the timepiece in her phone was more accurate than the analog clock on the wall but knowing the entirety of time on her phone would cease to exist in less than twenty-four hours because her phone battery would die. Why didn't she wear a windup watch on her wrist? Why depend on something that died every twenty-four hours and could be dropped or lost or left on a counter? Why did everyone depend so much on technology without ever planning for a backup? Disaster could strike at any moment. Disaster did strike. Holly was in it.

She googled *hourglass*, not thinking she'd start tracking time with one, but thinking instead it might be a good thing to have around as part of the decor, maybe set it on a coffee table, watch the sands of time fall through the bottleneck. She supposed she shouldn't be surprised to find both *hourglass* and *astrolabe* in the same article about navigating the high seas, but she was. To think, she'd lived her whole life never hearing the word *astrolabe*, and now there it was, front and center, in an article that also described the role of a young boy on a shipping vessel charged with keeping time by tipping the hourglass once the sands had run out. If he fell asleep while on duty, all sense of time on the voyage would be lost.

EMAIL—Time Sent: 3:40 a.m.

> TO: Psychic Betty, Psychic Hotline Network
> FROM: Holly Banks
> SUBJECT: Heartbroken
>
> Dear Psychic Betty,
>
> I thought you should know—my mom is in the hospital.
>
> Her beautiful heart wasn't beating properly, so blood pooled and thickened and formed a clot that traveled to her brain, causing a stroke.
>
> The sadness and worry I feel right now are almost unbearable.
>
> —Holly Banks

~

EMAIL—Time Received: 3:46 a.m.

> TO: Holly Banks
> FROM: Psychic Betty, Psychic Hotline Network
> SUBJECT: Heartbroken
>
> Dear Holly,
>
> I am so sorry.

With your permission, I'd like to pray in my own special way for you and your mother. There's a full moon out tonight, and you mentioned in an earlier email you're a Cancer. The moon rules Cancer, and one of the significations of the moon is mother-hood, intuition, and feelings.

It seems fitting that I step outside under the light of the full moon and ask Spirit to bring you and your mother peace in your time of trouble.

Would that be okay with you?

—Psychic Betty

Click HERE to connect with a stroke-survival sup-port group in your area.

~

EMAIL—Time Sent: 3:51 a.m.

TO: Psychic Betty, Psychic Hotline Network
FROM: Holly Banks
SUBJECT: Heartbroken

Dear Psychic Betty,

I would like that very much. Thank you.

I think I'll do the same.

How special there's a full moon out tonight. I hadn't noticed. I should pay more attention to celestial bodies—point my inner astrolabe in their direction. I never look up. Why don't I look up? Ancient people looked up. Why don't we? Psychic Betty, has humanity lost its sense of wonder?

My mother's stroke has taught me this: There's so much I don't know.

—Holly Banks

~

Checking on her mom, she found Greta asleep. Like the moon, Greta's gray hair spread like a halo on the pillow, surrounding her face. Her hand, browned and bruised from the IV, was resting on top of her blanket and lying across her stomach. Holly slipped her hand beneath her mother's, wove her fingers up and between Greta's until they were holding hands. "I love you, Mom," she whispered. Light of the full moon shining down.

The doctor indicated she'd be discharging Greta from the hospital and transferring her to an inpatient rehab facility down the road from Menander Medical. Sadie, due to arrive later that day, would travel with Greta to the rehab facility, then stay the next week by Greta's side before heading back home to Nevada, depending on Greta's status. Any discussion about moving Greta to Sadie's home in Nevada was off the table, as far as Holly was concerned, despite Sadie's assumption it was a done deal. With everyone taking matters moment by moment, it seemed too far reaching to make plans beyond next week—right? Holly knew now wasn't the time for childish sibling rivalry—this wasn't about that. Holly and Sadie loved each other, and Holly knew all discussions would be in the best interests of Greta. She just couldn't bear the thought of losing her at a time like this. Maybe if Sadie felt she had supervised Greta's transition into rehab, she'd agree to let Holly oversee Greta's at-home care?

Holly slipped quietly from the room, then stopped for a cup of coffee near the nurses' station. Returning to Greta, she noticed the blanket on her bed had slipped from the mattress, so Holly quietly and carefully tucked it back into place. How many nights had her mother done the same for her when she was a little girl? Too many to count, thought Holly, fighting the urge to crawl into bed beside her mom—"Oh, hey," said Holly, noticing Greta had opened her eyes. "Did I wake you?"

Still sleepy, Greta smiled, the corner of her mouth noticeably drooped but lifting.

"Do you need anything? What can I do?"

Greta pointed to a pad of paper. She wrote an *E* with some effort, followed by an *L*.

"Ella? She's fine," said Holly, remembering her phone call home, Jack giving the phone to Ella and Ella crying when Holly said Greta was too busy with doctors and tests to talk. Ella not understanding, showing her age when she asked about Greta's *broke*—not stroke. "She misses you."

Holly swept Greta's hair from her forehead—grateful time stopped long enough to give her a moment in the cool, still quiet of the hospital room.

"I told Ella the doctors said you'd be fine. You're strong." A sting in Holly's nose—*don't cry.* "You're so strong, Momma."

Sadie would arrive soon. Sadie wouldn't blather and blubber like Holly had been. Sadie would be stoic. Authoritative. She'd make decisions. Follow nurses down the hallway. Pull answers from the doctors. Leave no stone left unturned. Holly? All Holly could offer were questions with emotions stuffed inside.

Beyond the window, full moon showering the night sky.

"Are you hungry? I'm hungry." *Stop mumbling,* Holly told herself. *Don't cry.* "Let's get you something fresh to drink. Are you thirsty?" *I don't know what to do.* "Do you want me to call a nurse? Are you cold? Tell me what to do. I don't know how to help you." *Stop crying—you'll upset her.* "What do you need, Momma?" *Stop calling her Momma. You haven't called her Momma since you were a little girl.* "Mom?" *I'm all grown up. But I still need you. I'll always need you.* "Mom? I love you."

32

Penelope Pratt
Feathered Nest Realty

—ENCLAVE ALERT—

THE VILLAGE OF PRIMM HAS GONE PLATINUM!

Pop the cork—the Village of Primm Enclave Tour is now at full capacity with all twelve enclaves achieving platinum status, each with four homes on tour. Gratitude to village philanthropist Mary-Margaret St. James, whose tireless work on behalf of our quaint little village has once again allowed Primm to shine! I'm happy to report advance ticket sales are strong, and things are certainly looking up for our flowered feathered friend, the peacock we all know and love—Plume.

33

October

Meeting Jack and the contractor at the house, where work on the foyer and living room opening was set to begin, Holly left Sadie to tend to Greta's first day at the rehab facility, taking this time to catch up on a few things, like swinging by the bookstore for a book she had on hold for Ella. It was Monday, and in the three days that Holly had been at the hospital with Greta, Jack had allowed Thom to work with Struggle, taking Struggle out during the day for a few hours of ore dog training. Holly was looking forward to touching base with Thom to see how the search for the missing discs was going. It was hard to believe Struggle unearthed the first disc two weeks ago. So much had happened since then.

After purchasing Ella's book, she felt oddly drawn toward the back of the store, where a door opened onto The Quiet. Thinking she might take Frank Mauro up on his offer to visit his store to see a replica of an astrolabe, on her way toward the door, she passed an employee handing out bookmarks with the bookstore's storefront and logo above a list of recommended books to read as part of a village-wide reading challenge the bookseller was promoting. Holly flipped to the back of the bookmark as she walked, spotting a crossword puzzle clue.

<u>ACROSS</u>
NUMBER 7. READER'S PLACE KEEPER (EIGHT LETTERS)

Arriving at the exterior wall at the back of the bookstore, Holly slipped through a door that opened onto a wobbly courtyard made of stone, and for the first time since moving to Primm, she saw the series of smaller, older shops known collectively as The Quiet. Why had she waited until now to see this? *Greta would love this,* thought Holly, deciding she'd definitely be bringing Greta here once rehab was complete.

The Mappamundi awning darkened the narrow entryway, leading Holly to step with caution down a tiny uneven stoop made of three stone steps. She reached for a brass doorknob placed unusually low on the glossy beet-red door slathered through the years with thick paint. As Holly opened the door, the faint vanilla scent of paper mixed with a muskiness as the door sweep hooked a rug placed inside the shop and too close to the threshold. Holly pushed the door, and the door pushed the rug, dragging it forward as she stepped through and into the small oddball space.

"Mr. Mauro? Hello?" she called into the empty shop. "Frank? It's Holly Banks."

She spotted the time on a grandfather clock on the opposite wall. It was almost ten in the morning, but the shop was so cast in shadows you'd think the sun was going down. Tacked to a bulletin board, a flyer for astrolabe and compass enthusiasts caught her eye. Maybe *that* was the astrolabe community Eliza Adalee was talking about?

"Holly Banks, yes, the woman with the dog," said Frank, emerging from the shadows through a doorway covered in thick velvet curtains. "You must have received my letter. Come in! Come in."

"Thank you," said Holly. "I'd love to see a replica of an astrolabe. But also, I'm wondering, do you sell hourglasses?"

"Yes, of course. They're dispersed throughout the shop," he said. "Make yourself at home."

The floors of the shop were uneven and covered in thin old overlapping area rugs. The low-hung ceiling was made of rough-hewn planks, and around the shop, wooden bookcases with glass doors and oversize brass locks with protruding keys displayed globes, compasses, maritime sextants, and other navigation instruments. This was a cartographer's work space more than a shop, though there were items for sale—paper tags with penciled prices tied carefully to the objects. On a small table in the corner, Holly found an hourglass—blue sands encased in mercury glass. She checked the price. Quite reasonable. She didn't have interesting conversation pieces in her home and thought maybe she'd like to add a few. A small map of Primm might be nice.

After Holly had made her purchase, Frank shuffled to a bookshelf across the cluttered shop, before unlocking the door with the turn of a long brass key. From a brass stand on a glass shelf, he retrieved a wide-bellied metal object about eight inches in height. "I thought you might like to hold an astrolabe," he said, handing one to Holly. "This is just a replica. Nowhere near the value of the old ones."

She turned it over in her hands. The metal made it heavy; the roundness made it feel like an oversize pocket watch with no numbers but rather elaborate circular scrollwork you could rotate, turning it like a dial.

"Imagine holding that up like so," said Frank, extending his arm as if lifting a lantern to light a path, "and then imagine pointing it toward a celestial object in the sky. If you turn the dial like so—" He showed Holly the pointer, turning it to point toward the celestial object they were pretending to measure. Then he lowered the astrolabe to show her the engraved markings on the discs. "See all of those engravings? They show you everything you need to know."

"It's beautiful," said Holly, admiring the complexity of the object.

"The Hopscotch family established Primm. Merchant Meek Hopscotch the Third? They were shippers of tea. Seafaring people. So, of course, they would survey using an astrolabe in the early days of

Primm. I suspect that's why Meek is sponsoring a team of treasure hunt-ers. To him, the astrolabe is a precious family artifact stretching back across the generations. Oh, but then, he's been sponsoring treasure-hunting ventures like this for years. Mind if I ask you a question about your dog?"

"Go right ahead."

"I heard the dog's been seen around town with a dog handler. Is that someone you've hired?"

Holly remained quiet, not quite sure what to say. Everything between Thom and Houston seemed so buttoned up—Thom con-cerned he'd breach his contract with Houston. She liked Thom. And Houston was growing on her. Frank? She had no connection with him beyond this moment and their first meeting on The Lawn, when he called the media and wouldn't let go of Struggle's yellow bathrobe tie. "I love my dog," she offered, keeping things light and casual. "But she's in desperate need of obedience training."

"Hmm. It didn't sound like obedience training. I got the impres-sion the dog is out searching. Is the man with the dog part of Meek Enterprises—or is someone else in town trying to find the tympanum discs?"

"Why are you asking?"

"No reason. Just making polite conversation. Goodness!" said Frank. "This place is a mess. Do you know how hard it is to preserve paper objects? I have maps in here so old they keep me awake at night worrying I might do something to ruin them or fail to do something to protect and preserve them. That"—he pointed to the astrolabe in Holly's hands—"is much sturdier. Only problem? Back then, there were no safety-deposit boxes. Surveyors often kept records in their private homes. And many people, not trusting fledgling institutions, would bury things. But then they'd die, and often the location of the buried object died with them."

Holly wondered if, perhaps, Houston's grandfather Clive *did* steal the astrolabe and the three discs and set fire to the Land Survey Records Department, but then he buried the pieces, dying with the knowledge of where those pieces were located.

"Oh! Great news," said Frank. "The shop made the Enclave Tour thanks to your dog. Penelope called to say two words on the crossword puzzle are connected to this shop. I suppose I need to tidy up before the crowds arrive. You know what they say: consumer spending—"

"Stimulates the economy. Yes, I've heard," said Holly, thinking shops in The Quiet deserved more attention than they were receiving. She looked around, taking in the sights and smells of the cartographer's shop. Such an eclectic corner of Primm.

"Wait here." He slipped once more behind the heavy velvet curtains, before returning with a rough sketch of a map of the Village of Primm in one hand. In the other, two sheets of paper printed front and back with cutout directions detailing how to make and use a paper astrolabe. "The eight-by-eleven-inch map will be a line drawing in black ink with touches of watercolor. I'm thinking I'll sell the maps for five dollars but give the astrolabe instructions out for free."

"Very nice," said Holly. "I'll be back for both when they're ready."

"Thanks," said Frank, his demeanor brightening, presumably at the idea of someone visiting his shop—and at the thought of maps and low-tech "old ways" of knowing and navigating coming back into vogue, if only for the length of a weekend-long Enclave Tour.

ACROSS
NUMBER 1. IT HAS A KEY AND A LEGEND (THREE LETTERS)

DOWN
NUMBER 2. NAVIGATIONAL TOOL. SEXTANT FORERUNNER
(NINE LETTERS)

Readying herself to leave, Holly said, "That map you created of Primm is really beautiful."

"I have other maps of the village. Would you like to see them?" he said, coming off a bit clingy and persistent. "They're right over there." Maybe he was lonely in The Quiet. Holly wouldn't know, but there stood the possibility she'd be his only customer that day. She thought, maybe, she might like to buy a map of Primm and have it framed for the living room. Depending on the price, of course.

"I have a cabinet and table dedicated solely to maps of the area going back a few hundred years. I'd suggest you start with the maps on the table. Would you like to spend time with them?"

Spend time? How charming. Of course she'd like to spend time with some maps. Wouldn't everyone? "Thank you," she said. "That would be lovely." She followed him to a corner of the shop, where he gave her a pair of white gloves to wear while handling the maps.

"So nice of you to drop by. I was hoping you would," he said. "Spend all the time you like. And let me know if you see something that interests you." He left her to explore, disappearing behind the same claret-colored drape she first found him behind, presumably covering the doorway to a small office.

The maps were beautiful, each one different from the last. She admired the care that went into creating each map, enjoying the way her mind traveled as she looked back on Primm through the years. A few minutes into looking, something caught her eye—a particular map, the words *Penumbra Over Primm* printed at the bottom.

34

Holly rushed home from Mappamundi, eager to speak with Thom and Houston about what she'd found. Arriving home around eleven, she assumed she'd walk right into the middle of construction, but when she pulled into her driveway, there was no sign of the contractors. Did she have her days mixed up? It was possible. The last seventy-two hours with Greta had been both exhausting and sleepless. Walking up her sidewalk, she got the distinct impression everything felt calm. Oddly calm.

He must have seen her pull in because Jack greeted her on the porch. "Hey," he said, kissing her. Wringing his hands in that "Jack" way he did when he was up to something.

"What's going on?" asked Holly, suspicious.

"I have a surprise for you," he said. "Close your eyes." She heard the front door open. "Okay, now open them!"

Her eyes went *immediately* to the foyer ceiling. She gasped. "Oh, Jack!" There, before her, was a perfectly put-back-together foyer—no sign that anything had happened. "It's beautiful! Painted and everything. How'd you manage? I thought the contractor was coming today."

"When—you know, with Greta—I explained everything and asked him to come early and finish early. He agreed. And in exchange for my help with the project, we came in under budget. Can you believe it? And the wall between the living room and dining room is fixed too.

You'd never know anything happened. Both are fully supported and done the right way."

"You remembered," she said, rolling up on her tippy-toes to give him a kiss and hug him. "The chandelier I fell in love with at Feathered Nest Realty. How'd you know it was that one?"

"I called Penelope and described it to her the way you described it to me. She knew exactly which one it was, and get this—she didn't charge me. She said it was a gift from Feathered Nest Realty. A token of her dismay the home inspector didn't pick up on the bathroom remodel that was done without support, caulk, or proper plumbing."

"I'm speechless. Truly speechless." She stepped inside. There, in Holly's foyer—in the foyer that belonged to Holly Banks, not Collette— hung a stunning chandelier made of gilded twigs forming a bird's nest in the shape of a ring. Hanging from the twigs in differing lengths were twelve pot-bellied glass birds, their bellies illuminated with tiny clusters of light, almost as if the stars themselves were forming the night sky in Holly's foyer. She couldn't *wait* to tell Online Psychic Betty.

"Wait, there's more," said Jack. "Ella and I have been working non-stop preparing for you and Greta to come home. We washed all the sheets, did all the laundry, and the refrigerator is stocked full. You won't have to shop for two weeks. We even made meatballs. Bills are all paid, junk mail tossed. And I fixed the holes in the fence, so Struggle won't get out. Knock on wood. She's out back right now."

"Knock on wood," said Holly. "Jack, thank you. Thank you so much." She reached out to touch the freshly painted walls. "I like the color." It was just a shade or two different from what Collette had. It was *better* than what Collette had because it was Holly's. Holly's home on Petunia Lane.

"Here's what I figured out," said Jack. "No need to be upset with Collette or her husband. They're just like us. They tried their best. They were missing proper support, and I was missing proper support." He nodded toward the wall he took out between the living room and dining room.

"Sitting with my mom for the last three days has *completely* changed my perspective," said Holly. "A plumbing leak from an upstairs bathroom that reveals the need for a support beam? Big deal. We have the support of each other, of family. That's what matters. To me? That's a big deal."

35

About two hours later, after a call to Sadie to check on Greta and a long hot shower, Holly answered a text from Caleb.

CALEB: Hey. How's your mom?

HOLLY: Good. They moved her to rehab.

CALEB: That's good, right?

HOLLY: Yes, most definitely. We're hoping she'll come home soon.

CALEB: What's the matter?

HOLLY: Nothing.

CALEB: I can detect it in your text.

HOLLY: Since my mom's stroke, I've changed my perspective on quite a few things. I'm trying not to compare myself to others, but the thing is, I have to make a wedding dress for Ella and I feel so lame. Based on what I'm seeing online, other parents go way overboard for this thing called a Q&U Wedding. I ordered a bunch of wedding favors to be shipped to the school, but I keep thinking I should be doing more.

CALEB: Like what?

HOLLY: A few years ago, a Primm mom ordered custom wedding invitations from Primm Paper. People are still talking about it. The teacher sent home a bag filled with black felt letters. All of them are either Qs or Us. What am I supposed to do with that? She said they were leftovers from something a parent did last year. I don't have to do anything with them, but I feel like maybe I should. Maybe I'll glue a few to Ella's wedding dress.

CALEB: I can take this off your plate. I'll come by for the bag of felt letters.

HOLLY: What? No. Why? What are you going to do with them?

CALEB: I'll do something film-worthy. Trust me, Holly. I got you.

Doing something with the bag of *Qs* and *Us* was optional. If she didn't like what Caleb did with them, she could leave them at home, and Miss Bently wouldn't be upset in the slightest. Holly did wonder if Q's mom received a bag of letters . . .

A few minutes later, she was greeting Thom at the door, there to pick up Struggle.

"Hey, Thom. How are you?" she said, letting him in through the front door. "Ta-da! New foyer."

"I know." He smiled, indicating he had witnessed the activity over the weekend. Jack said he was great about taking Struggle out of the house so she wouldn't bother the contractor.

"Thank you so much for sending flowers to the hospital. They really brighten my mother's spirits." She hadn't seen him since Greta's stroke but was touched by reports from Jack that Thom had called the house a few times to check on Greta and offer assistance.

"Well, I'm really sorry to hear about your mother," he said. "A similar thing happened to my dad years ago. Jack said she was moving to a rehab facility?"

"Today, yes," said Holly. "My sister is with her right now. She flew in from Nevada. We have reason to be optimistic, but it's still worrisome."

"Well, I've been praying for her. And for you too. For your whole family."

"Thank you," said Holly, reaching out to touch his arm. "I really appreciate that."

Funny, it was often the people you hardly knew that stepped forward to offer support in your time of need. Holly supposed it wasn't the length of time you had known someone but more likely the type of person they were. She was grateful to have met Thom.

Tail wagging, Struggle ran to Thom as he knelt to greet her.

"Hey there, old girl," Thom said, rubbing Struggle behind the ears.

Three days of their working together had turned up nothing. No missing discs, and to Jack's chagrin, no discovery of gold, although Thom insisted that wasn't what they were searching for. Not that Jack truly believed Struggle would find gold in Primm, but still. As Jack had said more than once, wishing never hurt anyone.

"Does 'Penumbra Over Primm' mean anything to you?" Holly asked Thom.

"No, why?" he said, rubbing Struggle behind the ears.

"I think we should call Houston," said Holly, reaching for her phone. "Do you know his number?"

"Yeah, sure." Thom followed her into the family room, where she called Houston.

Within ten minutes, Houston arrived, joining them in the family room. They spoke for a few minutes about Greta before Houston asked Thom, "Did you tell her?"

"No. Absolutely not," said Thom. "I signed a nondisclosure agreement." Thom looked at Holly. "I told you everything I could. I've been nothing but honest with you." And then he said to Houston, "Likewise. I didn't breach our agreement. I said what I was allowed to say, and then I told her she'd have to get the rest of the story from you."

"Well, how about this," said Holly, a bit miffed at having found a *map* no one told her about that matched an *engraving* in the *ring* on Houston's finger. "You're both using my dog for search and rescue, and I think it's high time you both tell me everything I want to know," she said, mostly to Houston. It was her dog that was being used to solve the decades-old mystery. Her dog that had uncovered an artifact that would benefit Houston. And yet, Houston didn't feel it was necessary to tell Holly all that was going on? She felt confused, frustrated, and used.

"If Thom didn't breach our nondisclosure, then I don't know why I'm here," said Houston.

To which she countered, "Well then, I guess you don't need my dog anymore." She looked at Struggle, sitting on the floor at their feet, her ears tucked low, and her eyes sad, as if she were a child watching her parents fight. Struggle definitely understood English.

"Holly," said Thom, his eyes appearing sincere, the expression on his face earnest. "I don't know what 'Penumbra Over Primm' means."

"Is that what this is about?" asked Houston.

"Why? What did you think this was about?" asked Holly.

Houston fell silent.

"Jeez-us. I have a right to know," she reminded him. "You're using *my dog*." Had he been using her mom? Exploiting her friendship to get to Struggle?

"What do you want?" asked Houston. "Do you want to be compensated for the dog's time? Do you want a portion of the proceeds? What?"

"No," said Holly. "For now, I just want to know what's going on. I think I have a right to—my gosh, Houston. I said yes to letting some guy named Thom from Nevada take my dog during the day. The last person who should be kept in the dark is me." *And you better not be taking advantage of my mom.* "Now tell me what's going on?"

"Fine," said Houston. "I inherited mineral rights to land around the water tower from Grandpa Clive. He was a gold prospector and poker player—among other things."

Holly already knew Clive was a gold prospector. Thom had already told her.

"So you're interested in the gold?" said Holly. "That's what you're using my dog for?"

"No, absolutely not. They're not searching for gold," Houston assured her.

"We're not, Holly," said Thom, validating what Houston said. "You have my word. We're only searching for the two missing discs. Just like I told you."

"But why?" she asked Houston. "You care that much about the water tower?"

"Actually, no. I don't care about the water," said Houston. "I care about who owns the land. I care about making sure the right people know I'm taking an active role to protect my interest in my rightfully inherited mineral rights. Do you have any idea how long those mineral rights have been caught up in the courts since my grandfather died? It's been a nightmare. I got tired of pouring legal fees into it, so I gave up years ago, but now that ownership rights might be resolved, unlocking my mineral rights from land deeds going back generations over disputed land claims has, yes, piqued my interest. My grandfather won those mineral rights in a *poker game*. It's very complicated."

"Is the *water* part of your mineral rights?" Goodness, what a mess if it was. Two towns fighting for water only to find out Houston Bonneville-Cranbarrie owned it?

"That question doesn't quite apply because the water that's in the tower is pumped in from the water treatment facility, so no one is concerned about the water per se. It's not like they're drilling for water beneath the tower or taking it from the waterway that's beside the tower. They are concerned about the tower itself, which is basically a simple machine—but one that's very large and expensive to operate and maintain. But to answer the question, no," said Houston. "Subsurface water usually isn't part of someone's mineral rights. But gold? Yes."

"Got it," said Holly.

Houston continued, "Usually, people own both surface rights *and* mineral rights. But if they are separate, as they are in this case, then whoever owns the surface rights owns the surface of the land and any structures on it—that's what everyone in town is concerned about. The land beneath the water tower grants ownership to the structure on the land—the water tower. But honestly, I doubt anyone in this town is even thinking about the fact that I own mineral rights. Only a few old-timers would even remember the rumors about gold, and from what I understand, all it ever was—was rumors. I have no idea if there's actually gold there to be mined or how much any of it would be worth. This could all be a huge waste of time, but hey, if you own mineral rights, you pay attention."

"So if you have mineral rights, you can just walk onto someone's land and start digging?" asked Holly.

"Pretty much," said Houston. "Remember, surface rights grant you the surface and any structures, but the owner of the rights to the minerals in the soil can excavate a mine for precious metals or drill for oil or natural gas on that land."

Thom nodded his head in a way that indicated he knew a lot about this. "A lot of my work is done for mineral rights owners that do not also own surface rights. Sometimes they're leasing the mineral rights for a specific length of time."

"Are you planning to mine for precious metals?"

"Me? Probably not," said Houston. "I'm old and lazy. But I might sell or lease the mineral rights if I can extricate them from the courts." He cleared his throat and paused long enough to collect his thoughts.

"So why didn't you tell us any of this?" Holly asked. "Why keep the mineral rights a secret?"

"One, because I didn't want the media up my arse. Two, they're still caught up in litigation, so it's hard to claim you have something when you might not. And three, Grandpa Clive has a bad reputation in this town. Remember, he was implicated in the 1941 fire but died swearing he was innocent. I don't have the energy to answer the onslaught of questions that would come my way. I've enjoyed the peace and quiet."

"So why hire Thom?" asked Holly. That had to be expensive.

"Two reasons. One, if all of this is about to finally get settled, it's important from a legal standpoint for me to be active in helping to lay claim to what's mine. And two, I'm kind of hoping if I'm the guy who produces the remaining two discs—or at least one of them"—the glance he gave Thom was a bit terse—"then I was sort of hoping to right a perceived wrong. Grandpa Clive's not here to defend himself. I'm hoping to settle this score."

"Understood," said Holly. "You want others to acknowledge your participation. Proof you're doing all you can to help the village." She'd joined the Enclave Tour for much the same reason.

Taking advantage of a moment of silence, Thom asked Holly, "So what does 'Penumbra Over Primm' have to do with any of this?"

Houston told Thom, "Penumbra Over Primm is an inscription in the ring I wear." He pulled it off to show him. "This is my grandfather's wedding ring. Before he died, he gave it to me, telling me to lay claim to treasure by wearing it."

"Um, Houston?" said Holly, waiting for him to finish showing Thom the inscription. "Do you know anything about a map?"

"Map?" His eyebrows crumpled as he struggled to recall. "No, why?"

Holly walked over to the counter by the refrigerator, returning with the Penumbra Over Primm map she purchased from Frank Mauro. "I think this map is your grandfather speaking from the grave."

"Whoa," said Houston, stunned by the find. "This must be what he forgot—what he struggled to remember before he died but couldn't. I had no idea there was a map. None whatsoever." He took a closer look, pointing. "That's my grandfather's handwriting. This is his map. There's no doubt. Clive Cranbarrie made this map. Can I have this?"

Not *quite* trusting Houston just yet, Holly said, "So long as you're working with my dog, and I'm still trying to figure this whole thing out, I'll keep possession of the map. It's mine. I purchased it."

Houston folded his arms across his chest but said nothing.

"I can't pretend to know what your grandfather's involvement was or wasn't in the 1941 fire," said Holly. "And I have no way of knowing if he did or didn't steal the astrolabe and scatter the discs. But I think what we're looking at isn't *just* a map. I think it's a treasure map." Holly looked at Thom. "Take Struggle to the places on this map, and I bet you'll find what you're looking for. Here. Let me show you."

She laid the map on the kitchen table as Houston and Thom gathered around.

"I asked Frank Mauro what he knew about the map. He said he knew nothing. It was just an old map they'd had at the shop for quite some time. He thought maybe his dad had come across it somehow—he didn't know."

Houston was nodding. Holly figured either he was following a train of thought or maybe he was simply agreeing with her.

"It doesn't look like it's been tampered with," said Holly. It was a fairly simple map drawn in black ink on now-faded paper. "And from what I can tell, besides the very circular design of the map, there aren't any special markings. I assume all of these buildings and landmarks were buildings and landmarks known to be in existence when Clive made the map?"

Houston leaned in. "I think so . . . yes. I'd say that sounds about right."

Holly found it interesting to see a map of Primm before the newer shops on The Lawn were built. This map showed the shops in The Quiet bordering an open area with no North or South Gazebo.

"So where should I begin?" Thom wanted to know. "Search every landmark? Pick one, and get started?"

"I don't know. Maybe," said Holly. She asked Houston, "Did your grandfather frequent any of these establishments?" As Houston bent over the map, canvassing every nook and cranny of Primm as it existed when the map was created, she kept a close eye on him for signs he might be hiding something.

36

Wednesday morning, the day of the Q&U Wedding, Ella ran into Holly's bedroom, landing hard on top of Holly, a big fat *aw, hail no* as far as Holly was concerned, having stayed late with Greta the night before. "Go back to sleep," Holly whined, pulling the covers over her head as Struggle barked beside her bed. Five thirty in the morning and Ella was awake? No. That never happened. Struggle, on the other hand, routinely woke them up in the morning by running around the edges of the bed to lick their faces. This morning? A white feather boa was wrapped and knotted around Struggle's belly.

"She's a bride! Struggle is marrying Charlotte today," Ella said with a high-pitched, shriekish giggle that somehow knocked her backward on the bed until she was rolling into a quasi-sideways-somersault *something* who-the-heck-knew between Holly and Jack. Waaay too much energy for five thirty in the morning. The last time Ella shrieked like that, they caught her drinking Jack's Pepsi.

"Why do dogs lick your face like that?" wondered Jack, sitting up from his pillow after Struggle had licked his cheek. Scratching his head, he postulated in that armchair, professorial "Jack" way he so often did by saying, "Maybe she's dehydrated, but because she's a dog, her keen sense of smell is telling her to lick *salt* from our skin."

"Or," Holly offered, angry at being woken up so early, "maybe she's hungry and thinks your cheek looks like a chicken breast."

"Get up, Mommy, get up," implored Ella. "It's my wedding day!"

"No, actually," said Holly, attempting to make her point by lifting a finger in the air from a lying-down position, "it's not your wedding. It's the letter *U*'s wedding. You're just standing proxy."

"What's proxy?" Ella wanted to know.

"Proxy means this isn't about you. It's about the alphabet. Jack?" Holly reached over to tap his arm. "Back me up."

Jack lay back down, pulling his pillow over his head, clamping it like a vise while mumbling, "Q's no good, Ella. You deserve better."

"Five thirty, Ella? Really? Let's get you some breakfast," said Holly, throwing back the covers.

Jack sat up. "Ella, let's let Mommy sleep. She was out late with Gammy. I'll get breakfast, Holly. You go back to sleep."

"No, I've got it. I'm up now," she said, reaching for an elastic to pull her hair back. She wanted to put the finishing touches on Ella's wedding dress—white T-shirt with a black letter *U*, white leggings, white sneakers, a veil fastened to a headband, and one ginormous mound of white tulle springing out in all directions from around Ella's waist. At the request of the bride, instead of flowers, for her bouquet: a pink basket with *My Little Pony* stuffed animals tucked inside. "Ella, honey, wait till Mommy brushes her teeth."

As she carried Ella down the steps and into the kitchen, "What's that noise?" asked Ella, pointing toward the dining room. Holly walked with her into the dining room, then peeked inside Charlotte's box. "Kittens!" Ella cried, squirming to get out of Holly's arms.

"Whoa, slow down a bit," said Holly, wishing Greta were there. *Where was Greta? Greta should be here. She was Charlotte's doula.* "Ella, honey, shhh. We have to be super quiet. And stop jumping. Be soft—act like a feather." She held Ella back a bit, keeping her from bombarding the newborn kittens. "Don't touch them, honey. Let's leave Charlotte alone for a bit." Holly took a look around; all seemed to be in order. All kittens arrived and well. New life. A miracle. "Do you think we should call Gammy?" asked Holly. "Tell her the good news?"

"Mommy, what's wrong?" said Ella, her finger pointing to Holly's face. "Your eyes are soggy."

"I know, sweetie—sorry." She tried stopping but couldn't. The tears seemed to come out of nowhere—hitting her strong.

"Are you sad?"

"No! No, I'm happy," said Holly, voice cracking. She forced a smile. Kittens had been born! This was a happy time.

"You're sad about Gammy's broke?" asked Ella, mispronouncing *stroke* again. She wrapped her arms around Holly's waist and buried her face against Holly's stomach. "She's not here. She's in the broke center."

Charlotte wasn't Holly's cat. Charlotte was Greta's cat, and Greta loved Charlotte enough to become a cat doula—whatever that was. And now, the moment that would have meant so much to Greta had come and gone. Greta had missed it. And Charlotte had missed having Greta by her side to strum on her ukulele, to say something goofy, to help should anything go awry. Greta had missed helping Charlotte with her kittens, and she would miss seeing Ella get married later that day. It all seemed so unfair, and it heightened Holly's awareness that there'd come a day when Greta *wouldn't* be there to witness the miracle of birth or the joys of a wedding. Overcome with emotion, Holly covered her face and burst into tears, letting go with a torrent of pent-up emotions.

37

"So, Rosie," said Holly, with a check on the time. "How's it going?"

"Great." Rosie smiled, looking up from her desk inside the school office. "Can I help you?"

"Yes, actually," said Holly. "Can you come with me? Outside? I have questions about the setup for the Q&U Wedding, and well, Miss Bently is busy with the children, so . . ."

"Oh, sure." Rosie nodded toward a woman at the copier.

Holly led Rosie from her place in the office, through a front entrance filled with children's tissue-paper artwork saturated with light beaming through tall windows like the stained glass you'd find in a church. Down the steps they walked, through a courtyard once flanked with topiaries. Parents were slowly filing in, holding polite conversation as they took their seats. The Q&U Wedding, a celebration of phonemic awareness, was set to begin at the top of the hour.

On the sidewalk now, "You needed something?" asked Rosie, looking around.

"Yes, actually. I was wondering. Are you going to the wedding?" asked Holly.

"I'd love to. Although, weddings are always more fun when you have someone to go with." Rosie glanced past her shoulder to watch the UPS man, with a sizable, robust package beneath his arm, hustle down the steps of his truck and then head in their direction. "I've given up on that one," she said. "The only thing he delivers is a shallow flirt."

"Whoa! Look at that," said Holly, pointing in the opposite direction, having to raise her voice a bit, because, like a shadow emerging from the sunlight—first, a blurry dot, then expanding, getting closer and closer and clearer and clearer as it swelled in size, took shape, and made noise. *Bzzzzz*. Like a lawn mower. Holly watched as Rosie lifted her attention away from the UPS man and his truck to shade her eyes in the late-morning light, lifting them to the clear blue skies over Primm.

If this were a film, if this were Holly's film, filmed for the Wilhelm Klaus Film Festival coming to Primm in a matter of weeks, Holly'd shoot the scene straight into the sun, dousing the flying object with penetrating light until you felt there was nothing *but* light. As the shape in the sky grew closer, so, too, the sound grew louder: *bzzzzzzz*. *Bzzzzzzz*. *BZZZZZZZ*.

And though Holly couldn't know what Rosie was thinking, Holly was thinking how remarkable it was *to her, Holly*, to see the flying object flying straight, not bouncing about, not swooping up, nor swooping down. No tipping side to side. Nothing needed correcting. There was no tilting this way or that. It simply grew closer and closer. Expertly. Until it was about a hundred fifty yards away. Then a buck twenty-five.

"What is that?" Holly asked, with a sideways glance toward Rosie. "Who is that?"

"I don't know," said Rosie, breathless, never noticing the UPS man had also stopped to watch and now stood only a few feet away from her. Parents, there for the wedding, rose from their seats and turned around, all eyes fixed in Rosie's direction—as if, as if. As if *Rosie* were the bride and this—her wedding.

Flying low enough to clip the tops of the distant magnolias upon approach, the aircraft came into view. Attached below hang glider wings, a giant, two-seater cabin frame—a cabin that *still* looked to Holly like a double-wide baby stroller. Inside the baby stroller, a pilot—with Rosie McClure solidly in his sights.

Getting closer. Seventy-five yards, then fifty yards. Half a football field from the grassy knoll where everyone stood. Forty yards. Then twenty-five. Upon approach, the ultralight aircraft made one large circle over the schoolyard, the pilot surprising Holly as he reached into a basket strapped to the seat beside him before sprinkling fistfuls of white rose petals mixed with felt *Q*s and *U*s on the wedding crowd below before circling back in preparation for landing. Ha! No one had ever done *that* at a Q&U wedding before. *Q*s and *U*s and rose petals falling from above? Film-worthy for sure. Holly puffed with pride, watching everyone snap photos. *Booyah!* Special for Ella and way better than custom invitations or anything she'd seen online. Although, Holly didn't like to compare.

From the aircraft came the cry of the pilot: "ROSIE MCCLURE, WILL YOU HAVE DINNER WITH MEEEEE?" The ultralight dipped slightly, then dipped again, bouncing ever so gently as it rolled to a graceful landing on the grassy knoll.

No *ka-pitz*.

No *ka-putz*.

No *ka-pertz*.

No *ka-chhhhhhhhhhhhhhhh* as the plane landed. The blades of the propeller didn't slash everything in its path; its back end wasn't caught up in a violent whiplashing, arse dragging, snagging, zigzagging its way across the grassy knoll the way it had across Holly's lawn. No. It was perfect. Caleb had executed the perfect landing, and he did it in front of Rosie. The speed, the energy, the forward momentum of the landing, all of it clearly left Rosie stunned and breathless.

Caleb killed the engine, the noises slowly winding down. He stepped out of the aircraft, grabbing a bouquet of flowers from the seat beside him.

"Rosie McClure," he said, presenting the flowers, GoPro camera fastened to his helmet—for posterity, he later told Holly, so their grandchildren would have something to watch. "My name is Caleb. We met last month at the Cherry Festival on The Lawn. I think you're the finest woman in all of Primm, and nothing would make me happier than having the honor of taking you to dinner."

Rosie gasped, and Holly could see a sparkle in Rosie's eyes—the start of tears, something. Holly imagined what Rosie must be thinking: There *were* guys like Caleb in the world, and it *was* her fate to meet one. And apparently, the good ones liked bird poetry. Who knew?

"Take a knee!" someone from the crowd yelled as others laughed and held up phones to record.

Always a good sport, Caleb took a knee, asking, "Rosie McClure, will you have dinner with me?"

"Yes!" Tears were welling in Rosie's eyes. "I'd love to." She reached for the flowers, pulling Caleb to his feet as everyone, including the UPS man, clapped. Rosie tossed in an "I do!" because why the heck not? This was, after all, a great day for a wedding.

It touched Holly, deeply, to see a great guy like Caleb appear so fiercely happy and fulfilled: Rosie laughing with delight in his arms as Jack whistled from the crowd, one of those two-fingered, tongue-pushed-back, earsplitting whistles. Caleb had set out to accomplish the one thing he most wanted to do: catch Rosie's attention. And on that day, he did just that. He set his sights, took flight, and piloted his destiny, for better or for worse. He once told Holly: "The sky's the limit." Holly was beginning to believe he was quite right about that. Quite right.

"Thank you, Holly," said Caleb, giving her a thumbs-up. Rosie in his arms, he closed his eyes, breathing deep the scent of Rosie's skin.

"You're welcome," whispered Holly, smiling, hand resting on her heart. *Hip, hip, Caleb. Hip, hip.*

~

Ten minutes later, all the guests seated, a different sort of wedding was set to begin: the marriage of two otherwise underappreciated letters of the alphabet: the letter *Q* and the letter *U*—better together than apart, if you asked Miss Bently.

And Holly would agree, in part.

As a Scrabble player, it was the "rule" Miss Bently was imposing that niggled Holly a bit, because *Q* managed to live life perfectly fine without *U* in Scrabble words like *QI*, *QAT*, and *MBAQANGA*. Greta agreed. She'd helped Holly explain to Jack that *U* didn't *always* have to come second when paired with *Q*, as Miss Bently was insisting.

But what Jack thought was niggling Holly was Ella's assignment to the letter *U*.

"Would you care," Jack wanted to know, "if Ella had been assigned the letter *Q* and the little boy the letter *U*?"

Holly insisted she'd feel the same either way, but Jack insisted it *was* influencing her. And sure, maybe it was. But it was more than that. This was Holly's first experience with Ella having trouble with something at school. It scared Holly, so she thought about it—a lot. And well, unfortunately for everyone, Holly supposed, she was a Scrabble player. She played with words one letter at a time. A particular letter, with a particular point value, played on a particular square within a particular word, lit up the Scrabble board. She'd told Miss Bently that.

"Ella flunked her pre-pre-reading test because of *phonemic* aware-ness—individual phonemes, the smallest units of sound," Holly explained to Jack. "So Ella's issue right now is at the level of the indi-vidual letter. If that's what Ella needs help with, then that's where my focus is. I'm a mom. If Ella needed to get to the moon, I'd build a rocket ship and become an astronaut if I thought it would help her. But her class is moving on to *phonological* awareness, which includes larger units of sound. So they're learning which sounds are produced when you pair certain letters together. Like pairing the letter *Q* with the letter *U*."

"I think you're overthinking it," Jack had said.

"I think Ella's a few weeks into kindergarten, and her class is already one step ahead of her," said Holly, knowing *that* would catch his attention. Knowing *that* might explain why she was so worried and "needling" (his word) the situation.

But then he replied by pointing out, "She's a few weeks into kindergarten. A lot can change." *Well, of course,* thought Holly, remembering what she had learned from Online Psychic Betty. *The moon travels fast.*

"I just want her to have a good, solid foundation," said Holly, thinking she might let Ella use her bullet journal and pens. Maybe talking about letters and their sounds while forming letters on a grid of dots would help. *Anything,* thought Holly. *Anything she needs, I'll give her.*

Caleb and Rosie took their seats beside Holly and Jack. Rosie would need to return to the school office after the wedding, but for right now? Caleb was beaming because Rosie was holding his hand.

Holly leaned toward Sadie to give her a hug and a kiss and to ask, "How's Mom?"

"Good," said Sadie, just arriving, tucking her purse beneath her seat. "Really good, actually. When she heard about the kittens, I almost expected her to check herself out and march home to Charlotte. I think they'll be very motivating for her."

"Maybe they'll help speed recovery," said Holly. Silver lining.

"Let's hope. When I left, she was sleeping. Could have sworn I saw a smile on her face as she slept. I think she's gaining muscle strength near the corner of her mouth. I just wish the muscle around her eye would lift."

"I'm glad you're here." Holly reached over to give Sadie's hand a tight squeeze. She missed her sister. Missed living out west and playing Scrabble and getting drunk on hoppy beer or a gutsy, grassy sauvignon blanc because it paired well with ultimate loaded nachos and Sadie's homemade guac.

The wedding was staged at the front entrance of Primm Academy with rows of white folding chairs fanning out into the courtyard and onto the sidewalk that lined the bus lane. All chairs faced the wide wooden doors, waiting for the bride and groom to appear. Beyond the bus lane behind them, a grassy knoll, smooth and even—with an ultralight aircraft parked between the school and a flagpole that stood in a courtyard that sloped gently downward as it approached the street that bordered Primm Academy. In attendance at the wedding were Principal Hayes and a handful of parents, including Shanequa and Malik. Mary-Margaret was there. As far as Holly could tell, she was slowly but surely getting her groove back. In addition to Mary-Margaret helping Penelope launch the Enclave Tour, it appeared she'd be hosting next week's PTA meeting too. Holly received an email about it just last night. In it, Mary-Margaret asked Holly to bring cupcakes, as a member of the board and all. Gluten-free, soy-free, sugar-free, nut-free, dairy-free, paleo- and keto-friendly cupcakes, of course.

"Dearly beloved, we are gathered here to join the letter *Q* and the letter *U* in phonemic awareness," said Miss Bently, speaking from a podium to the left of the doors. And so it began, Holly's first wedding as mother of the bride. With Jack recording the wedding on his phone and an empty chair on the other side of Sadie where Greta would have sat, Holly pulled a tissue from her purse to dab a tear that was forming at the corner of her eye. She leaned toward Jack, resting her head against his shoulder for comfort.

"Are you okay?" he whispered.

"I'm fine," she said, wiping her nose. "I just wish Mom was here." She reached over to hold Sadie's hand. And then she sat upright: back straight, tears wiped, realizing parents in attendance might think she was going *waaaaay* overboard with emotion witnessing her daughter star in a school literacy activity. This wasn't a *real* wedding. Ella was just the letter *U*, for Pete's sake.

"Well, I think this is a horrible day," said Jack. "I don't want Ella to get married. Ever."

"Oh, stop," said Holly. "Today is a beautiful day." And it was. The day was so beautiful that Holly imagined a real wedding for Ella—twenty or so years into the future—would also be beautiful. "I love you, Jack Banks," she whispered. "Thank you for living this big, beautiful life with me."

"And I love you, Holly Banks," he whispered back, lifting her hand, kissing the ring he'd placed on her finger the day the wedding they were attending was for them.

Miss Bently left the podium and opened the doors to the school, and there, where everyone was expecting to see a bride and groom, stood only the groom, looking a bit snot nosed and bored. Where was Ella?

"Oh, no," said Holly. She leaned forward to get a better look, intuiting the sky was about to fall on Ella's wedding. She glanced across the seats toward Shanequa.

Where's Ella? Shanequa mouthed. Holly returned a look that said, *I don't know.*

She tapped Jack on the leg. "Ella's not where she's supposed to be. Jack—something's wrong."

"One moment, please," Miss Bently said, smiling sweetly. "It appears we're missing a bride." The crowd murmured and chuckled a bit as Miss Bently stepped over the threshold of the door and into the school lobby to look for Ella.

"Should we do something?" asked Jack. "Maybe we should check—"

But Holly was already on it. She shot up to move swiftly toward the open door, slipping past the groom and into the front entryway of the school.

"I'm the mother of the bride," explained Holly, moving past a teacher's aide and into the front office, where she found Miss Bently kneeling to speak with Ella, who was clinging to a leg of the school nurse.

"Mooommmy!" Ella, a puffy, poofy ball of white tulle, released her grip on the nurse.

Holly, open arms, knelt to absorb Ella's body and billowy white veil and skirt as Ella crashed into her, shaking she was so upset. Was it nerves? "Honey, what is it?" asked Holly, sensing Jack arriving behind her.

"I miss Gammy."

"Oh, honey. I do too. But we're going to see Gammy this afternoon, and you can tell her all about it."

"Really?" asked Ella, whimpering a bit, not quite letting go. Holly felt Ella turn her head to look up at Jack. "Hi, Daddy."

"She doesn't want to get married," Jack announced, speaking quickly. Urgently. "Do you, Ella?"

Seriously? What's this about?

"Listen to your heart, Ella." He bent down behind Holly so he was face to face and eye to eye with Ella. "Is your heart telling you not to get married?"

"Jack, shhh," said Holly, glancing back at him with a stern look. "Of course she wants to get married." She assured Miss Bently and the school nurse, "She does. She's been looking forward to this for weeks."

"Because you don't have to," Jack continued. "I got a good look at the groom. He seems like a nice kid, but you don't have to do this, Ella. You can come home with me."

"Seriously?" Holly attempted to turn around while still kneeling with Ella in her arms. "Stop saying that. What are you doing?"

"You and me," said Jack to Ella, father of the bride to the bride. "We can leave this place right now. I won't let anyone take you."

"Jack!" snapped Holly. "Stop. You're upsetting the bride on her wedding day." She looked up at Miss Bently, who was exchanging odd glances with the nurse. Was this getting weird? This was getting weird, thought Holly. She pulled Ella from her shoulder until Ella was standing in front of her. "What is it? Are you scared?"

Ella nodded.

"She's just scared," Holly told everyone in the room—as if they hadn't heard. "That's perfectly understandable. I was scared on my wedding day too."

"You were?" said Jack, rising to his feet. "I didn't know that."

"But do you know what made me feel better?" Holly said to Ella.

"What?" Ella tried to slip her thumb into her mouth, a habit they were *still* trying to break, but she couldn't, because Holly had taken hold of her wrist, so as soon as Ella lifted her thumb to her mouth, Holly would pull it down again. Thumb up, thumb down. Thumb up, thumb down.

"I found someone who loved me," said Holly, "and that person walked me down the aisle. And I wasn't afraid anymore."

"Your dad?"

Holly nodded, trying to be brave for Ella, trying not to cry. "Yes. For me, it was my dad. But that special person can be anyone. Your mom, a grandparent, a friend, an uncle, an aunt. Anyone you want."

"Struggle?"

"Um, sure," said Holly. "Lots of people walk down the aisle with their dog. But Ella, Struggle's not here right now."

Holly noticed Ella was looking at Jack.

"Do you want your dad to walk you down the aisle?" asked Holly, hoping it would be okay with Miss Bently because now it was out there.

"Ella," Miss Bently said, "let's let your mom have a seat outside so your dad can walk you down the aisle. How does that sound?"

"Don't let them force you," urged Jack. "They can't make you. You don't have to do this, Ella."

"Seriously, Jack? Stop," muttered Holly. "She's the letter *U*. You want her to learn how to read, don't you?"

"Are you ready, Ella?" said Miss Bently.

"No! She's not," said Jack—and he wasn't kidding. He was utterly and completely serious. "She's not ready."

"Because I think you can do this," said Miss Bently, not quite ignoring Jack, instead focusing on Ella. She gave Ella a fist bump.

"Okay, then," exclaimed Holly, placing a firm, flat hand on Jack's chest to push—or rather, guide—him out through the door of the office and into the main corridor. "I'll go take my seat. Good luck!" She gave Ella a big hug. "Be brave, Ella Bella Cinderella. You got this."

She mouthed *thank you* to Miss Bently and the school nurse and then smiled at Jack, touching his cheek for a moment, thinking: *You poor guy. Be brave, Jack. Be brave.*

Once seated, Holly gave Shanequa the thumbs-up, Holly's eyes passing quickly toward Mary-Margaret, who, surprisingly, winked and smiled at Holly. The verdict was still out with Mary-Margaret, but Holly suspected there might be signs of light.

Miss Bently returned to the podium. "Let's try that again," she said, closing the doors to start the ceremony over again. "Dearly beloved, we are gathered here to join the letter *Q* and the letter *U* in phonemic awareness."

She opened the door. And there, in the doorway, dressed in black pants, a white shirt, and a black tie, stood a little boy with a ginormous letter *Q* pinned to his chest. On his face was a look that implied he had *no idea* what was happening at that moment, giving everyone the impression he was just doing what he was told to do—stand there and wait for the bride.

As the traditional "Here Comes the Bride"—the "Bridal Chorus" by Wagner—played, stepping into full view of the audience and in sync with the music was Jack, taking careful, deliberate steps toward the groom, all while holding Ella's pink basket filled with *My Little Pony* stuffed animals in place of flowers. Here came the bride, all right—arms and legs wrapped around her father's leg, clinging for dear life, her face tucked and hiding, refusing to look at the crowd as Jack walked. Right leg first and then left leg swinging forward, bride attached, her feet never touching the ground.

The crowd oohed and aahed and laughed at the tiny, scared little bride. Ella, on her wedding day, an adorable cloud of white tulle with a bag of *U*s carefully glued by Holly and cascading the length of her gown.

Holly smiled at Jack, and Jack smiled back. She could sense by the look in his eyes he might be feeling how most dads felt on their daughters' wedding days—pride, love, the feeling time had passed too quickly.

"Will you, letter *Q*," Miss Bently began, "partner with the letter *U* to form words like *quit*, *quake*, and *quiet*?"

The little boy standing beside Jack said, "I do."

Miss Bently continued, "And do you, letter *U*, agree to partner with the letter *Q* to form words like *question*, *quibble*, *qualm*, and *quarrel*?"

Quarrel? Holly glanced at Sadie. "Did she just say what I thought she said? Seems like a poor choice for a wedding ceremony." Why'd Q get the easy words?

Ella was expected to say the words *I do*, but she refused to let go of her dad's leg or to look at the crowd. With everyone waiting for her response, and figuring the show must go on, Jack shook his leg to jiggle Ella, hoping she'd pipe in with an *I do*. Some people in the crowd started to laugh, but that only made Ella cling more fiercely to Jack. When it appeared all might be lost, Jack saved the day, chiming in the way a ventriloquist would with a girlie voice that said: "I do."

Bringing this wedding to an end, Miss Bently said, "Children in the kindergarten class at Primm Academy, do you—"

"Wait!" yelled Ella, showing her face to the crowd for the first time, while still not letting go of her dad's leg.

"Yes, U?" Miss Bently asked. "Do you have something you want to say?" She leaned down, placing her microphone beneath Ella's chin.

Ella took hold of the microphone, her breathing loud and distorted because she was holding the mic too close and breathing *super* freaking loud. "This is for my Gammy," Ella said. And then, with only the slightest of pauses, she added, "Quizzical. Quadrilateral."

"Whoa!" said Sadie, as a good number of people started to clap. "Did you just hear that?"

"I did," said Holly, proud momma—playing it over and over in her mind: *QUIZZICAL freaking QUADRILATERAL! Squee!* She leaned toward Sadie. "What are the odds Mom had something to do with that?"

"I'd say pretty high." Sadie smiled. "She's training the next generation of Scrabble players."

Miss Bently picked up where she'd left off by saying, "Children in the kindergarten class at Primm Academy, do you promise to *always* place the letter *U after* the letter *Q*?"

"Ouch," said Sadie.

"I know. It's painful." Holly closed her eyes, wanting *really, really, really* badly to raise her hand. *Leave it alone, Holly,* she could feel Jack thinking. *Leave it alone.*

In unison, the kindergarten class shouted (at the top of their lungs, some of them screaming), "WE DO!" before erupting into wiggles and giggles and all sorts of mayhem.

"Classroom voices. Library voices, please." Miss Bently placed a finger to her lips. "Shhh." She waited until every last wiggly body had settled down. All day long with a crowd of five-year-olds. *Teachers are amazing,* thought Holly.

Miss Bently pressed play on her phone, held it up to the mic, and then blasted Mendelssohn's 1842 "Wedding March" in C major while proclaiming, quite loudly, to all those present: "Joined in phonemic awareness, it gives me great pleasure to present to you—Mr. and Ms. /kw/!"

Everyone, including Jack, clapped and celebrated.

And yet, with Jack and Ella up there on the altar, Holly couldn't help but think: *So that was it. Ella's first wedding.* She felt—something. Melancholy. No, not quite melancholy. Sentimental. Nostalgic. Something. She wasn't quite sure.

Of course, she knew it wasn't a *real* wedding. Ella wasn't *really* Ms. /kw/ now.

She was sweet Ella. Sweet, quizzical, quadrilateral Ella.

What is it with womanhood? Holly wondered. *Motherhood, raising children? Being a sister, a daughter, loving and then helping your parents as they age? Loving a man, loving your family, loving the home you've built? What is it with life? Time passes as we etch and notch moments. Often, it's the marking of significant moments—milestones like weddings and proposals—that causes us to pause and reflect. But other moments make up a life: smaller moments like letters inside a word. We should pause to consider them.*

38

The kitchen phone rang.

"Hello?" said Holly, standing at the counter by the refrigerator, where cluttered piles of paper once were. At Mary-Margaret and Penelope's suggestion, Holly had purchased a desktop file, something that matched with the kitchen and could easily be carried to the table or family room when Holly needed to process paperwork, pay bills, or update the family calendar.

"Ms. Banks? Eliza Adalee here, VOP News," said the chipper, spunky voice pursuing the story from the other end of the phone line. "Would you care to make a statement?"

"About what?" asked Holly, checking on Charlotte and the kittens, missing Greta. "About interest rates? Lowering the volume on the radio so I can see better while driving? Or would you like for me to comment about why I see a price tag I clearly can't afford but act like I'm still considering it?"

"Excuse me?"

"My mother's fine," said Holly, pulling free from the canvas work gloves she was wearing while clearing a spot in the backyard for the she shed scheduled to arrive and be installed later that day. "She had a stroke but is expected to make a full recovery."

"I don't understand," asked Eliza. "Muggles had a stroke?"

"We have kittens now," Holly continued, wishing Eliza would realize there was more to Holly's life than her dog's sense of smell. "Mother and kitties are healthy and resting. Four of them. Thank you for asking." Although, Holly couldn't blame Eliza. She was just doing her job. "My mom missed it. She missed helping Charlotte through birth."

"Have I reached the Banks residence?"

"You have." Curious, Holly changed her response to "Why? What happened?"

"The second disc was discovered today. Inside the Clock Tower Labyrinth."

"Well, I don't have a comment at the moment," said Holly. "But maybe later."

She said goodbye, then hung up.

"Jack?" she called out. "Have you talked to Thom?" No response. "Jack?"

She checked her texts. Found a group text Thom sent to both Jack and Holly.

THOM: Eureka! Found another disc.

Holly replied.

HOLLY: Don't talk to the media.

THOM: Too late. Guy from the municipal department ratted me out. They know—but I haven't said anything to them.

HOLLY: Have you told Houston?

THOM: I did. Had to. He's bankrolling the search.

When Thom returned with Struggle, the dog barreled through the door and headed straight for Ella lying on the family room couch, where she was playing with Pinkie Pie, her favorite *My Little Pony* pony. After a moment of checking in with Ella, Struggle's miracle snout kicked into

296

gear, and she turned her attention toward the dining room but then got confused when she didn't detect Charlotte and the kittens, Holly having moved them to a safe location upstairs.

Jack, after having spent most of the day with the she shed installers so that Holly could join Sadie at the rehab center, joined Thom and Holly in the kitchen, catching Struggle by the collar as she ran past them through the kitchen. He hooked a leash on her, sliding the loop beneath a leg of the table to keep her from looking for Charlotte.

"Mind if we call Houston over?" asked Thom, pulling the dirty disc from his pocket.

"Yes, of course," said Holly, respecting the fact that Thom had been hired by Houston to do the work in Primm.

When Houston arrived, they all sat down at the kitchen table to discuss next steps.

After pulling a soft bandana from his back pocket, Thom applied a gentle touch, brushing the crusted dirt from the astrolabe's disc. "Well, that makes two out of three," he said, looking at Houston. What everyone knew, but no one said, was that Thom's time in Primm was coming to an end soon. "Thoughts?" Thom asked Houston. "I figured, maybe a few more days? I could take Struggle along the banks of the tributary. Maybe search the border of the Topiary Park? We found this one on the hill by the water tower."

"Water tower?" said Holly, confused. "Eliza Adalee called asking for a statement. She said a disc was found in the Clock Tower Labyrinth. That wasn't you?"

"No, definitely not. We were at the water tower all day," said Thom.

Everyone exchanged glances.

Houston offered, "Maybe one of the treasure hunters from Meek Enterprises found it? I don't know. It's just a guess."

"Does this mean," asked Holly, "that all three discs were found?"

"It does," said Thom.

"So now what?" asked Holly, hoping this would be over but not wanting to say goodbye to Thom just yet. He'd grown on her these past ten days or so. "What do we do now?"

"Hand it in to the Land Survey Department and wait for the results," said Houston. "I'll call my attorney, and we'll make my claim to the mineral rights known. When clean and legal ownership to the land is determined, it'll make my life a lot easier."

"I hope Primm owns the water tower," said Holly. "I don't want everyone mad at me."

"No one will be mad at you," said Jack.

"Well, I don't know about any of that," said Thom, a smile growing on his face. "But you might find it interesting that Struggle and I also found *this*."

He pulled a small vial from his pocket, then handed it to Holly. After opening the vial, Holly tapped into the palm of her hand a gold nugget no larger than Ella's pinkie fingernail. It looked like a chewed-up piece of bubble gum painted gold. Thom pulled a second vial from his pocket.

"How many of those have you got," said Jack, peeking over.

Thom laughed. "I'm afraid this is it. Not exactly the motherlode."

He handed the second vial, filled with *maybe* half a centimeter of teensy tiny trace amounts of what looked like gold flecks, to Jack. "Very cool," said Jack, holding the vial up to the light to get a closer look.

"Keep it," said Houston to Holly and Jack. "We want you to have them. As a thank-you."

"Oh, no. We couldn't," began Holly.

But Jack held his hand up. "Hey," he joked. "Speak for yourself."

Thom smiled. "We thought Ella might get a kick out of it. But hey, know this: Your dog is legit. She's the real deal."

Conversation continued for a few more minutes, Thom recounting how the day went with Struggle, offering a few training suggestions to Holly and Jack. "I'd love a chance to work with her further. She's a talented ore dog, but I agree: she's very, shall we say . . . 'energetic.'"

Something on the television caught Holly's eye. "Hold up," she said to Jack to stop the men from talking. She pointed to the television. To Eliza Adalee reporting.

"This just in," Eliza told the camera. "The tympanum found earlier this morning in the Clock Tower Labyrinth was a fake. Early investigating by VOP News indicates Frank Mauro, Village of Primm cartographer and owner of Mappamundi in The Quiet, may have planted a historically *insignificant* disc in the labyrinth, hoping to throw off or possibly alter the outcome of the reading."

"I knew it!" yelled Houston.

"Knew what?" asked Holly.

"He's Francis Mauro's son. I knew he couldn't be trusted. *Frank, Francis*." Houston mocked the similarity of their names. "Same difference. Like father, like son, I always say—the cheats. They'd probably do *anything* to prevent this mystery from being solved. Let me see that map," Houston insisted. "I bet he altered it. Frank Mauro probably altered the map to throw everyone off. And he knew you'd be the one to come looking for it." He pointed to Holly. "You got hustled."

"Whoa," said Jack. "I suggest you lower your voice, Houston."

Holly looked at Thom. He put both hands in the air as a sign of surrender, shaking his head. "I know nothing," he said. "Honestly, I don't. Yes, I looked at the map, but I couldn't make heads or tails of it. Struggle's the one who led me to the second disc. It's authentic. It's definitely authentic."

Houston exhaled, taking a moment. "Holly, I apologize. And Jack, you're right. I was out of line. I'm an old man, and I'm upset. All my life I've lived in this town, and no one gives me the benefit of the doubt. They always think I'm lying because I'm Clive's grandson."

Stressed, he rubbed his temple. "May I ask? How'd he get you into his shop?"

"He invited me," said Holly. "He wrote me a letter, and I happened to be in the bookstore picking something up for Ella, so I dropped by."

"And did he ask you about Thom?" Houston wanted to know.

"He did. But I didn't say anything. Houston, Francis Mauro is Frank Mauro's father. He's dead," said Holly. "What could he possibly have to do with any of this? How is he involved?"

Houston took a moment to look at the faces of all those present before saying, "Years ago, Frank Mauro's father, Francis Mauro, lost all of his mineral rights to Clive Cranbarrie in a poker game."

"Two dogs chasing one bone," said Holly, thinking of a popular plot device used in the film industry. "You believe the mineral rights are yours. He believes they're his. Until now, neither of you could do anything about it. But if clear and legal ownership rights beneath the water tower are established, one of you can exercise those mineral rights. The question becomes: Who?"

"Exactly," said Houston.

"Then why is Frank Mauro sabotaging everything?"

"Because he knows my family's reputation. He knows no one in this town will believe a Cranbarrie won mineral rights fair and square from a Mauro." Houston pointed out, "There's only one person in this town still alive who was at that poker game and watched it happen."

Holly asked, "Who?"

"He was a young kid at the time," Houston started to explain. "He could barely see over the card table, if you know what I mean."

"Who was it?" Holly asked.

"Merchant Meek Hopscotch the Third."

"Wow. That guy gets around," said Holly, with a glance toward Jack. To Houston, she said, "When I was at Mappamundi, Mauro speculated someone from Meek Enterprises hired Thom—now I'm assuming he thought it could have been you. I'm sure it's been driving him crazy watching treasure hunters canvass the town. But in all these years, why hasn't Meek said anything?"

"Card players don't announce in the public square what happened during games," said Houston. "It's bad form. No one will play with you anymore. And besides, Meek was a kid at the time. It was all but forgotten by everyone until your dog unearthed the disc."

"Then why is Meek funding the treasure hunt?" asked Holly. "*He* wants to prove ownership rights?"

Houston waved that suggestion off. "Nah, he doesn't care about any of that. He knows there's an astrolabe to be found. He's going for the big stuff. And besides, *technically*, the astrolabe belongs to the Hopscotch family."

"So Meek is in it for the astrolabe," said Holly. "And Frank Mauro is *pretending* he wants the discs found, when in fact, he wants to *delay* their discovery until after Meek has died because Meek's the only living witness that could testify to the transfer of the mineral rights from Mauro's father to your grandfather in a poker game?"

"Correct," said Houston. "Meek has never been called to testify because no one has ever *legally* fought over mineral rights, because the moment the Land Survey Records Department burned to the ground and the astrolabe and tympanum discs went missing, ownership of the land and water tower structure fell into question. The way the mineral rights were written, permission by the owner of the land needs to be given before any mineral rights can be exercised. No owner? No permission. No digging for nothing. Boy, I wish I was there to see the look on Mauro's face—I bet he nearly choked on his sandwich the minute he realized your dog dug up what my grandfather buried."

"So it was your grandfather who hid the discs?" asked Jack.

Until that moment, Houston had never admitted to that, and as far as Holly knew, no one in town knew who stole the astrolabe, hid the three discs, or burned down the Land Survey Records Department in the 1941 fire.

Houston nodded. "That's right. After the poker party, once Mauro sobered up and realized what he lost, he started making trouble for my grandfather. Threatening him. Saying things about Petunia. Mauro soiled *both* the Bonneville *and* the Cranbarrie name."

"What a jerk," said Holly.

"I don't know what he thought would happen. Did he think my grandfather would cave and give it all back to him? My grandfather wasn't that kind of man. And besides, he won those mineral rights fair and square."

"He won gold in a poker game," said Holly. "Sounds simple to me."

"Nothing's ever that simple," said Jack.

"When that didn't work," explained Houston, "thinking he could buy more time to win back what he lost, old man Francis Mauro set out to muck up ownership rights—knowing mineral rights can't be exercised unless ownership rights are established. So Francis Mauro stole the astrolabe and discs and set fire to the Land Survey Records Department—making it appear as if my grandfather did it. Mauro set him up!"

"Wherever there's gold, there's a story," said Thom, shaking his head.

"But wait—you just said your grandfather buried the astrolabe and discs," Holly pointed out. "If he didn't cause the fire at the Land Survey Records Department, how'd he get them?"

"He stole them from Mauro," said Houston. "Hey, I never said the guy was a saint."

"But wait," said Jack. "If your grandfather had the astrolabe and discs, he had everything he needed. He could prove ownership rights and then exercise his mineral rights. Why in the world would he hide them?"

"To keep from going to jail," said Houston. "The entire town assumed he was guilty. If he got caught holding the astrolabe and discs—they'd take it as *proof* he stole them from the Land Survey Records Department and started the fire. They'd toss him in jail. No questions asked. I know they would. This way, he keeps from going to jail, passes the mineral rights to the next generation, and hopes they're smart enough to find what they're looking for on a map."

"But somehow, the map was lost," said Holly.

"And that's the part that might never get solved. My grandfather's memory was failing him before he died. I never knew there was a map, and I may never know how the map fell back into the Mauros' hands," said Houston. "I suppose, if they've stolen once, they can steal again. And besides, they are in the map business, so if anyone in town came across the map or passed it through shady dealings, I'm not surprised it would end up in their collections. They are, after all, cartographers."

"And that's why your grandfather engraved the name of the map—Penumbra Over Primm—inside his gold wedding band," said Holly. "Instructing you to keep proof of when he did it."

"That's right," said Houston with a nod. "The receipt to the engraving is in a safety-deposit box in Menander. Around my finger is proof of my grandfather's link to that map."

"The map was lost mysteriously, or at least, knowledge of what happened to it died with Clive Cranbarrie. The Penumbra Over Primm engraving and receipt were kept with care in the desperate hope the next generation would recover the map and find the astrolabe and discs," said Holly, piecing it all together. "It's a good thing the younger Mauro didn't know what he had. That Penumbra Over Primm map was hidden in plain sight."

Houston started to laugh. "A cartographer—duped by a map."

Holly understood why Houston didn't like the Mauros. Still, she didn't like him *laughing* at Frank Mauro. Despite all that had occurred between the two families, there was something about Frank Mauro that Holly liked. "If you don't mind my asking, why in the world have you been so secretive about all of this?" Holly asked Houston. "Didn't you trust us?"

"I'm sorry, Holly. Truly," said Houston. "But that's how I've been getting by all of these years in the Village of Primm. Have you ever had something to hide? The village is full of secrets. Have you ever kept a secret?"

The questions made her a bit uncomfortable. Of course she had something to hide. She had secrets. Didn't everyone? She was keeping one right now about the spread of the chilli thrips.

Houston changed his demeanor. *He's hiding something,* thought Holly.

"Here's the truth," said Houston. "At first, I was a suspicious neighbor. You moved here a month ago, and your dog kept getting out to dig in my backyard. Now, I know there's got to be all sorts of things back there—I get it. Clive didn't trust people. And neither do I. I thought you might know something or someone. And then, a plane landed on your front lawn, and I thought: *This is nuts. And why is Maeve Bling so provoked?* And then—and then—after all these years, your *dog* unearths the first disc while Mauro, of all people, just happens to be there eating his lunch, and like that," he said, snapping his fingers, "everything is brought back into the open again. Secrets once buried are revealed. Truthfully, I didn't know what to believe or who to believe."

"So you started dating my mom," said Holly.

"That's real," he insisted. "I'm crazy about her. That has nothing to do with any of this."

"Well, I'm sure all of this has been difficult for you," offered Jack.

"You know what's difficult? I still don't know why my grandfather always told me autumn is the season to hunt for buried treasure. He said look for a clue hidden in plain sight. I never knew what he meant by it, but if there's still a third disc out there, I say we put our heads together and figure out what he meant when he said autumn was the season."

Holly shrugged. "I'm game. I'd love to put this to bed. Let's figure this out."

"And, well. There's something else," said Houston. "I haven't been completely honest with you."

Oh, jeez. "What now?" said Holly.

"Grandpa Clive hid the discs," said Houston, reaching into his pocket, "but kept the astrolabe." And with that, he set a shiny brass astrolabe on Holly's kitchen table.

39

The fact that Houston had the astrolabe all along made the work of the treasure hunters pointless. Unless, of course, they wanted to stay on to search for the third and final disc, which was still missing now that Frank Mauro had been found guilty of planting, and then "discovering," a bogus disc. Houston speculated that Meek had put up a reward for the *discs* simply to motivate the treasure hunters when what he really wanted was for one of the treasure hunters to find the valuable artifact—the *astrolabe* that once belonged to the Hopscotch family when they were settling Primm.

The plan now was to find the third disc. The moment the third disc was found, Houston would turn the astrolabe and discs in to the authorities, explain everything that had happened between the Mauros and the Bonneville-Cranbarries through the years, and finally stand a chance of being believed now that Frank Mauro had proved himself to be untrustworthy. If the disgraced Frank Mauro tried to discredit Houston's explanation that Clive Cranbarrie won the mineral rights fair and square in a poker game against Francis Mauro, Meek was still alive to testify it had happened. Once the tympanum discs and astrolabe proved which town had ownership rights of the land where the water tower stood, Houston and his attorneys could finally execute the mineral rights—either selling them or digging for whatever might still be in the ground.

Holly was intrigued by the whole matter, but for Houston, this was turning out to be a redemption story. In a town as old and as small as the Village of Primm, to Houston, that redemption might be more valuable than the mineral rights.

For the first time, Holly felt truly comfortable with Houston, so she let Jack create photocopies of the map for the four of them to pore over. The four sat at the table, continuing to search for anything that would pair with the three clues left by Clive.

Penumbra over Primm . . .

Hunt for buried treasure in autumn . . .

Look for a clue hidden in plain sight . . .

Penumbra, penumbra, penumbra, thought Holly, considering the word and looking for any possible clues within the map that would explain why someone would name the map Penumbra Over Primm in the first place.

Penumbra—the lighter outer lining of a shadow. So, if you were looking at a solar eclipse, for example, when the moon passed between the earth and the sun, the moon's shadow would form a dark central umbra surrounded by a much lighter penumbral ring. Much like the gold wedding band Houston wore? Or a penumbra depicted on a building or structure in town? Did something on this map look like a shining light beyond shadow?

The first disc Struggle found was near the compass rose on The Lawn. Interesting, it had only just occurred to Holly that the compass rose was surrounded by a brass ring along its outer edge—a clue hidden in plain sight.

The second disc was found near the water tower. An entire structure built as a circle, and, too, no coincidence a disc would be found there—the lost discs surveyed *that* specific area of Primm.

But the third disc, the fake disc planted by Frank Mauro, was found in a labyrinth. The Clock Tower Labyrinth, which was round. It was no wonder Frank chose to hide the bogus disc there. He probably figured a labyrinth was the perfect place to pretend someone had hidden something—because no one would question it. Labyrinths were mysterious and puzzle-like. In many ways, it was the most plausible location in all of Primm.

For that same reason, Thom had already taken Struggle there to hunt for the disc before Holly had even found the map. It had seemed obvious at the time. Although, when Thom had been there with Struggle, they'd found nothing. Replica or not, the disc Frank had buried was still a metal. If it had been there at the time of Thom and Struggle's visit, Struggle probably would have found it. It wasn't that large an area to search, and Thom was a pro working with an apparently gifted scent dog. So, Frank most likely had not yet hidden the fake disc when Thom and Struggle had searched the labyrinth. Maybe Frank had been caught off guard when he realized someone had come to town to work with the dog. Maybe he felt uneasy watching treasure hunters search The Lawn with metal detectors. Things were happening too quickly. It was in his best interest to delay, delay, delay and hope Meek would eventually die, so he couldn't testify. Eventually, Mauro probably panicked and scrambled to bury the bogus disc, hoping to delay, confuse, end the search, and maybe, just maybe, render the survey results inconclusive for now.

So where did that leave things?

One missing disc.

One map of Primm and a maddening hunt for circles.

Holly's mind wandered, thinking about Merchant Meek as a young man at a poker table where mineral rights changed hands between Francis Mauro and Clive Cranbarrie, both now dead and unable to speak on the matter. But Meek—Meek was there. And then, just as she was thinking about Meek—and Penelope and Mary-Margaret and the legacy of the Hopscotch family in Primm—her mind wandered to Hopscotch Hill, where the twelve homes of the Hopscotch family still stood.

"I've got it," she announced, looking from Jack to Houston and then to Thom. "I think I've figured it out. I know where the third tympanum disc is buried."

40

Holly led them to the dog park. Holly, Jack, Ella, and Struggle in one car. Thom and Houston in another. Gripping the map, Holly pointed straight ahead at the transition in the road from winding streets to a tree-lined road that curved, eventually leading to the gate that began the ascent up the hill toward Hopscotch. She had driven that stretch of road more than once but had never—to borrow a phrase from bullet journaling—connected the dots. Nor had she noticed it on the map. Why would she? The circular road was clearly marked on the map, but the trees? The trees were hiding in plain sight.

"They're sugar maple trees," said Holly, as everyone gathered on the grass at the park. "And look—golden leaves. Clive said hunt for buried treasure in autumn, and look for clues hidden in plain sight. Without those valuable tips, no one would guess a disc was buried there. To see it on paper, it looks like a perfect curve in the road. But to see it in real life, you see trees lining that road. And when you see those trees in autumn, you see the penumbra. The penumbra is the golden leaves!"

"Whoa," said Houston, in utter disbelief. "That's incredible. It's like the map just came alive, but only during the fleeting moments of autumn."

"Much like the penumbral ring that forms around an eclipse," said Holly, "it's temporary. You have to be standing before it to see it—when it occurs."

"Holly, great job," said Jack, giving her a high five.

"Yeah, Mommy, great job," said Ella, having no clue what they were talking about but still wanting to give her mom a high five.

"Wow, that's such a risk," said Thom. "What if someone cut the trees down?"

"Always a possibility," Holly agreed. But trees lived a very long time, so there was a good chance a bank of trees would still be standing from one generation to the next. And those trees were positioned in a place where no one in their right mind would cut them down. You couldn't build a house there, and Holly doubted the Hopscotch family would ever agree to have old, established sugar maples cut down, especially because they were so beautiful and led to a place that was sentimental to them. "In many ways, it wasn't a risk. It was Clive's insurance policy. Anyone looking at the map, and only the map, might have noticed the curve in the road, but there are lots of curves in roads. He was relying on a natural phenomenon—the changing golden leaves of the sugar maples every autumn—to illuminate a golden penumbra on the map. It's brilliant! Houston, what was the date on the receipt—the date Clive engraved *Penumbra Over Primm* inside your ring?"

"September 21, 1941."

"I bet that's the date of the autumnal equinox—marking the first day of autumn." She googled it on her phone. "No, that's not right. The autumnal equinox was two days later, on September 23. Hmm. Hold up." She performed another search. *"Whoa,"* she said. "Look!" She held her phone up for all to see. "On September 21, 1941, the date *Penumbra Over Primm* was engraved inside your ring—there was a total eclipse of the sun!"

Houston's ring—made of gold—when held up like an astrolabe and pointed toward a celestial object, in this case, the sun during a solar eclipse, would match. They'd line up. That same ring, acting symbolically as the penumbra of light around a solar eclipse, served as a secret key or code or clue for the map itself—a map where treasure was buried in circles—the compass rose, the water tower, and the circular road that colored every autumn with the golden leaves of the sugar maples. Clive was a gold prospector with mineral rights. He'd built a system of clues, including a treasure map, using an astrolabe as his inspiration highlighting what an astrolabe did best—navigate using celestial objects and phenomenon. As all the pieces of the puzzle fell together, Holly felt as if she were invoking the spirit of a bygone age. Using the ring and the concept of an ancient instrument, the astrolabe, she'd taken information from the sun—the knowledge that penumbras formed during eclipses—and then she laid all of that on Earth, like a survey conducted across a piece of land using a celestial object as a waypoint. From beyond the grave, Clive had pointed them in the right direction. And from across the distance of time, an astrolabe was back in use in the Village of Primm.

"Well, I say, let's get this ore dog hunting!" said Thom.

Jack opened the car door, and Struggle came barreling out; Thom immediately seized control of Struggle through a series of commands. He clipped a leash on her, and together, they all rushed to the sugar maples, Thom guiding Struggle as they wove their way around the trees. "Go, Struggle, go!" Ella cheered, Struggle's tail wagging madly.

About fifty or sixty yards into their walk, Struggle's nose low and curious, she began pulling hard on her leash, tugging, tugging, until Thom broke into a run with Struggle, headed straight for the gate that began the ascent up the hill toward Hopscotch. Meek lived up there. His whole family did. Maybe Clive hid a disc close to Meek to remind him of what he witnessed that day.

Struggle—whimpering, whining, crying. So *overly* animated it looked like Thom was having trouble maintaining control. The excitement almost more than Holly could bear. And then—Struggle, barreling headfirst behind a tree, began pouncing on the ground. Tail wagging, barking, growling. Struggle starting to dig, dig, dig.

They all gathered close as Thom got on his hands and knees, crawling behind the tree to help. As Struggle dug, Thom stuck his hand in to help loosen the soil, and then—holy criminy. She found it! Struggle found the third and final disc!

41

Holly told Houston she'd handle getting word to Meek that the third and final disc was found so he could call off the treasure hunters. Houston was reluctant to make the call himself, for fear Meek would ask the whereabouts of the astrolabe, and Houston would have to admit he'd had it all along. It might come out later, Houston had said. He just wasn't up to answering questions about it from Meek, so Holly agreed she'd send word.

She picked up her phone to send a text.

HOLLY: Hey. I have news your grandfather might find interesting. I tried Penelope but she's not picking up. Can you do me a favor?

MARY-MARGARET: Maybe.

HOLLY: Can you send a message to your grandfather?

MARY-MARGARET: Maaaaaaybe.

HOLLY: Can you tell him the third disc was found?

MARY-MARGARET: Maaaaaaaaaaaaaybe.

HOLLY: And will you tell him he can suspend the search for the astrolabe? That's found, too.

MARY-MARGARET: Maaaaaaaaaaaaaaaaybe.

HOLLY: Why are you saying it like that? Are you trying to mess with me?

MARY-MARGARET: Maaaaaaaaaaaaaaaaaaaaaybe.

HOLLY: Will you stop?

MARY-MARGARET: Maaaaaaaaaaaaaaaaaaaaaaaaaaaaaybe.

42

Ordered a little more than a week ago, and now fully installed in the backyard, the she shed arrived already painted white with black shutters, so it matched Holly's house perfectly. Like having House One in front of House Two, although, yes, of course, the sizes were a bit different—but not by much, mused Holly, planning to give the shed a playful address and paint 12½ on its soon-to-be-*blue* door. How she wished Greta were here to see it. Soon, she kept telling herself. Soon.

Jack installed the beginnings of landscaping and cut a pathway from the shed through the side gate so people could enter the backyard from the driveway and walk a gently winding path to the shed, never needing to walk inside Holly's house.

Leaning against the top of his shovel, "Let's wait to see how things shake out," Jack told Holly, referring to his employment and the cost it would take to make this improvement, "but I think we should pop some landscape lighting along this path. If you're working late, or someone is leaving after dark, the distance from the shed to the driveway will seem pretty dark." He turned to consider the back exterior of their home. "I'm going to mount a motion sensor light up there and angle it toward the shed."

"I was wondering about security," said Holly. "How are we going to lock up? Dead bolts? Wiring with alarms?" The she shed kit they ordered was minimal and basic—it wasn't a That's What She Said she shed. It was what they could afford.

"Already have that all figured out." He smiled. "The shed is anchored with L brackets, screws, and Rawl plugs to prevent tipping or—and I know this sounds crazy, but hey, it could happen—stealing."

"That is crazy," said Holly, trying to imagine how someone would steal an entire shed.

Jack continued. "The screws in the gate hinges were replaced with nuts and bolts to deter someone from trying to pry open the door. And on the inside of the shed, I used Loctite on the nuts and bolts. The lock the shed came with was basic and easy to cut with a bolt cutter, but I don't want to overdo it with some ginormous lock you need to type a code into, or that might broadcast to someone valuable stuff is inside."

"Everything inside is valuable."

"I know. I picked up a shackle padlock from the hardware store in Southern Lakes. You can't break into the shed with bolt cutters and saws with a shackle padlock because only a small portion of the padlock is unprotected. So that leaves the issue of the windows."

"Oh, jeez."

"Motion sensor alarm for around the shed, door sensor, window sensors. All with crazy-loud sirens, but Holly, I'd bring your computer and most expensive cameras in the house at night. To be safe. I'll pick up a site box next week to store smaller items of value, and it wouldn't hurt to get a bike lock you can wrap around larger objects."

"I hate thinking someone would break in," said Holly. She felt safe in the Petunia enclave. Safe in the Village of Primm. But sure, with valuable film equipment and computers and things she wanted to protect sitting out in the open like that—she was glad they were being overly cautious. "Don't make it look like Fort Knox."

"Just a precaution. You're listed on the Enclave Tour," he pointed out. "Better to be safe than sorry."

Though Holly had to get used to the idea the shed might attract unwanted attention from the wrong kind of people, in many ways, the she shed was a better solution than establishing a film studio in the dining room. The foyer, the load-bearing wall, and having to take the living room and dining room film studio off the Enclave Tour all felt devastating at the time, but in the end, it led Holly to where she was now—in a much better place and even more excited. Silver linings. Penumbras, if you will. Bands of light at the outer edges of a shadow.

"Oh, hey!" Holly turned around when she heard Shanequa and Malik open the side gate with Talia. Jack and Malik shook hands, united in friendship but also as coaches of the Bubble Gummers.

"Wow. This is surprisingly spacious," said Shanequa.

"I know, right? So spacious," said Holly, stepping into the shed with her. Holly whispered, so Jack wouldn't hear, "Did you drop the stuff off? I can't wait to show him. He's going to be so surprised."

"I did," she whispered back. "We made it look nice." Talia tugged on her arm. "Talia, honey, one minute." To Holly, Shanequa said, "She's dying to see the kittens but told me she's not allowed to look at them without a grown-up with her."

"Ella must have told her our rules."

"Talia!" yelled Ella, running toward them from a play area she had created beneath a tree. She handed Talia a Hula Hoop, and the two went straight to playing.

Jack had spent the morning building a cute table for Holly to paint and stage for the Enclave Tour. The entirety of Holly Banks Productions wouldn't be installed until after the crowds and photo ops wrapped up and the Enclave Tour ended. Mapping what it would look like and what it would take to finish in time for the tour, Holly created an inspiration board on Pinterest, using it to collect and then install decorative items that told the story: This was a shed fully equipped to handle still shots for clients, with a green screen where custom backdrops could be used behind multiple options for sitting or standing should you want to shoot live video. The green screen rolled up when not in use as part of a bracket-and-pole system that also folded up and could be stored. Holly imagined many of her future clients would want to shoot on location—in their craft rooms, kitchens—so the shed would serve dual functions: a place to work and a place to store her equipment without cluttering up the house. Inside the shed was a small workstation with equipment for handling production: a computer, editing software. It wasn't big and fancy. It was small and cute: a creative space where Holly felt inspired and oh so *freaking* excited about developing a series of short stop-motion films for a website she needed to launch pronto. Things were looking up, and Holly couldn't be more excited.

"So what do you want from us?" asked Shanequa. "How can we help? Put us to work."

"Awesome. Well . . ." Holly looked around, feeling pretty confident most of the work had already been done. "I made a list in my bullet journal—"

"Woot!" Shanequa fist-bumped Holly. "Bullet journal!"

"I know, right?" Holly laughed. "It's the prettiest things-to-do list I've ever created. Only took me two hours, but wow. You should see the pendant triangles strung across the top of the page."

"What did you use for a title?"

"She Shed," said Holly. "Although, I screwed up on the *d*, so I covered it with washi tape, tearing the washi tape into what I'm hoping looks like flower petals. I stuck the *d* above it."

"Good, good. Sounds good." Shanequa nodded, somewhat impressed, but knowing there was *lots* of room for improvement.

"Actually," said Holly, "it looks pretty bad. It looks like: *She She* with a blop of tape and a random *d* on top."

They laughed.

"I almost wrote *That's What She Said* across the top," said Holly. "And then I thought, if it was *Jack* out here in the shed, it would be a *That's What He Said He Shed*." The whole thing sounded deliciously ridiculous. When they finished laughing, Holly thought: *Good gravy. What would this town be like without Mary-Margaret?* "Let's do one last check against the list of things needing to get done. And then I thought we could all kick back and relax while the girls play."

"How's your mom?" asked Shanequa.

"Good. Good. Thanks for asking," said Holly. "I watched movies with her last night and brought breakfast to her this morning. She's hanging in there. We were lucky."

"Well, if there's anything you or Jack need, shout."

"Thank you. Truly. That means the world to me," said Holly, taking a moment to bask in the realization of just how much she was grateful for her new friendship with Shanequa. Talia and Ella were two peas in a pod. And Holly was sure Jack wouldn't survive the Bubble Gummers without Malik.

"Think I should show him now?" Holly asked.

"Most definitely!" said Shanequa, joining Malik as they followed Holly as she led Jack down the path from Holly Banks Productions to the doors of their garage.

Holly tapped the code in the keypad, garage door opening to a cooler filled with beer and a large commercial coffee roaster still in the package.

"Whoa!" Unable to contain his excitement, Jack walked immediately to the coffee roaster. "What is this?"

"It's the start of your new man cave," said Holly. "I know it's not much, but I thought we could clean this place up and create a space in the house for you to enjoy the things you love."

He lifted his attention from the roaster to move swiftly toward Holly, before wrapping her in a tight embrace. "Thank you," he said, but then, as Holly knew it would, the moment passed quickly into Virgo practicality. "Holly," he said. "You shouldn't have done that."

"You love roasting," she said.

"I know, but this feels a little indulgent. It's just a hobby."

She knew he'd say that. She knew he'd somehow feel it wasn't right of him to take time and resources away from the family. "Hobbies are important," said Holly, looking at Shanequa and Malik for backup. They both nodded in agreement. "Evenings and weekends are important. Time alone to connect with what you love is important. Everyone needs something that's uniquely theirs. And you helped us save some money on the renovation. You earned it."

"Yeah, but it's not like this is my job," he pointed out. "I can't support a family on coffee beans."

"Some people do. And why do you have to make money at it? Why can't you simply enjoy it?" she asked.

She knew he wasn't going to come right out and say it, though Shanequa and Malik already knew—Jack was between jobs. Spending hundreds of dollars on a coffee roaster probably wasn't the best idea at the moment. She'd tell him later there was money left on the business loan—that she had tightened her budget when ordering camera equipment to make room for the purchase. And besides, she was simply equipping her film studio with a coffee machine for the employee break room, right?

"It'll be fine. Even though it's still in the box, I got it secondhand from a wholesale warehouse, so it was a bargain," Holly assured him. They still had a six-month severance package, given all that he had done for the firm. "I love what you love, Jack," she said. "You do so much for this family. If what you love is roasting coffee, then roasting coffee just bumped to the top of our family's priority list. And don't worry about turning it into anything. Just enjoy it."

43

Pushing through the etched-glass double front doors into Feathered Nest Realty's stately, chandeliered entryway, Holly met with frenzied activity as vendors and Enclave Tour organizers hurried about. A long line of banquet tables topped with Feathered Nest Realty gift bags had no fewer than six associates busily stuffing the bags with promotional items.

Penelope spotted Holly near the reception desk. "Come quick!" she said, signaling for Holly to join her. Into Penelope's office they went, moving swiftly across the pale silk rug toward Penelope's desk. "How is your mom?"

"Good," said Holly. "I was just there. I brought a bag of Scrabble tiles for her to work with."

"She's playing Scrabble?"

"Not yet—she's just sliding them around on a tray. The therapist suggested it as a 'high motivation' fine motor activity. She has a motley crew of friends who visit every day. They're strategizing a takedown at next month's Scrabble tournament. She's up and walking—slowly. Getting feisty. Tired of squeezing a stress ball every hour to build strength. We figured out if we bring Ella and her coloring books every day, we get a good half hour of fine motor therapy out of her with no complaints. One step at a time. We're very lucky."

"New coloring books to colorganize."

Holly laughed. "Exactly."

"Will she be ready to play in the Scrabble tournaments?"

"I don't know. I hope so," said Holly. "The doctors said recovery is different for everyone, and she's a fighter. So who knows. We have to wait and see."

"Have a seat," said Penelope, walking toward her thick, clear-glass desk with gilded legs like gold balls stacked one on top of the other. She plopped into a tall chair made of tufted upholstery and on wheels so she could glide about with ease and sophistication. Above Penelope's desk were the bulbous, curlicued rods and big bang bubbles made of blobs of molten glass forming the Big Bang Bubble chandelier designed by Calista Weaver. The chandelier was truly a remarkable splendor in gold-speckled, iridescent peacock-green glass, its reflection mirrored in the ceiling's ultraglossy, ultrablue paint with a shiny pearlescent finish like the sky reflected in a clear mountain lake. To Holly's mind, it wasn't as special as the chandelier she'd fallen in love with, but it was certainly exquisite.

"Penelope, thank you for the chandelier. You didn't have to do that."

"Nonsense, Holly. It was my pleasure."

"Well, it looks beautiful hanging in my foyer. Thank you. How are the auction items performing?" asked Holly, knowing they were posted within the app and had been live for at least a week now.

"Vacation packages are topping the list, followed by themed gift baskets. And, yes, a few bids on your commercial film shoot package." She pointed, attention turning to a stack of folded T-shirts and matching bumper stickers on her desk. The T-shirts were solid white with black block letters inside a black oval outline—matching the white oval bumper stickers with the same black lettering and black oval outlines.

"Aren't they cute?" asked Penelope. "Something for everyone as a thank-you for attending the Enclave Tour. We're unveiling them for sale tomorrow in shops across Primm. You can order them on our website too. Something to wear . . . ," she said, then took a moment to snap open each of the six white T-shirts, modeling each one by holding it up to her body. "This one says *SOLA* for Southern Lakes," she said, pointing to the *SOLA* black lettering in the black oval splashed across her breast. "We have *ME* for Menander, *QUIX* for Quixotic, and *DOOL* for DooLittle. We were going to print *DOO* but worried someone would buy two bumper stickers and place them side by side." She picked up the last two T-shirts. "And here are the crowning glories, if I do say so myself: *VOP* and *PRIMM*. We're selling them in various colors. Aren't they cute?"

"Super cute," said Holly, reminded of how close she came to living in SOLA. How would a *SOLA* sticker look in the back window of her Suburban compared to the *VOP* or *PRIMM* sticker she was sure she would soon be buying? She supposed it was a lot like choosing a college—how one decision changed the course of bumper stickers for the rest of your life.

"Oh, Holly. Great news!" said Penelope, dropping the shirt to plunk down in her seat. She slid her chair forward toward her desk, placing both arms out and across the desk to captivate Holly's attention with her body language. "Earlier today, when I was finalizing media and PR for the Enclave Tour with Eliza Adalee, she said the results of the land dispute beneath the water tower are expected to be announced Friday by the Land Survey Department. Village of Primm versus Southern Lakes. I know it's quick—but from what they're telling me, it's pretty decisive. Anyway, they're announcing preliminary findings, then community hearings will begin if necessary, and then further litigation if it gets to that point, but I doubt it will. They wouldn't make an announcement this fast if they weren't certain there was overwhelming evidence. I think it's an open-and-shut case. One town will overwhelmingly prevail."

"Really? Wow," said Holly, her mind wandering. One step closer for Houston. Clive must be smiling down.

"So get this: Eliza Adalee of VOP News as well as media from Southern Lakes, Menander, Quixotic, and DooLittle are all expected to be present for the land-dispute announcement. Expect a call asking if Muggles—"

"Struggle. Our dog's name is Struggle," said Holly.

"Sorry. Struggle. Anyway, Eliza Adalee is going to call you asking if Struggle can be present for the unveiling of ownership rights, but I reminded Eliza your shed was on the Enclave Tour and suggested you might be too busy to bring your dog by the Land Survey Department. She then let it slip your dog will be given a key to the village. A key to the village! You know what I think that means? I think that means the Village of Primm is about to be declared owner of the land beneath the water tower!" Penelope squealed, before quickly adding, "Oh, but we can't know that for sure because when I said that to Eliza Adalee, she told me that she asked the same question and was quickly shot down by the guy at the municipal office. So there's no guarantee—the key is simply to recognize the dog's service. Anyway, I suggested Eliza contact the Land Survey Department and ask that they move their announcement to the she shed behind your house. That way, Mugg—*Struggle* will already be there, and maybe you can make a few comments on behalf of the dog. What do you think?"

"I don't want the media at my house," said Holly, anxiety rising. "I have a better idea. Rather than host the media event at my house—and thank you for that. That was very generous of you to offer—why not hold the event in the Topiary Park? Perhaps at the base of Plume? After all, that's the primary reason we're all doing this."

"Good point," said Penelope, taking a moment to consider it. "Okay, yes. You're right. Decision made. You're a stop on the Enclave Tour just like everyone else, but you won't be a featured media event. All of the excitement and announcements will happen at the Topiary Park with Plume. As it should be."

"I have a question to ask," Holly said. "Confidentially, of course."

"Of course," said Penelope, rising from her chair behind her desk to join Holly on the Chesterfield Leather grand armchairs. "What is it?"

"If Jack and I were thinking about selling the house—like for job transfer or something or maybe to return to our hometown in Boulder City—how long do you think it would take for you to sell our home? Should we need to sell in a hurry." Holly braced for the bad news.

"Well, assuming you addressed the situation in the foyer—"

"We have."

"And assuming all goes according to plan with the rebuilding of the Village of Primm—which assumes a successful Enclave Tour to rebuild the Topiary Park Petting Zoo so that tourists will return and help stabilize the shops on The Lawn, which will in turn stabilize the local economy . . . oh! And *if* the folks at Neem Oil can assist with eradicating the chilli thrip infestation that's sweeping the village—on the other side of all that, then I'd say about two weeks."

"Two weeks?" said Holly. "That's great news!"

"Maybe three. The Village of Primm is a sought-after community thanks to Primm Academy, and the Petunia enclave is within reach for some young families."

Whew. She was worried they might lose their shirts or go underwater with the bank. If they needed to cut and run, it was comforting to know they could.

"Oh, but Holly," said Penelope from her Chesterfield Leather grand armchair, finger wagging to make her point, "be glad you didn't buy that colonial in Southern Lakes. Southern Lakes is saturated with colonials, so the supply of houses is greater than the demand, which is killing prices for the homeowners trying to sell. Often, they're competing with an identical floor plan down the street, so it's all boiling down to how the homes are staged. And remember, Southern Lakes doesn't have Primm Academy. Had you bought that other home, selling it would have taken a lot longer. I'd say four? Maybe five months?" She reached over to hand Holly a yellow, some might even say buttercream, VOP

T-shirt. "Keep it. I think it's the best one of the bunch. Don't you agree?"

"Thank you," said Holly, stunned by the news the Southern Lakes home would have taken longer to sell. She felt an easing of the knot she so often felt inside her chest.

Maybe the skies *had* aligned in her favor. Maybe it *was* her fate to have purchased the home in the Village of Primm when her free will was exercised to do so. Who knew? Who knew what, or how, or how come, or why not? The more she searched for her place in the world, the more she wondered about something bigger than herself at work in her life. Holly suspected the only thing that mattered in this world was the who. Who you placed your faith in—not what.

"One more thing," Penelope added, handing Holly an envelope. "I have four new listings scheduled two weeks from now—the homeowners are making final preparations. One in Pram, two in Gilman Clear, and one in Parallax. I need aerial and interior photographs. Also, I'd like to shoot live video of myself at each residence introducing the features of the home, and I'll need short clips produced for the beginning and end of each. But the most significant project coming my way is the opening of the Stone House and Glass Studio property. Highlighting them the way we have while promoting the Enclave Tour has piqued interest *and* ruffled a few feathers." She nodded toward the chandelier above her desk. "I suspect Calista Weaver will be coming to town. If that happens, things are bound to get interesting. Are you ready for that? Is that she shed of yours up and running?"

"Yes, of course," said Holly. It wasn't, yet, but it would be.

"Good. Pull Caleb into the fold and dedicate a corkboard or some sort of production calendar to Feathered Nest so you can schedule listings when I send them."

Holly didn't know what to say. In that moment, Holly Banks Productions picked up its first customer. A good customer—a great customer. Feathered Nest Realty. Wow.

"I sense a strong buying-and-selling season in real estate is coming, and well, a little birdie told me ultralight aircraft is far better than drones." She smiled.

Holly smiled, too, readying herself to leave.

"Before you go," said Penelope. "Collette Williams wants to build an entire YouTube channel dedicated to the work she's now doing to her home in Dillydally. She wants to pin, shoot, and post every nook and cranny of that house across all of the major social media channels. IGTV, content marketing. It's a huge project. And she wants you to handle it."

"Penelope, you didn't call her about the foyer, did you?" *No, no, no.* "Because that's not what I wanted," said Holly.

"Trust me when I tell you I handled it with sensitivity. I was very delicate with my words," said Penelope. When Holly started to protest, she raised her hand to stop Holly from continuing. "Holly," she said. "Give people the opportunity to right their wrongs. I know a certain someone who added her home to an Enclave Tour—a home she had hardly unpacked—because she felt bad about a situation she may or may not have knowingly taken part in."

"But—this is embarrassing. I can't take her money. I feel horrible. I never meant for that to happen."

"Funny," said Penelope. "That's exactly what Collette said."

44

Jack getting Ella ready for the school bus and the Wilhelm Klaus late-entry deadline looming, Holly slipped from the patio door with a renewed sense of purpose, heading to her she shed in the backyard to put the finishing touches on the stop-motion she'd been working on. She set her coffee on the worktable in her shed, and then before she began, she texted Sadie.

HOLLY: How's mom?

SADIE: Good. Thanks for taking my shift to sit with her last night.

HOLLY: Of course. You practically moved in with her. I'm happy you finally got a night in an actual bed. Is she still coming home at noon? Nothing's changed?

SADIE: That's the plan.

HOLLY: Awesome. We're ready for her. Want me to come now?

SADIE: Not yet. I'll text when she's back in her room. She's down the hall in physical therapy right now. She's dying to see the kittens and hang with Ella more. I'd say come around eleven?

HOLLY: Not sooner?

SADIE: Eleven is fine.

HOLLY: Okay.

Sadie ran the ship. Always did. Oh, well, thought Holly, trying to put a positive spin on it and not let it bother her—this gave her time to finish the film and hit submit.

All her shots taken and imported into film-editing software, she just needed to tweak a few things, add credits, export it in the correct file format, and then upload it to the Wilhelm Klaus Film Festival website. Not too long ago, this would have overwhelmed her, but she'd been tinkering with the software. Trying things, making mistakes. Making lots and lots of mistakes, but also figuring out a few things along the way. And though she had jumped from *Henny Penny* before capturing a live shot of the clear blue skies over Primm, she was happy with the layered-paper effects she made for the sky. Not quite the real thing but good enough.

Picking up from where the story left off, with the Audrey character and her dog hailing a taxi, Holly edited the final scene of her stop-motion with her paper-cutout character walking down a cobblestone walk Holly had fashioned with tiny pebbles she and Ella had collected, then glued to card stock. A row of twelve houses made with decorative papers and found objects—button doorknobs and paper clip shutters—lined the walk, each with a distinctive chandelier viewed through a front window. Like welcome signs, enclave names were painted on each of the doors: Peloton, Blythe, Hopscotch, and others.

—WILHELM KLAUS FILM FESTIVAL ENTRY—

FADE IN:

SCENE 7 — EXT. SIDEWALK — TWILIGHT

    Stepping from a taxi, AUDREY visits
    each home, pausing, not to knock on

the door but to peer longingly inside each window at the chandelier hanging within. From the leash in her hand, no longer her dog, but the words "HAVE NOT," a reflection of how she feels when she compares what she has to others.

Audrey arrives at the final paper house, a small home with "Petunia" on the door. She peers inside, finding a FAMILY of three, a GRANDMOTHER, a DOG, and a CAT with KITTENS. As she watches the family, she is filled with delight. Above the family, a chandelier made of gilded twigs forming a haloed circle. Hanging from the golden circle, twelve pot-bellied glass birds filled with light.

Reaching inside the window, she takes hold of the gilded nest as the chandelier breaks free of the structure, floating through the roof, and pulling Audrey along with it, the word "NOT" catching on the window ledge, falling to the ground in a pile of broken letters.

Still on her leash, a new feeling, a joyous feeling, a feeling of gratitude, the word "HAVE" follows Audrey as she floats up, up, up through the roof as twilight turns to night, Audrey still clutching the chandelier.

SCENE 8 — EXT. SKY — LOW ANGLE (shot from below, looking up)

The glass BIRDS free themselves from the chandelier to take flight, each finding their place as a glass bird "star" in the night sky. As AUDREY floats, she places the gilded ring of twigs onto her head and wears it like a crown. Together with the birds, she forms a constellation in full acceptance of her fate: "at one" with the universe, grateful to "HAVE," thankful for her life on earth; her journey; her one beautiful, miraculous, at times quite peculiar life.

SCENE 9 — EXT. SKY — CLOSING SHOT

AUDREY lifts the gilded crown from her head, placing it above her, letting it shine like a penumbral ring in the sky.

At the close of the shot, three letters shuffled their way across the screen, forming the word FIN, a French word often used at the end of a film. A little word, a simple word that meant so much: "the end."

She did it. Holly had *finally* reached the end. Holly saw the word she most longed to see.

She leaned back in the chair she'd bought to support her body during long hours of film production and editing. "I did it. I freaking did it," she whispered the moment she clicked submit and then watched as a confirmation notice popped onto the screen—entry 63.

Sixty-three? Good gravy, that's a lot of entries.

She wouldn't place. No way. Not with that many entries. And that was fine by Holly because sometimes, it was about crossing the finish line—not letting everyone else pass you by because you were bogged down with self-doubt, fear, procrastination, a foolish pursuit of perfection, and the tendency to always, habitually, compare yourself to others—to what they had and what you did not.

She texted Caleb.

HOLLY: How did it go with Rosie?

CALEB: Amazing. Took her to dinner Friday. We've been texting NONSTOP. And get this—she likes BIRD POETRY! It's like—we're fated or something. I mean, how was I to know she liked bird poetry? I just grabbed a book off the shelf. I didn't know. That's destiny, right? And get this: I rented a powder blue tuxedo.

HOLLY: Was the dinner that fancy?

CALEB: I wore a button-down shirt and my best cargo pants to dinner—Holly. You should have seen her dress. I couldn't speak for like—ten minutes. She looked like an actress from the Golden Age of Hollywood before the decline of the studio system. Her shoes had a strap across her ankle—who are those dancers who kick?

HOLLY: Radio City Rockettes?

CALEB: I was so nervous I dropped my keys. Twice. But then, she held my hand and I was like—I don't know. She knew I was nervous, but she didn't laugh. She said it was nice, and once, I thought I saw her tearing up a bit, but she was smiling, and kept asking me where I came from. Not like, did you come from Chicken, Alaska or Booger Hole, West Virginia.

HOLLY: Booger Hole?

CALEB: Those are real towns.

HOLLY: Get back to the powder blue tux.

CALEB: She told me at dinner her favorite poem was titled Blue-footed Booby—true story. That's a real bird. And get this—this dude has blue feet. The whole poem was about a blue-footed booby looking for his soulmate on Galapagos Island.

HOLLY: So you rented a powder blue tuxedo?

CALEB: Yup!

HOLLY: So you're a blue-footed booby.

CALEB: Yup! I wore it to bring her to Mitch & Lucy Creamery for ice cream on Saturday. Guess what flavor she ordered?

HOLLY: No idea. Chocolate?

CALEB: Blue Moon.

HOLLY: Ahhh. Nice one!

CALEB: Bird poetry. Trust me, Holly. You gotta try it.

HOLLY: Well, guess what—Wilhelm Klaus. I just clicked submit.

CALEB: Congrats! Are you happy with the finished product?

HOLLY: I am.

CALEB: Think it will place?

HOLLY: Definitely not. I can already think of ten things I'd change if I had more time.

CALEB: So, how does it feel?

HOLLY: It feels amazing. Like, really, really amazing.

CALEB: Awesome.

HOLLY: Caleb?

CALEB: Yup.

HOLLY: None of this would have happened without you.

CALEB: Aw, sure it would.

HOLLY: No. It wouldn't. Second week of October? Having only lived in the VOP since August? I'd still be spinning my wheels with Ella in school and settling the house. Flipping channels, watching movies, wishing I was creating. Instead, I just submitted a stop-motion to the Wilhelm Klaus from a she shed home office for Holly Banks Productions. I'm so grateful I met you, Caleb. You're the best thing that's happened to me since moving to the Village of Primm. You've changed my life, Caleb. You really have. If there is ever anything I can do . . .

CALEB: I know!

HOLLY: What.

CALEB: Fly with me.

45

Friday morning, first day of the weekend Enclave Tour, Holly asked Jack, "What's got you so happy this morning?" as he placed a cup of coffee in front of her. They were up before everyone else, Greta and Sadie still sleeping in Greta's room. Ella asleep in Holly and Jack's bed after climbing in around five that morning. Holly took a sip. "Um." She wasn't quite sure what to say.

"I scorched it," he said, dejected. "You don't have to drink it." He moved to take the cup from Holly's hand.

"Hold up," she said, appreciating the effort. The stop-motion she'd submitted, were it a batch of coffee beans, definitely wouldn't come out perfect straight out of the gate. There was a lot she'd be learning, exploring, and trying as she ventured further into the craft. "No way are you taking this from me—this is your first official batch. I want to enjoy it."

"I think the charge temperature was too high," he said, his face appearing worried, but Holly suspected he was loving every moment of it. Learning, exploring, trying. "There were burnt patches on the flat sections of the bean."

"It's delicious." Holly reached over to squeeze his forearm. "Smoky."

"I'm so happy this Enclave Tour thing will be over in seventy-two hours," he said. "Can you imagine? Strangers coming inside the house when we just got Greta home?"

"No, actually. I can't," said Holly, feeling encouraged that the doctors said Greta looked so good. "It's so nice to have her home again."

First thing Greta had done when she got home was check on Charlotte and the kittens. Holly convinced Greta to sit in her favorite chair in the family room, Jack moving the box with Charlotte and the kittens next to Greta. When Ella got home from school, the first thing she did was climb into the chair with Greta, eventually falling asleep in Greta's arms just before dinnertime. It was easy to underestimate how tired a busy life made you until that tiring life stopped the clock and asked you to sit still for a while.

Javina, Lottie, Ruth, Henry, and Darnell had come over, as well as Houston—full of requests for more Crock-Pot Pit Stop gatherings—along with Aahna and her husband, Raj Patel. Raj was every bit as warm and lovely as Aahna, who brought *gulab jamuns* made of heavy cream, cardamom powder, and rose water. Greta took one bite, accused Aahna of hooking her on crack, then asked how she could get more. After the motley crew left, Houston lingered, sitting with Greta for a while, spending one-on-one time with her in the family room. When he left, he kissed the top of her hand and said, "Get better, kiddo. I miss your company. And don't forget. We have clients who need us."

In the kitchen that Friday morning, enjoying their coffee while the family slept, Jack said to Holly, "I'd love to learn what'll happen to that Frank Mauro character." He brought Holly the sugar to sweeten her coffee.

"I doubt anything will happen. I don't think he broke any laws, did he?" Holly thought about it for a minute, remembering the scene he created on The Lawn when Struggle was found digging. He called the media. And then he did everything he could to stay in front of the camera. "For someone who spends his days in The Quiet, I suspect he's enjoying the limelight. For better or for worse."

"I'm looking forward to returning to our private life." Jack took a sip. "I need a job—and that sucks—but if I'm being honest, I didn't like the one I had. In the end, maybe a new job will lead us to a better place."

"Yeah, maybe," said Holly. "Although, I kinda like it here in Primm."

"I talked to the headhunter. She's lining up a few interviews in the surrounding area, so hopefully, this won't take long, but who knows? We might have to relocate."

"Maybe it wouldn't be so bad to head back home," said Holly. "I think Mom might be leaning toward recovering at Sadie's house. I can't say I blame her. Besides the new ones she's made here, all of her friends are there. But it still makes me sad."

She took an eensy weensy sip, trying her best not to choke.

"So," said Jack. "The big day has arrived: the long-awaited Enclave Tour. What happens now? How can I help?"

"Tonight should be pretty chill. Judges will swing by between five thirty and seven. I'm sure I'm not winning any awards, so it'll just be a formality. Nothing for you to do, but would you mind bringing Struggle and Ella to the kickoff at the Topiary Park Petting Zoo?"

"I think it's so crazy Struggle's getting a key to the village."

"I know, right?" said Holly. "I've already told Houston, and Houston called Thom. They're going to the ceremony, and Thom is giving a statement. I thought he could explain ore dogs better than you or me."

"Got it," said Jack, giving Holly two thumbs up. "And they're announcing the results of the land survey?"

"Of course. It's a big media draw for Penelope. That announcement alone should draw people to the event from both towns. Maybe even Menander, DooLittle, and Quixotic if they're following the story. I told Penelope she should have a promo piece created this weekend so she'll have something to use should she decide to run another tour next year. Caleb is shooting footage all weekend. And next week, we start production."

"Quite the entrepreneur."

"I'm trying," she said, turning her head so she could listen over her shoulder to the sounds coming from upstairs. "I think Mom's up." She set her mug down, readying to leave the table to help Greta.

"Before you go," he said, "I just wanted to say kudos for getting that stop-motion submitted. I know that was important to you, and you've had a lot going on around here."

"You're the one who told me to live my art." She touched her fingertip to the tip of his nose. "Do you remember telling me that? On the porch the first week of kindergarten?"

"I do. I told you to live your art—because it was certainly living you."

She reached down to take hold of his hand, telling him over scorched, garage-roasted coffee, "I love you, Jack Tavish Banks. You're my best friend."

"And you're mine," he said, bringing her hand to his mouth to kiss her ring. One of those "Jack" things Jack so often did.

~

Later that night, with Jack, Ella, and Struggle at the Enclave Tour launch event at the foot of Plume in the Topiary Park, Holly, Sadie, and Greta made their way to the she shed to wait for a team of judges to arrive.

"You got this, Ma?" Holly asked, walking backward, facing Greta while holding on to Greta's hips as Sadie steadied Greta from behind. Struck by how small her mother was, Holly found it hard to decide: Was she small and frail and weak now that she had been compromised or strong and resolute, a fighter? Both, of course. "Take your time. There's no hurry."

Holly's shed was one of only two she sheds on the tour—what were the chances she'd win against Mary-Margaret's That's What She Said she shed? Absolutely zero. Zip. None. Nada. But really, *who cared*? Holly had agreed to have an entry on the tour, and she'd followed through despite having an ultralight aircraft rip across her lawn, trashing her curb appeal. Despite a leak in her ceiling that later dropped on her head, dousing her with water when the dog flooded the upstairs bathroom. Despite the removal of a load-bearing wall, calling the very structure of her home into question. Despite purchasing paint for the living room and dining room, and wood for bookshelves. Despite taking out a loan for camera equipment that was purchased and living room furniture that was not purchased because she repaired her foyer and bought a she shed instead. And hey—that was just her home. Never mind Greta's stroke, Jack's job loss, Holly's business launch, the creation of her first film and its entry into a film festival, Ella's wedding, Charlotte's kittens, and the decades-old mystery she found herself at the center of due to Struggle's adventures in Primm. Holly had been busy.

If she had learned anything these past few weeks in Primm, it was this: don't compare yourself to others, do the best you can, and if you don't get your priorities straight, the universe will straighten them for you.

Who gave a flip about winning first place in a she shed competition? Or a film festival, for that matter? Holly was happy she had survived the events of the past month. And besides, as Shanequa had said that day at Mitch & Lucy Creamery, it wasn't about the result—it was about the process. And what a "process" that last month had been. Not just bullet journaling and colorganizing, Holly had built a business from the ground up—quite literally: a she shed now stood in her backyard housing Holly Banks Productions. More important, at a soul level, ever since Jack had encouraged her that day on the front porch during Ella's first week of kindergarten to "live her art," she had one burning desire: to write the word she most longed to see—*FIN*, "the end" in the film industry. And she did it. She finished her first film. And soon, others would see it, and they'd experience a small part of her. A part of her she'd share with the world and hope the world would be kind. Holly supposed life was a lot like the creation of a stop-motion. You had to take it step by step, one frame at a time. With Sadie's help, she guided her mom through the backyard, telling Greta, "One step at a time, Momma. I got you."

Sadie held the lawn chair still as Holly held Greta by the armpits, Greta lowering herself into the chair. "I'm fine," said Greta, who kept waving them off. "You're fussing too much."

"What now?" Holly asked, once they had all settled into their chairs. "Mom, do you know your plans?"

"Hmm. I don't know," said Greta.

Holly looked at her sister, trying to read from the expression on Sadie's face what Sadie thought Greta would do. Did Sadie know something Holly didn't? Though Holly wanted Greta to recover at her house, all parties involved intuitively knew without anyone outright saying as much that if either Holly or Sadie was to become Greta's primary caregiver, it would be Sadie. And it didn't matter if Holly lived in the Village of Primm or their last home in Boulder City, Colorado. Sadie was Sadie. Greta was Greta. And Holly was Holly. That was why Sadie descended upon Greta the moment she was admitted to the hospital. That was why she slept most nights by Greta's side and sent Holly home while saying she was doing so because Holly had a family to care for, whereas Sadie's family was back in Nevada. It made sense at the time, but the underlying question for Holly had become: Did Sadie not trust Holly to oversee Greta's care? Or did Sadie think, in some ways, Greta and Holly were cut from the same cloth? Hmm. Holly wondered.

Greta moved her arm toward Holly, reaching out to take her by the hand—in part, Holly presumed, because she wanted to show Holly and Sadie that she could.

"What is it, Ma? What's wrong?" Holly asked.

Greta squeezed Holly's hand—it was slight, but it was a squeeze.

It took a moment for Holly to understand what was happening.

"Seriously?" said Holly, wanting to throttle Sadie, realizing the decision had already been made. She turned her head to look away. Away from Greta, away from Sadie, and toward the shed, swiping a tear with the back of her hand.

For the longest time, she couldn't look at either one of them—though she loved her sister, she couldn't look at Sadie without getting mad, and she couldn't look at Greta without crying, so instead, the three of them sat. In lawn chairs. Outside of Holly's new shed.

"Okay, fine," Holly said at last, voice shaky, chin about to quiver. "But *Sadie* tells Ella. I'm not telling Ella. No way."

"I'll be back," whispered Greta. "I promise."

Another squeeze. Slight, but a squeeze, nonetheless.

46

EMAIL—Time Sent: 12:03 a.m.

TO: Psychic Betty, Psychic Hotline Network
FROM: Holly Banks
SUBJECT: My Mom

I thought I'd write to tell you my mom is home from the hospital. After three days at Menander Medical, she spent a week in rehab, is now home, and scheduled to continue occupational, physical, and speech therapy on an outpatient basis. She moves slowly, seems weak, and though the muscles around her mouth appear to be strengthening, her eye still looks droopy, and is showing no sign of improvement. I know I need to be patient, but it's hard, and I worry.

The problem is, she's leaving me to go home with my sister Sadie.

I know I should take a cosmic perspective on things and point my inner astrolabe to the heavens and all that, but truthfully, I'm sad. She's my mom. I need her and I'm going to miss her. I want her to stay here. With me.

Tell me a story. Say something that will make everything seem all right. Maybe, tell me about the Big Bang or something. Can you do that, Psychic Betty? Tell me about the Big Bang? I want to know where all of this began so I can figure my way out of it.

~

EMAIL—Time Received: 12:50 a.m.

TO: Holly Banks
FROM: Psychic Betty, Psychic Hotline Network
SUBJECT: Your Mom

You want me to tell you about the Big Bang? All right, here it is. The complete story of the Big Bang. What it is and how it happened. Are you ready? Here we go.

A metric shit-ton of stuff happened, and now, tah-dah! Here we are!

I suppose hearing about the Big Bang doesn't make you feel better. I suspect that's because you're asking big questions when sometimes, life has a way of answering by "bringing it in," drawing you close, asking you to sit still, remain small, and hunker down beneath the light of the moon. Quite the opposite of the Big Bang lives we tend to live.

Consider this. As far as celestial objects are concerned, nothing stands between the moon and the earth. Why? Because the moon is the closest thing to earth. She's closer than the sun. Closer than the stars. And she's always there. She's right there in the night sky, tucking you in with the tides. She's there in the daytime, too. Though you often can't see her, she's there.

Look out your window from time to time. Step outside and look up.

Miraculous things surround you.

Click HERE to order the Big Bang platter. Corn on the cob, melted butter, and a jumbo lobster holding a fistful of lit firecrackers. BANG! (I'm guessing that's not very appetizing?)

Alrighty then.

Click HERE to order a platter of Dizzy's Crescent Moons. Tasty seafood dip spread inside crescent rolls and baked to perfection. Yum!

~

EMAIL—Time Sent: 1:01 a.m.

TO: Psychic Betty, Psychic Hotline Network
FROM: Holly Banks
SUBJECT: Where Are You?

Though it doesn't change the fact my mom is leaving, it brought me great comfort when you said, "She's closer than the sun. Closer than the stars. And though you often can't see her, she's there." I'll miss my mom when she's gone, but I know she's always with me.

Thank you, Psychic Betty. You're a good friend.

I'd like to eat at Dizzy's Seafood sometime.

May I ask? Where is it?

~

EMAIL—Time Received: 1:05 a.m.

TO: Holly Banks
FROM: Psychic Betty, Psychic Hotline Network
SUBJECT: Where Am I?

Dear Holly,

I'm closer than you think.

—Psychic Betty

Click HERE for coupons to Dizzy's Seafood.

47

Penelope Pratt
Feathered Nest Realty

—ENCLAVE ALERT—

THE VILLAGE OF PRIMM HAS BEEN SAVED!

On behalf of Feathered Nest Realty, it brings me great pleasure to announce the successful end to the Village of Primm Enclave Tour.

Welcoming tour-goers from our own Village of Primm, as well as Southern Lakes, Menander, Quixotic, DooLittle, and others, the residents of enclaves Ballyhoo, Blythe, Castle Drum Tower, Chum, Dillydally, Gilman Clear, Hobnob, Hopscotch, Parallax, Peloton, Petunia, and Pram—each achieving platinum status with four homes per enclave on tour—have much to be proud of.

Ticket sales far exceeded expectations and shops throughout the village received a much-welcomed influx of business, thanks in part to merchandise designed to complement the Enclave Tour Crossword Puzzle.

To the forty-eight star-studded homeowners, four each from the twelve enclaves, who showed their love for the Village of Primm, showed their desire for the replanting of Plume, and showed their commitment to the reshaping of the Topiary Park Petting Zoo, I say this: the fate of Primm was in your hands, you rose to the occasion, and we couldn't have done it without you.

As a token of our gratitude, these forty-eight homes will be receiving mailboxes crafted in antique nickel, mimicking the look of platinum, forever commemorating your willingness to put your private home on public display for the sake of others. I encourage every HOA to approve the installations of these mailboxes. I feel certain the dedicated individuals across the village who work tirelessly through the Hello Note program to ensure that every single HOA rule for their particular enclave is followed at all times will move heaven and earth to see that these special homeowners receive the recognition they deserve. Let's let the next Hello Note taped to a mailbox be a Hello Note of congratulations and gratitude.

This just in from horticulturists at the Topiary Park Petting Zoo: orders have been placed for boxwoods, moss, holly, laurel, and privet. Not to mention the beloved flowers that will adorn Plume once more: Liberty Classic white snapdragons, white begonias, purple pigeonberry, sky-flower and golden dewdrop, blue lisianthus, fragrant verbena, sweet viburnum, and more.

The Grand Reopening of the Topiary Park Petting Zoo is upon us.

The Village of Primm is open for business.

All of us can say once more: there's no place like home!

PLEASE NOTE: Results of the land dispute beneath the water tower bordering the Village of Primm and Southern Lakes are NOT the topic of today's Enclave Alert.

48

On the hill above the Clock Tower Labyrinth, in the empty, open field where hot-air balloons took off, with trees sloping toward the orchards on the other side of Pip's Mountain, Holly sat in the passenger seat of *Henny Penny*, seat belt buckled, flight suit so huge you could fit another person inside it.

"Are you sure you want to do this?" asked Caleb, *Henny Penny* off and resting but perched and ready to roll at the end of the runway the moment Caleb fired her up.

"I'm sure," said Holly.

"I'll stay low, keeping about five or ten feet above the treetops," he told her. "But Holly, no jumping."

Embarrassed, Holly acknowledged, "No jumping. I promise."

She lifted the helmet from her lap, placing it on her head before buckling the strap beneath her chin. She was nervous. Nervous AF.

Caleb handed her the goggles.

"Thanks," she said, hooking them across her helmet but leaving them at her forehead the way Greta wore her Red Barons, thinking she still felt she was about to ride in a double-wide baby stroller. After watching Caleb land *Henny Penny* at the Q&U Wedding, Holly had a wee bit more confidence they'd return to this spot unscathed. At least, she hoped so.

Caleb handed her an in-flight snack: Nutella and pretzel sticks.

"Let's confirm our flight plan," he said, unfolding a map of the Village of Primm, knowing Southern Lakes, Menander, and the dueling resort towns of DooLittle and Quixotic were not on the itinerary. Things felt calmer now that the Enclave Tour had ended. It had only been a few days, but Holly welcomed the chance to focus on other things. Like time spent creating and exploring her art, launching Holly Banks Productions, and settling into a new normal with Greta no longer living with them. Greta, Charlotte, and kittens had left earlier that morning with Sadie in a rental car because it was too soon for Greta to fly. Ella was almost inconsolable, but Greta promised her she'd FaceTime every day, and she promised all of them—especially Ella—she'd be back, "just as soon as the yoga returns to my legs, the ukulele to my fingers."

With his finger, Caleb pointed to the locations they'd fly over so Holly could catch footage she'd incorporate into her future portfolio of stop-motion pictures. With Pip's Mountain behind them, they'd fly first over the Clock Tower Labyrinth, making sure to swing past the Topiary Park and the Topiary Park Petting Zoo, capturing Plume (if her wire frame was still in the courtyard; they'd skip it if she had already been rolled into the shed to await her replanting once proceeds from the Enclave Tour had cleared).

And though Caleb *technically* wasn't allowed to fly over congested areas in an ultralight, no one seemed to care, not even Officer Knapp, so next, they'd swing by the hidden-in-plain-sight penumbra created every autumn when golden leaves brightened the sugar maples that lined the circular road leading to the gated entrance to the twelve homes on Hopscotch Hill—passing over Penelope's home, Tryst on Hopscotch Hill, as well as Mary-Margaret's That's What She Said she shed—before heading into the center of town as they passed Feathered Nest Realty.

They'd begin in-town footage along the road that eventually led to Southern Lakes, the same road that lined The Lawn near the South

Gazebo. The South Gazebo, flanked at its roofline with twelve embroidered flags, each representing an enclave in the Village of Primm.

Holly wanted footage of Primm Paper and Mitch & Lucy
Creamery, but also Mappamundi in The Quiet and the compass rose
on The Lawn, where Struggle had unearthed a whole host of problems
stretching back through the decades and across family lines. While they
were there, they planned to circle Primm Academy, site of the Q&U
Wedding at the north end of The Lawn near Primm's Coffee Joe and
the North Gazebo.

Before returning to the open field where they were now, Holly also
wanted to capture footage of all twelve enclaves: Ballyhoo, Blythe, Castle
Drum Tower, Chum, Dillydally, Gilman Clear, Hobnob, Hopscotch,
Parallax, Peloton, Pram, and last, but certainly not least: the Petunia
enclave, where Houston Bonneville-Cranbarrie, Raj and Aahna Patel,
and the ever-lovely Maeve Bling—Hello Notes at the ready, nippy Pom
at her feet—all surrounded the Banks family at numbers 12 and 12½,
headquarters of Holly Banks Productions.

"Don't forget the water tower," said Holly, then fell quiet as she
wondered what would happen between Houston Bonneville-Cranbarrie
and Frank Mauro now that ownership rights beneath the water tower
had been brought to light by the three newly recovered tympanums
and the astrolabe they slipped into. She assumed this would become an
issue for the courts to decide. She assumed, too, that Merchant Meek
Hopscotch III would be called to testify.

"You know, right? You heard the outcome?" asked Caleb.

Holly had been with her mom and Sadie, but Caleb was *at* the
Enclave Tour launch event beneath a vacant twenty-five-foot-tall wire
frame of Plume, where Jack, Ella, Thom, Houston, and a crowd of
onlookers watched Struggle receive a key to the village—which turned
out to be a jumbo-size knotted rawhide bone she took home to eat in
an hour and which later gave her diarrhea.

Caleb was shooting footage of the ceremonies alongside Eliza Adalee of VOP News, the guy from the podcast division of Radio SOLA, and reporters from the *Primm Gazette* and the *Southern Lakes Daily Dose* tabloid.

"Jack told me. Shocking," said Holly, eyes open wide. "I really expected another outcome."

"The Village of Primm—dry. Southern Lakes—wet," said Caleb, longtime villager. "Score one for Southern Lakes, I suppose." He shrugged. "Meh. Maybe they deserve it. They're always getting the short end of the stick. At least the Enclave Tour was a success."

"And the neem oil appears to be working. And Plume and the beloved topiaries will be replanted," said Holly, relieved her involvement in the chilli thrip infestation was never brought to light. Welcome to the Village of Primm: tuck that secret beside the others. She exhaled, glad the chilli thrips were quickly becoming a thing of the past.

Flight plan established, Caleb folded the map before tucking it down the zipper of his flight suit. "Ready to fire this girl up?" asked Caleb.

"*Henny Penny*'s a girl? Hmm. I guess I always thought of her as a boy," said Holly, calming her nerves by centering her breathing as she looked up to the underside of the glider wings above them. "You do know how the folktale ended, don't you?"

Caleb gazed at the runway, thinking. "No, I don't think I do."

"It's a folktale with a moral about hysteria and paranoia, warning against mistakenly believing that disaster is imminent. There are a few endings, but the two most common endings either have all of the animals—*including* Henny Penny—getting eaten by a fox. Or all of the animals—*except* Henny Penny—getting eaten by a fox. In that version, he runs away while the last of his friends is getting eaten."

"Hmm," said Caleb. "I don't know what to make of that."

"Neither do I," said Holly. "But it's interesting to think about it. Nothing was going right, and I thought the sky was falling. It felt devastating—until my mom had a stroke and Jack lost his job."

"I'm sorry to hear that," said Caleb, picking at something beneath his fingernail, presumably because he didn't know what else to do. "Do you think Penelope Henny Penny'd the Village of Primm into believing the sky was falling?"

Holly considered it. "I think in this case, the sky was falling. I think she was smart to sound the alarm and rally the troops. Score one for Penelope. I think she saved Primm. I really do." Holly smiled at Caleb. "Ready to roll?"

"I am."

"You know I'm scared spitless," said Holly, not wanting to think about her death-defying leap into the bushes.

"I do." He smiled. "And it's okay to be scared. I think there's a lesson inside the folktale about being brave. I also know this is just the beginning for you. I believe you're going to tell great stories through your filmmaking, Holly Banks. You have a particular fate to fulfill. Walk toward that destiny. Who else would face their fears and return a second time?"

She took hold of his hand and squeezed. "You're a true friend, Caleb."

Holly's mind drifted to Shanequa, Malik, and Talia. To the friends Greta had made in such a short time. She thought about Online Psychic Betty and the warmth of their email exchange when Greta was in the hospital. Penelope was a friend and mentor. Mary-Margaret was a work in progress, but Holly was feeling more comfortable asserting herself when Mary-Margaret was around. Baby steps. Holly was grateful to be supported by friends—online, and off.

"Camera ready?"

"Camera ready," said Holly, holding it up, then sliding her goggles down and giving him a big thumbs-up.

Caleb got busy, preparing for flight, firing up the propeller, which began whirling behind them, causing the entire contraption to hum and vibrate, making loud noises like a souped-up lawn mower: *bzzzzzzz. Bzzzzzzz. BZZZZZZZ!*

Holly thought she might puke.

They set out. *Henny Penny* rolling down the runway. Holly closing her eyes every time she feared the sky would fall. *Be brave, Holly. Be brave.*

Bumping along, not wanting to admit that the swiftly moving tree line was scaring her, she closed her eyes, channeling the memory of the old-timey airplane flying over the Cherry Festival and those dash marks in the sky that had inspired her.

"You ready?" yelled Caleb as they taxied down the runway.

Holly was sweating. Contemplating the length of the runway, the ledge at the apogee that awaited her. "I'm ready!" she yelled, eyes still closed as they reached the end of the runway, feeling *Henny Penny's* nose lift as Holly leaned back until she was *up, up, up* in the air—eyes open now, feeling herself *breathe, breathe, breathe* until everything leveled out and she found herself flying through the clear blue skies over Primm.

I'm okay.

I'll survive.

The sky isn't falling so long as I'm in it.

Thank you.

Thank you for this beautiful, miraculous, and at times quite peculiar life.

ACKNOWLEDGMENTS

I will never be able to adequately thank the two people at the center of my writing life: my literary agent, Joëlle Delbourgo, for her expertise, advice, and support, and my editor, Alicia Clancy, whose guidance, skill with words, and keen insight into story touched every page of this novel. I'd also like to thank Gabe Dumpit, Brittany Russell, and the exceptional team at Lake Union Publishing for their continued support and second-to-none talent in transforming words into books. For the gorgeous book covers, Liz Casal, thank you. Thank you, Brilliance Publishing and Brilliance Audio. Kathleen McInerney, for giving Holly her voice in audio, I am absolutely thrilled to have you as part of the team.

Immense gratitude to the following people, who were instrumental in introducing Holly Banks and the Village of Primm to readers while I was writing this book: Kathleen Carter, Stephanie Elliott, Judy Gelman, Sandy Kenyon, Vicki Levy Krupp, Logan LeDuc, Zibby Owens, and Michelle Wolett. Superhuge dot com shout-out and more to Cara, Scott, Emily, and the rock star crew at Rocket Pop Media. To the book influencers who continue to wrap both Holly and me in a warm embrace, how can I ever thank you enough? Two kind souls, in particular, helped turn up the volume: Michelle Jocson @nurse_bookie, for the incredible introductions, warm welcome, and continued fun; and Gina Pelz @readingirlreviews, for the safe-place, "I got you, girl" friendship and for introducing Holly Banks to the book-loving Disney Princess, Belle, in Disneyland, Florida. Stephanie Caruso and Vanessa Esquibel, enormous gratitude for the by-my-side things you do. For the collective think tank, Bookish Road Trip authors Melissa Face, Libby McNamee, and Mary Helen Sheriff. For years of sisterhood and writerly support, Beach Babes Samantha Bailey, Josie Brown, Eileen Goudge, Francine LaSala, Meredith Schorr, and Jen Tucker. Special shout-out to book influencers Melissa Amster, Kristy Barrett, Dany Drexler, Suzanne Leopold, Susan Peterson, Kate Rock, and Vanessa Vicente. Readers in the Kinloch Book Club, James River Writers, and Lake Union Author communities, for the camaraderie and shared love of books and the reading and writing life.

I am blessed beyond measure to be surrounded by family and friends who have been there for me in countless ways. My parents, Bill and Jeanne Breitbach. My sisters and their husbands, Sarah and Skip Sneed and Jill and John Taylor. Beth Cuzzone, Jamie Valerie, extended family and friends I hold dear, thank you. For believing in me, Stephanie Litzerman—there are no words. Thank you, Rayelynn Banks, for sharing with me the story of your daughter, Holli Banks, and the courageous fight she fought. It touched me deeply to learn Holli and I were born the same year. Sunflowers, always.

Emma, Noelle, Holden, and Porter, you are my whole world. Andrew "Michael Michael" Valerie, college sweetheart, husband, father of my children, love of my life, best friend. The lyrics of Tom Waits's "Little Trip to Heaven," which we danced to on our wedding night, say it all.

To my readers, the mere thought of you inspires my every word.

BOOK CLUB QUESTIONS

1. In what ways do the concepts of luck, fate, and destiny play out in the novel? Do you believe events in life can be fated? Are value judgments such as "good luck" or "bad luck" helpful? Have you ever felt a relationship was destined or that you were destined to do or become something?

2. How does the folktale "Henny Penny" play out in the novel? Who behaved like Henny Penny, either feeling or warning others "the sky is falling"? Were those feelings justified? In the final scene of the novel, Holly takes flight in *Henny Penny*, realizing: *I'm okay. I'll survive. The sky isn't falling so long as I'm in it.* What do you suppose she meant by that?

3. Throughout the novel, a fundamental question is asked: What is worth fighting for? Caleb shares his views with Holly on the drive to Feathered Nest Realty. Penelope explains further when she and Holly meet with Mary-Margaret in the she shed. Is the Village of Primm worth fighting for? Why or why not? What would have happened if nothing had been done to save the village?

4. The family dog is at the center of Holly's "struggle" to conform and fit in to her new community. Because of

Struggle, Holly must interact with neighbors Houston Bonneville-Cranbarrie and Maeve Bling, but also with the town and the media, drawing an ore dog trainer named Thom to the village. In what ways did Struggle's actions impact the characters and events in the story? In what ways do family pets impact our lives through their actions?

5. A central theme in this story about community is the value of adult friendship. Who has or is developing real friendships? For better or for worse, how did the following friendships begin, what is holding them together, and how do you see them evolving in the future? Holly and Caleb? Holly and Penelope? Holly and Mary-Margaret? Holly and Shanequa? Greta and Houston? Greta and Aahna, Javina, Lottie, Ruth, Henry, and Darnell? Jack and Malik?

6. At the heart of the mystery is the search for a centuries-old astrolabe and its three missing tympanum discs. This search challenges Holly, Thom, Houston, and Struggle to hunt for missing treasure using a map and the clue *Penumbra Over Primm*. What role did celestial phenomena play in the solving of the mystery?

7. Holly intuits Greta's health might be compromised but is unable to penetrate Greta's insistence there is nothing wrong. Have you ever found yourself caring for a loved one but unable to prevent a medical event that could have been managed or prevented with early intervention? Discuss the complexities of adult children caring for the health of their parents. Does the parent-child relationship complicate the role each must play?

8. Why did the author juxtapose a decades-old conflict over natural resources—water, land ownership, mineral rights,

and gold—against the current conflict of lost financial resources in the local economy of Primm? In what ways are resources a form of currency and vice versa? Can conflicts over resources ever be avoided?

9. To save her community, Penelope launches a village-wide campaign under the premise *consumer spending drives the economy*. Do you agree? Disagree? To what extent should members of a community support locally owned businesses?

10. What role do you think Online Psychic Betty plays in Holly's life? Is she merely an online psychic advisor, or is she a mentor and friend? Do you find her advice helpful, insightful, or silly? Was there anything that Online Psychic Betty said to Holly that caused you to think differently about your own life? Do you think you will follow her advice to "look up"?

11. Holly and Caleb spur each other on to do things they are afraid of while also bearing witness to and supporting each other when bold actions are taken. How do they help each other achieve their respective goals? Do you feel their friendship strengthens their courage? Would either have achieved their ultimate goal were it not for their friendship?

12. How do Holly, Penelope, and Mary-Margaret differ in their responses to the chilli thrip infestation devastating Primm? What do they have in common? How are the differences in their roles in the chilli thrip spread affecting their responses to the aftermath of this disaster for their community?

13. Off-grid tiny homes, she sheds, and man caves are frequent topics of discussion in the novel. Do these structures represent a desire to downsize, lead a simpler life,

reduce our reliance on resources, claim a room of our own, have a place to escape or create, or something else? What is behind each character's interest in these structures?

14. Holly fixates on chandeliers, referring to them as bright, sparkling constellations you can hang indoors to remind yourself the sky's the limit. What do you think it meant to her to see that specific chandelier hanging in her foyer in the place where she felt the sky had fallen? In her stop-motion entry to the Wilhelm Klaus Film Festival, after the word *not* fell from Audrey's leash, what did the chandelier symbolize?

15. Knowing the complexity of Holly's feelings toward Collette, were you surprised to learn it was Collette and her husband who performed the shoddy home renovation? In what ways did Holly's opinion of Collette evolve throughout the novel? Were Jack and Holly justified in their feelings? How did Jack's removal of the load-bearing wall influence their views on the matter? How did Greta's stroke change Holly's perspective? Do you feel it was Penelope's place to tell Collette? In what ways did Penelope and Collette attempt to make amends?

16. How did you feel when you learned Greta was attending funerals of people she never met? Though Houston introduced Greta to a group of friends who tended to the departed, Greta told Holly she also attended by herself, even played her ukulele. Do you find this to be an act of kindness? Loneliness? Philanthropy? What do you suppose motivates Greta and others to do this?

17. What is beneath the tendency to overdo things? In what ways did the Enclave Tour consume the village and put pressure on homeowners? Why do you suppose Ella

learned so much about weddings from the girls on the playground? Why did Holly feel pressure to perform as the mother of the bride in the Q&U Wedding?

18. The desire to get organized is so strong that Holly is willing to make herself vulnerable and expose herself to potential ridicule when she invites both Penelope and Mary-Margaret into her home. And yet, she stands her ground when challenged to downsize her collection of coloring books. Do you colorganize? If not with coloring books, with something else?

19. In many ways, the first two books in the Village of Primm series depict Holly Banks coming to terms with the demand to give her time and effort in volunteer labor, first to the school in *Holly Banks Full of Angst* and then to the community as a whole in *The Peculiar Fate of Holly Banks*. What was your response to these demands being placed on Holly? Were they justifiable? Excessive? An opportunity for personal growth and belonging? Have you ever experienced a similar pressure to contribute or volunteer? How has this played out in your life?

20. Despite everything happening in Holly's life, she remains steadfast and focused on both opening Holly Banks Productions and submitting an entry to the Wilhelm Klaus Film Festival. Can you think of a time in your life when you persevered against all odds? How was your experience similar to Holly's?

ABOUT THE AUTHOR

Photo © 2018 Kim Brundage

Julie Valerie is the bestselling author of *Holly Banks Full of Angst*, Book 1 in the Village of Primm series. She serves on the board of directors for James River Writers; earned an editing certificate from the University of Chicago Graham School; and has a master's degree in education, a bachelor of fine arts in fashion, and certification in wilderness first aid. A former trend forecaster, Julie enjoys books, the study of wine, hikes on the Appalachian Trail, and travel. She married her college sweetheart, and they live in Virginia with their four children and two English Labradors. Learn more about Julie at julievalerie.com.

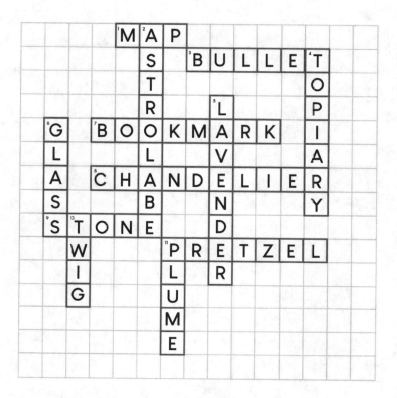

ACROSS

1. it has a key and a legend
3. typesetter's dot
7. reader's place keeper
8. branched hanging light
9. you can skip one on a lake
11. twisted treat

DOWN

2. navigational tool - sextant forerunner
4. botanical sculpture
5. plant prized for its scent
6. half-full or half-empty
10. chickadee's perch
11. nom de _____; pen name